Quake

Lou Cadle

Quake
Copyright © 2014 by Cadle-Sparks Books

This is a work of fiction. Names, characters, and incidents are a product of the author's imagination. Any resemblance to actual persons or events is entirely coincidental.

http://www.loucadle.com

Books by Lou Cadle

The Gray Series:
Gray, Part I
Gray, Part II
Gray, Part III

Erupt
Quake
Storm

41 Days: Apocalypse Underground

Crow Vector (May 2017)

The Dawn of Mammals Series:
Saber Tooth
Terror Crane
Hell Pig
Killer Pack
Mammoth

Audio books:

The Gray Series (coming soon)

Chapter 1

Bash

Bash clamped a dishtowel over the top of the blender and gave it a pulse. The pale yellow banana half and bright green kiwi disappeared into the orange juice and fat-free yogurt. Several more pulses and the smoothie was done, the color turning out a pastel he might call toasty salmon or shrimp mousse.

That made him long for a plate of fresh seafood. But the nearest ocean was a thousand miles away now. He could add oceans to the things he missed about California, a list already long enough to stretch the whole distance from here to there.

Gale came into the kitchen in his kimono, scrubbing at his face with his hand, one of the big, muscular hands that Bash had fallen in love with twelve years ago. He tried to love them again, right now to stir up that old warm feeling, but years and overfamiliarity and the last few months of unhappiness made it impossible.

Bash made an effort. "Smoothie?"

"I'll make myself eggs."

"Do we have any?"

"Dunno." Gale opened the fridge and peered in, came out with a carton of eggs. "Plenty," he said. He set the carton on the

1

counter and stuck his head back into the fridge. By the time Bash sat down with his liquid breakfast, Gale had piled up a hill of food—eggs, butter, green peppers, mushrooms, salsa, and two kind of cheese. He shut the fridge door with his hip.

"I'm jealous."

"You can have some."

"No, I promised myself I'd get rid of this gut. I'm getting middle-aged and fat."

"You're fine," said Gale, sounding weary more than sincere.

Bash, wounded, ran through several responses in his head. I am not. I used to be better than fine. If I'm fine, why do you not seem to love me like you did a year ago? All whiny answers, which Gale would hate. And who could blame him? Bash hated the needy words that came out of his mouth these days too. He swallowed down those words with a swig of smoothie. "What's up with work today?"

"Meetings, meetings, and more meetings." Gale pulled down the French omelet pan and set it on the burner.

The smell of butter melting in the pan made Bash's stomach growl. He drank more smoothie while he imagined a greasy-spoon breakfast of bacon and hash browns and buttery toast. No, not until his little poochy gut had gone away. He would not turn into his father, whose gut had grown more than a little poochy. "Just wait until you turn forty," he said.

"It can't be that different from thirty-eight."

"Just wait," Bash said. He watched as Gale chopped his vegetables and grated his cheese. "You making any headway on your building code thing?"

Gale turned his head and met Bash's eyes. In fact, the question had been innocent. As Gale continued to stare, Bash's forehead muscles began to ache with the effort of holding his innocent expression. "Don't burn your omelet," he said.

Gale returned his attention to the stove. "It'll happen when it happens." He banged the spatula on the edge of the pan. "I'm working as hard as I know how to."

"I know." Bash felt guilty for turning them back into the same old argument, was worried about their relationship, was lonely, and was desperate to leave this little Midwestern town as soon as possible. But before they could leave, Gale had a list of accomplishments he felt he had to achieve.

Gale was already launching into his end of the argument. "And I have to stay two full years, even if I get everything done I want. And it might not happen in two years anyway. We've been over this."

Bash nodded miserably, though Gale, stabbing at his omelet with a spatula, couldn't see him.

"Look, another ten or fifteen months and then I can start sending out resumes."

Bash tried to sound grateful. "I'm counting the days, dear."

Gale's shoulders rose and fell with a quiet sigh. "Maybe you should quit counting."

The words burst out of him. "But I hate this place."

"Bash." Gale's voice was weary.

It was almost as if someone else were in control of his tongue. "I want to go back to California. Or on to New York or Chicago or somewhere cosmopolitan. I want my friends, and parties, and a community again. I want—"

"Then go."

That was new. It stopped his outburst cold.

They were both silent while Gale finished making his omelet. He slid it onto a plate and put the plate on the table. He turned back to the counter and got out the French press, went through the ritual of making himself a cup of coffee. Bash sat watching his husband's eloquently angry back and blinked back tears. You stupid old queen, don't cry. Sometimes he hated himself as much as he hated this town. When had he become such a nag?

Gale sat down with his coffee and took a deep breath. When he opened his mouth to speak, Bash, afraid of what he might say

3

next, interrupted.

"I love you."

"Then support me."

"I do."

Gale's eyebrows shot up.

"In my heart, I do."

"How about your heart and your mouth have a little chat, then."

"C'mon, don't you miss L.A.?"

"Damn it, Bash." He slapped his coffee cup down. "Of course I do. I don't love living in the Bible Belt any more than you do. I have a higher hill to climb at work here, and I struggle with making connections because of the antediluvian attitudes here."

"The city manager knew you were gay when she hired you."

"And she's been great. But I have to deal with the Council and developers and architects and homeowners and the community at large, far more than you do."

"I do too. I work with the public."

"Not like I do. Your patients need you. Nobody needs me—I need them. My job is all politics. It's all about schmooze. And it's a hard job, and you only make it harder by pushing me. I need a goddamned break here."

Bash stood up and grabbed his smoothie. He went to the sink and poured the rest down the drain. He couldn't swallow food when he was fighting Gale. He turned on the faucet.

"Leave it. I'll do the dishes. Just go to work."

Bash turned off the tap and slumped out of the kitchen. Damn this place. He and Gale had never fought like this before. He was being a bitch, and he knew it, but he couldn't seem to stop himself. He ached for the old world like a shy little kid dumped at summer camp ached to go home. Again his eyes stung.

Don't cry. Do something. Something good. Something useful. Something to make things better. Do something for Gale, or do something for yourself. Quit complaining and *do something*.

Problem was, he had no idea what that should be.

* * *

Bash sat at a stoplight, tapping his fingers to the jazz ballad playing off his flash drive, James Williams on piano. He tried to let the music float away the residue of fear and anger the morning's fight had left, but not even music was helping. His emotions felt like a poison, souring his stomach and mouth, leaving a vinegar taste.

The front wall of the cancer center came into view, a shiny round curve of glass, a pretty building, one that Gale had complained about almost every time he saw it. "All that glass in tornado and earthquake country," he would say, shaking his head. He was probably right—he knew his job—but Bash liked the building. It was a stylish splash in a boring city.

He punched his code into the employee door, and it snicked open for him. A dim utilitarian hallway led into the locker room. He shrugged off his jacket, took out his blue uniform tunic and slipped it over his t-shirt. A stethoscope went around his neck.

He was pushing the morning's fight over breakfast to the back of his mind, but his mood hadn't yet caught up to work, which was seldom cheerful either, though it was sometimes rewarding. Since he couldn't quite force a pleasant expression just yet, he grabbed an old issue of the pediatric oncology nursing journal out of the top of his locker for camouflage. Locker door shut, dial spun, and he was ready for the day, Bash walked to his shift pretending to read the magazine. As he entered the public spaces, the morning light streamed through all the windows. He made it to the elevator, backed in, and sighed with relief that he was alone.

Too soon. A hand stopped the closing doors and in walked Suze, of all people, winding her dishwater blonde hair into a bun

5

and stabbing it through with plastic chopsticks.

"That's an old issue of JOPON," she said. "I read it ages ago. There's a good article on sibling grief you should read."

Did I ask? This is what he disliked about Suze—indeed, two of the things he disliked about her, in addition to the Ozark accent. First, no hi, how ya doin', pretty morning, isn't it? No attempt to establish a give and take of normal human conversation. Second, always the "shoulds." Adults, in Bash's opinion, did not give other adults unsolicited advice. If I want to know which articles to read—and he had read this issue months ago—I'll ask.

She simpered at him and stepped off the elevator onto the second floor, patting her pale hair.

Even California blond seemed different than Missouri blond, he thought, as the elevator opened again on the third floor. He turned left.

The staff supervisor, Meggy, was coming down the hall toward him, cradling a tablet computer. "Sebastian, may I have a word?"

"Of course."

She motioned him into an open doorway. "Alene's sick again."

"Is she okay?"

Meggy gave the tiniest of shrugs. Everything about her was tiny—she was four feet ten, probably a size 2, had small hands, the tiniest gold studs in her ears he had ever seen, and standing next to her made Bash feel like a bouncer in comparison. "She won't be in today. I'm shifting staffing. Can you stand two shifts in chemo?"

"Once in awhile, sure." He had been drawn to the job not only for its day-only work, but also for its philosophy of rotating the staff at midday to avoid burnout, but he could do this. He was a reasonable and flexible person. No matter what Gale would say about that.

"Something wrong? Just say no if you have a problem with it."

She was a hawk with reading expressions. "No, no. I'm fine with it." Bash thought himself fairly sensitive to others' moods, but Meggy was almost mystical in her abilities to read her staff.

She peered more closely at him for a moment, seemed to be satisfied that whatever was wrong wasn't her concern, and gave a sharp nod. She walked away, tapping at her tablet.

He passed the waiting area and smiled at Trevor, one of his youngest patients, sitting at his mother's feet. Mom, a chunky woman in canvas shoes and sweat pants, was on one of those dollar-store cell phones, a sweating Big Gulp beside her on the table. Trevor was on the floor with a primary-colored wooden train, but he caught sight of Bash and waved and smiled at him. What a cute kid. His bad mood evaporated with the boy's smile.

Trevor had ALL—a common form of leukemia in children. And there were drug shortages on the preferred drug for chemotherapy, had been for months. Chemo was worse on kids, as the drugs target not cancer cells but all rapidly dividing cells, which is why there are side effects. Kids had more rapidly dividing cells than grownups—their bodies are trying to grow up, poor babes. Trevor, being on Medicaid, got a cheaper drug, an older drug with even more side effects.

On the other side of the waiting room was an African American couple he didn't know, the woman hugely pregnant and glowing with health, the man thin and tired-looking. For an instant he had the wild notion that she had stolen her man's health, but that was silly. The man was sick with cancer, or with its treatment, and the disease was his succubus, not his pregnant partner.

He sat down beside the receptionist, Jo, and said to her, "Great hairstyle today."

She beamed. "You like it?"

"Very much." More than the actual style, he liked that she experimented with it. There were so many staid and boring and stuck-in-their-rut types around here, a little thing like changing hair every week was a radical and brave statement in southeast Missouri. "Who's up first?"

"Trevor. Then Mr. Witherspoon." She pushed him a note with the new patient's DOB and file number.

"Thanks." He went back to the treatment rooms to make sure everything was in place—some of his coworkers left the rooms in less than perfect order, and Bash was a stickler for detail. And a stickler for cleanliness and professionalism and order and—well, he was anal about his work, he admitted that. Only a few bits of tidying this morning were needed, and he was ready to go. He sat at a computer terminal and called up the new patient's info, made sure there wasn't anything special that would require a special room or schedule—but no, pretty standard protocol, stage II gastric, antiemetic and two meds.

He called up Trevor's chart, though he had the older parts memorized. Treatment protocol was same as the last five times. No new hospitalizations, so good. His own notes, including the ongoing problem with hydrating the little guy. He made sure all the meds were lined up and went to get the boy. This time, Trevor did not look up, though Bash knew he saw him. Bash didn't blame him. If only we could all ignore what we didn't like in life and focus intently on the toy train until the bad thing went away. Right there with you, kid.

Trevor's mom saw him and clicked off her cell, then gathered her things and spoke quietly to Trevor. The boy's head hanging, he got up and trudged over to Bash.

Bash squatted down and said, "Hey, buddy, what's it going to be today? TV or a game or…?"

"The hospital has PlayStations."

Bash smiled. "I know. I'm sorry we don't have them here."

"My mom brought a book. It has dinosaurs. It's really good."

"She's a wonderful mom."

Trevor nodded.

Bash stood and walked back toward the treatment room. With a sigh, Trevor followed him. What a little man he was. Bash remembered his own morning meltdown and felt ashamed of himself, an adult with tiny problems compared to this brave little kid with real problems.

He got Trevor settled into a recliner, his mom got him to sip from the Big Gulp—good going, Mom—and started the antiemetic IV. And so another work day began.

* * *

By ten, he had five infusion rooms filled and two more patients in the waiting room. The new man, Mr. Witherspoon, had slowed him down a little, as Bash refused to leave him alone for long. Until he felt certain that he wasn't going to react to any of the meds, he checked him compulsively. And then there was the pregnant wife, who had been a problem since she stood up to go in to treatment with her husband.

"You can't go into the infusion room," Bash said. "You're pregnant."

"I could at the last clinic."

"They were wrong," Bash had said, wondering how much more rural and backward such a place had been than this. Ye gods, he had thought it was bad here—he couldn't count the number of times he had seen medical staff cross a sterile field, for instance. But to allow a pregnant woman into a chemo room? Ack! Might as well be working in some third-world country. "You have to think of the baby," he said.

"The baby is fine. She's kicking right now."

Bash would believe that she was fine when he saw her born alive, without defects. "Let's keep it that way. No chemo for babies."

The woman looked mutinous, but the patient stepped in. "If it's about the baby, hon, maybe you should wait outside. Go shopping."

"For what, more tents?" She plucked at her maternity dress.

"Baby clothes."

"We have plenty to start."

"Go for a walk then, or window shop."

"I want to be with you. And if not with you, then here, in this building at the very least. What if you need me?"

The cancer patient grabbed her hand and kissed the back of it. "Do what the doc says."

Bash didn't correct him about not being a doctor, and the woman finally rolled her eyes and said, "Fine." She stuck a finger in Bash's face. "But you take good care of him."

"The best," Bash promised. And he had kept the promise after he had guided the woman to the central waiting area. Running out to her every twenty minutes for updates had slowed him further. Didn't they own cell phones? They could talk to each other the whole time if they did, but apparently not.

In Infusion Room 1, Trevor grew more restless and bored, and he balked over drinking enough. Bash hated to hurt him more, but he started an IV line for fluids in the free arm. This limited the kid's movement further, which made him more bored and fidgety and mad. Bash liked to see his anger—much healthier than acquiescing to everything in a stupor. When his mother tried to admonish him, Bash motioned her out into the hall. "The anger is a good sign."

"I don't want him to be a brat."

"He couldn't ever be. Your son is a doll. But that he's fighting and mad, that tells me he's still strong. We like to see a little fight in him. If there's none at all, that's bad news. Of course you should discipline him normally, over tantrums or harsh words or whatever, but know that I see it as a good sign."

She took the information in. She really was a good mother, and she would see the boy through this, Bash felt sure, if the chemo worked. Nodding, she returned to the room.

Bash caught up on charting from the last hour, sitting next to Jo at her receptionist's station, typing as fast as he could. He was standing up to get the next patient from the waiting room when the earthquake struck.

* * *

For the first three seconds of the earthquake, Bash did what any normal California-raised person did—he stood still and observed, poised to move into action. Most of the time, three seconds was all it took, and the earthquake subsided, and you unfroze and went on with life, forgetting it by the next day. If it lasted for longer than a few seconds, that's when you dove for cover.

This one lasted for more than three seconds. Bash dropped down and crawled under the counter. Jo still sat in her chair, so he grabbed her leg and yanked. "Get down here!" he yelled.

She slid off her chair to sit next to him, white-faced.

"Only an earthquake," he said. "Not a terrible one, I don't think." He glanced at his watch—it was 11:38:15—and figured four seconds had gone by. He kept staring at the sweep second hand—a holdover habit from taking pulses without electronic doodads—and watched seven more seconds pass. The quake eased off and stopped. "Twelve, fifteen seconds at most. Probably less than a 6.0, if it was centered nearby," he said, patting Jo on the knee. He crawled out from under the desk and looked out at the reception area. A huge pane of glass had popped out of the exterior window. At least it hadn't fallen inside, but he wondered if anyone outside had been under it.

He was curious to see, but first things first. "Come on," he said. "Take care of the people out in reception. Point them to the exits. No elevators. Stairs only. Tell them to get well away from the building and to watch for broken glass."

"What? Why?"

"There could be an aftershock. Pull yourself together. We

have patients to help." He hurried down the hallway to the treatment rooms. Boy, good thing he had just charted. What if they lost electricity? He hoped the system had saved his morning's notes. He turned around to Jo, just now getting to her feet. "Where's paper, pencils?" She pointed mutely to a drawer and he yanked it open to find blank paper headed with a pharmaceutical firm's name. He'd double chart everything, do it on paper too, and keep it the paper copy with the patient, just in case.

Back to the treatment rooms. He did a quick triage of everyone. Mr. Witherspoon had vomited, mostly into his emesis basin, but Bash left the cleanup until he made sure no one else was in worse shape. Trevor was the last he checked, now on his last med, five minutes from done. Good. That'd be his next job, discharging Trevor. He'd let the bag empty, and he'd hustle Mom and Trevor out, leaving four patients.

What to do after that depended on two questions. Was this the only earthquake they'd have? And was the building seriously damaged? They still had electricity, good news there. He tried to think. Okay, if the electricity went out, he'd have to not only chart by hand but switch a couple procedures over. Best to prep for that at the first opportunity. Hope for the best, prepare for the worst.

Back to Mr. Witherspoon, then, who was apologizing for vomiting as Bash opened the door.

"No, no, that's fine," said Bash. "I'll get it cleaned up in no time."

"I'll help." The man tried to lever himself out of his recliner.

"You'll sit." Bash glanced up at the television. A DVD was playing. "I tell you what you could do for me that would be a big help. Grab the remote, stop your movie, and turn it to a local station, see if we can get some news."

"Good idea."

Bash yanked on one new glove, took the basin and dumped it, rinsed it, and got some paper towels damp to help clean up the man's shirt. He was turning to do it as the pregnant Mrs. W stormed in. Damn.

"Are you okay?" she asked her husband.

"I'm fine. Are you?"

"I'm good." Mr. Witherspoon took a tissue and dabbed at his shirt.

"Let me do that," she said.

"You shouldn't be in here," Bash said, but gently. He'd want to rush in too, under the circumstances. He was a bit worried about Gale, who was healthy and earthquake-savvy, but he'd check on him too, if he didn't have responsibilities here. "Everything is okay."

"I'm fine, honey," said Mr. Witherspoon.

"You've sicked up," she said.

"Just a little," he said. "I feel better now."

Bash butted in again. "I know how worried you are, ma'am, but the best thing you can do is to leave the building, just in case."

"In case what? If I should leave, he should leave."

"As a precaution," said Bash. "If there's another quake, it'd be better to be outside, and far enough from buildings that you don't get hit by falling glass or bricks. Don't stand under a power line, either."

"I want you to come too," she said to her husband.

"I'm hooked up," he pointed out.

She turned on Bash. "Unhook him."

"It's better for him to finish the protocol. Just twenty minutes, he'll be done."

"Go on, honey," said Mr. Witherspoon.

Bash left them to fight it out. He had other patients to deal with first. He hoped she would get out, but he wasn't going to wrestle her out the door.

Outside. Damn, he'd forgotten. He hurried over to the windows where the glass plane had popped out and looked down, half afraid he'd see a decapitated person lying there. But no one was under the fallen glass, and there were no pools of blood. Another two panels had popped elsewhere, one lying on the bushes and one on the walkway, split into two neat pieces. Whoever built the place had chosen the glass wisely. He drew his head back inside and made a plan.

First, he'd finish up with Trevor. Then if he hadn't heard from Meggy or someone else in administration, he'd try and figure out what they were supposed to do next—continue the treatments to the end, or stop after the current meds?

Trevor had gotten over the initial shock at the earthquake and now thought it was cool. "It was awesome!" he said, as Bash took out his lines. "A real earthquake and everything!"

"Say 'ah,'" Bash said, unable to keep himself from smiling.

"Ahh," Trevor said, a real pro by now at obeying medical instructions.

His mouth didn't look dangerously dry any more. Bash said, "Hand, please," and Trevor offered him his small hand. Bash pressed on a nail, watched capillary refill. He got a BP and pulse and jotted them down, put cartoon bandages on his arms, and said, "Ready to go. You were a good boy, Trevor."

"I'm always a good boy." He glanced at his mother and flushed and said, "Almost always."

Bash laughed. He said to Trevor's mother, "Someone picking you up?"

She shook her head. "Bus."

"In case there's another quake, don't stand next to a phone pole or under electric wires while you're waiting for it, okay?"

"Will do," she said. "Thank Mr. Hill, honey."

"Thank you," Trevor said.

Bash thought, Gee, thank me for hurting you. He loved kids, and he hated seeing them sick and hurting.

"Get yourself a nice cold drink real soon now," he said.

"Thank you," the mother said, and then they were gone. Bash

did a whirlwind clean of the treatment room, not to his usual standards, but then, he wasn't sure what was going to be happening in here the rest of the day. Why hadn't he gotten a call or directions? It had been ten or fifteen minutes since the quake.

As if someone had been reading his mind, Jo stuck her head into the room. "Got your boss for you on line two."

He hurried up front, gratified to see an empty waiting room. Before he picked up the phone he said to Jo, "Sorry if I snapped at you earlier. Good job clearing them out."

"No, no, it's okay. I was shocked. It took me a second to get in gear."

"While I'm on the phone, can you poke your head in all of the rooms for me, make sure no one is in trouble? Tell me if there's any emergency."

"They have call buttons."

He lowered his voice, despite there being no one in sight. "Make sure no one is passed out on the floor or seizing, okay?"

"Oh, right," she said, and hurried off to check.

He picked up the received and poked at the blinking button. "Meggy?" He heard her talking to someone else. He waited for a pause, then said her name again, louder.

"Yeah. You okay down there?"

"Shaken up, but no one got hurt. What's the plan?"

"We're going to evacuate the building, until we get someone here to check on the structure. We don't like that we lost windows, and everyone up here is feeling nervous."

"Oh. Okay, what do I do with my patients?"

"Try and call their docs first, get updated orders. Electricity is working, so we lucked out there. Document everything. But without other problems, get them out of here as soon as you reasonably can."

"They'll be happy about that."

"And call me if you have questions."

"Will do."

15

"We have some minor ceiling damage up here on four. Three injured people. When you get yours out the door, come up and lend a hand, would you? Don't worry about setting up rooms again, not right now. Just dispose of medical waste and leave the rest."

"Done," he said. He made calls to three doctors, got through to none of them—no surprise—and went back to shut off the infusions of the newest patient. Working backward, he got to Mr. Witherspoon last, and the last of his drug was dripping.

The pregnant woman was still there, though.

Bash didn't yell at her for staying in the room. What was done was done. He said, "We'll have you both out of here in a minute, two at the most." He charted on paper while the last few drops of drug dripped. Out with the lines, bandage, check vitals, jot those down, and he was done.

He repeated his warning to the Witherspoons about power lines, telephone poles, elevators, and so on, but he didn't think either of them were listening. The man was too sick, the woman too focused on her husband.

He followed them out into the reception area, where Jo was gathering her things. "I'm out of here," she said. "I canceled afternoon appointments, and they told support staff to go home."

"Keep safe," he said.

"You too. See you tomorrow." She hurried to the stairwell and was gone. The Witherspoons followed more slowly.

"Do you—" Bash began. He was going to say, "need a wheelchair," but no, if they were going down steps, that made no sense. "Need help? I'm not sure which of you is helping the other, here."

Mr. Witherspoon managed a chuckle. "We're a pair, all right."

The woman looked grim-faced and said nothing.

A little alarm went off in Bash's head. He went over to them and reached out toward the woman's arm, not quite touching her. She didn't seem the type who wanted a pat on the arm. "Are you all right?" he said.

"I think maybe not," she said, her voice tight.

"What's wrong?"

"I think I'm in labor."

Chapter 2

Gale

Gale's assistant, Angela, stuck her head in the door. "Woodham is here," she said, and raised her eyebrows in a question.

Gale shut his laptop, picked up his landline, punched the five to keep it from ringing and motioned for her to send him in.

When Woodham strode in, Gale raised a finger and looked serious as he said into the dead phone, "Yes. Will do." Ridiculous, the act of the fake phone call, but Woodham was the sort who was influenced by appearances, so Gale appeared to be in demand, a man who was doing a favor, not asking for one. He hung up the phone and rose, walked to the front of the desk, and shook hands with the developer.

"Ten-thirty, Swanton," said Woodham, checking his watch. "We should get going."

More games, thought Gale, each of them trying to establish dominance. Sometimes, he thought, they should all just whip 'em out and take a piss on the wall. As with dogs, whoever could hit the highest spot would win and get his way. He nodded, grabbed the accordion folder with the printouts he had prepared, and gestured for Woodham to go first.

He flashed a smile at Angela as he passed. "Hold the fort," he said. She gave him a two-fingered salute.

Woodham had a brand new metallic Lexus, shining in the morning sun. The locks clicked open and Gale sunk into a cloud of new-car smell. Sitting on the soft copper-toned leather seat, he thought this was probably the most expensive car in the whole county. He imagined the lease—surely it was leased—would run about the same as the average mortgage payment in town.

He'd have to remind Bash that was another positive part of living in Missouri, affordable housing. He thought back to their tense words this morning and winced with guilt. He knew Bash was unhappy here, and he really should be trying to avoid making him even more miserable. Damn. He'd call him later and apologize. Maybe they'd go out tonight, drive up toward St. Louis, get a nice meal, maybe Italian, and find something to laugh about.

Woodham took some time to get the seat and climate controls set up to his satisfaction, but soon they were driving west on Brown Street, talking about the weather.

"Injun summer," Woodham said.

Gale made what he hoped was an agreeable noise though he winced inwardly at the racism. "Must be good for construction."

"Damn spring was so wet, we need it to catch up on building before the sleet comes."

They were at the development site within ten minutes—another vast improvement over L.A. was that everything in town was at most ten minutes' drive away—and Woodham pulled into a packed-dirt parking area. He popped the trunk and handed Gale a yellow hard hat. "Leave your jacket," he said, and Gale stripped it off and lay it on the pristine carpet of the trunk.

They walked toward a street with active construction, Woodham reciting specs and jabbing a finger here and there. "Durable poured-concrete foundation walls, structurally engineered joist floor and roof trusses, foundation drainage system with sump pump, spray foam rim insulation."

Probably word for word from the sales brochure, Gale thought.

Woodham added, "And no brick."

Well, at least he'd taught the guy enough about the dangers of unreinforced brick construction in earthquake country that Woodham had remembered to make the point. "There's brick on that one," said Gale, pointing to the nearest house, the most finished.

"First-story features and porches on the top models, sure. But nothing structural. Let's go down to the far end."

They walked toward the houses that were still empty frames. As they walked, they passed teams of men working—bricklayers, roofers, carpenters. A flatbed loaded with Sheetrock sat in the middle of the unfinished street. Inside the nearly finished houses, there must be plumbers, electricians, drywallers too.

Woodham said, "Thirty men employed full-time. Others part-time."

Gale nodded. "Sold many units yet?"

The hitch in Woodham's step suggested not. "Enough," is what he said.

"Important to the city's economy," Gale said.

"I'm glad you recognize that."

"Oh, I do. I'm not your enemy, you know."

"You merely want me to spend more money than I can afford."

"I want people safe. I know you do too." Because it would save you lawsuits, he thought, if not for any compelling moral reason.

"I think you worry about earthquakes so much because you're from L.A."

"That's the truth," Gale said. "Live through two good-sized ones, and it changes your perspective."

"You won't live through two here. I've been here fifty years and only felt one, and it was a dinky thing."

"It only takes one, one bad one."

"There's a scientist says the earth is done moving here. That the 1820 one was the end of it."

1811—but he didn't correct Woodham. And yeah, an irresponsible fool was saying that about the location of the nation's worst earthquake swarm ever, and Gale wanted to kick that man. As if you can hope plate tectonics will shut themselves off, and that wishes will keep you safe. As if there weren't small quakes every year here, below the threshold of human feeling, perhaps, but not below the ability of instruments to detect. Where's there's smoke, there's fire, and where there are several 3.5 earthquakes, that's an active fault. Hoping it all had gone away was another version of sticking your fingers in your ears and LALALAing away the truth. What he said to Woodham was, "We certainly can hope so. And prepare well in case he's wrong and all the other experts are right."

They had reached the end of the street, a cul de sac where the houses were still skeletal.

"Basements would have been nice too," said Gale. They were in the middle of Tornado Alley as well as on a fault zone, but at least everyone was conscious of that threat.

"The ones who want can build storm cellars—it's allowed in the CCRs."

Gale could predict many would actually do that—only one or two in the whole subdivision. But he'd save tornado issues for another day. He wanted to present earthquake-proofing ideas today.

"Okay, let me show you some affordable ideas that others have used to harden residential housing against quakes. They're doing some marvelous things in Japan."

They spent an hour at it, and Gale was grateful Woodham gave him that much time. Gale went back and forth between hands-on description, walking around one of the new frames, and pulling out full-color illustrations to show him. Convincing people to change was a slow process, and it demanded a surprising number of pretty pictures. He longed for a 3-D printer too, to create models overnight. But not on the measly budget he had to work with.

They both knew that Woodham wouldn't be making any changes on this project, but Gale was in it for the long run. He wanted to accomplish two things: to change Woodham's behavior in the future, but more importantly, to soften him up for the major zoning law change Gale had put together and would propose this winter. Woodham was the biggest builder in the county, and he'd probably be the loudest voice in the opposition. So what Gale was doing here today was mostly whittling away at the man's resistance.

When Woodman glanced at his watch for the third time in five minutes, Gale wrapped it up. "Give it some thought," he said. He took out his phone and checked the time, 11:38, and turned on his ringer to vibrate again. "Can I buy you lunch? I know it's a bit early."

"Not early in the construction business. But no, I have a luncheon meeting in an hour. I'll drive you back to your office—"

The ground rolled beneath Gale. He glanced up, saw there was nothing about to fall on them, and held his ground, knees flexed to absorb the ground motion. He counted to himself, one thousand one, one thousand two. It was a healthy shake for about eight seconds, but then it tapered off, and in twenty seconds he felt nothing at all.

He looked at Woodman, whose arms were out like he was on a surfboard. The man's usually florid face was paler, with two spots of white over the cheekbones. Gale said, "You okay?"

"If I were a superstitious man, I'd have thought you somehow brought that on."

Gale barked a laugh. "From talking about it? Not nearly that powerful a person," he said. "Excuse me while I call in. I'm supposed to get to the EOC, I imagine. I need to check."

"EOC?"

"Emergency Operations Center. Everyone in city hall has a job, and mine is to coordinate non-emergency services."

"Like what?"

"Infrastructure."

"So water lines, sewer, gas, and so on?"

"Exactly, and government buildings."

"Surely it wasn't that bad."

He shrugged and listened to his phone. The phone call didn't go through. He checked the bars, and he had a signal. "No dice. Probably everyone in town is on their cell phone."

"I should check on my men before I can drive you back."

"Yeah, let's walk up that way, make sure nothing fell on anyone."

As they strode up the curve of the drive, the flatbed of drywall came into view. A few bundles had cascaded off the top of the pile and were lying tilted against the trailer's side or burst open on the ground. Men in hard hats—and only one woman he could see—were milling about in the street. No one was hurt.

"Everyone accounted for?" shouted Woodward.

A man in shirtsleeves and jeans stepped forward. "Looks like it."

"Check. Count off. Check against the sign-in sheet from this morning."

"Yes, sir," the man said, and hurried off. Woodward followed him.

"Anyone hurt?" called Gale.

"Just my pride," said one man, pointing at a nearby house. "I was up on the roof there and screamed like a girl. About pissed myself too."

The guys laughed more than the small joke deserved, easing their own tension. Gale remembered Bash after the last L.A. quake, joking endlessly in public, and very wittily too, but waking up with nightmares at night and quick to tears over every broken plate he threw in the trash.

Gale tried his phone again. Nothing. He had to call work, but he wanted to call his husband. At least with this quake, he and Bash were likely the only ones in town at risk for earthquake PTSD. A quake this size in LA, crisis phone lines would get overwhelmed with calls from survivors of the bad ones.

"Anybody get a cell call out?" he said.

"I did, right after," said a man, a bricklayer from the look of the mortar that dotted his green coveralls. "Left a message."

"Mine's in the car," said another.

"Nope, just tried," said the woman, sounding worried. "I wonder what's wrong."

"Overuse," said Gale. "Don't fret. System is jammed with too many calls. It'll free up in a short while." He punched a note into his phone to get something done about this too. If a minor quake overwhelmed the cell system, they needed a better one.

And then it hit him. He nearly slapped himself on the forehead for being an idiot. Of all the people here, he had the right information, and despite it being a small earthquake, the adrenaline had made him forget everything he knew, like how to make cell phones useful at such times. "We should be able to get texts out," he said, and punched one in to Angela. He forwarded it to the city manager too. still at bldg site. need me for EOC? u ok? The texts went through, and he nodded, satisfied. To Bash he sent, love u. u ok?

He glanced up. Around him, the crew was texting or rushing to get their own phones from cars.

The supervisor was walking up with a clipboard, yelling at people to stay together, but that didn't stop them from going to get their phones. By the time they were all gathered together again, his phone buzzed in his hand and he felt a rush of relief. He glanced down to see a text from Angela. all well. c.m. says no on EOC.

Woodham stood while the supervisor checked names against his list. "Everyone present," he said. Woodham gave a curt nod. "Get back to work, then. Good job." He jerked his head toward the parking lot and said to Gale, "I can get you back now."

They returned to the Lexus, Gale retrieved his jacket and started to hand back the hard hat, then thought better of it. "I know this is an inconvenience, but can I borrow this for the day?" At least until he could get his either from the EOC or the one at home in the garage.

"Why?" said Woodham.

"Just in case."

"In case?"

"Something happens before I can get back to my office."

"Something? You mean another quake?" He blanched again.

"It's possible. There's an outside chance this is a preshock, the quake before the real one."

"Keep it, keep it as long as you want," Woodman said. "Your offer for lunch still open?"

"Sure."

"I have that lunch deal later but you could buy me a drink."

Gale grinned. "You're on." If he ever, in his whole career, got a better chance than this to educate a builder about earthquakes, he'd be surprised. Strike while the iron is hot.

"And you can take the opportunity to lecture me some more."

Gale's grin turned sheepish. His mind had just been read.

"I'm not as dumb as you think I am."

"I never thought you were dumb, Mr. Woodham. You're among the most successful men in the county. All along I thought you were a savvy businessman."

"It's a good line of bullshit, at least. And call me Ron." He slammed the trunk. "Now, that drink."

* * *

25

He got back to the office from the drink with Woodham, having had only a cola himself, at about quarter to one. Angela was gone to lunch, so he dropped off his files, tucked his hard hat under his arm, and strode down the hall, pleased with what he'd accomplished today.

He stepped into the city manager's suite. Her assistant was gone too, maybe out to lunch with Angela. The inner door was open six inches. He tapped on it lightly and looked in.

Evelyn, the manager, was at her desk, eating a sandwich and scrolling through a computer screen. When she caught sight of him, she waved him in.

"Can't be too bad if you're still here and not downstairs at the EOC," he said, sitting down across from her. "Everything okay?

"For us, yeah. Fire department did the windshield survey. Some bricks down, some broken windows. No damage to hospital or schools. Fire station and police department intact. Most of the 911 calls were only panic. One possible concussion the only injury called in. The hospital might have others at the ER."

"My other stuff fine? I mean, water, sewers? Anything I need to do?"

"Nothing the windshield showed, and nothing we've heard of. Power and phone company are checking their own gear—give them a call in a half-hour or so. At least we're not Caruthersville." She turned her monitor for him to see and started up a video.

He was watching a news video of a helicopter flying low over a small town. There were tumbles of bricks onto the street, and as he watched, they flew over a burst water main. Water bubbled up and ran in a stream down the street, going downhill, seeking the Mississippi.

"I heard on TV at the restaurant that that's the epicenter."

"They think almost exactly."

"Any deaths?"

"None they're reporting yet."

He watched the video play out and fade to black. "That could have been us."

She took a swig of coffee, nodding. "I was a convert to your ideas already."

"Maybe I should propose the zoning changes next council meeting."

Her face turned thoughtful. "Hadn't thought that far ahead. You're a better politician than me sometimes."

"Hardly."

She grinned at him. "See, even that was politically astute, buttering up the boss." The grin faded. She fiddled with her earring while she thought. "They're not going to love it, no matter when you take it to them. But yes, this is the time. Still not confident about it going through the first time, but let's try it now." She took a decisive bite of her sandwich.

"Heard from the council or the mayor?"

"All but one. Mayor's taking off work early and coming in at 3:30 to meet with me."

"Do I need to be here?"

"No."

"Good. I'd like a late lunch after my assistant and I meet, and then a personal hour."

"Okay." Her tone implied the question.

"While I'm thinking of it, I want to refresh all my earthquake kits. I've been lax, done nothing in the year since I set them up. New water, boxed food, fresh batteries, all that, switch it all out and consume what was in there."

"Update the main office stash too, and you don't have to take personal time."

"Sure. Happy to."

She pointed. "What's the hard hat about?"

"I got it from Woodham. He needed a drink after the quake, and I let it sit on the table as I hammered home a few choice points."

"Ah, the big yellow reminder."

He smiled. "Right where he couldn't miss it. I never said I was subtle."

"Probably not the day for subtlety. But why do you still have it?"

"In case I need it."

Her eyebrows shot up. "You expect another quake? This some kind of California earthquake-fu prediction?"

He shrugged. "It's caution. But make sure your kit is up-to-date at home too, would you, Evelyn?"

"I'll put the twins on it. They'll love it."

"They okay?"

"Yes. I got a text from them finally, right before you walked in. How about Bash?"

"Haven't heard from him yet. But he's probably busy." Or still mad at me from this morning.

"Okay, what else you got going before the weekend?"

They turned to talking of other matters and in a half hour, he left her. Already, life was settling back down. He hoped by the time the council next met, they wouldn't feel too settled about the quake. Was it awful to hope for a couple small aftershocks to remind them of the danger? He should take pictures of any damage he saw around town to add to the presentation, and make sure to play that Caruthersville video, maybe on a loop behind him.

* * *

A few minutes before 3:00, he finally made it out of the office to run his errands and get lunch. He had connected with Angela and checked the EOC survival supplies, which were extensive, including several five-gallon water containers, MREs, and a few sleeping bags and folding cots. The only expired item was the chocolate, which was likely still good, considering it was in the basement and always cool, but he'd replace it anyway.

He drove the same route he'd taken this morning to the building site but pulled in at the Walmart, parked, and went into the Subway to grab a small turkey sandwich to eat as he shopped. He loaded six 2.5-gallon containers of water onto his cart, which in a pinch could last him and Bash two weeks, six large containers of anti-bacterial wipes to use in lieu of showers or hand washing, several no-cook boxed meals, and a variety of boxes of crackers. He got the chocolate bars for work, and a hazelnut bar as a present for Bash.

When he'd taken the hardhat from Woodham, he realized he could store it in his car trunk along with an extra pair of boots, cheap but solid. Over half the injuries from earthquakes and tornados came from stepping on broken glass, so it wouldn't hurt to duplicate the boots and hardhat to store in his car. He and Bash already each had hiking boots and hardhats under the bed, along with heavy-duty flashlights. Their other survival supplies were stuffed into a 64-gallon wheeled trashcan in the garage.

He steered his cart to the shoes section and found a pair of mustard-colored work boots, sat down to try them on and paced the aisle to make sure they fit okay. Ugly as sin and only $23. Good enough. He'd probably never use them. And Bash would probably scream when he saw how horrible they looked. Gale smiled at the thought.

At the checkout he grabbed fresh batteries, D and AA. He had the bored cashier check the work chocolate separately and paid cash for it, tucked the receipt into his wallet to submit to work, and charged everything else to his credit card. It came out to less than a hundred dollars, which was damned cheap for some extra peace of mind.

As he left the store, mostly mothers with children in tow were coming in. Elementary schools must have let out. He packed his trunk full of personal supplies and grabbed the chocolate for work to take with him. Easing the car carefully around a group of preteens heading away from the McDonald's carrying fast food, he steered back onto Brown.

He had gotten two blocks when the second quake hit.

Chapter 3

Bash

"Labor," he said to Ms. Witherspoon. "You're sure?"

"No," the pregnant woman said. "It's my first baby. But my back hurts and I'm cramping."

"When's your due date?"

Mr. Witherspoon said, "In two weeks, two days."

Bash said, "Okay, I'm going to walk you outside, get you safely away from the building. Then I'll call an ambulance."

"Oh, no, don't do that."

"I'd rather. I hate to be blunt, Ms. W, but I'm not confident either of you is fit to drive."

She looked at her husband. His eyes were weary, the skin around his mouth gray. "I think I can manage," she said.

"Let's debate it outside," Bash told them. He wished his cell phone wasn't in his locker. He'd be able to call an ambulance if need be, could call Meggy to tell her he was delayed as he walked them out. And he should check on Gale too.

He pushed through the fire door and held it for the couple, eyeing them both as they passed. Mr. Witherspoon was slow and shuffling. She held her hand against her back but was upright. He followed them onto the landing and said, "Ms W., you go first."

"Yeah, better if I fall, I don't crush you two with my big ol' pregnant self."

"You think you're going to fall? Do you feel faint?"

"No. It was a joke."

Bash let out a tense breath. He could only stand next to one of them, and he'd done the triage for that—it was Mr. Witherspoon who needed a hand most. He said to the man, "Hold on to that banister," and stood beside him, not holding on, but with his arm in the air, poised to support the man if he stumbled.

Slowly, they made their way down the echoing stairwell. Ms. W was going faster, but she stopped at every landing to wait for them and rub at her back. The two flights of stairs took them five minutes to navigate, and Bash was relieved when she pushed through the exit bar and daylight flooded the lowest landing.

"Neither of you has a cell phone?" he asked

"In the car, charging," said the woman, gesturing to the patient parking lot.

There wasn't a bench at this exit, wasn't anything but a trash can to break up the concrete expanse. Just before the door closed, he thought to jam the trashcan in the opening, leaving the door cocked open so he could get back in without his keys. He couldn't leave the couple standing here, and he couldn't phone anyone for help now. "So we'll walk to your car." They all began the slow trek in the direction she pointed.

"I'm feeling well enough to drive," said Ms. W.

"I'd feel more comfortable if you let me call an ambulance."

"Knowing this damned insurance the way I do, I doubt they'd pay for it."

She was probably right about that. Insurance companies were the bane of good health care. It was maddening for Bash to have to choose between the right treatment and financial reality. Choices like that had driven better people than him out of nursing.

"And it's only four blocks to the hospital," she said.

And traffic looked light out on the road. "You'll take it slow?"

he said.

"I'll be careful."

"How are you doing?"

"I'm fine. I may not even be in labor. Maybe it's a false alarm."

"Best to get it checked out. Call your OB right away."

Mr. Witherspoon wasn't saying anything, and Bash had his eye on the man. He looked washed out and chalky, and his shoulders were slumped with weariness. A few drops of sweat had popped out on his forehead. Bash wanted nothing more than to go with them and make sure both of them were okay, but he had other obligations.

It was a relief to make it to the car and get Mr. Witherspoon settled in the passenger seat. "Don't walk farther than you have to. Drive up to the emergency entrance and both of you get out. Let the security guy park your car, okay?"

From the driver's seat, the pregnant woman nodded. "Thank you," they both said, together.

"Be safe," he said, and with a wave turned and jogged back across the lot to the door. He shoved the trashcan back in place and ran up the stairs past his own floor and to the fourth. Only as he pushed through to the floor did he stop to think he should have detoured to get his cell phone from his locker. Damn.

He found Meggy in the big conference room, which was also a first aid station at the moment. There was a young woman in an aide's smock with bandages on her head, another nurse attending to her. An older woman sat with a handkerchief, dabbing at her eyes. An elderly man was fighting to catch his breath as Meggy and two other staff members hovered nearby.

When Meggy saw Bash, she stepped away from the man. "I was starting to worry about you."

"I had a medical situation down on my floor."

"Anything serious?"

"A patient's wife thought she had gone into labor."

"Good grief." Meggy shook her head. "Everything okay?"

"I got them headed to the hospital," he said. "What's going to happen now?"

"I called admin. A structural engineer will be here about 3— we're closing down most services until then. We already sent most of the support staff home. What I'd like to do the rest of the day is, first, get these people out, and second, have a meeting with professional staff, review emergency procedures."

"Okay," said Bash. "What can I do to help?"

She tapped her tablet with a stylus as she thought. "We're okay here. I know it's a big favor to ask, but can you run out and order food? Most people will have missed lunch."

"For how many?"

"Twenty-three. So maybe five or six pizzas, or fifteen big deli sandwiches sliced in half, something like that? Real food, in any case, not just dessert. I hate to ask you, but the few support staff left are swamped."

"No problem. Want me to take petty cash or charge it or what?"

"Can you pay for it, and put in for reimbursement?"

"Sure? What's the timeline?"

"I doubt we'll be ready to sit down and meet for an hour." She glanced at her watch. "Better make it 3:30 to be safe. That'll give me an extra half hour to get organized, and I can get us all out of here on time."

"Great. I'll clean up my treatment rooms better, order food about 2:30, then run out to get it."

"Thank you so much," she said. "I hate to impose."

"No imposition. You're sure I can't do anything to help here?"

"No, We got one patient to the hospital. Ashleigh there is cut, and her cousin's going to come get her. The gentleman is a patient, mesothelioma, and the upset lady is his wife. He refused hospitalization. A daughter is on her way to fetch them, and he says he will get himself on his oxygen back home." She shrugged

34

and her lips tightened, conveying a good deal to Bash—the elderly man was likely a terminal patient who had made his end of life choices, and the crying wife was upset with more than the earthquake.

He took the time to run down to his locker and grab his lunch and cell phone. He powered up the phone and saw the message from Gale, which was a relief. He hadn't been worried very much about him—there hadn't been a cacophony of ambulances arriving at the hospital, which Bash would have heard from so near, so he thought probably no one in town was seriously hurt. He started to punch in a message but then hesitated. He wasn't entirely sure why. It was mean to let Gale worry longer than he needed to. But he was embarrassed about seeming weak and whiny this morning, and he didn't want to emote all over the text message now too. He erased the message he had begun, and typed in just I'm ok and sent that. He didn't want to think about his personal problems right now.

He ate his healthy low-cal lunch alone—he'd skip the food at the meeting—then cleaned his treatment rooms to his usual standards. Trevor had left a coloring book, so Bash took that to the front desk and put a sticky note on it. When the treatment rooms were spotless, he ordered pizzas and left to pick them up, passing a crew of three men outside in putty-colored overalls picking up glass. You had to hand it to the administration here, Meggy and the facility administrator, Joanne. They ran a tight ship. In two days at the outside, he predicted, they'd have the glass replaced, the building's integrity confirmed, and everything would be running smoothly once again.

The pizza place smelled like heaven. This calorie-watching was tough on him. He loved food and missed being able to eat rich foods. Pizza would be cheating, but if he held it to one slice, that wouldn't be too awful, would it? He'd just have a small salad for supper, to make up for it. The counter clerk slapped a bell, called his name, and Bash paid for the stack of five extra-large pizzas. He picked them up with an, "*Oof.*" They were surprisingly heavy. He had to set them on his car's roof while he cleaned a space for them in the back seat. Gods, those clothes from Macy's he was going to return, purchased in an attempt to improve his mood—had to get them back to the store soon, or they wouldn't take them at all. He was a bit of a pack rat, if he didn't keep after himself, and he'd have to clean out his car soon. This weekend, he promised himself.

The drive back to the clinic was slowed by the start of school traffic, temporary 20 mph signs slowing him down, crossing guards stopping him, and double the normal number of cars, with parents going to pick up their youngest children. In a little bit, high school seniors would be adding their cars to the mix. He was a few minutes late for the meeting when he pulled into the staff lot at work. He opened the back door of his car to retrieve the pizzas, and the second earthquake struck.

He knew immediately that it was something else entirely from the earlier quake. First there was a great sound, like a million pieces of Styrofoam being ripped apart at once, or a distant train wreck, at the same time both low and loud and full of squeaks and creaks. And then the earth beneath his feet lurched, and as suddenly was gone from underfoot, and he felt himself falling. At the same time, a flock of birds whirled overhead, screaming, screaming. A giant snapping sound came at the same time he hit the ground, hard, on a hipbone.

He found himself lying on his side on the asphalt, looking out beneath his car at the nearly empty parking lot. The earth was rippling like an ocean, waves of asphalt coming at him. He flinched. Then he realized nothing was coming at him. It was an illusion of the ground pumping up and down, in literal waves. The asphalt split apart at a nearby wave peak as he watched. His car bounced on its shocks and he yanked his head back from the edge of it, fearing he'd be brained. Fighting his way to his hands and knees, he crawled away two feet from the open car door before the shaking forced him to lie flat again, on his belly.

A hard shock shook him so that he was rolled involuntarily over onto his back. In the sky, the screaming birds wheeled, turning the blue sky black for an instant. A hundred car alarms shrilled and honked. Out on the street, there were drivers laying on their horns. The sound of cars colliding, metal on metal. And the roaring beneath him continued, an angry giant coming awake. The cacophony was maddening, like nothing he'd ever heard before. The ground kept rolling, as if an angry fat guy was jumping up and down on a waterbed beside him. His hands grasped at the ground, trying to find purchase, but there was nothing to hold on to and he was shaken, like an abusive father shakes a baby to death, unable to do one thing to protect himself.

Still the ground rolled and moaned. It was Northridge again, from his childhood, but Northridge times ten or fifty or a hundred. His head smacked against the pavement, and he saw a burst of light. *Sit up, sit up,* he told himself, but the best he could manage was to roll over to his belly, brace his palms on the ground, and lift his head clear of the pavement. To his left, a thousand tinkling bells went off, and he looked over to see the clinic being shaken apart, the last of the glass raining down out of the windows, shimmering in the afternoon light, steel supports bending and twisting, the roof coming down to rest at an angle. Meggy, he thought, with a wrench. The rest of the staff. The men who had come to check the building. All inside.

And still the earth shook. It went on forever and ever, long enough for him to get religion, to lose religion, to know he was going to die, and to think a hundred times of Gale. In his mind he apologized to his husband, he called out to him, he raged at him for putting them in this hellhole, he begged forgiveness for every stupid thing he had ever said or done, he told him he loved him. He told him to live. Live, he thought. Live, Gale. Please live. I'm so sorry I didn't call you.

His eyes burned. The air stank of sulfur, he realized, as the shaking barely paused before it intensified yet again. As he stared toward the clinic, a light pole at the edge of the parking lot bent in half, and a Mini halfway across the lot jumped like a kangaroo, coming down three feet away from where it had been. The whole world was coming apart.

He felt himself floating out of his body and saw himself from above, a frightened man clinging uselessly to the ground, a man whose ass was widening with encroaching middle age, whose fingers tried to dig into the surface of the parking lot. Poor thing, look at him, so scared. And then his consciousness zoomed down and slipped back into his body and he felt the shaking easing off. Easing off more. A final hiccup, and the world came to a rest.

Holy fuckoli, Batman, now *that* was an earthquake. He started laughing. But he clamped down on it right away, knowing it for hysteria. He didn't have time to be hysterical. He didn't even have time to worry about his husband. He was a nurse. He had to try and save lives.

And I'm alive. I'm alive! He felt great giddy relief and joy at the thought. Had it struck five minutes earlier, or thirty seconds later he probably wouldn't be. His sunglasses had been shaken off his head early on, and he found them an arm's length away and pulled them back on his face. He grabbed the car door, pulled himself up with it, and slammed it. He began to run for the half-collapsed building but, after two steps, though better of it and went back to open his trunk. He had to mutter instructions to himself to help himself focus.

First, push aside the disaster survival kit—might need that later. Grab the old plaid wool blanket and toss it out, and now dig underneath empty plastic grocery bags to get to the spare tire well. He snatched up the jack and tire iron, tucked them under his arm, and slammed the trunk. He took up the old blanket and draped it over his shoulders.

The trip across the parking lot, clean and barely six months from its last resurfacing, was like a trip across a land-mined war zone. The asphalt had buckled and split in several places, and the surface was no longer even. A great hand had shaken the surface like a bedspread and not bothered to smooth it out afterward. He hopped over peaks and jogged where he safely could. A twisted light pole—the very one he had seen fall—sputtered with electrical sparks, and he detoured well around it.

The driveway that circled the clinic was less damaged than the parking lot. When he reached it, he had to stop to look at the fallen glass, which had splintered and scattered out past the edges of the drive. Steel columns remained upright, the beams stretching between them. A few sections of the top floor were recognizable as straight lines, but they were now down at the level of the second floor, pancaked. Every single bit of glass had fallen from this side of the building, a flat side, hundreds of panes. Dust hung in a cloud over the wreck of the building. Past that, he could see the rounded side of the building had taken less damage. As he moved into the dust cloud, Bash started coughing.

He put down his paltry set of rescue tools and stripped off his scrub shirt. Underneath, he wore a plain white t-shirt. He stripped that off and tied it around his face as a mask, then pulled his scrubs back on and picked his way over the debris in the drive.

Though the building was altered beyond recognition, he knew about where he was. The main entrance was over there, the visitor's lot in front of it, with only one car left in it, luckily. The conference room, where he thought everyone in the building had been when it struck, was at the rear of the building, to his left, where it had overlooked the next building.

* * *

He made his way around the building, calculating his best chance of finding survivors. They had been on the top floor, at least. Bottom floor this side, and they'd be smashed under tons of fallen building. He stepped around a file cabinet that had launched itself out of the building but somehow landed upright. It seemed barely damaged.

As he reached the end of the building, his heart fell. The side of the building facing the street, with the rounded curve of glass, was still standing nearly to the top. Everything else fell off toward the staff lot. If there were survivors, they could be under the debris of the roof, or they might have rolled down into the real mess at the edges in this direction, or they were dead somewhere—anywhere—in that mess. At the far front end of the building, there was a section of the first and second story that looked almost intact. Something from the roof—a big air conditioner or heater, maybe—sat precariously balanced half on and half off that little intact section. He tried to think of what had been in that area, couldn't, then shook off the thought. Rescue—that was what was important.

He could imagine Gale screaming at him for trying to do this alone, without equipment, without much training. But he couldn't sit and wait. And wait for whom? It was him or nobody. A single glance down the street told him what the rest of the town was like. Buildings were down, cars were wrecked, water gushed down a street from a broken water main. In a town of 45,000, probably a third were dead or seriously injured, and anyone left trained to effect rescue was as likely to be among injured as not. Those few who were alive would not need to look farther than their own noses for work that had to be done. No one was coming soon to help him here, and five minutes' work right now might matter to someone's survival.

He needed both his hands, so he set his jack and tire iron down outside of the debris field. They looked pitifully small compared to the tons of stuff that had to be moved.

He waded into the debris, climbing carefully on hands and knees, trying to get up to the top of the mess. A section of drywall slid under his right knee, and he could do nothing but freeze until it quit sliding. He edged to the left until he found more stable purchase on a beam. His heart was pounding hard—had been pounding hard all along. He realized he felt sick from the constant rush of adrenaline, almost poisoned by it. His mind cast over his schooling, trying to remember how many minutes of the hormone the body could supply before it merely ran out, or when all the available receptors would fill up in his brain and fear would max out. It was a pleasant distraction from where his mind wanted to go, which was thinking about being crushed to death.

If he found someone hurt, it was only four blocks to the hospital. Maybe he could find some uninjured bystanders and have them carry someone over. He was higher up now, and he looked over in the direction of the hospital—and saw nothing. It was a seven-story building, and he knew where it should be, but it wasn't there.

Brick. Shit, the hospital was brick. He realized it was gone. Collapsed. He saw a denser cloud of dust where it had been, though he couldn't see the collapsed building itself. Between him and the hospital, the parking structure and two other medical buildings had also sustained serious damage. Facades had peeled away. Roofs had collapsed. There was orthopedics, across the way, also badly damaged, the roof fallen into the center of the building, the edges intact. His building and the others in the complex, unusable. But the hospital—it was just gone. Who was going to take care of the injured? And where?

He heard a voice, behind him, and to his left.

"Help," it said clearly, if faintly. "Help me."

"I'm here," he called. "Hang on, I'll be right there." The dust was settling, so he yanked his makeshift mask down around his neck.

He followed the beam back and then had to leave it to move toward where the voice had been. "Say something."

"I'm here," the voice said. It wasn't ten feet away, but look as he might, he couldn't see a person-shape among all the building debris. Gingerly, he picked his way closer.

"Again," he said.

"Bash?"

Someone who knew him. His heart leapt in joy. "Who is it?"

"Suze. I'm right here, looking right at you."

He looked toward the voice and finally made out her face, filthy with dust, half-hidden behind a grid of small orangish PVC pipes, maybe part of the sprinkler system. He couldn't help but smile in relief at finding a survivor. "You're going to be okay."

"What happened?"

"Earthquake, honey. I'll get you out." He hoped he wasn't lying.

"But what happened?"

"Is your head okay?"

"My head's fine. My leg hurts. I can't move it."

Bash tugged at the grid of pipes, gently at first, then harder, but they wouldn't budge. He traced them back to where they disappeared under a section of roof. Anything he tried to move could send more debris cascading down. What he needed was a saw, a chainsaw, then he could cut out sections of the piping. This way, it was like playing a game of pick-up sticks, a very dangerous one where dislodging a pile of sticks could mean death for them both.

But he had to try something. He grabbed the pipes and began wriggling them back and forth, back and forth, trying to ease them out from whatever pinned them. After a few seconds, they began moving, and suddenly he felt a give and was able to slide them away to the left, away from her face. A hand came out and he grabbed it. "You're fine, you're good."

"How is everyone else?"

"I don't know yet. I'll get you out of there, and you can help me find the others."

Her upper body was tucked into a free space in the debris. From the crotch up, she was unpinned and uninjured, as far as he could see. Merely dusty. Her legs were underneath fallen debris, he hoped not crushed. Or gone—he flashed on blood pumping out of severed legs and forced the image out of his mind. He held her hand up to the light, pressed the fleshy part of her thumb, and was relieved to see quick capillary refill. "I don't think you're bleeding."

"It hurts."

"I know." He studied the situation some more. "Look, I think I can crawl in there with you, if you don't mind my butt in your face for a moment."

"As long as you can get me out, I'll even kiss it."

He barked a laugh. "Hang on." He pushed at the debris above her, testing it for stability. He didn't want to get in there, bump into something, and bury them both. Once he was as certain as he could be that it was safe, he wriggled forward to drop over the lip of the space she was in, and he eased himself down on her— well, half on her and half next to her. "Sorry," he said.

"I'm fine. And it's your knee in my face, not your butt."

He rolled more weight off her, but there wasn't room for them to be side by side. "Move my knee to where you can stand to take weight." He felt her take hold of his calf and shift it.

"Better," she said. "What do you see?"

"I'm waiting for my eyes to adjust to the light," he said. He should have grabbed the flashlight from his glove compartment.

"I have a lighter in my pants pocket," she said.

"No no no," Bash said. "There could be pockets of gas. I'm seeing better now. Give me a second more."

His eyes were adjusting, and he could see where her nearer leg, the right one, disappeared into to the debris. He reached a hand down and slid it along the top of her leg. There was space at first, then it narrowed down. From her knee down, she was pinned. He prodded at the lowest spot he could reach, but she made no protest. He pulled his hand out and looked at it. No blood.

"I'm moving around you." He twisted himself until he was splayed across her lower body, reaching for the other leg. There was more space there. It was as free as far as he could reach. And to the left, there was more empty space still. He wriggled backward and levered himself out of the space.

"I think your left leg is going to be easy to free. Your right, that make take some time. Here's what I want you to do. Really slowly, wiggle your left leg toward the left. There's some extra space there, and you might be able to get it out yourself."

"You sure?"

"I'm sure about the space. I couldn't get down to your left foot. Does it feel pinned? Does it hurt? Numb?"

"I think it's okay."

"So try and get it out on your own. I'll be right back."

"No!"

He paused and smiled at her. "I need something to help us. It'll only be a second."

As fast as he could do it safely, he scrambled back to where he had left the tools.

"Hey!" a voice called.

He looked up to see a man jogging toward him.

"You a doctor?"

Bash shook his head. As the man neared, he said, "I'm a chemotherapy nurse."

"I need some help over here. There's someone hurt."

Bash felt torn. He'd be needed in a hundred places at once right now, but he could only be in one. "Very next person, I promise. I have a trapped nurse I need to get out first." And if her injuries weren't too severe, there'd be two of them to help other people.

"He's bleeding."

Shit. "Okay, here's what you do. Find a clean cloth, and press down on the bleeding. Keep it under pressure."

"Someone is doing that already."

"Terrific. Where are you? I'll be there as soon as I can."

He pointed. "The green Toyota over there, smashed into the

light pole."

"I won't be long," Bash said, and he turned back to the collapsed building. The jack slowed him down, but he was figuring out how to navigate the debris better too. A few more times for practice, and he'd be scampering up and down like a monkey.

He made it back to Suze.

"I did it!" she said. "My left leg is out."

"Fantastic."

"I tried to push with it to get my right leg out, but I can't. It's really pinned."

"Good job." He handed her the jack. "Take hold of this." When she had it, he handed down the tire iron. "And the handle. Don't drop it."

"I won't," she said peevishly.

Probably a good sign that she was her usual self. "I'm coming down."

One again he wriggled his way toward where her leg disappeared under the debris. "Jack," he said, reaching his hand back.

"Forceps. Scalpel," she said, mimicking a surgeon, then, "Oh shit," as she must have thought of the possibility of what a scalpel might be used for at this moment.

"You're going to be fine," he said, jamming the jack into the space by her leg. No, that was too far back. He had to have space to work the handle. He reached his hand back again. "Handle, Suze." When he had it firmly in hand, he worked it into its slot and pumped the handle until the jack slowly rose. When he started to feel resistance, he stopped and wriggled forward to check the jack.

"Okay," he said. "I'm going to try and relieve some of this pressure. I have no idea what'll happen, so be ready for anything." He hoped he didn't bring a pile of debris down on his own head, trying this. He could be making his own tomb. "We'll go slow. If you think you can move your leg, do it. Take the first chance you get."

He began to pump the jack handle again, slowly and steadily. A snap made him stop. He heard tiny bits of gravel or debris rolling downhill. He glanced back at the light behind him, hoping it wasn't the last look at sunlight he'd ever see. "Anything?" he called back.

"Still stuck."

"I'm trying again," he said, and he pumped the handle once more, twice, and Suze's knee shot back and smacked him in the nose. "Ow!"

She crowed with joy. "I'm alive, I'm alive."

"I think you broke my nose." He touched it gingerly. No, not broken.

She pounded on his butt. "Damn! You did it!"

"Stay still, for pity's sake. Let me out of here before the world crashes down on my head."

He cranked down the jack until he could get it out and passed it back to her. She was laughing in hysterical relief. Bash crawled backward until he could lever himself out once again, and then Suze passed him up the jack and handle. He didn't want to lose them. If they worked once, they would work again. "Can you use the leg?"

"Yeah, I can move it. The foot's a little numb and it really hurts along my shin. I think it'll be okay."

"Bend your knee and bring it up to the light so I can see."

She did, holding her leg in place at the thigh. Bash raised her pants leg and saw a dark line, bruised already. It was going to hurt. She'd probably limp for a while. But there was barely any blood. "Move your toes?"

"Yeah, I can, I think."

"You're going to be fine." This time, he felt more certain. He wished he knew more about crush trauma, compartment injuries, and how to treat them—especially without a hospital. Without drugs. Or an x-ray machine. Or any equipment. The reality of his situation came home to him.

"I know I am fine." She was still giddy with relief. "I don't think it's broken."

"Suze," he said, serious. "There were twenty people with you in that room. You're the only one I've found."

She sobered. "Are they—?"

"They might be dead. They might be trapped. We need to find the survivors, before nightfall. I have to go over to a car wreck on the street for a second, but you start looking for them, okay? They're up the hill of debris, I think, over here to your right." He yanked the t-shirt off from around his neck. "This is all I have for you to clean your face with."

"Okay, okay. Go on. I can get out by myself."

"I'll be back as soon as I can. Be careful. We need to help our friends, but we need medical workers too, Suze. The hospital is gone, and we both need to stay alive."

"What you do mean, gone?"

"Just what I said, *gone*. You'll see, when you look over there once you get out. I'm sorry, but I'm going to leave you to do it on your own. I have to see about this accident," he said, and worked his way back down to street level once again.

Chapter 4

Gale

Flat tire, he thought, as the car lurched to the right. His foot automatically went for the brake pedal and he steered to the right. Then ahead, not five car lengths, a power pole came crashing down onto the street, crushing an SUV's roof. He braked fully, and his car kept rocking, and that's when he knew for sure. Earthquake. A big one this time. Looking to the right, he saw another power pole waving, and he inched the car forward and back into the center lane until he was as far from it as possible. It put him closer to the downed lines, which were probably live. He shifted into park, then took his hands off the wheel and watched the world go mad.

Everything was shaking, and then shaking more. This wasn't like the earlier quake. This was serious. With every few seconds—he thought to look at his watch—something else came down, the windshield like a movie screen showing a Hollywood disaster movie. A restaurant sign crashed spectacularly down, glass spraying for dozens of yards. Facades peeled off strip mall stores. People who had missed being hit by that debris were thrown to the ground. A few fought their way back to their feet but were thrown down again. Ahead of him in the crushed SUV, there was no motion. He feared whoever had been in there was dead.

Another power pole fell farther down the road, and the line snapped, sparking and whipping around, slithering across car roofs and the sidewalk. A woman in a red Ford leaped out of her car, and the line danced across the car as she was shutting the door. She jerked and her hair instantly burst into flames. She fell, out of his line of sight, surely dead. The power lines stopped slithering, the power gone from them.

And still the earth shook. Where his car rested was still up a few hundred yards up off the lowest river bottom land, but down there, it must be shaking harder, the sandy ground liquefying. He checked his watch again, struggling to read it while being bounced about, and it turned over another minute. The quake had been going for at least a minute—meaning it was a really big one. Behind him, he heard an enormous crash in the distance as something came down, a building probably, from the sound. In the Walmart, there must be—what?—hundreds of people in there right now. A thousand?

He should feel something more, panic, or horror, or fear for his own life, but he felt only numb as he rode out the last seconds of the earthquake as it tapered off. When it was done, he glanced at his watch again. Another minute had ticked off, so the quake was somewhere between 2 and 3 minutes of shaking. The magnitude was going to be really big, somewhere between 8 and 9, he thought.

All around him, people were injured. He stepped out of the car to look behind him and saw what the crashing noise had been—the interstate overpass, two blocks back, had completely collapsed. Anyone under there was dead. He turned. The SUV—maybe someone could be saved in there. No. He had to ignore that, ignore all of it. He had a job back at the EOC. The normal human reactions, to help, to run from the car and ask strangers if they were okay—those had to be quashed. In the long run, keeping the city's infrastructure up and working would save more lives than anything he could do right here in the next ten minutes. It went against every human instinct toward decency, but he got back in his car, put it in gear and drove around the fallen power pole and the crushed SUV and toward downtown.

The pavement was buckled and cracked in many spots, but he was able to steer around the worst of it. Stopped cars were the bigger hazard, many sitting in the travel lanes, some with doors open, their drivers gone. In some, the driver seemed in shock, sitting still and doing nothing—in others, a parent was leaning back over the seat to check on kids. Soon his head was hanging out the window as he shouted at people to clear the road for emergency vehicles. It seemed to take forever to get them moving, and he got a lot of angry and defensive shouts back, but as long as they moved, he didn't care how irked they were at him. He had the oppressive sense of seconds ticking by, and unimaginable hours of work that all needed to be done right now, this very instant.

He drove through a landscape that at first looked a bit like the video of Caruthersville had looked, a river of water from broken mains, some downed houses. But as he drove down the hill toward downtown, he could see the damage on the river bottom land was much worse. Whole blocks had been turned to rubble, with a building standing here and there or sometimes just a single wall in a whole block. Many two-story frame houses had the upper levels collapsed into the lower level. Every single brick house had been turned to rubble. After two or three minutes of hard shaking, that was no surprise to him. Water from broken mains ran past him, seeking lower ground. He thought about the drinking water in his trunk and realized it could mean life to him, to Bash, while others might die from drinking contaminated water. He had no doubt it would be weeks before safe water was running out of taps again in this part of the city, maybe months. Not that there would be all that many intact houses with taps left if it were working. What a horrible mess.

He pulled out his cell phone and texted Bash, but it didn't go through. Again, he felt the urge to turn his car and drive out to Bash's clinic, but he clamped down on that desire too. He had a job to do, a crucial job. He turned the phone off, conserving the battery, which might have to last him a week or more, fumbled for his charger and plugged it in to the dash. He punched the radio on and set it to scan. Local stations would be out, but he'd probably catch a St. Louis station. The radio found a signal.

An announcer was saying, "The President was in a staff meeting when he was informed. He immediately canceled his meeting and began making calls to the FEMA director and six governors. A White House official said everything possible was being done..."

He half-listened, hoping for something certain, a number maybe, a magnitude. Then he shook his head at himself. Whatever the number was didn't matter. The situation was whatever it was. Having someone call it a 7 or 8 or 9 didn't change what he had to do next.

The road worsened as he approached City Hall. He was driving at a crawl. At one point, he came upon two cars nose-down into a broad crack in the road, and decided to back up and take another street. The next street over was no better, nor the next, but on that one, the sidewalk was buckled but clear, and he drove up onto it to get past the bad patch, crunching over a patch of broken glass. His teeth rattled as he came hard off the curb, and he shoved the car into park as he opened the door to lean down and look down at his tires. All intact and inflated. He drove on.

He passed the fire station, a concrete and steel building. It was standing, but many cracks showed in the concrete. One body lay under a blue tarp, and four uniformed firefighters were pulling debris off a fire truck half in, half out of the bay. He hoped they were going out for the windshield survey of the damage once they had it out. That was their job, and he'd have to trust them to do

51

it right.

As he turned back onto the block where City Hall was, Gale's stomach sank. The brick building was badly damaged, despite having been retrofitted. A whole exterior wall was gone, office furniture still tumbling out of canted floors, pipes and wires stretching out of the hole and lying along the wreckage. The facade had rained down heavy slabs that would have crushed anyone beneath them. A patch of the street in front of the building was gone, and in its place was a half-circle of sand. Holy shit, he realized, it's a sand blow. He'd read about them but never seen one, except pictures of excavated ones from history. It had come right through the pavement or maybe the front lawn of City Hall and left a big patch—maybe forty yards in diameter—that went from the far sidewalk and all the way over to the front of City Hall and disappeared under the rubble. It stank vaguely of sulfur.

He rolled up his window and parked the car well outside of the sand blow. As he approached City Hall, he could see the whole building was canted. Liquefaction, he thought—this whole left front quarter has sunk into the ground.

There was no way he was going to be able to get into the Emergency Operations Center. It was gone, and the supplies and generators and radio equipment might well be buried and out of reach.

What to do? Should he dig through the rubble and look for survivors? Try and find Evelyn? He counted rooms. Her office wasn't among the worst damaged. Maybe she'd survived. But where were the survivors? It had been ten minutes since the quake, he thought, maybe more. Surely there'd be someone crawling out of a door or milling around outside.

As he had the thought, there was a crash of glass, and a wheeled office chair came sailing out a front upper-story window, the window on the central hallway.

He jumped back.

A head appeared. Angela's. "Hey!" he called up to her.

"Gale, is that you?" She leaned forward. Her hair was covered with dust.

"Be careful of that broken glass in the window frame."

"I will. How should I get out of here?"

"Stairwell?"

"They're both blocked."

"Is Evelyn there?"

"Hang on." Her head disappeared, then reappeared. "No, but I sent someone to look."

"Can't you get out the fire escape?"

"It's gone. Fell to the ground along with the back wall."

"How about rope or—no, wait, there's a fire hose? In a case? Clear all that window glass out, every single bit first, and then maybe you can use the fire hose as a rope." He tried to think if they had emergency fire ladders anywhere inside, those foldable metal things, but if he hadn't thought to get one, he doubted anyone else had. Two staircases and a fire escape had seemed like plenty of ways out.

She turned again to talk to someone, then back. "We're on it." A voice behind her, distant but shrill. She yelled at him, "Be right back," and then she was gone.

Another face appeared, one of the city clerk's assistants, and she cautiously started picking shards of glass out of the broken window, using the sleeve of her cardigan as a glove. She stopped for a second, then came back holding her shoe, and began whacking at the remaining glass. Gale stayed well clear as bits of glass rained out.

In a few moments, the woman was replaced by Angela. Her voice was steady as she said, "Evelyn's office is totaled. I don't see how she could have made it, unless she's unconscious under a bunch of debris. I'm sorry, Gale. It's not safe to try and find her. The floor is tilted out toward the back."

"Shit." Poor Evelyn. Her poor twins. He thought of the fire

truck he had seen with a twinge of regret. They had their own priorities—the survey, any real emergency that could kill hundreds, like a toxic chemical leak to be sealed, then a more careful check of schools and hospital, power plant and water treatment plant, trying to keep basic services up. Only then they could start pulling debris off people, starting with the schools and police station. If Evelyn were hurt and awaiting rescue, she'd have to keep waiting a little while. Just like everyone else, probably everyone from St. Louis to Nashville, and beyond. Gale and the surviving City Hall staff were on their own. There was no 911 to call, no rescuers to rely on, only yourself and the people standing next to you and whatever tools you could pick out of the debris.

"Gale," Angela said, grabbing his attention back to the moment. "She was with the mayor. He was in there too. I think they're gone. It means you're the acting city manager now."

And in charge of all Emergency Operations for the city? Oh, shit. But he straightened his shoulders and nodded. "Okay, you have that window clear yet? Let's get all of you out." Before the first aftershock, he thought, but did not say.

The tan hose came slithering out. He stabilized its end as the office staff, one by one, climbed down it or, as with a couple, fell off it, luckily without serious injury. The city clerk, a very large woman in her 50s named Kay, refused to even try. "I'm not the fat lady in the freakin' circus!" she said. "I'll wait until someone can get me a ladder. A big, sturdy ladder that I won't break."

"Can you check every office, then?" he called up to her. "Collect food, water, candles, battery-operated radios, anything that will help us survive. Don't be shy about going through drawers. See if anyone has one of the emergency radios in their office. And don't hurt yourself trying, but then figure out if there is any way at all down to the EOC, okay?"

"I can do that," she called, and disappeared from the window

A few of the workers were moving off toward the parking lot. "Hey!" he yelled at them. "Where are you going?"

"To check on my kids," said one.

"Oh, right." This was the problem with emergency staff. They were people too, and they wanted to know, as he did, if their loved ones were okay. "Look, I know it's hard, but the instant you know they're okay, get back here. There's work to do. If we've set up an EOC someplace else, I'll leave a sign."

He turned to the others. "Those of you without small children, I'm begging you, hang with me for now. We'll take off in shifts, to go check our houses and husbands and pets. But we need to get to work now."

"Doing what?" a male maintenance worker asked, looking around at the destruction all around them. "Sweet Jesus, is there anything *to* be done?"

"We're the government. No one is going to come rescue us for days, more than likely. St. Louis and Memphis, maybe Paducah, they'll get attention first. We're on our own, and we have to be the ones to make sure services are provided, that food and water are distributed fairly, that medical care is available. We have to contact FEMA somehow. We have to prioritize, and take on big jobs, and get it done somehow, even what seems impossible. Everyone here will have to do important work, crucial work. Some of you will have to recruit and direct volunteers. We'll all be working crazy long hours, and we'll all be making tough decisions." He looked around and held every set of eyes for a few seconds. "I know we can do this. Are you with me?"

Nods all around, a few "Yes, sirs" and Angela half-smiling at him. No one looked mutinous, at least not yet.

Now all he needed to do, to follow up his little motivational speech, was to figure out what the *hell* they were supposed to do first.

"Anybody have something to write with? I need to make a list, give assignments."

"Smartphone," said one woman, holding hers up, and a couple others nodded, pulling out phones and a tablet computer.

"Okay, good. But we'll be out of power for these eventually," he said. "And we'll need to be making signs and duty rosters and so on too. What we need is to pretend it's 1960 or so. Markers, poster board, chalk maybe."

An older woman from finance piped up, "I lived that time. I know what we need."

"Great. Try and get Kay's attention. Have her send down all the markers and big paper of any sort she can find for posters. Notebooks and pens and pencils. Strapping tape. Staple gun." He wiggled his fingers, asking for other suggestions.

"Push broom," said the maintenance guy. "Wrench."

Oh shit, thought Gale. "Wrenches first. We need to get natural gas off, everywhere we go."

The older woman—Jeannine, Gale thought her name was—went over to the building to try and get Kay's attention.

"Oh God, gas. My house," said one woman, sounding on the verge of panic.

"I know," said Gale. "Just stick with us a bit longer. Either someone there will turn it off, or a neighbor will do it for all the others on the block, or the utilities guys will be out, turning it off street by street."

She looked mutinous for a second, about ready to turn and run away, but then her shoulders sagged. "My husband should get it."

"Right. Try sending texts to home, all of you. Tell them you're okay and to turn off the water main, the gas, preserve the water in the hot water tank by shutting its feed off—that may be all you have to drink for a while. If the texts don't go through, turn the phone off and try again in an hour. Conserve your phone batteries." His own house would have to burn or stand, whatever fate decided, though he felt a twinge at the thought of losing so many beloved things, photos and keepsakes, antiques, clothes. He hoped at least the garage had made it and that the trash can full of survival gear wasn't crushed. Two people could live for ten days off that, with another week using what he had just bought.

He glanced around at footwear. Two-thirds of the women had running shoes on or sensible flat shoes. The other third were in heels. "You need better shoes," he said, stabbing his fingers at the impractical ones. He made a mental note to make a rule to ban high heels henceforth at any workplace as part of the emergency operations plan. Screw fashion.

The maintenance guy pulled a multi-tool off his belt. "I can just yank them heels off, if you want."

"These are Blahniks," cried one woman, backing away from the maintenance guy.

"I have my sneakers up in my desk," said another.

"Add it to Kay's list of things to toss down," he said, and that woman and another went over to speak to Jeanine as she paced the front of the building, still trying to catch Kay's attention.

The maintenance man studied his multi-tool. "I'll see if I can manage to get gas off here with this somehow."

"Great, thanks. Someone, take some notes on your phones for now please. I have to get this straight in my own mind. Priorities. Police, fire, ambulance—coordinate with them. Map of navigable roads, probably from fire department, updated with their survey. Tow truck to move abandoned cars. Water and food for us, here in the EOC. Location for EOC. Radios. Sanitation. Health care. Morgue." He saw shocked faces at that word, but he plowed on. "Generators. Camp stoves or someplace to boil water. Water purification tablets. Cots, sleeping bags for EOC. Big tents for temporary shelter for us."

The woman with the pricey shoes said, "Thank you, Jesus, that it's not cold."

He nodded. "For October, we're lucky. Anyone remember the forecast?"

Angela said, "Rain, I think, tomorrow night. And a cold front."

Damn. He forced a smile. "At least it's not January."

"Or August," said Angela.

The dead bodies, he thought, in a hot Mississippi Valley August—yes, that'd be bad. But he didn't mention the thought. "Okay, I know you're all anxious to check your houses, so what we need to do is get a list together and send half of you on a mission for supplies, and we'll pick something to find near your house. But you need to swear to me to come back. No matter what." He didn't want to say it aloud—Even if your whole family is dead. "You come back here. We need you."

"We can't stand in the middle of the road and direct operations," said the shoe woman.

"No. But we need to stay outside. We can't go inside any building. There will be aftershocks."

"Aftershocks? Bad ones?"

He looked at a sea of worried faces. "Some could be as strong as the first one. There could be dozens of them, and a lot of buildings that didn't come down the first time will come down the next time, or the next." He glanced at the building. "We have to get Kay out of there as soon as possible."

"Let's just go back in the park" said a woman. She pointed to the green space behind City Hall.

He'd have to get all these names straight eventually—he hadn't needed to know everyone in City Hall until now. A few seconds alone with Angela, and he'd grill her on that. "Good. But we won't be easily findable by the public, hidden back there."

Angela said, "That might not be a bad thing."

Kay appeared at the front window and started tossing down trash bags. "Unbreakable stuff," she called. She hauled the fire hose up. The older finance woman started shouting up their new list of items to her.

"Map!" he called over. "And I need letterhead and some official seal, a stamp or embosser or something that we can prove we are who we say we are."

"To who?" asked the woman who had expressed her worry about the gas at her house.

"Shop owners, whoever. If you're going to demand camp stoves or a generator or bottled water without cash money, you need some authority."

She nodded, thinking it through. "Yeah, I guess credit cards aren't going to work today."

"We may need to—" He hesitated, looking for a delicate way to put it, but realized being blunt would be better. "Not declare martial law, but be insistent. I mean, point out we need the goods and tell them to keep track and bill the city government later. And we need to get on it now, before dark." After that, it'd be too late, he thought. What stores there were would be emptied out by tomorrow.

"It won't be that bad," protested the shoe woman.

"It might be very bad indeed. Is the bridge still up? Add it to the list, would you? Bridge, airport, rails, highway. Without any of those, nothing will get to us—no rescue, no supplies. The food and bottled water, juice, colas—what's in town may have to last everyone in town for days." He thought that body bags would be as important as food. Mass graves or mass funeral pyres would not be out of the question, but he wouldn't bring that up yet. These people hadn't yet seen the destruction across the city, the completeness of it, but they would soon enough. Some of the bodies to be disposed of would be people beloved by his EOC staff—Bash could even be among them. No, don't think of that. Get the work done. Take each hour's tasks as they came. Each moment's tasks.

"Anything else on the list?" asked a woman with her smartphone in her palm.

"Sewage," he said. "We'll probably have to dig pit toilets before long, or recruit people to do that."

"One pit won't do it," said Jeannine, back in the group now. "Not for forty thousand people."

He wondered how many of the sandy bottoms had intact houses with septic fields. Subtract the dead, and he thought he still needed to think about sewage issues for as many as 20,000.

A young woman said, "You know what we need? Something like block leaders. People who can, neighborhood by neighborhood, organize sanitation and child care and first aid. Someone should try and put that together. Use neighborhood watch leaders if they exist—if not, go around and knock on doors and give people a list of things to do. Maybe there are ham radios or walkie-talkies to keep in contact with them."

"Medications," said the older woman. "My husband's a diabetic. Insulin needs to be kept cool."

Angela said, "And managed. If there's any at the pharmacies, you can't let a few people grab it all."

"We need the police," Gale said. "And I want to meet with the fire chief too. Most of them seemed okay over at the station when I drove past. And everybody keep track of any ham radio people you run across."

Kay appeared at the window. "Letterhead and an embosser from the clerk's office," she called, waving another plastic bag and dropping it out the window.

"We need some sort of uniform," said the shoe woman. "I mean, matching jackets or something to identify us. It'll automatically say we have authority too, like the letter."

"We need to get you all hardhats and work boots, hiking boots, something sturdy," said Gale. "And that's first thing, before you go walking through debris."

The maintenance man came back. "Fire chief got the gas off for the whole block. He wants to meet with you."

"Can you please run back and tell him ten minutes?"

Gale took the ten minutes to dash off two letters declaring the holder of the letter to be an official representative of the city government, with emergency powers. He tried to find wording that demanded cooperation of the reader in a way that would be least likely to incite refusal or resentment but that conveyed it *had* to be done. People were going to have to get used to, very quickly, a different world for a few weeks, to losing some freedom in order to keep the most people alive, to taking orders without having a long democratic discussion first. They'd be cooperative for a couple days, he had learned, in emergency management courses, and then they'd start to balk as stresses overwhelmed the urge to do communal good. He needed them to act like soldiers, but they'd act like frightened people.

"Reservists, National Guardsmen," he said, as soon as the thought crossed his mind. "Add it to the list. If you know anyone who is one, have them report to the park, in uniform if they can get to theirs. We'll need them too." He was sure they'd be called up officially, but until those orders got through to them, the city could put them to good use. He'd talk to the police and fire chiefs about splitting them up and assigning them out. He didn't envy the police their jobs these next few weeks.

When he had two letters written, he handed one to Jeannine and one to Angela and asked them to make thirty copies each, signing his name. Then he asked for volunteers who did not have a family to check back home, and he got only two hands, a sturdy middle-aged woman who said she had cats she wanted to check on eventually but that could wait until last, and a girl barely out of her teens, who said her boyfriend was a truck driver and on the road out west. He set them to mapping where his staff lived and what sorts of stores were close by to them. He had someone else send Kay to toss out a phone book. He wanted to find a party supply place that might have big tents. Someone from Parks said there was at least one out at each of the two biggest parks, stored, for rentals. He had the rest of them except the two without families count off one-two, one-two, and said the twos would be going out first. When they got back, he'd let everyone else go home and check on things. Tomorrow, in shifts, he'd give them some time to clean up whatever messes they had at home. He'd take a short shift at that himself, but he knew for the next twelve hours, he wouldn't be leaving the city center.

Everybody had pads of paper by then, and pens, and they were taking notes on what supplies to find, addresses to stores to check, getting shoe sizes from the rest of the high-heeled women, and doing darned well, he thought, considering how worried they must all be about loved ones. "We'll set up back there," he said, pointing to the green space and picking out three people randomly. "You three get that started. The rest of us, do not put yourself at risk, but see if you can find any other survivors in City Hall. Walk around the edges and listen for voices. Look, listen, but no more than that. That building is a menace. And if you see something useful in the edges of the debris, pick it up." He wanted Evelyn to be found, and found alive, but he wasn't counting on it. "Try to develop a list of who is missing in this building. Don't forget to list the mayor. I'll be back in fifteen or twenty minutes."

He was ten yards down the street when he had another thought. "Power company," he called. "Put that on the list too." He had to talk with someone there and see what was going with power, or what kind of emergency power they might be able to supply to part of the town, or at least to the EOC.

He was halfway to the firehouse when he had another thought—jails. First, who was in them, who would care for them, were they dangerous enough people to need to keep locked up? And second, as people started looting, which he imagined would be starting very soon and escalating as normally decent people got more desperate, enough cells to hold the looters. He honestly didn't give a damn if that type got fed or not, but they'd have to see to it anyway.

There was so much to do—and ninety minutes of daylight left to get too much of it done. He turned back one last time, but they were out of hearing range now. "Flashlights," he said to himself. "Everybody needs the biggest flashlight you can find, and plenty of batteries."

Chapter 5

Bash

Bash jogged across to where the green Toyota coupe was smashed into the light pole. The car was surrounded by three people—the man he'd spoken to before and a pair of frightened teenaged girls, one white, one Asian, hands gripped together. A middle-aged white woman was leaning into the driver's side window. As he approached them, the man said, "Thank God. I think he's pretty bad."

"Have you tried opening the door?"

"Jammed tight from the damage," the man said. "I think he might have panicked and accelerated into the pole. Or been speeding. I mean, look at it." He pointed to the crushed front of the car. "They aren't supposed to accordion like that at city speeds."

Bash edged up to the woman, who was holding a blood-soaked rag against the man's head. The steering wheel had pinned him upright in the seat. The driver was unconscious. He wore no seatbelt. It didn't look good.

"I don't think I've helped," she said. "And I can feel things moving around that shouldn't." Her voice shook at the last phrase.

"You did great," Bash said. "Hang on for a second." He palpated the neck, found a thready, rapid pulse, checked the pupils, glanced at his near ear and felt around to the far one for cerbrospinal fluid. Listening for breathing, he caught a reedy sound with a hitch, totally wrong. Gentle, he palpated the chest, thinking, *I need gloves, hundreds of gloves, and a stethoscope. And the jaws of life and a damned operating room for this man.* But gloves would be a start.

"Did you undo his seat belt?" He nudged her hand aside and palpated the skull. Fracture, definitely.

"No, it was off already."

Here it comes, he thought. *This is the start of it, and it's going to go on and on and on for me. I don't want to do it, but I have to. Triage.* He needed tags. Black for this guy—he was a goner. Pneumothorax, maybe injury to the pericardium or heart, and a serious head injury. This guy needed a surgeon, and fast, and an ICU. And much as they all might wish for it, that wasn't going to happen. Bash checked his phone. No signal. No way to call for helicopter evacuation from elsewhere, even if they could get one with all the competition he knew there'd be.

"You can step back," he said to the woman, making his voice as gentle and as kind as he could.

She pulled back a bloody hand and stared at it, a confused expression on her face. Blood was barely seeping from the wound now that the blood pressure low.

Bash sighed and patted the injured man on the shoulder. "I'm sorry, fella," he said. He stood up and faced the four people. "He's not going to make it."

The man blinked at him. "What do you mean, he's not going to make it? We'll get an ambulance—"

"Cell phones are out," said the white girl.

"I'll run down to the hospital and get an ambulance," said the man. "Should have done it before." He shot Bash an angry look.

"There is no hospital," said Bash.

The woman looked up from studying her bloody hand. "What?"

"It's gone, just pile of bricks now."

"But what about—?" she said.

"I'm sure at least half of the patients and staff are dead. Some are pinned or trapped. Some are injured. Some are—" He was going to say, "Some are going to die waiting for help," but he couldn't be that blunt. He looked round the group. "I'm so sorry. Did you know him?"

They all shook their heads.

"But how will people get help?" the woman asked. "Without a hospital?"

The man muttered, "Fuck," then looked at the girls and flushed.

Bash suspected the girls had heard the word before. "I'll help. Other nurses and doctors who survived will help. We'll save as many as we can, I promise."

"But where?" said the woman. "Where will you help them?" She gestured to the catastrophic damage to the buildings all around them.

"That's a great question," he said. He glanced around. He knew about aftershocks. He could see the condition of the buildings along hospital row. The sandwich shop across the street looked intact, but that was the only building. Hmm. He could use the food in there. He needed that to become the hospital cafeteria. And if an aftershock took it down, better not to put patients in there. He looked behind him at the nearly-empty visitor lot to his workplace. He pointed at it. "There."

"Outside?" She sounded shocked.

"It's safest," he said. He looked at the four of them, assessing. Then he pointed at the two girls. "You two need to check in with your mom and dad."

The white girl cocked her head at the Asian one. "She's an exchange student living with us, Haruka."

"Do you speak English?" he asked the girl.

"We learn English every year in school," she said, clearly, though with a strong accent.

"You speak it very well," he said. "I'm sure your parents will be terribly worried about you."

She nodded.

"Have you texted them?"

She nodded. "But it does not work."

"It will, eventually."

The white girl spoke again. "My mom works over in Johnstown."

A town a dozen miles away, but up in some hills. "Ah, well, she's probably okay then. But it might be some time before she can get back here."

The girl nodded.

"You checked in with your families?" He aimed the question at the man and woman.

"I will. I'll go now," said the woman. She threw a miserable glance at the injured man inside the car.

"You did what you could," he said. "Don't blame yourself."

"I'll pray for him," she said. "And for you."

Bash nodded. He raised eyebrows at the man.

"I'm not from here. I'm from Marion."

"That's in Illinois?"

"Yeah. I fix photocopiers."

"I'm sure your people are fine, then. Far enough from the quake."

"Yeah, ex-wife has the kids there. But..." He gestured helplessly about him. "I can't just leave. There's so much to do here."

"Are you willing to stay and do some of it?"

"Absolutely," the man said.

"Thank you," said Bash, meaning it from the bottom of his heart. "I need help. I need you to walk up medical row here and collect every walking medical person you find, every support person, every receptionist, everyone who is willing to work. Send them here unless someone has already gotten something better set up elsewhere, in which case come get me, please. I'm going to set up for first aid in this parking lot. And if you find stretchers intact, or even office chairs with wheels, a pile of blankets, a table sturdy enough to use as a bed, anything like that, wheel them over here, please. Get people to help. Bring me anything that looks useful, anything like medical supplies. I need it all. Bandages, splints, syringes, everything like that, and pens and paper, something to write with."

"Will do. I know some of these offices from fixing their copiers." He took off toward the east.

The white girl said, "We'll help."

"You sure?"

She nodded, decisive. "We can do anything he can do."

Bash smiled at the attitude. "Thank you. Think about what you see in your first aid supplies, or what you've seen in doctor's offices. I'd need all that, and I have none of it. And don't forget gloves. Look for boxes of latex gloves, boxes and boxes of them. And if anyone tries to stop you, my name is Sebastian Hill, BSN, Cancer Center, and have them come and complain to me instead."

"Sure, I get it," she said. She tugged on Haruka's hand and they went down the street.

"What's your name?" he called after her.

"McKenna!" she shouted over her shoulder.

Bash ran back to his collapsed office building and yelled up, "Suze, you okay?"

"I found Meggy," she called down, but from where, he couldn't see. "She's dead, Bash." There was a catch in her throat.

"Can you hold on alone for five minutes?" he called.

"If I have to."

Bash ran as fast as he could over to the sandwich shop. The

glass in front was cracked in several places, but the one-story building looked solid.

"Hey," yelled someone. "There's no one in there." A tall young black man, early 20s, came up to him, dressed in a white shirt and clip-on bow tie. He came up to Bash. "You want a sandwich now?" he asked, incredulous.

"No, no. I came to ask a huge favor. You're the manager?"

"Assistant manager, but yeah, in charge today."

"I'm going to be setting up a first aid station—temporary hospital, really—over there in that parking lot. I'll be blunt. We're going to need this food."

"Need it? For...?"

"For patients and staff. We need you guys to be our commissary, our cafeteria, for as long as that food in there stays good."

The fellow cocked his head, thinking. "We have a freezer. Big freezer, big fridge too."

"Then we probably have three days, maybe four or five, before the food all goes bad."

"The cheese and salami, chips, like that, should stay good even without being cold, as long as they don't get real hot." He rubbed his neck. "But I was going to go home, you know. I can't stay here and serve people."

"No one needs to be served right now. But I don't want anybody else to get to that food. It'll be a life-saver. Literally."

"Well, shit," the young man said. He rubbed his neck some more and looked around. "I hate to think what the owner would say. He's a greedy asshole."

"He may be a dead asshole now for all we know—and in any case, not worried foremost about his sandwich shop."

"Oh, he owns a dozen places. This isn't the biggest or the one he'll be thinking about first."

"So you'll help us?"

He made a quick decision. "Hell, I'll give you the key." He

dug in his pocket and came out with a big ring of keys. "I locked her up. You can get in easiest out back, by the dumpster."

A dumpster! He'd have his newly recruited workers borrow it, for sure, wheel it or drag it over to the parking lot if they could. He'd need a place for medical waste. He needed so many things.

"You're saving lives," he told the young man, as he pocketed the keys. "You're a hero."

"Nah. I'm just—well hell, I tell you, if I can get back here tomorrow morning after I check on my people, I'll give you a hand too. You keep the keys, but if I can come back, I'll make you up some sandwiches. You probably want to eat the potato salad, cold slaw, like that, first."

"You're right. And I thank you, really, from the bottom of my heart." He shook hands. "What's your name?"

The man pointed to a nametag. "Nathan."

"I'm Bash. I hope your family is okay, Nathan."

"Yeah, me too," he said, and held a hand up in farewell as he went back to his car.

"Food," muttered Bash. "Dumpster. Medical supplies. Personnel. I need a tent. A nice big tent." As he got back to the fallen building, he glanced at the employee lot and saw 20 cars, including his, sitting there. And he thought, Those are beds for the healthy or walking wounded. Beds for staff to catch a few winks between long shifts. Those cars are temporary housing, that's what they are. Even if their owners are dead, and please no, let them not all be dead, those cars will keep someone dry and warm.

"Suze," he shouted up. "We need their car keys too!" He climbed the pile of debris to explain the situation to her.

* * *

She hadn't taken well to his demand that they paw through corpses of their friends for car keys, and he couldn't blame her. It was grisly work and not terribly useful after all. Most must have had their keys in purses or the lockers. If he got a minute, he'd see if he could find the lockers amongst the debris.

Seeing Meggy's corpse was awful—he really had liked her—and she had been crushed beyond recognition by equipment from the roof. Only her size, plus her skirt and shoes and the electronic pad in her lab coat pocket, had let Suze identify her. Her face and chest were under a slab of roof and another big metal box, air conditioning or heating or whatever. It didn't matter what it was—it had killed her.

Suze was crying silently as she worked, tears trailing down her checks from time to time. "Don't you care?" she asked when he didn't cry with her.

"I just—" He shook his head. "I care. I'm thinking about what to do next, Suze. It's an ER. Our life has just become one big ER, and everything has to be triage now. I'll grieve later. It's way down my triage list."

She had shaken her head at him and they had gone back to searching the debris. They found another dead nurse, Rikki, an older woman who had kept to herself. They heard no voices calling for help, which made Bash's heart feel heavy with dread. No one was banging on metal, trying to get their attention, either. Twenty more staff members in the building, and he feared none of them were left alive.

Suze's leg was obviously hurting, but on her hands and knees, she managed well enough. With her bad leg, she wasn't much help in lifting heavy debris. He had found an electrical cord attached to a projector, one of those things you plug your laptop into to give presentations. He had, with some effort, yanked it out and used it to strap his jack and handle to one of the bare beams, so they didn't get lost in the debris field.

They had found their third body, they couldn't tell who, only one leg without a femoral pulse and the rest buried under rubble, when he heard someone screaming from the street, "Nurse

Sebastian, where are you?"

Carefully, he stood up and saw the two teenaged girls wheeling a trolley along the cracked sidewalk, like a mail cart or something, piled high with boxes. He waved his arms overhead until they caught sight of him. "I'll be right back," he said to Suze.

"Does it matter if you are?" she said, with a fresh welling of tears. "I don't think we're going to find anyone alive here."

He scrambled down the debris pile. When he hit the ground, he glanced at his watch. It had been 30, 35 minutes since the quake. The sun was getting lower. Shit, damn, and every other bad word he could think of. He needed light. A generator and lights. He needed too damned much, and he was only one man. One man, one weepy nurse, and three civilians. That wouldn't begin to fix things.

When he got to the girls, he saw that Haruka looked pale.

"You okay?" he said to her. He thought she'd probably seen dead people, horrible sights, and it was getting to her. As it would anyone who didn't have training at pushing it aside temporarily. It got to everyone, eventually, even the trauma-trained.

McKenna said, "She's afraid of me."

"Why's that?"

"Because I just killed a guy," the girl said, and burst into tears, launching herself at Bash.

Bash took her in his arms and patted her back, shushing her as she wept. He looked at Haruka, who, to his shock, was nodding.

Haruka said, "She did."

McKenna wrenched herself out of Bash's arms, dashing angrily at her tears. "That asshole."

"I'm sure you didn't do anything," said Bash, thinking she was feeling guilty for not helping an injured person, or maybe even moving someone who was dying.

"I hit the bastard over the head," she said, sniffing, then rubbing snot off her face with her shirt. "With one of those round metal bar things that you see, those ridged things, like from a wall."

"Like a rebar?" Bash said, feeling a bit dizzy at this confession.

"Yeah. That bastard," she said, furious.

"He was stealing drugs," said Haruka.

"What?"

"There is druggist store," she said.

"A pharmacy," said McKenna. "And I knew the kid. He used to go to our high school but dropped out last spring. Or maybe got kicked out. And he had these—" she pointed to two grocery sacks hanging off the handles of the cart she had been pushing "—and he says, 'Hey, you two girls wanna party? I got some tasty stuff here.' And he said that about what was in the sack. And I thought about people who would need drugs, I mean, really need them, and I picked up the bar and I started hitting him. And hitting him and hitting him—" She faltered. "And I think I killed him."

"He is not moving, Mr. Sebastian," said Haruka, touching her head to indicate, he thought, the injury to the drug thief.

"Call me Bash," he murmured, as he picked up one of the bags and looked inside. Oh, smart kid, that thief. There was Vicodin, and Oxy, and Percodan and Dialudid and—holy crap—fentanyl skin patches. He held up a box of those to show McKenna. "Chances are he would have killed himself with these anyway," he said. Addicts had before, many times. He closed the bag and took the girl by the shoulders.

"Look, I'm not suggesting you beat up more people, but he may be fine. Maybe he's only unconscious. Maybe someone will bring him in for first aid."

She shook her head.

"Or maybe you killed him," he said, hoping it wasn't so. "But in doing that, you've saved a bunch of other lives." He pointed to the sacks. "That stuff there, that's going to allow us to set bones and do minor surgery and is going to let people who are hurting get to sleep for a little while. It will save lives, really." He held her eyes. "Many, many lives."

Great, he was thinking, first triage deciding who can live and die, and now he's jury and judge over criminal matters. Where does a guy apply for godhood, he wondered? I'm moving myself in that direction. "But don't—" He gestured vaguely. "Try not to kill anyone else, okay? I have enough patients as it is."

She laughed. "You're weird." The tears were done. For now.

"I am that."

"You gay?"

"I am that too."

"Fine by me," she said. "But you might not want to tell some of these people around here."

"I appreciate the advice," he said, though he hardly needed it. This was a bizarre conversation to be having right now. Back to work. "You two did great. But I want you to avoid going back wherever that guy was. If he wakes up, he's going to be mad at you. Did you keep your...er, weapon?"

"I left it there."

"Hmm." He hadn't thought that sending them out for supplies would be dangerous, but he realized now how naive that was. Carrying a weapon for self-defense might not be a bad idea, but a better idea would be to try and keep these two out of harm's way, and nearby. "You did great, but I have another job for you. There's a dumpster behind that sandwich shop over there. See if you two can manage to move it over here. If not, let me know. Don't strain anything. I don't need more patients."

The girls nodded. McKenna hesitated.

"Questions?" When they shook their heads, he said, "You did fine. Put it out of your mind for now if you can."

McKenna nodded and the two of them turned to go across the street.

Bash was looking at the cart of supplies, thinking about taking the drugs over to his car to lock them up, when he looked up and saw the man from the wreck leading a line of almost a dozen people, three in lab coats, two in scrubs. Had he asked the man's name? He needed to jot down names, and he realized he had Meggy's pad computer still, where he'd stuck it in his pocket to get back to her family eventually. Well, screw it. He turned it on, relieved it needed no password, opened a notes document, and typed in McKenna and Haruka's names.

Then he turned to greet his new staff.

* * *

In twenty minutes he had six tables—taken from inside the sandwich shop—set up to hold supplies and act as reception. He also has his first dozen patients, who were sitting on chairs also taken from the sandwich shop and, in one case, lying across three waiting room chairs, a rotten substitute for a bed but better than nothing, and a situation that had to change soon. His staff had no doctors, but one very experienced ward clerk, who was organizing the heck out of everything, supplies and staff names and drugs, using the girls' school notebooks to write in and make signs. He had everyone on the lookout for indelible markers in black, red, yellow, and green, in addition to everything and everyone else they were trying to find, beds or blankets or cots most of all. He was going to mark people for triage right on their foreheads as it got busier. He had one nursing assistant doing all the nursing and he himself was triaging, diagnosing and, right now, suturing cut feet using a woman's purse sewing kit and cotton thread doused in alcohol. It was field promotions for everybody and everything. Finally, at least, he had gloves to wear. And the clerk wasn't letting them throw gloves away. "We might have to reuse." So she had a bag of used gloves being collected.

A fire truck inched by and Bash yelled up from his suturing, "Somebody stop that truck!" But it was coming to a stop anyway. He put the last two stitches in, tied off the thread and told the patient, "Don't move. Don't walk on those. The nurse will come over to wrap them." Though she was busy with someone else, she made eye contact with him and nodded to show she had heard. She was a sharp one, and Bash was relieved to have her. He needed Suze, but she was using the last of the daylight to hunt for their friends and would not be dissuaded. Bash had given up hope on that front. And even if he had hope, triage was the place for him to be.

He hurried over to where a fireman was getting down from the truck. Someone was pointing at Bash, and the fireman strode to meet him.

"You're in charge here?"

"By default, it seems."

"The hospital is gone, you know."

"I know. We need..." He gestured helplessly. "Everything. Anybody you can save from there. Any equipment. Any equipment you can spare from your own stores. Beds. Portable lights and a generator. Patients."

"Oh, they're coming. More than you'll want."

Bash thought that one more would be more than what he had the staff to treat. "How about lights?" he said to the firefighter.

"I'll radio in to the command center. The police will set you up."

"Is there anyone else doing this?" Bash pointed behind him. "Emergency care?"

"A few individuals here and there. You're by far the most organized. And this space is good, and safe from building collapse. And it's close to the hospital, so anyone driving someone in there from this direction will see you. Let's call this the new hospital. We're going to spray directions on the street and walls in either direction to point here, so people can find you."

"Gods, I didn't even think of that."

"You can't think of everything," the fireman said. "I'd like to get my chief on the radio and have you two talk. Oh, and I have a patient for you, in the truck. I'll get her out of there and into your hands."

Bash nodded and started trying to organize his thoughts. What did he need, what should he ask for from the fire chief? What could they do for each other? Might the fire chief spare him a paramedic or two? Thinking furiously, he followed the fireman over to the truck. Two men were helping a woman down. He was shocked to see he knew her.

"Ms. Witherspoon!" he said.

"Small world," the woman said, holding tight to the arms of the men on either side of her. They lowered her weight to the ground.

"Are you hurt?" he asked.

"No, having a baby," she said.

A fireman said, "Irregular contractions."

"I want my husband."

"We'll get him here, ma'am," said the other one. By his tone, Bash thought he'd be happy to be rid of Ms. W.

"Put her on a chair over there," said Bash. "I'll get right with you, Ms. W."

"Well call me Melba if you're going to be putting your hands on my privates."

Bash smiled, despite his worries.

The first firefighter leaned out the truck's door and said, "I have my captain on the radio now."

Bash climbed into the cab, realizing how achy he was as he hauled himself in, sat down and took the radio. He and the chief worked talked things through, and he was reassured that a generator and lights were on their way. The truck and these three men were headed up to the hospital for rescue work, and with any luck they'd find more medical workers trapped but still able to function. Every police and fire unit would be on the lookout for doctors, nurses, dentists, anyone who might be able to join the makeshift hospital. For now Bash was its director, and everything that could be done to help him would be done.

When they had all that settled, Bash couldn't stop himself from saying, "I have family at City Hall."

"It took a pretty bad hit. All that brick. But most made it out."

"His name is Gale Swanton."

"Yeah, I know him. I talked with him earlier."

"He's alive?" Bash's throat closed and he had the force the next words out. "Thank you. Tell him I am too, next time you see him, would you?"

"Sure." The fire chief signed off.

Bash thanked his fireman. He wanted, more than anything, to go to Gale, but he had work to do. He was alive, though, alive! The knowledge eased a weight Bash hadn't acknowledged he'd been carrying, and he felt a burst of renewed energy.

As he stepped down from the truck and saw two ambulances pull up, he knew he was going to need every bit of energy he could summon.

Chapter 6

Gale

It was full dark when the first sizeable aftershock hit. A woman moaned in fear nearby—Gale wasn't sure who. A cascade of bricks fell down from City Hall first with a rattle, then a loud thud. Exhausted, Gale let himself sink to the ground and sat, cross-legged, waiting out the quake. It was a strong one, the strongest yet. For fifteen seconds, the ground beneath him moved. A 6.5, he guessed, or thereabouts. He wondered why the numbers still mattered to him. Habit. As it faded, he heard a distant crash as some other building a block or two away came down.

They'd had tremors all through the late afternoon, and each one brought a rush of adrenaline. You tensed, Gale thought, no matter if you wanted to or not, and when it backed off and didn't turn into another major quake, you still felt rattled from the burst of your own fear chemicals. The first few times, it fueled the work you had to do, and that was fine. About the fourth time, it started to wear on your mind and your body. You started to hurt all over, all the time, like you'd been working out for hours at the gym. But awful as the aftershocks were, as exhausting as the chronic adrenaline was, the aftershocks reminded you not to go indoors, even though part of you wanted to, like an animal wanting to crawl into a cave. It was not safe anywhere but outdoors.

Earthquakes don't kill. Buildings do.

They were working in the light of three large flashlights set on their ends, functioning as torches, and someone had brought them a box of strap-on LED reading lamps for doing paperwork, but it wasn't much light. They had dragged every park bench over to serve as a work area. They hadn't gotten a tent from Parks yet, or organized any furniture. In the morning, he was going to dig through the edges of the debris of City Hall and try to build a more organized office space out here, with a desk or two, a filing cabinet or maybe plastic boxes he could label.

He had been checking in staff as they returned with supplies, trying to learn their names, and sending two out for every one who returned, even people who'd already been out once already, until his staff was down to six, where he'd keep it until morning. Not everyone had returned. He wondered if the ones who hadn't were okay, if they'd fled town, if they were searching for lost family, or if they'd gone home to face a death and were emotionally incapable of returning.

He also had three family members of Vinya, the expensive shoe lady, bedded down in the park. Their house had been leveled. The family was lying on blankets on the lawn, close together, covered with a quilt they had rescued from the ruination of their home. It was early, but she had said she wanted to get the little ones to sleep, so she had lay down at dusk, the two children bracketed by their parents. He hoped they had slept through this aftershock. And he was reminded, thinking of them, that they also needed small tents for camping here, along with ground sheets and sleeping bags. Several people had said their houses weren't safe to stay in. If they wanted to, when the rains came, they could sleep here, but they'd need cover.

People had been understandably anxious to start the clean up at their homes, so he let them, as long as they all came back at dawn. It wasn't as if they could accomplish all that much in the dark anyway. Angela had said she'd wait until last to check on her house and husband, along with Megan, the lady with the cats, and Sophie, the girl with the trucker husband. The next staff member who returned, he'd send all three of them home. The unlucky ones like Vinya had no homes.

Gale wondered if he did.

The whole town was hunkered down for the night, it seemed, while firefighters continued to rescue people and police prowled the city with searchlights. The rescuers had finished with the schools and were working on the hospital now as well as the buildings all around it. The injured were taken to the temporary hospital. The dead were put into body bags and taken to the old cemetery two blocks from the hospital where they lay along the roadways, shoulder to shoulder, Dan, the fire chief had told him. "And we'll be out of body bags and stacking them naked in the roads before too long." Just as Gale had feared, there were that many dead.

Water mains were broken. Almost no one had water, and the few who did had to boil it, though there was no easy way to get that warning out to people. No electricity. No landlines or cell service yet. Nerdy ham radio operators were suddenly the most popular guys in town, and Gale kept in touch with police and fire via a handheld radio from the police department. Sewage was going to be a problem soon. People in the county with septic systems were in the best shape. Every port-a-potty they could find had been commandeered. A half-dozen were taken to the temporary hospital, which was seeing heavy business now. One was here. The others had been distributed in badly-hit residential blocks downtown. But port-a-potties didn't last long without cleaning. Tomorrow morning, they'd have to pick sites to dig latrines. In consultation with the police chief, Flint, they'd found a Guardsman who had some relevant experience overseas to lead the project, recruit volunteer diggers, and explain their use to what was going to be a very reluctant populace, used to gleaming clean porcelain and running water. Soap-free hand cleaner and anti-bacterial wipes were more valuable than gold right now. They had to think avoid spreading disease, which would tax an already overwhelmed health care system.

The interstate's overpasses at the west side of town were collapsed or unsafe. Any random one that was still up would only allow you to drive to the next collapsed one anyway. You could get around, but many roads were in bad shape, especially on the river bottomland. A third of the city streets downtown were blocked off to all but foot traffic. Spray-painted detour signs had started to go up. The fire department had found a stash of particleboard to use for signs. When they'd swung by to help Kay down from City Hall around sunset, they'd left him two cans of spray paint for any sign-making he and his people needed to do.

The town was cut off from supplies from the world outside. The train tracks, running right along the river, were underwater. The fire department had found breaks in them in both directions. One chunk had sunk into the soil with liquefaction, disappearing entirely. Where the interstate had collapsed onto roadways blocked east-west travel too, for now. Anyone driving under a remaining overpass during a serious aftershock was risking his life. The fire department couldn't even get out to the airport to check, but radio contact from there told them there was buckling and cracking of the runways. So if a brave cargo pilot could land safely there, which was unlikely, there was no way to get food or other supplies in from the airport. They'd have to get supplies via helicopter or by airdrop.

The river was of little use for travel, as the ground beneath it had shifted, and formerly clear channels were now shallow and filled with sandbars. The last dam along the river had been damaged beyond use, they had heard on commercial radio, and levees had been damaged, including one eight miles north of town. The filthy Mississippi was seeping over the lowest parts of town, and every day that towns upstream had sewage disposal problems of their own, it'd get filthier and carry more disease. Gale worried that if they ran out of bottled water, people would start trying to drink boiled river water, and they'd have epidemic disease on their hands, not to mention the certain cancers down the road from drinking who knew what awful chemicals. The bridge was still standing, but both approaches to it had collapsed.

They were on their own.

He looked back over toward the silhouette of City Hall, still far down the list for rescue and recovery until the buildings of hospital row had been cleared. His mind kept drifting back to Evelyn, and her twins. He hoped a neighbor had taken the twins in—if they were even alive. The elementary schools had already emptied out when the quake hit, but some kids at the middle school and high school had been there after the final bell, for band or play practice or detention. Some hadn't made it out. A number of teachers had been crushed in school buildings, most of which were brick.

A quarter of their fire force was dead or missing, and a full third of the police force. At least Guardsmen and Reservists had brought those numbers back up. So far, public order wasn't a problem. But it would be. Of that he had no doubt.

"Gale," he heard. It was Angela. "The aftershock is over. You can get up now."

"Right," he said, but made no move to stand.

Angela dropped down and sat next to him. "You need food. I need food."

She was right. The fire department had brought them a stack of cases of drinking water, but no one had eaten, at least not the four of them who hadn't gone home yet. "My car," he said.

"Mmm, sounds good, lovely crunchy car."

"No, no. I have food in the trunk of my car. And boots. I should get those on. And lots of chocolate."

"Now that's the best news I've heard all day."

"I'm getting up now," he said.

When he didn't move, she snorted a laugh. "How 'bout we do it together?"

"Sure," he said, and slowly levered himself off the ground. Angela popped up with more alacrity. "Why am I so tired? It's not even eight o'clock yet."

"Stress, probably."

"Maybe so. I'll be back in a flash," he said, and he walked toward City Hall, using the faint light from the sky to navigate. He glanced up at it and realized he could see hundreds upon hundreds of stars. No light pollution, so the sky was filled with light from distant suns. He could see the Milky Way. It actually lit the night so well it cast faint shadows. He thought about how far that light had come, and about beings that might be living out there around those suns, not knowing or caring about his problems. It comforted him a little, helped him realize that these days would pass, that his troubles didn't add up to all that much if you backed up and got a wider perspective.

At his car, Gale changed into his new boots. Then he grabbed some of his personal supplies and the office chocolate and took them back to share with his staff. It wasn't the healthiest of meals, crackers and chocolate, but it was fuel. He put multivitamin pills on his mental list of things to find. He should have bought some at Walmart, but he'd never thought to add them to his earthquake kit, not back in California, and not here. Of course, he'd been thinking about supplies for three days or a week. He was afraid this would last longer.

A half hour later a pair of staff came back together. "With the dark, there wasn't much we could do at home," said one.

"My husband and kid are camping out at the house," said the other. "He's afraid of looting."

"Yeah, that'll happen, I'm afraid," said Gale.

Megan said, "Not in a small town like this. We all know each other."

84

"If people get desperate for food, or blankets, or medicine, they'll do whatever they think is justified to find it." And a few idiots would loot for the joy of it. Gale sighed. "Angela, Sophie, Megan, I want the three of you to go check your homes, and your husband, Angela, and your cats, Megan."

Angela was reluctant to leave, but he shooed her off and sat on a bench with the returning staff, bringing them up to speed. He wished there were more they could do in the dark, but all they could do was accumulate knowledge as it dribbled in on the radio or from visitors. Gale felt as though precious time were slipping through his fingers, but he couldn't think of a thing more to do without light. He was anxious to hear back from power and water about the status of repairs, but he knew they'd call when they knew something more.

About nine, they got a visit from a power truck, a supervisor coming to report what was being done. In brief, everything possible, but nothing very useful. The power plant was on the river, a coal burner, and they were fighting flooding there from the levee breach and liquefaction. Lines were down all over, and for safety's sake they'd shut all off power to the town. Crews were fixing lines, but they would run out of replacement poles and line before long.

"And if we get many more aftershocks like this last one, I don't know that the replacements will stand for long, either," said the power guy. "We had a guy injured with that aftershock. A safety line came loose and he fell twelve feet. Broke an arm."

"They take him to the hospital?"

"Such as it is," said the guy. "They've got it outdoors. They can't operate outdoors, can they? And if it gets colder, how will they keep people warm there?"

"Everybody is doing what they can," Gale said. "And I'm sure your man is getting good care."

"Yeah, but this earthquake pretty much sucks."

A master of understatement. "Agreed."

"I mean, everything is screwed up. Water and the hospital and the roads."

Buddy, you haven't seen the half of it yet, Gale thought. But he merely made sympathetic noises.

The power supervisor took off then, his truck grinding gears at the end of the block, and Gale went back to the open-air EOC. He checked in with fire and police again on the radio, and he tried to get his staff to sleep on the benches, or at least lie back and close their eyes until the next emergency arose. A few more had trickled back.

By eleven, he was the only one awake. Someone should stay up, and he was in charge. But he'd have to get sleep at some point. Alone, in the dark, he had a powerful urge to talk with Bash, to be with him, to hold him for five minutes and reassure himself that he was okay. Bash had suffered from earthquakes in the past, and Gale hoped he was holding up emotionally. He wished he could be there for his husband to lean on. But he had a job to do and couldn't indulge himself with personal concerns.

At midnight, Angela came back, carrying a pile of blankets. "Some of these are pretty ratty," she said, "and one of them used to be my dog's, Flake, who died last year. But they're clean and I thought we could use them."

"It's great. Thank you for thinking of it," he said. "How's your house?"

"Inside, a mess. Could be worse, though. It's wood. Man, you really don't want a brick house in one of these, do you?"

"Not even one tiny bit, no."

"Did you think of that when you two bought here?"

"That and location. Nothing on river bottom. And I ordered a geologist's report, made it a contingency of my offer."

"Then your place should be okay."

"I hope. You can do everything exactly right and some damned thing will happen anyway, reflection of quake waves at that very spot, or whatever."

"You should go check it. Doesn't look like much is happening here."

"I wish more *were* happening. I wish we could do something useful. We're going to regret in a few days what we didn't do fast enough, I'm afraid."

"We pretty much are relying on others to do something, right?"

"Yeah, technicians. Power, and water, and cell phones. Fire, rescue and medical. For some of what needs to be done, we need daylight. Or a hundred generators dropped from the sky so we can see."

"Have you had a chance to talk with Bash?"

"No." He waved the thought away. "Tell me about your house. Michael is okay?"

"Yes. He made it home on foot a half hour before I got there." She went on to describe the damage she had seen walking there and back, and concluded, "We'll know better in the morning, of course."

"Everybody on staff will get some daylight hours at home."

"I know." They sat in silence for a few moments. Then she said, "You talk to FEMA again?"

"No. I need to in the morning. I keep thinking of more we need."

"Get some sleep now," she said. "I'll stay awake." She handed him an old blanket.

He nodded. He took the blanket, which smelled faintly of motor oil, and moved to a free bench and lay down. With his eyes closed, the initial quake replayed in his mind, the falling telephone pole, the crushed SUV, the stunned faces he drove past. The collapsed City Hall, and he couldn't help but dwell on all the useful EOC equipment buried and out of his reach. Without opening his eyes, he said, "Bulldozers, Angela. A temporary site for debris."

"Fine. I'll write it down. Now go to sleep," she said.

He pushed the images aside and tried to remember something else, something soothing. He remembered their wedding, out on a beach, how crazy windy it had been that day, whipping the hair of the officiate around, the gulls diving crazy circles through the wind, how happy he had been. Bash's eyes, bright with unshed tears. Their friends applauding the kiss. And he drifted into sleep.

Another hefty aftershock woke him some time later. He found himself grabbing on to the seat of the park bench before he was fully awake, his heart in his throat. He rode out ten conscious seconds of shaking.

And then he was wide awake.

He found his headlamp where he had hung it over the end of the bench and strapped it on, then sat up, rubbed his eyes, and went to look for Angela. He found her sitting up, where he had left her.

"You ready for some sleep?" he asked.

"I can't. I'm too wired."

He checked his watch. 2:02. "Anything happening?"

"Not a thing. A firefighter got injured hunting through the hospital. The chief told his guys who were on the day shift to get some sleep. I don't think they liked it."

"No, they wouldn't," he said, knowing the commitment of rescuers to their jobs. "The chief is going to have a lot to deal with in the next few days."

"You mean searching all the fallen houses?"

"That too. I was thinking of the psychology of his men. People who are trained to save lives get terribly depressed when they're only finding bodies. And they'll all be overworked and short on sleep, like the medical people. Like us, for that matter. Are you sure you can't sleep now?"

"I'm sure."

He sighed. "Then I'm going to leave for an hour, or ninety minutes maybe, if you don't mind. I want to drive by my house, see if it and my earthquake kit survived. And drive by to see Bash too. Just for a second."

"Absolutely. You need your turn too."

"And I'll try to dig up food for us all. I'll be back before dawn. In time for you to get some shut-eye while it's still dark."

"If I ever can sleep again while these aftershocks last."

He squeezed her shoulder and left. On the way past the sand blow in front of City Hall, he could smell sulfur again. He leaned down and shone his headlamp on the belched-up sand, wondering if any of it was new, coming from the aftershocks. He saw a lighter patch several feet away and walked over to it. The sulfur smell was definitely stronger here. On a whim, he reached down to touch the sand. Hot. He snatched his hand back, then realized, no, it hadn't burned him. Tentatively, he touched it again. Maybe 110 degrees? Something like that. Superstitious people seeing this would be talking about belching from the fires of Hell. He brushed his hand off on his slacks and went on.

The streets were nearly empty as he drove up to the house, though twice he saw people congregated in small groups, talking. And he saw tents, camping tents, as people set up camp in their own yards. They were lucky it hadn't gotten cold yet. It didn't feel any worse than 60 right now. He didn't even need to turn on the car's heater.

Driving time to his house was doubled, partly because he had to slow at every intersection with a dead traffic light, and as he approached this house, his stomach clenched in sick anticipation. He expected the worst. Bumping over a cracked sidewalk, he pulled into his driveway and was relieved to see that the house and garage still stood. So the emergency supplies were still accessible. He dithered about what was in his trunk. Part of him wanted to hoard, to take that stuff in the trunk and put it with the old stuff and keep him and Bash alive and healthy, no matter what. But there was a week of supplies in the house, and even if the water had passed its stamped expiration date, it'd still be fine. Lots of foods were fine past their sell-by date, just not as tasty.

He'd leave the old stuff for the two of them for now, and the supplies in his trunk, he'd leave there. If he needed to share it with the staff, if he couldn't find another way to feed them, it'd provide maybe one light meal.

He left the car's headlights on, illuminating the house, and opened the garage. First thing, he shut off natural gas—though if it hadn't burned down yet, it probably wasn't necessary. Then he shut off the feed to the hot water tank. Since no one was running water, that should still be uncontaminated, certainly safe enough to wash hands and do dishes.

Then he turned on his headlamp again, and took a tour around the house's exterior. The first thing he noticed—how could he not?—was that there was another garage in his back yard. Up the slight slope, someone's detached garage had jumped its foundation and slid its way through his cedar fence. Its back wall had collapsed and brought it to a halt. It wouldn't be moving any farther. He shook his head. Deal with it another day. Or another week or even another month, more than likely.

The worst damage to his own house was the chimney, which was the only brick on the house and was now a pile of brick and mortar rubble flung out from the back wall. On the bedroom end of the ranch house, there was a cracked window, and he thought the window frames looked out of true.

Now for the inside.

He got in his car, hit the garage door opener and when, after a few seconds, it didn't open, he slapped himself on the forehead. No electricity. The front door into the house was stuck and he had to yank on it. It had been shaken out of alignment. He wondered if the house was safe to live in, and if the damage would be fixable. The door opened at a hard yank. He flipped on the light switch as he entered house and shook his head at himself again. Automatic, to hit the lights, mere habit. He made it through to the garage, found the lantern flashlight right where he had left it, and turned it on. It took him ten minutes to figure out how to disconnect the automatic garage door opener so that he could manually raise the door. He went back into the house.

The kitchen was a mess. Almost every drawer had been vibrated open, and one had fallen out, strewing spatulas and whisks and wooden spoons over the tile floor. A glass vase with silk flowers had fallen from a shelf and smashed over the counter. The refrigerator had danced halfway across the room and unplugged itself. The dishwasher door had popped open. He left it all as it was.

The living room was odd. The TV was down, and everything on that wall and the opposite wall, every painting, a ceremonial mask from Zaire, a knick-knack shelf, all were down. But on the other two walls, everything was still where they had left it, though canted, making the direction of the earthquake's waves obvious.

He went quickly through every room and saw similar damage. A wall of bookshelves had puked out the books, but the shelving all still stood because he and Bash had bolted it to the studs of the wall. He was looking at three days' work of picking up the house, but he didn't have time to do it now. In the spare bedroom, he muscled a reluctant closet door open and pulled down old blankets and pillows, and a pile of older towels that matched a bathroom back in California. He grabbed a 12-pack of toilet paper, only two rolls gone, took out half, and piled those rolls on top of the towels. The other half he'd take in to work.

Moving faster now, aware of the minutes ticking by and Angela sitting up at the EOC, he changed clothes, putting on jeans and a long-sleeved ribbed t-shirt, then putting on his new ugly work boots. He grabbed a sports jacket in case he needed to look slightly more official. He went back into the kitchen and found the stack of paper grocery sacks they had kept wedged in between the fridge and the cabinets, and snapped open three. He opened the fridge and started cleaning it out. Almost everything went in the sacks. No reason to hoard food that would go bad within a day. He'd feed his staff and their families that had come along breakfast, and a weird breakfast it'd be. There were still eight eggs, and he'd make "everything" omelets, light on the eggs and heavy on the everything. All that went into a picnic cooler and then into the back seat of his car.

In the garage he found a tiny hibachi they took camping, and two bags of lump mesquite charcoal, one full. He grabbed the nearly-empty one. He was rushing now, feeling the clock spinning away on him, and wanting to lay eyes on Bash just once before his responsibilities to the town took control of his life again. Back in the kitchen for the cast iron skillet they kept in the oven, and then he dug through a cabinet for a gallon-sized Dutch oven—one of Bash's good pans, which he'd likely get chewed out for taking. And then he grabbed at the scattered utensils on the floor, finding a spatula, a big spoon, a bread knife, a long fork, and he tossed them all into the Dutch oven and took them to the car.

One last look around the garage and he spied a hatchet. He thought about fuel for cooking, as the charcoal wouldn't last even one day, and he thought of all those nice trees in the green space. Some of them could do without their lowest limbs. He grabbed the hatchet.

He slammed the garage door and turned the handle to lock it. His back seat was full of supplies. He was headed to the hospital in no time flat, checking his watch as he drove. 2:43. He could only spare ten or fifteen minutes for Bash, but he had to see him.

As he turned onto hospital row, he saw the lights glaring from two spots—in the distance, two fire trucks working at the hospital and emergency lights were illuminating where they were still doing rescue. Nearer was the makeshift hospital and its emergency lighting. He could hear the generator as he pulled up. A National Guardsman was there to direct traffic. People were still bringing in their injured family members.

He pulled over and rolled down his window. "Where can I park for ten minutes?" he called.

The Guardsman—woman, actually—came over. "You have someone injured?"

"No. Family member in the medical staff. I wanted to check on him."

"Park over in the lot by the sandwich shop," she said, pointing, and backed away from the car.

He did, and jogged back across the street to the makeshift hospital.

It was controlled bedlam. An ambulance, silent but lights flashing, pulled onto the sidewalk, and the driver leapt out to help unload a patient on a stretcher. Gale hung back until they'd moved the patient out. To the far left was the row of turquoise port-a-potties. At the center of the area fronting the street, what looked to be a reception area. Piles of boxes on tables behind reception were being opened by a young woman with a clipboard. She glanced in one, made a note, wrote something on the box, and then she carried it to a new spot, under a different table.

Family members milled about, looking anxious. They didn't have a place to sit. Every chair seemed to be taken with a wounded person, waiting for treatment that Gale thought, from the looks of things, might take a little while. The medical staff— at least the ones who were dressed for that role—didn't seem numerous. He wondered how many they'd lost in the hospital collapse.

The receptionist was busy with the new emergency patient, so Gale went to the clipboard woman. "I'm looking for Bash Hill? Sebastian Hill? He's a nurse."

"He's back there, in surgery, I think." She pointed to a bright light off to the right side of the parking lot. "You shouldn't go back there if you're not sterile."

"I won't get close or interfere," he said. His heart fell. He hadn't thought through that he might not be able to get near Bash. But of course he was busy. They'd have to make do with a wave, maybe. He wanted to hold him, to feel for himself that Bash was okay.

The woman shrugged and went back to work, too busy to argue with him.

He wound his way past injured people. A broken leg being set. A woman weeping over an unconscious or dead child lying across two chairs serving as hospital bed. A man moaning in delirium or pain. Two smocked medical workers holding down another man who seemed to be going nuts, raving and fighting them. "Hold him still!" one snapped at the other. "I'm trying!" was the reply. Gale thought of stepping over to help, but no. He had no idea what was going on there, and he'd probably hurt more than help.

He kept moving toward the light of the surgical area. A pair of teenage girls sat in chairs, watching the surgery, as if the audience at a play. A pair of white porcelain bowls sat at their feet.

As he moved past them, he felt a tug on his pants leg. "Hey," said one of the girls. "Where you going, buddy?"

"I'm trying to find someone."

"Who?" she said, challenge in her voice.

"Bash Hill."

"Oh." She looked him up and down. "You must be the boyfriend."

"Husband."

She gave a nod and the expression on her face said, "You'll do." He felt, oddly, that he'd passed a test.

"They're almost done. Look, he's not squeezing stuff into the patient's IV any more." She stood and rolled her neck. "More instruments to wash."

The other girl spoke softly. "We need more bleach."

"We'll tell them," the bossy one said.

Gale glanced at his watch. When he looked up again, Bash was looking his way. Gale could see him smile, even under the mask. He felt his own eyes go damp and he smiled back, blinking back tears of relief. That was silly. He had been told Bash was okay. But there was something about seeing him with his own eyes.

Then the doctor said something, and Bash's attention snapped back to his work.

Chapter 7

Bash

At sundown, Bash had climbed the debris pile with a bottle of juice from the sandwich shop. He handed it to Suze. She looked like hell, washed out, disheveled, but she also had a stubborn set to her jaw.

He was afraid to say the wrong thing to her, so tried, "Dusk is coming on."

She nodded, slurping down juice.

"We're set up for treatment now."

"I can see that."

"I'd like to get a better look at your leg."

"I'm fine."

He cleared his throat. "The firefighters are doing search and rescue now. They'll be able to get up here soon with equipment."

"I don't think it'll do any good," she said. "How much time has passed?"

"Three hours," he said.

"It seems like longer."

"I know." He wanted to pat her arm or give her a hug, but everything in the way she held herself said not to.

"I haven't heard a thing."

"I'm sorry?"

"Here," she snapped, waving the juice bottle around the remains of the clinic building. "No cries for help, no moans, nothing."

"Oh, Suze," he said. "I'm sorry."

"Are you?"

"Of course. I have friends in there too."

"Can corpses be friends?"

"Maybe someone is alive but unconscious. With their lights and equipment, the rescuers have a good chance of finding them. But you don't, not in this light."

She jerked her head in anger.

"And I want to look at your leg, and get you some aspirin if you need it."

"Is there an orthopedics guy down there?"

"We only have one doctor, a retired GP."

"It's just you?"

"And an LPN with cardiac care unit experience, a hospital aide who was running late to work at the hospital, and an orderly. And a chiropractor, a dialysis tech, and an ophthalmologist, and don't tell anyone this, but we have a veterinarian taking pulses and temps and BPs."

She coughed a sound that was nearly a laugh. "You're not joking, are you?"

"Nope. Everybody is working at the very far end of their training, or beyond. And I'm not the only one there digging all the way back to nursing school to try and remember stuff. If you're okay, we'll need you too. Seriously, desperately need you."

"I'm fine. I can work."

"Examination first. And how about checking in at home?"

"I don't need to. The kid is with his father this weekend. Left this morning for a long hunting weekend. Youth deer season."

"Where are they?"

"Safe, I think, up in the mountains."

"Good. That's one thing off your mind at least."

She drained the juice and said, "Okay. I'll come down."

"I'm right beneath you. Yell if you need help."

He backed off and crawled down in the waning daylight. When it was obvious Suze could get down by herself, he called to her, "I'll be right back to check that leg."

He made his way to reception, which was lit with a variety of flashlights. "Fire department isn't here yet with our lights?"

"Nope."

"Going to make it hard to treat patients. Anyone new?"

"In triage." She waved vaguely behind her.

"Here comes someone," he said, watching two dim forms approach. Oh! "McKenna, I thought I sent you two home."

"My mom isn't there. And the house is a wreck."

Haruka said, "It's not safe inside, Mr. Sebastian. We left many notes for her mother."

"Bash," he corrected her.

McKenna said, "And we thought we might help. Find more stuff for you."

"Not in the dark." He thought, Well, why not? Two healthy bodies. Surely he could put them to some use. "I'll assign you some work. In a second."

He jogged back over to the clinic and gave Suze an assist toward the chairs. She could walk, but she was limping. She started to give him instructions on what to look for on her leg. Her Suze-ness was reasserting itself. But he didn't argue, just got her seated.

At that moment, the fire truck drove up. Two men jumped off and began to unload equipment. A third man—no, a stocky woman firefighter—picked up a small limp form and walked it over. "Where do I put her?"

Bash grabbed a flashlight and shone it back to the treatment area. "Follow me."

As he walked away, the clerk at reception said, "You bring that flashlight back when you're done."

"Head injury," the firefighter was saying. "Pulse 45, pupils fixed."

Bash ground his teeth in frustration. One more serious injury they didn't have to equipment or personnel to treat. "Here. I'll push these two chairs together and we'll use it as a stretcher. Has she seized or regained consciousness at all?"

"Not while the rescuers had her."

"What hit her?"

"They couldn't say. She had tumbled free of the children's wing of the hospital. Could have hit her head on the way down." She set the girl down. "Looks to be about eight. God only knows what she was in for in the first place."

"Right," said Bash. Could be cancer or infection or anything at all, something bad enough to have her in pajamas in a hospital. He shone the light on her face. The firefighter hesitated, then said, "I would offer to help, but I really have to...." She sighed as she waved back in the direction of the truck.

"You did great. Thank you."

"We'll have your lights set up in no time." As she walked away, he heard a generator roar to life.

He hoped someone would remember to bring them gas for it from time to time. If there was gas to be had. With no electricity, how do you pump gasoline out of the ground? He pushed away the question. Not his job. His job was here in front of him. Without turning his head he yelled, "McKenna?"

"Geez, I'm right here, you don't have to scream," she said, from not four feet away.

"I need a blood pressure cuff, and some tongue depressors, and three sets of gloves. I'm going to teach you two how to glove up."

"Okay," she said, and disappeared into the deepening dark.

Haruka said, "I know little about first aid, Mr. Sebastian."

He didn't correct the name this time. Let her call him

whatever made her happy. "I'm not going to make you do surgery. But I am going to teach you how to soak used equipment in bleach. But you have to pay strict attention to me. No matter what, you stay away from needles. I don't want you sticking yourself, hear me?"

"Yes, sir."

"You understand what I mean by needles?"

"Yes."

"Or anything sharp. You keep the gloves on, and you stay away from needles."

"Yes, sir."

"And keep reminding McKenna. I think she's a little more of a risk-taker than you."

"I heard that," said McKenna as she walked up. "Here. And somebody handed me this too." She thrust out an otoscope.

"Great. I wonder where they came up with this." The retired GP had bought a bag, and he had sent his wife out to hunt down more equipment from colleagues. Maybe she had returned with much-needed supplies.

Suddenly, the area was flooded with light. Not enough to see this patient very well, but it was a start. The light shifted as they moved the light stands around. Bash waved the girls to either side to move and leave him the best light.

"Watch how I put on these gloves," he said. "Okay, never touch the gloves with a dirty hand. Never touch a clean glove with a dirty glove." He pulled on his gloves and examined the girl. "Pulse 45—remember that, Haruka." He pumped up the ancient blood pressure cuff next. "McKenna, you remember blood pressure 100 over 66. Say it back to me."

"One hundred. Sixty-six," she said.

He went on examining the girl, palpating her skull carefully. He found where she had hit her head, and there was a golf-ball-sized lump. No fracture that he could detect—no displaced fracture, at least. No spinal fluid leaking from the ears. He began to wonder if her unconsciousness might have a cause in whatever condition had put her in the hospital. No chart and no way to know. No parent to ask. He also thought that the last time he had read what to do for TBIs had been over a decade ago. Treatment modalities had doubtless changed since then.

"Can you do anything for her?" asked McKenna. When he turned to look at her, she said, "A hundred over sixty-six. I didn't forget."

"We need to make sure she doesn't roll off these chairs. And put her someplace where I'll pass by her from time to time. But no, otherwise, I don't know of a thing to do."

"Will she die?" asked the girl.

Bash stood. "I don't think so." Not immediately, but she might not wake up with her full faculties. "Okay, watch how I take my gloves off. Remember, never touch a dirty glove with your hands." He did it slowly while they studied him. "And what do you never, *ever* touch, Haruka?"

"Anything sharp like a needle."

"Exactly." He tucked his dirty gloves in his pocket and pulled out the notepad he charted on. Cauc. Female, approx 8 years old, identity unknown, parents unknown. Moderate head injury. He charted her symptoms. "Pulse," he said.

"Forty-five," said Haruka.

"Blood pressure 100 over 66," chimed in McKenna. "You didn't say a temperature."

"I don't have anything to take temperatures with," he said. "But she didn't feel hot." He finished charting, then pulled out the roll of strapping tape and a pocketknife he had gotten from a patient's husband. He waved it to draw the girl's attention to it. "Something sharp. A knife. Stay away from it and anything else sharp," he said to the girls. He cut off the sheet of paper with his charting and laid it on the girl's chest. "Haruka, you hold that in the center, gently." Once she did, he cut off two lengths of strapping tape and taped the chart to the girl's pajamas. It was the safest way, he had decided, to do charting, out where any medical person could see. Any stranger could see it too, but screw that. This was not the time to worry about such inconsequential things. He had told the staff, anything really sensitive—STD, mental health issue—write on the reverse and put a big arrow at the bottom. That's how we'll tell each other there's more to the story.

What a way to practice medicine.

Then he had the girls put on their gloves while he watched. Gloves were precious, and he didn't want to dirty several pairs getting this done, and he wasn't going to have them touch patients at all. Only equipment, used gloves, hemostats, and so on. He coached them through the glove procedure and they did well. "Fantastic," he said. "Now we'll find you a trash bag for trash and something to hold what stuff needs to be washed, like my old gloves or any instruments. And when I get a minute, I'll teach you how to set used instruments and gloves to soak and keep track of the times they are soaking."

"Just like chem class. We can handle that," said McKenna.

"I have no doubt you can, or I wouldn't be asking you to help. Let's drag one more chair over here to keep the girl from rolling off." When they had done that, he wound his way toward where he had left Suze.

The chiropractor was finishing an exam of her leg.

"What do you think?" Bash asked him.

"Contusion, not too bad. Under normal circumstances, I'd tell her to stay off it for 48 hours, but now?" He stood up and shrugged.

"I can work," said Suze.

"I'll wrap it," said the chiropractor.

"I'm glad you're okay," Bash said to Suze. He wanted to say more to her, to try and forge a better connection with her, but he didn't know what to say. And there was too much to do.

He turned to the girls. "Okay, before we get more patients,

I'm going to show you two what I want you to do and how to do it right. And what's the number one rule?"

"Nothing sharp," McKenna said.

"No needles," said Haruka.

"Exactly. And second most important, don't touch dirty things with your bare skin. Third, don't touch clean things with dirty gloves."

It took only fifteen minutes of instruction before he was satisfied they knew what to do. It'd save professional staff some time, and get some of the pavement cleaned up. There were flecks of gauze and empty wrappers and all sorts of debris lying on the parking lot. If someone saw that, they'd fire him from his job.

Ha. As if there were anyone to take his place.

He went to check quickly on Ms. Witherspoon. Her husband had arrived, catching another ride somehow, and he was sitting and watching his wife as she paced, her hands on her back.

Bash said, cheerfully, "Coming along okay?"

"What the hell was I thinking?" she said. "Getting pregnant?"

"You couldn't have predicted the earthquake," he said.

"Man, this is going to hurt, isn't it? I bet you don't have an epidural in your bag of tricks up there," she said.

"I'll tell everyone to keep an eye out."

"Yeah, that sounded hopeful."

"I'm sorry."

"Women had babies before epidurals, honey," said Mr. Witherspoon.

"You want cancer *and* to be missing all your teeth?" she snapped.

He grinned wanly at Bash. "She's in a little mood."

Bash winced, readying himself for the response to that, but she must have thought better of it and kept her reply to muttering. He kneeled by Mr. Witherspoon. "You feeling okay?"

"The nausea is pretty much gone from today. I'm tired, is all."

"I'll find you a blanket and you can lie down, if you don't

mind lying on the ground."

"I think I'll stay up for now. Be with Melba."

"The two of you went through delivery coaching classes?"

"Oh yes, we did. So I can help her breathe and rub her back, if she ever lets me near her."

Ms. W's mumbling got louder. "Help me breathe, as if..." And then it faded as she paced away again.

Mr. W said, "She's been saying she's hungry."

"Hungry!" Bash smacked himself on the forehead. "I have just the thing. I'll be back soon." He went up front, calling for McKenna and Haruka.

He found them in the stacks of equipment, watching over soaking pans of gloves and various small instruments. "Fantastic," he said. "And the ground is all picked up already. You two are great."

"I'm bored," said McKenna. "You said we have to wait a half hour with this stuff." Haruka held up her cell phone where a stopwatch app was ticking down the time.

"Deglove, without touching dirty gloves remember, and add those to the gloves soaking," he said. "And then I have something else for you to do." He coached them again through safe degloving, then praised them. They were being so sweet, willing to work and willing to learn. He loved kids. He thought, not for the first time, that Gale and he should have adopted or found a surrogate in L.A.

"Pizza," he said, when they were done.

McKenna snorted. "I don't think we can feed your cravings now."

He grinned. "But you can. I have a stack of pizzas in my car, a few hours old. I want you to get them, and get a slice each to the couple back there, the Witherspoons—she's the pregnant lady in a temper. And then hand them out to staff, a slice each. But no other patients until medical staff say so. Not everybody is okay to eat." He handed over his keys and told them how to find his car.

"Bash," called the receptionist. "We have new staff."

He smiled at the girls and turned to greet his new staff. An occupational therapy assistant, who could surely do temps and pulse and assist, and best of all, a plastic surgeon, a Dr. Shah.

"You're the surgeon," Bash said.

The man looked puzzled.

"I mean, you're our *only* surgeon. You're going to have to do it all."

"I see."

"You up for it?"

"I don't see as we have another choice." He had a faint British accent.

"Great." Bash did triage in his head again, thinking of his red-tagged patients and who would benefit most.

"I need a surgical assistant or nurse, of course."

Bash looked around. Well, shit. "I guess that would be me for now, but I'm not at all expert." Suze couldn't stand for that long. An LPN wouldn't do. He wished he could clone himself. "Okay, first, I think we have a compartment injury, both legs, and I don't know that much about them."

"Nor do I," said the surgeon.

He led the man around the parking lot and let him re-examine all the red-tag patients and decide for himself who he could help and who would go first. McKenna came up to him with the stack of pizzas, now only three boxes tall. "You said not to feed patients until you could go with us and tell us who can eat," she said.

He wished he could clone himself in three.

* * *

The night got busier as both the fire department and individuals uncovered trapped people. The good news was, they uncovered some medical workers who needed minimal care and were at least able to sit and take vitals, though with head bandages and a sling in one case, so a couple of staff looked as bad off as their patients. A pediatrician in private practice had arrived, unhurt and ready to work. When he got some time, Bash would try and foist medical director duties onto him. They'd added two dentists to the team too, who were perfectly capable of giving injections and dressing wounds. For surgery, though, they had only the plastic surgeon and Bash to function as nurse.

The worst surgery was the first, a nasty compound femur fracture with vascular damage. Not only were they both uncomfortable about operating in the open air, where for all they knew a bat overhead might poop into an open wound, but a bad aftershock hit in the middle of the surgery. The surgeon backed off, his hands in the air, and Bash held on to the table to keep the patient from shaking off.

Without McKenna and Haruka, the evening would have been much harder. They refused to leave him alone, so one was always with him as the other scoured the ground for trash and for supplies to sterilize. They seemed to enjoy having something useful to do, and they actually were useful. They ran messages, they took instruments off to soak in bleach, and they brought new supplies. They were getting a nursing practicum without the benefit of the two years of education first. He wondered if either would go on to become a doctor, if this night was making them into something they hadn't been yesterday.

Ridiculous. Of course it was. This night was making *everybody* over several hundred square miles into someone they hadn't been at lunch. McKenna kept him updated on the news from outside that trickled in from the paramedics and from people with access to battery-powered radios. She had sharp ears and a good memory for detail. Memphis, terrible shape, raging fires sweeping through downtown. St. Louis, better than that but bad enough. Paducah, bad. Even Little Rock and Nashville and Cincinnati had taken serious damage. As with the big quakes here of 200 years ago, it had rung church bells all the way out on the east coast. They'd felt it in Toronto. Millions of people had had their lives changed. Based on what they were seeing here, he imagined tens of thousands had died in the big cities.

The surgeon's swearing brought his attention back to the moment. "Move the light, would you?" he said.

Bash grabbed a four-by-four package and used it to adjust the maglight in the makeshift lighting stand they'd rigged. Though he'd sterilized the flashlight's case the best he could, he was taking as few chances as possible and not touching it directly with his gloved hand.

"Better."

He put the package down and waited for the next instruction.

"I wish we could evacuate this one. This nerve damage needs an expert."

"Morning, maybe, when helicopters can fly, they say."

The surgeon snorted. "With all the injured in the big cities? We'll be lucky if they notice us."

"Oh, they'll notice," Bash said. He had faith that Gale would make their needs clear. The question was, were there resources to respond? Were there enough helicopters available in the whole Midwest to evacuate every serious case to a safe hospital, like in Chicago or New Orleans or Kansas City? He thought not. Not the first morning, at least. And every hour that passed, they were losing golden hours. Like with the head-injury girl, who still hadn't woken. The pediatrician had his eye on her now.

They finished with the patient and took another, an abdominal injury. He was too busy to think as he set up the IV and prepped the patient while the doctor put him under.

As the surgery began, he wondered how Ms. Witherspoon's labor was advancing. How Suze was holding up.

The surgeon's voice cut through his reverie. "I said sponge."

"Sorry," said Bash, putting his attention back on the open abdomen ahead of him. He was losing focus.

"Fuck a duck," snarled the surgeon, but not at Bash. "I'm not going to be able to save this spleen. And he's going to bleed out if I don't hurry. Prep for splenectomy."

"Yes, doctor," Bash murmured, and snapped himself out of his mind-drifting. The next half-hour he worked alongside the surgeon—they were slowly finding each other's rhythm—and they got the bloody organ out. He added it to a bucket—literally, a square white bucket that had once been used for potato salad at the sandwich shop—of human waste at the edge of their operating area. Forget pathology. This was meatball surgery of the worst sort.

They needed a roof for the surgery. A tent, a fold-up camping gazebo from Walmart. Something. They were out here, visible to any passerby, not so much as a shower curtain hiding the patient's internal organs from view.

The patient was almost done, the closing going quickly, the surgeon muttering about scars, again—poor guy, plastic surgeon, he wasn't used to stitching with anything less than exquisite care. And that's when he looked up and saw Gale, standing behind McKenna and Haruka.

He swallowed back a lump in his throat. He wanted to leap over there and hold his husband, to fall apart in his arms. But he couldn't, not while he was in surgery. And not in public anyway. Still, the urge made him feel weak, set cracks in his carefully constructed fortress of competence and professionalism.

"I'm sorry, doctor, but I need a fifteen-minute break after this one," he said, as the surgeon backed off and ungloved.

"No. That's fine. I need to take a whiz anyway."

Now that he mentioned it, so did Bash.

He cleaned up after the surgery as quickly as he could. When he took off the plastic apron and tossed it in the trash, Haruka stood up, holding out her pan for the dirty instruments. He carried them to her, peeled off his gloves, and his mind drifted to the bloody bucket of human bits, wondering how the hell they'd dispose of the accumulation of those.

Then Gale was there, and they were hanging on to each other, and all thoughts of his responsibilities fled for precious seconds.

Gale pushed him away and studied his face. "You're okay? I mean really okay?"

"Haven't had time to be anything else," he said, forcing a smile.

"Yeah, I know. Take care of yourself too, while you're taking care of everyone else."

Bash nodded, but he didn't know how he could. There were so many people to care for and so few to do it.

He saw McKenna staring at them, and moved a step away from Gale. "How's it going, kiddo?" he asked her.

"Good," she said.

He wondered if she'd ever seen two men embrace each other. Probably only on TV, if that. He supposed they should move into the dark and spare people the horror of seeing such forbidden love, screw their narrow little minds. He turned to Gale. "Can we leave Missouri, now?"

Gale laughed. "Not for a few days, at least." He looked Bash up and down. "You need a new uniform. You're bloody."

Bash looked down at himself. "You're right. I'm probably terrifying the patients."

"Should I get one from home? I wasn't thinking when I went there."

"We still have a home?" His heart lifted for the first time in hours.

"Pretty much, yeah."

"Because of you. How careful you were picking one, getting the geologist and all."

Gale waved that off. "You sure you're okay?"

"You sure *you* are?"

"Now that I see you, I'm much, much better."

Bash saw McKenna out of the corner of his eye. "Let's take a short walk."

McKenna said, "That pregnant lady is asking for you."

"Thanks, hon," he said. "Please tell her I'll be there as soon as I can." He took Gale's hand and tugged him toward the street, then over to the sandwich shop and behind it, out of the view of strangers. They stood, holding each other, rocking each other, for too few minutes.

"I'm sorry, but I have to get back in a minute," Bash said.

"I heard. Pregnant lady. Take some time for yourself too."

"I'm lucky I can find time to take a sip of water."

"Wear yourself down to nothing, and you won't be able to help anyone."

"I know. And the same to you. Have you slept at all? What time is it?"

"Quarter to four." They walked next to each other, back toward the lights of the makeshift hospital. "And I had a nap until an aftershock woke me up."

"Those!"

"Be prepared for worse."

"You know something the rest of us don't?"

"I know that in 1811 and 12, they had three earthquakes of 8.0 in a few months. Don't stand under a brick wall."

"Is there a brick wall left?"

"Nope." Gale laughed bitterly. "I'm two or three years late in getting these zoning laws changed."

"You've only been here a year. And you tried."

"Not hard enough."

He grabbed Gale's forearm and gave it a little shake. "Stop it. You did your best."

Gale made a frustrated sound and led them back toward the hospital. They were nearing the reception area again. "There's this term in earthquake-proofing a city."

"Yes?"

"'Hardening off.' It's a polite way to say, everything dangerous has fallen down already, and what's left is pretty good construction."

"Charming."

"We're hardening off here now. You have to go, I know." Gale took his hand and gave it a squeeze. "Stay safe."

"You too." There were a hundred questions to ask, and no time to ask them in. "Can we set a time to meet?"

"I'll pick you up at, say, two tomorrow afternoon, if you're still here, or as near as I can make it. Sleep before that, however you can, but we'll go home for an hour or two then and look around the house while there's daylight."

"Deal."

"I love you." He mouthed the words.

"Me too. I'm sorry I've been such a bitch lately."

"You've been fine. You're great. We're great. Stay safe, love."

"You too."

Bash watched him walk away for ten seconds he didn't have to spare, then he turned and wove his way back to his little maternity ward of one. He was going to be later than he promised for the next surgery, but he had to do this too. And he desperately wanted to go around and give the staff pep talks and make sure no one was falling to pieces.

This first.

Mr. Witherspoon was dozing in his chair as Bash walked up. Melba was pacing still.

"You've probably walked a marathon by now," he said to her.

"I sit down some. But it hurts more when I do."

"How're the contractions?"

"Like a session in Abu Ghraib."

"Are you timing them?"

"That's why I asked for you. I think I'm in transition."

He dithered about how honest to be. "It's been awhile since nursing school. Tell me how you mean."

She began to tick off items on her finger. "One, I—" And

then she gasped a short breath and quit talking. Her arm shot out, and Bash moved forward to give her something to lean on. Her face was set in obvious pain.

"Breathe," he said, and she shot him a look, but she did take a shaky breath. Bash started counting, one thousand one, one thousand two. From the time he started counting, it lasted 68 seconds.

She blew out a sigh of relief. "Help me sit down," she said.

He guided her to a chair and squatted down in front of her.

Her husband jolted awake. "You okay, hon?"

"I've been better."

Bash said, "How often are they coming?"

"It dropped under five minutes between. That's when I asked that girl to bring you over. And they're hurting more."

"What I'd give for a midwife," Bash said.

"What I'd give for an epidural," Ms. W said.

"Or an anesthesiologist," he said. "I'll ask the surgeon about pain meds, I promise, and if there's anything safe for you and the baby in our stockpile, you'll get it. This is your first?"

"My first baby, yes. I had an abortion about eight years ago, but real early."

"We need to see how far you're dilated. It might be hours yet, or it might be soon, and I don't want you...." He searched for a nice phrase.

"Poopin' a baby out on the sidewalk with no warning," she suggested.

"Now, Melbs," Mr. Witherspoon said.

Bash jumped in before she could snap back. Ms. W was not in a good mood at all, not that he could blame her. "I'm going to send the pediatrician over here to examine you. That's as close to an OBGYN as we have."

"Right here in front of every stranger in town, eh?"

"We could...." He cast his mind about for a way to ensure ten minutes of privacy. He stood up and felt the keys shift in his pocket. "I know," he said, smiling at her. "Be right back."

He turned and called, "McKenna?"

"Yes, boss," the voice came.

"I need you guys," he said, walking toward the voice.

He dug into his pocket and found the two spare sets of car keys he had taken off the bodies of his coworkers. "Out there is the staff parking lot. Here are two sets of keys that match two cars—I don't know which. Can either of you drive?"

"We don't drive until we are eighteen in Japan," said Haruka.

"I can if it's an automatic," said McKenna.

"Do you have a license?"

"Does it matter?"

He supposed not, since she'd only be moving it a few feet. "We'll hope one of these is an automatic, then. Hit the panic button on each key, find the cars, pick the biggest. Drive it out into the driveway and park it over there, by the pregnant lady." He pointed. "Slowly. And brake in plenty of time to avoid hitting anyone." The car's back seat would serve as a bed, and the open door would shield prying eyes. The pediatrician would have to figure out lighting by himself. "You guys are the best," he said to the girls.

"Damn straight," said McKenna cheerfully.

As they strode into the night, he wondered where the girl's mother was. He hoped not dead. He hoped—well, too many people to do hoping for to get started down that road.

He detoured past the surgical area, where indeed Dr. Shah was looking pretty impatient. "Five minutes," he called at him, and he went to look for the pediatrician. He explained the Witherspoon situation to him, and turned back toward the surgical area as an ambulance pulled up with lights flashing.

A paramedic jumped out. "Emergency here."

Bash looked around. There was no one else but him to check and triage. He stepped forward. "What is it?"

"Crush injury, lots of bleeding," said the fellow, a

firefighter/EMT. He lowered his voice. "It's an amputation situation, I think, if we want to save this one." Bash followed him to the back of the van and watched as the two unloaded a teenaged boy, a tall kid, lean. He was moaning and tossing his head.

"Bring him directly over to surgery," said Bash, once he had taken a look at the patient. Whoever was up next was going to have to wait. As he walked alongside the stretcher, he said, "We're developing a medical waste problem. With an amputated leg, it'll be beyond bad." Another leg in the bucket, he thought, a little hysterically. "We have sharps, we have bloody bandages, we have a spleen, maybe a leg next. The medical waste service isn't going to be driving up any time soon. So what do we do?"

"Shit," said the other man, a fellow in street clothes. "We'll call it in, see what the chief suggests."

Bash should have mentioned it to Gale, get him started on it. But they'd had so little time. "We at least need sealable bags. Big ones."

"Maybe it should be incinerated," said the street-clothes guy.

"Where?" said the medic.

"Fuck if I know," said the other.

They were at the surgical area, and the medic ran through the vitals and condition of the patient for Dr. Shah. Bash got ready to drug the poor kid.

An hour later the teenaged boy was dead, bled out. The surgeon was tight-lipped and angry.

"We need blood."

"We need refrigeration for that."

"Some way of taking a pint from relatives and getting it into patients."

"How do we type and match it?"

"This is ludicrous," said the surgeon, snapping off his gloves and tossing them down, angry.

Bash knew it was not directed at him. "It's what it is," he said.

"I hate that phrase." He drew a deep breath and let it out. "Though I suppose it fits here. We can only do what we can do."

"That's right. You're doing great."

"I need coffee."

"There's some bottled iced tea from the sandwich shop."

"That'll have to do too, I suppose." He reached a hand up as if to scrub at his face, then thought better of it. "Long night."

Tell me about it, Bash said. He turned around and looked over the makeshift hospital. He thought there were twice the people there had been the last time he looked. He hoped some were visitors, looking for missing family members. Lights, but still no tent. He glanced at his watch. 5:36. "Dawn soon," he said.

"Like being a resident again, this no sleep business."

"I feel like I should check with Suze. She's doing triage for us right now."

"Sure, go ahead. I'll get your errand girls to find me the tea." He glanced over at where Haruka and McKenna sat. Haruka was asleep, her head on McKenna's shoulder.

"We should let them sleep."

"*We* should sleep. But, as you say, it is what it is."

Exactly. He needed to check his staff and set up shifts. They'd go on 12-hour rotations, maybe. He'd find the best administrator or assistant available and work it out with her, then hold a five-minute staff meeting with as many as he could pull away from patients.

He thought this through as he cleaned up after the surgery, then realized he was staring at a dead body that had to be removed. Damn, he wished they could have saved the kid. He couldn't be 18, and this morning he had had his whole life ahead of him. Bash would flag down the next fireman or medic and have them zip him into a body bag, and leave a few body bags here too. He could feel himself detaching from the patients as people, and hated it and welcomed it in equal part.

Unless they had body bags already? He stripped off his

disposable apron and stuffed in into the waste bag and turned to go find out.

McKenna was staring at the bloody body with a pale face, her eyes wide and filled with horror.

He felt like kicking himself. What had he been doing to these poor little girls? He could become professionally detached in the face of blood and death and screaming, but they certainly couldn't. What had he been thinking?

Chapter 8

Gale

Gale stared into the eastern sky, watching the stars fade away as the thinnest of gray light stole into the sky. Good. He wanted daylight.

And he dreaded it and what it would show.

There was too much to do today, and what they did or failed to do would determine how the community made it through the next week or two. At worst, he could make a decision that could kill people. At best, what he did would today speed recovery over the next months. He knew, having been through disasters, how long it would be until life was normal again for everyone, but he thought the people around him would be in for some unpleasant education on that topic.

After he had returned from seeing Bash, he had checked in with the fire and police chiefs via radio and set a face-to-face meeting for 6. a.m. He had made a list of everything for his staff to do on a yellow legal pad. It ran to four and a half single-spaced pages, and he was afraid he'd forgotten a lot.

Then he spread those sheets out and organized the tasks into twelve logical groups. He'd appoint a supervisor from his staff for each area, delegate to them, and they would delegate further, recruiting family or random citizens or other city employees who might be out there, parks workers or others who didn't have offices in City Hall. He himself would liaise with police and fire, coordinate, troubleshoot, and cope with unanticipated crises, of which he knew there'd be many.

He didn't know most of his staff, or what their strengths or weaknesses were, or very much about the office politics, so he woke Angela with an apology and worked with her until they had tentative assignments that used people's strengths. Some might have to be shifted, depending on who did not come back today, or who might fall to stress in the coming hours. She suggested since he wanted them on 12-hour shifts, switching at noon, he should have co-leaders, and from 11:30 to 12:30, twice a day, they'd overlap and be able to communicate what was in process, what the next priorities were, what problems had to be solved. She was right. It'd create a smoother transition between shifts.

She offered to make more copies of the plan, said that 30 copies would be what they needed, but he said five would serve, one for her, one for him, one for police, one for fire, and one to keep at the EOC to refer to. The co-chairs would copy out their own responsibilities. "When we have time," he had told her, "we'll make a one-page summary to pass out to the public, starting with radio operators and then to any citizens who request it. And we'll put in cell phone numbers on those, in case we get service again." She said she'd take photos of every page when the light was good, and if the cells came back on, she could simply mail them to people. But for now it was hand copying, tedious and slow work.

He was lucky to have someone as clear-headed as Angela by his side. He told her so, and she waved the praise off and set to making handwritten copies.

More stars faded from the sky and he stretched, turning to look at the ruin of City Hall. That was a top priority too, and he was going to advocate for its search at first light. If there were any chance at all that the missing staff—seven of them, counting Evelyn—and the mayor were still alive, he had to make sure they were found before it was too late to get them medical help. His worst moment last night was telling a group of returning workers not to crawl over the debris in the dark to look for coworkers, telling them they had to wait for the people with equipment and for full light. He was blunt. "One of you is sure to get injured, maybe die, in the attempt. Don't do that to your families. And the people of this town can't spare any of you." If he didn't get help on the rescue—recovery, he feared—from the fire chief, and soon, he was going to have to fight that fight again, and he suspected he'd lose this time. Some of his staff had good friends still in there.

It was time to get to that meeting. He told Angela he'd be back in less than an hour, and he walked down to the firehouse, where the fire chief, Dan Bickham, and police chief, A.J. Flint, stood on the broad drive in front of the firehouse.

The three of them, the city's Triumvirate, he thought, were joined by an executive from the power department. They began with a radio report from the water treatment facility, an engineer talking about broken lines, breached levees, sulfurous water seeping up from the bowels of the earth. The water facility had divers ready to check their filtration tank just minutes from now. The old water tower had water, but that was the city's only certain safe supply. The bottom line was this—the water in hot water tanks in the homes and whatever bottled water there was in stores? That was all there was to drink. They needed backhoes and workers to repair mains or lay new pipes, but even then, there was no guarantee they could get safe water flowing again any time soon.

Flint said, "What if we get a single line working, from the tower, north through south through town? Put in public faucets along the way, or just one, to control it. People can walk down to it and fill bottles and carry them home, stand in line if they need to. And we can put a Guardsman on each tap to prevent hoarding or waste."

The radio crackled. "They aren't going to like that much. They'll want to turn on the tap at home."

"They'll like it fine when they start to get thirsty," said Flint.

Gale liked his no-nonsense attitude. "I concur," he said.

"Do it," said Dan. "We have maybe two days to get that done, maybe two days of bottled drinking water for people in apartment buildings and the nursing home. And the second priority is getting a water line direct to the hospital. They're swamped with patients."

The water exec said, "You know, we aren't even thinking about sewage lines at this point. Getting the water restored has to be our priority. But assume there are breaks in sewage. Get reports back to us if people smell sewage or see any seeping out of the ground. We'll do what we can, when we can, with that."

"Without water," Gale said, "at least no one is going to be flushing."

"Exactly so," said the water exec. He signed off.

Dan said, "What's next?" Then he answered himself, "We need to get a tent over the hospital."

Gale said, "Do they have a radio?"

"Yeah, now they do," Dan said.

Flint said, "We're asking every person we see if they're a medical worker or ever were one, trying to get them in, at least for a day or two."

Dan said, "We're going to have more injuries today as people climb around in debris. Or injuries from aftershocks."

Gale said, "What about food? Are there any stores that didn't take a bad hit?"

"Walmart," said Flint. "And a Schnucks up on Oak is pretty solid."

"Are they secure?" asked Gale.

"Both are closed, if that's what you mean," said Flint.

"What I mean is, do we have enough control of them to keep looters out, and control how the food in those stores gets distributed."

"You're talking martial law?" asked Dan, frowning.

"I'm talking survival. We need to manage what food there is and get it parceled out fairly. Think about the damage to rails and rivers and roads. Who knows when we'll get more?"

The three of them sat in silence, thinking about what they should do. Or, Gale thought, what they had to do. And how their decision would look in a week, or a year.

Dan sighed. "Okay, I get it. How do you two think we should manage this?"

Gale said, "We'll deal with the political fallout later."

Flint said, "That'll come." He slapped his hands on his thighs. "Okay, I think we can get police wives—sorry, spouses—and military spouses in on this. They're public-minded folks and as trustworthy as anyone. We'll take some National Guard guys, in uniform, with weapons, and station them at the stores. The ladies—spouses—can bag up food. Every household gets a bag."

Gale said, "Starting with what can spoil. Only then move to bags and boxes and cans."

Dan said, "We have other stores. Convenience stores. The dollar stores."

Flint said, "I'll check, if I have the manpower." He grimaced. "But if anyone loots, we'll arrest their asses. We don't have the manpower to protect more than the two bigger stores full-time."

"We need a list. City directory, map, something, to keep track of who shows up for a bag, check them off."

"Maybe start with our map on the wall," said Dan. "I'll show it to you in a minute."

"That list can also serve as way to record survivors," said Gale. "If we can post it, or get it out on the short-wave radio so it can get posted on the internet, that'll be a kindness to a lot of anxious people out there outside the quake zone. We'll need the numbers of survivors for FEMA anyway, as we request food and drinking water later on."

The other two men nodded.

Gale went on, "And until we know when we're likely to see more supplies from the outside, you might want to tell people to go easy on the food, like 1500 calories a day for adults, 2000 for children, something like that."

The fire chief said, "I'm glad it's not me convincing the Walmart manager to give away food for no money."

The police chief tightened his lips and said, "He'll do it."

They moved on to review search and rescue operations, and after the fire chief's report on what they had done overnight, Gale put in his request for City Hall to be searched next. "If there's any chance the major and manager are still alive," he said, "we have to find them, and now."

Flint said, "They'd fire our sorry butts for not getting them out sooner."

"We can hope they're alive to do it," said Gale.

Dan said, "I'll order the search. But realize, there are apartment buildings with more people trapped and missing that I'm delaying because of it."

"I know. I'm sorry. But just half a day—"

"Three hours, one small crew," said Dan. "That's all I can give you."

Gale knew he was lucky to get that much.

Dan said, "If we don't find survivors—I mean anywhere, not just at City Hall—before sunset tonight, we're probably not going to find them as survivors. I'm told my crews to grab two hours' nap last night, but every man and woman is on today. And at sunset, every man and woman is off or in bunks, to get sleep and to see to their own families and deal with their own houses, however they can in the dark. We'll recommence recovery operations tomorrow morning at dawn, but I'm not going to lie to you. It'll be recovery, not rescue, unless there's the rare miracle."

"How about all the dead?" asked Gale.

"What do you mean?"

"I mean, what are we to do with them?"

The three of them talked about body bags, which were running out, and graves, how to coordinate with clergy and morticians, how to get the bodies into the ground quickly, without upsetting people over religious traditions. Gale resented having to tiptoe around such things while risking disease and contamination from rotting bodies, but this was the Bible Belt, and people had to have things just so. What he'd give for a city of Muslims who wanted the bodies in the ground within 24 hours. That'd be healthier, though how to accomplish that big of a task?

"I hope we don't have to have mass graves or the like," said Flint. "They'll riot."

Dan said, "We need volunteer grave diggers or more machinery. We need someone from the cemeteries to deal with that."

"I had that on my list," said Gale, and explained the list that Angela was copying as they spoke. He gave them a quick rundown of his twelve areas. Sewage and latrines. Tent cities in the parks for people whose homes were gone. Neighborhood leaders. Graves and funerals. Communications within the city structure. Trash. Logistics and supplies. And so on. "Let me know if I'm stepping on your toes any way. I don't mean to."

Flint shook his head at that. "We'll have enough to do with managing public safety. It'll get worse."

Dan said, "And we—someone—needs to reestablish some sort of schooling by Monday, or kids will start getting into trouble and getting hurt farting around in the ruins."

"And classes would be good for normalcy, good for mental health," said Gale. "Get them back into a routine. We need the head of the school board or the high school principal or someone to coordinate that for us."

Dan shook his head. "The high school principle is dead, and a dozen of the teachers there. The high school took a terrible hit. Kids practicing b-ball, kids there for meetings, trying out for a school play. More than 50 dead. The middle school fared better, and one of the elementaries. The other elementary school was brick—flattened, but at least all the kids were out."

Gale wondered what it'd be like to be a parent who survived such a loss, who woke up this morning to realize they'd never see a beloved son or daughter again. He felt the pressure of tears behind his eyes and forced them back. He couldn't be the weepy faggot here, or he'd lose standing with these men. He was tired, he knew, and emotions were nearer the surface for it.

"Have either of you had any sleep?" he asked.

The fire chief rolled his eyes.

The police chief said, "Two fifteen-minute power naps—that's what you Californians call them, right?"

Gale said, "We have to sleep too. All of us need a second-in-command, and all of us need to start sleeping six hours, at least, starting tonight. Eight hours would be better. We need something in reserve when the next bad thing happens."

"You have a name for that bad thing?" said Flint, squinting at him.

He shrugged. "Could be anything. Giant explosion of a propane tank. Toxic chemicals flowing downriver. With the levee breaches, that'd be bad—could be effectively something like a gas attack, depending on the chemicals. Riots. I know that you know, Chief, that after a couple golden days, everything you had to deal with before is going to come right back, and worse in some cases. Drunks, family violence, whatever."

"I know it," he said. "I hope every liquor bottle in town fell off a shelf and got broken."

Dan, "Then we'll need a DT ward in the hospital, the way some people around here drink."

Gale went on, "And my vote for the most likely bad thing?

Aftershock. A big, big aftershock."

As if he'd conjured it, the earth beneath them rumbled for a few seconds.

He shook his head as it faded. "Not that. I mean a real one. One nearly as big as the first. Or one worse than the first. In 1811, there was one as big a few hours later, and another a month later, and another after that."

"Four like the big quake?" Dan said, his face horrified.

"There's no way to know what will happen," said Gale. "But we know what *did* happen, and that makes a repeat possible. Yesterday's aftershock, however big that was—"

Flint said, "6.2, according to one of the ham radio guys."

Gale nodded. "We'll probably see dozens of those in the next six months. *Dozens.* And some of them are going to be the final straw for damaged buildings. They'll come down. People have to stay out of damaged structures. We have to convince them, somehow."

The fire chief said, "We need someone who can determine which structures are sound and which aren't. Structural engineers, like that."

Gale had forgotten that one. "Yes. Please have your people ask around for professionals like that while they're hunting for medical personnel. We have to find everyone in town who can help in any way. In fact, I'll write up a list of skills that might come in handy. Carpenters, backhoe operators, and so on. I'll do that first thing and get the list right back to you. And everyone without a specific skill who is willing to work, they're going to have to dig latrines or graves or volunteer somehow. We need to convince every functioning person to pitch in."

"Most will," said Dan, checking his watch. "We have to wrap this up. We all have work to do that can't wait." The sun had crested the horizon—there was light enough to read by. Behind them, the firehouse cast a long shadow over them. It was going to be another clear day.

The power department executive, who had sat quietly until now, gave his report. No one had power. They had flooding at the plant because of a levee breach. They were working on that. They'd string lines today too, but expect no power at all until tomorrow. "If then," he said.

"Gas for generators," Gale said, remembering. "We need to find a way to get gas out of the storage tanks and out to people with generators. And I'd love a generator for the EOC."

Dan said, "We'll deal with recovering the gas and diesel. We probably need to set up something like with the groceries, giving out a limited amount to people who line up, get them used to conserving it, give five gallons per day per household, something like that. I don't know how to pump it—not yet—but my guys can figure it out."

Flint said, "It'd be great if we could find a tax list or city directory, to check all this off against. Survivors, the lines for groceries and gas, burials, everything. A few copies of it too."

Gale said, "When we get back internet service, that'd be a snap." A generation earlier, there'd be hard copies of that sort of thing all over town. Today? Without internet access, they might not ever get that or to other crucial information.

The fire chief said, "I'll see what's in hard copy here, back in the office. Which reminds me." He pointed to Gale. "I need two minutes at the end from you. Are we done?"

Not nearly, Gale thought, but they'd dealt with enough for now and they all had more important things to do than talk. "We'll stay in touch via radio," he said. "Maybe meet again this afternoon, maybe about sunset."

The three of them shook hands, and the police chief marched off.

Dan motioned him along into the firehouse. "Let's hope there's not another quake like you promised while we're in there," he said.

Gale glanced up as he walked inside. It was such a weird thing about big quakes. In normal life, a roof was comfort, security, safety. It harkened back a hundred thousand years, he thought, was part of the hardwiring of the human mind. Give me a cave— protect my back. But with an earthquake, a roof was death, a wall at your back could easily collapse onto you, and once you'd been in a major quake, standing underneath either made your heart beat faster and your throat go dry. Swallowing past that dryness in his own throat, he followed the chief back to the offices.

Dan handed him a pile of soft material crisscrossed with bright yellow, reflective tape. "They're school crossing guards' vests. We got them from the middle school for you. And I have a spare permanent marker here. Figured you could write 'City' real big on them. You said you wanted some sort of uniform for your people, right?"

"Right. Thanks for remembering." He had forgotten himself that he had ever mentioned it. "You're good at this, keeping the details in your head."

"Short-term memory is pretty good," Dan admitted. "Didn't realize how useful it might turn out to be."

"Thanks for the vests."

"Also, speaking of markers, we're going to be marking buildings with paint—number of dead inside that we can't easily get out, hazards. Standard FEMA marking system, in orange."

"I have to admit, I don't remember it exactly. There's an X and some codes?"

"Right. I have copies of how it's done, the codes and all. I'll run one out to you later this morning. The police chief should have his own already, but I'll make sure of that too, that we're all on the same page."

Gale carried the vests back to City Hall and went directly to the work area, where people who had slept there overnight were stirring. The two little kids were running around a bench. He smiled to see them acting so like kids. It gave him faith that these days would pass, that he'd see a normal world again one day.

"Anybody up for making breakfast?" he said. And he started what he knew would be a long, long day.

By 8:00 a.m., the overnight staff was fed, and more were arriving for the day's work. There was Kay again, and Sophie and Megan, all people he was coming to rely on.

One of the smaller fire trucks with three workers began working at City Hall, searching for the city manager and mayor and anyone else who might still be alive. His chief of supplies, Jeannine, was hanging out by them, out of their way, but looking for a list of crucial supplies and pulling out any from the edges of debris that she could get to without risking herself. He glanced over from time to time, making sure she wasn't putting herself into danger, but she was being cautious.

He had Sophie, who claimed to have nice handwriting, print "City" on the back of the vests. He had other people set at various other chores, and the heads of department were sharing out the master list of tasks and copying their own responsibilities. He had to remind them to make paper copies and not to rely entirely on their smartphones or other electronic gadgets.

He was happy to see that everyone in his staff had good shoes today, and most had bike helmets or hard hats with them. Many were bringing food from their refrigerators, paper plates, boxes of plastic zippered bags from home, and trash bags. They'd eat well today, trying to eat up everyone's perishable food before it spoiled. Tomorrow, they'd have to start being more careful with calorie intake. And he had to remember to make sure his staff got to the grocery store and received their bag of food each today. A few of his staff had brought their husbands to lend a hand.

The maintenance worker, Oscar, had brought three teenage sons, who looked like between them they could lift a pickup truck if need be. He got introduced to everyone new, and Angela kept track of names for him. He'd have to study the names when he got a spare moment so he wasn't calling all these new people "hey, you" all day.

By 8:45, he had enough people gathered to hold a meeting. He put his fingers to his mouth and whistled and waved Jeanine in from the building, thinking, I wouldn't mind having a loud silver whistle, and a bullhorn. He made do with his own voice this morning, as he hit the highlights of the assignments for everyone to hear. He told the people who weren't on shift until 11:30 they could go home and work at their own cleanup until then, but only one couple left, apologizing, but saying they had yet to find their dog and wanted to try again. The other second shift people offered to start work early, making it another long day for them.

"I accept. And I appreciate it more than I can say. But after this," he said, "everybody take their twelve hours off. You need the downtime."

At the end of the meeting, someone requested a moment of silence for those who had died, and he motioned everyone to do so, but while their heads were bowed his own mind was spinning with lists of things to do. He'd honor the dead some other way, later on. For now he'd honor them by trying to not add to their numbers.

After the meeting broke up, he took individual meetings with his department heads. He and Angela had to fill in two slots with alternatives, as some of their staff had still not returned. First, he got his shelter people together, two people from the Parks department, one of whom had been out supervising groundskeepers when the quake hit and had a set of master keys for parks buildings.

"We need tents," Gale told him, "the kind of big tents they put up in reserved sites for weddings or big parties. One for here, for us. One to put in every large park for shelter for the homeless. We need to know where all the other shelter-size tents in town are, and we need tools like rakes and shovels, and we need you to dig up a big grill to bring here so we can feed our people, and you need to find fuel—charcoal, downed tree limbs, firewood, whatever. Bring us a supply and lock the rest of it away. When shelter tents go up, someone has to stay with them until they fill up, to make sure they don't get stolen." After five minutes of listening to their ideas, he broke it off, and sent them on their way, then took his next priority group. It took another hour and a half to get through everyone, and by then there were more people waiting to ask him questions.

By the time they were organized for the day, Angela had another list for him of what he needed to do. "FEMA wants you," she said. "I told them 11:00."

"Ye gods, is it that late?" he said, glancing at his watch. "Let me run over to City Hall and see how the search and rescue is going, then I'll go."

"They found Evelyn," she said. "And the mayor."

He knew by her voice. "Dead?"

"I'm sorry, Gale."

"I hope the twins are okay," he said. "Do they know yet?"

She shrugged. "There really isn't time, or the personnel. That no one has come to check on Evelyn...." She shook her head.

"I know. We have to trust that people are taking care of each other out there, somehow."

Another aftershock rumbled beneath them. It was at least the tenth this morning. "Have faith in people out there," he said.

She gave him a wan smile, and he jogged over to City Hall. He found three body bags lined up next to the fire truck and sighed.

He said a few words of encouragement to the staff who were still trying to dig out useful items from the edges of the debris. They had four mismatched chairs. A man—probably one of his staff's husbands—had a four-by-three wood table upside down and was working at fixing a broken leg with hand tools.

Two firemen were hauling down another body bag. Four lost. He spoke with the rescue workers, thanked them for their help, and checked his watch, feeling the precious minutes escaping from him. He drove to the address Angela had given him for the radio people.

There were few cars on the streets. He saw smoke from a distant fire and thought about how every firefighter who was fighting it would not be doing search and rescue. He didn't envy the fire chief, having to prioritize. Maybe the fire wasn't in a neighborhood, or threatening other buildings—maybe it was an unimportant warehouse, and he'd let it burn to the ground to keep the rescue going full-tilt, trying to save what injured people they could. It's what Gale himself would do, but he knew that would drive firefighters crazy, letting a fire burn. Not his problem to fret over. He had plenty of his own.

He found the address, an older one-story wood house. A big generator was audible from in back. A woman was waiting at the door, and she said, "You're the City Manager?"

"Yes," Gale said, realizing he was, now that he knew Evelyn was dead. He introduced himself.

"I'm Marilyn. My husband is George. He's downstairs with the radios."

The basement was a single bare room with a row of radio equipment that had to date back at least fifty years, in some cases. He even caught a glimpse of a device hooked to one that he was pretty sure was for sending Morse Code—at least, he'd seen such things in old World War II movies.

"I have them on the line," said George. "It's 11:02."

"Sorry," said Gale, about his tardiness, then he got on the radio. "This is Gale Swanton, acting City Manager," he said.

"Kansas City FEMA, Regional Administrator Eliza Hayes," she said. "How's it going there?"

A dozen chatty replies flew though his brain, starting with "could be better," but he kept it factual.

"We have—had—forty-two thousand people in the city. We don't have casualty numbers yet, but we may have as many as ten thousand dead, another ten thousand wounded, most of that walking wounded. We lost our hospital. Do I say over?" This last he said to the radio guy.

George nodded at him.

The FEMA administrator came back. "We've found three helicopters to do medical evacuations for your city," she said. "Coming your way from Springfield right now. And we're bringing medical supplies to you on each of the runs. What are your other priorities for supplies? Over."

"Body bags," he said. "Over." He realized he wasn't organized enough in his mind yet for this conversation. He cast about in his mind for what was small enough to fit into medevac helicopters and was needed most.

"Check," she said. "What else? "

"Ma'am, I'll be honest with you. I've been so busy setting up everything for the city, on no sleep, that I don't have my head on straight. I need to think, and check again with fire and police, and then I'll get right back to you. We need a lot. We're going to need food and water in three or four days, airlifted, if the roads or train tracks aren't clear by then. I haven't seen a television, so outside of the few square miles we've surveyed, I don't even know what's happening out there or how far out roads are damaged. "

"In brief, two million estimated dead," she said. "Memphis is on fire for at least two square miles, with no way to put it out. We've lost 32 bridges across the Mississippi and several on the Ohio. St. Louis is bad. I'll be honest, a lot of my resources are going to be going to metro St. Louis. I wouldn't trust the river water—not that I would ever—for drinking. But there are chemical and petroleum tanks leaking into the river upstream of you on the Illinois side. Over."

"I understand," he said. "Can I radio you back in a half-hour?"

"My assistant or I will be here," she said. "Out."

He turned to George. "Can you get me in touch with the police and fire chiefs? You have those kinds of radios too?"

"I have everything," the man said. "I could get you in touch with the International Space Station."

Gale was pretty sure that wouldn't help anything. "Police chief first," he said. Another aftershock rumbled around them and he glanced up, hoping this house wasn't about to come down on his head. It didn't. The shock passed, and he said, "And do you have some paper? A pen?"

"Can I ask you about gas?"

"I'm sorry?"

"For my generator. I heard on the radio how they're going to ration, but if you want me and Marilyn on the radios full-time...."

"Yes, yes, of course. I'll make sure to tell the police chief—no, fire chief—you need more."

"Twelve gallons a day should do it."

Gale jotted it down and returned to his list-making.

An hour later he was headed back to City Hall, with a guarantee from FEMA that supplies would be delivered to the temporary hospital in the evac helicopters. He and the other two men who were leading the city had come up with a list of portable, small, crucial items, including some bizarre part the power company needed that they swore was no bigger or heavier than a generator. After talking on the radio to the power exec and carefully writing down what he needed, Gale had radioed it all back to FEMA, set up a schedule for radioing her twice a day for the foreseeable future, and listened impatiently to five minutes of ass-covering and politicking, rolling his eyes at her need for it. At the end, he was twirling his hand at the radio in a "get it over with" gesture. Finally, the bullshit was over.

He turned to thank George, then said, "Oh. I'm sorry, I volunteered your radio equipment for twice a day. Is that doable?"

"Happy to help," the man had said. "Either me or Marilyn will be here, every minute. Just ask for whatever you need."

"I appreciate your service so much. So does everyone in the city."

Back in his car, he wondered how many local heroes there were, making survival possible. Bash was one too. He'd have to remind him of that, first chance he got. And when this all was over, he'd have to think of some way to acknowledge every volunteer who had kept the city going.

He'd be barely in time to catch the shifts overlapping at City Hall, if he hurried. He hoped someone had organized lunch back there. He was hungry. He felt like he shouldn't be, that needs like eating and peeing and sleeping should leave him alone for a few days, just until he got a handle on the worst of this, but it didn't work like that.

At City Hall, he was in luck with food. There was lunch, and people were seated at a dozen office chairs, with four solid tables set up in a "u" holding supplies and, at one end, the food. Other people were seated on the park benches, eating off paper plates. The kids—they were ten of them now—the two little ones from last night, the three teen sons of Oscar, and another five in between—were all sitting on blankets on the ground, making a picnic of it. Making his way to the food, he waved some flies off a pile of boiled ham and made himself a sandwich.

His staff called greetings to him, and one of them stood up to give him her spot on a bench. Most of his pairs of co-chairs were seated together, working over scrawled notes as they ate. He looked around and realized he knew better than half the names now. He'd get them all by sundown, he promised himself, even the spouses and kids.

Angela put down her sandwich and came over to him. She handed him a stack of paper at least twenty pages high. "While you were out," she said, with a wry half-smile.

"In only an hour?"

"Most popular boy on campus," she said.

He started flipping through the papers. "You ordered them by priority," he said. At the bottom of the stack was a note—"Five bodies recovered from City Hall." He glanced over there and realized search and rescue had moved on. Out there somewhere, if not in his town, in Memphis or St Louis and elsewhere, there were many people lying there, pinned, hoping for rescue that might never come. His mind flashed on the giant fire in Memphis and he imagined lying, pinned under a beam, smelling the smoke and knowing it was coming for you.

The sandwich turned to ashes in his mouth. But he kept chewing and swallowing, chewing and swallowing, getting all the food down. If he was running on no sleep, he couldn't run on no food too. He wiped his mouth with the back of his hand and stood. "Ready for more work?" he said to Angela.

"You could sit and have a soda. They're all warm, though."

"I'll sit tonight," he said. "And you'll go home this afternoon."

"For a while," she said.

"We need to do shifts too. You're my co-chair for administration, like every other group has their co-chair. I need you here from 8 p.m. to 8 a.m., from now on. So take a break while you can."

Oh man, what time had he said he'd come for Bash? He completely, utterly forgot. He needed to get him a message. "Does the hospital have a radio yet?"

"Yeah, they're on the police-fire radio net now like us."

He'd radio a message to his husband right after he met with everyone here, he promised himself. "I'll take off from 3:00 to 4:00, barring catastrophe," he said.

"Ha," she said. "Things are going to go wrong, no matter what. Take that hour for yourself, and then go home tonight for a while to get some solid sleep. You have a home?"

"It's standing," he said, "but I may sleep in the car in the driveway anyway, in case of aftershocks. How are you? Holding up okay?"

"I'll catch a nap this afternoon, and I'm sure I can sleep at night here."

"We both need radios," he said. "I prefer some separate, short-distance thing, like walkie-talkies, just for you and me, something strong enough to reach from here out to our houses, so we can keep in touch."

"I'll tell Megan and Ruth. They're communications, remember? Keep delegating."

"Right." He did have an urge to do everything himself, and as this morning had shown him, that was a pipedream. He barely had a chance to supervise. Shit, the FEMA call too—he had forgotten. "I have a five p.m. radio call with FEMA," he said.

"If we get three walkie-talkies, you'll leave one here, put someone in charge for that hour, and if they need you, they'll call you. If we can't find any radios locally, ask for some from FEMA."

"Good idea. Ideas." He shook his head, feeling like his logic circuits weren't working so well any more. He needed sleep, but he'd have to do without.

Chapter 9

Bash

Bash stood between McKenna and the dead patient. "You don't need to look, honey," he said.

"He just...died," she said faintly, staring blankly at Bash's chest as if she could see through it to the cadaver beyond.

Bash took her hands, carefully peeling off her gloves, then his. When he was done, he said, "McKenna, sweetie, look at me."

Slowly, her eyes recovered from the blank stare and met his.

"I'm sorry I let you see that. I shouldn't have."

"He bled so much," she said. "And you cut off his leg."

"I know, I know."

"I never saw anyone die before."

"I'm so sorry."

"He was an okay kid, you know? For a jock."

Bash's chest went cold with a deeper fear. "You knew him?"

"No, not knew him, not really. His name was Jared. He was on the basketball team—not the star, just a guy. Sometimes when the cheerleaders danced, he'd sort of dance on the sidelines, make fun of them. But not in a mean way. He made people laugh. And the assistant coach would swat at him with a clipboard, and people would laugh more."

"Oh, McKenna. I'm so very, very sorry."

Haruka began to stir to wakefulness.

Bash said, "I want you two to get some rest. Your mom hasn't shown up?"

"No," she said. "You don't think she died, do you? Like that." She pointed behind him.

He shook his head. "No. I imagine she's having a hard time getting here. The roads aren't passable."

"Is it horrible of me?" started McKenna, then clamped her lips shut.

Bash said, "Is what horrible?"

It took her several seconds to manage a reply. "That if my mom did die like that—that I'm glad I wasn't there to see it?"

Bash's heart was breaking. Mentally he kicked himself across town and back for forgetting these girls weren't trained medical staff, but smart teenagers who had taken on a new job and done it well. As a reward, and because of him, they'd probably have a lifetime of nightmares about tonight.

"I think the two of you could use some rest," he said, glancing down at his watch. It was 5:12. The sun would be up soon. He could use some rest too, but more important was getting the girls away from the blood and death. On the other hand, he couldn't send them out into the world alone. "The night's over. And you did great, but it's time for you to sleep now."

"I'd like to sleep," she said, her voice faint.

"Great. We can do that." He took back one of his hands and shook Haruka's shoulder gently until she pulled her head upright. "Take off your gloves, Haruka. We're going to call it a night."

He got the girls up and turned away from the body on the operating table, which he wanted to bag and hide from view soon. The living were always more important than the dead. He led the girls over to the staff parking lot and beeped open his own car. McKenna was the taller of the two, so he got her settled in the back seat and untied her sneakers. The clothes from Macy's that he'd never returned served as a pillow. Then he helped Haruka find a comfortable position in the front seat, tilting the passenger's seat back until it nearly touched McKenna's legs. He cranked down the driver's side window a few inches, closed the door, and stood peering in. Haruka was asleep again almost immediately. He thought she hadn't seen as much of the operation, so maybe she wouldn't carry as much trauma from it. McKenna traced her finger along the stitching on the seat back for a moment, then she curled her hands under her chin. Her lids fluttered, then closed.

Bash wanted to stay until she was asleep, but there was the body lying there on the operating table under a slowly brightening sky. He made his way to the operating area. Someone had tossed a plastic sheet over the body in his absence. Bash went to get a body bag and find someone to help him slide the boy in. He talked the OTA into assisting, and as they bagged the boy's body, she moaned a little. When he retrieved the amputated leg and put in the bag with the boy, she said, "Shit shit shit shit shit," until she ran out of breath. He didn't think she knew she was saying anything aloud.

Bash asked her to get a piece of paper and write, "Jared, H.S. basketball player," on it in permanent marker and tape it securely to the outside of the body bag. Along the way, in a town this small, someone would fill in the last name, he was sure. He went back to cleaning up the surgical area, getting it ready for the next patient. As he did, a big fire truck and two ambulances pulled up and rescuers started hauling down casualties. Some civilians, walking wounded, climbed off the truck on their own. As they moved into better light, he could see some were actually medical workers, in uniform.

Were they well enough to help? They must be rescued from the hospital or one of the medical office buildings. He checked his watch. They'd have been trapped or pinned for 14 hours, so psychologically they wouldn't be in the best of shape. But he'd been working for 14 hours straight, and he didn't know how long he could go on before he was doing more harm than good. He was desperate for more staff, and not too proud to beg them to help.

He bagged all the trash and turned off the flashlights. He kept his eye out for Dr Shah too, and finally saw him over near the street, talking to a woman with salt and pepper hair. The surgeon waved him over.

"This is Dr. Liz Eisenstein, orthopedics. Sebastian Hill, nurse. He's been pretty much running things here since the quake."

"Looks like you've organized it well."

"We did what we could. Are you from the hospital, or—?"

"Hopkins Medical Building," she said. She waved a hand at someone, motioning someone else over. "What can we do?"

"Honestly, you can take over. Or find someone to take over. I need a few hours' sleep, and I'm not an MD, and emergent medicine is not my field, and I'm so glad to see you." He realized he was babbling and clamped his mouth shut.

Another woman, in her thirties, very pale with wispy black hair, came up. The orthopedist introduced her. "This is Sonja, a PA. She's done some work overseas."

"I did a stint with Doctors Without Borders," she said.

"Would you?" Bash said. "Help? Take over? You must know a hundred times what I do about field hospitals."

"Shouldn't a director be an MD?" Sonja said, deferring to the two doctors standing there.

The surgeon said, "Bash here has managed well enough without an MD. We need someone to organize, assign staff, start setting up staff rotations, keep track of specialties, request equipment. And then we need an MD—you, maybe, Liz, to decide who gets evacuated with some smart triage. They'll have three evac helicopters coming in mid-morning."

We will? thought Bash. Things had been happening without his managing them while he was in surgery, so obviously he could back off his responsibilities. He wanted to. He felt guilty about it too, but he wanted to simply help patients and let someone administrate.

"We need to pick the six most critical cases to go first, within an hour," said Shah. "The helicopters will be back every two to three hours as long as they can be spared. With luck we might get 20 or more people out of here today."

The two doctors talked about how to go about assessing patients for evac. Bash trailed behind, half hypnotized with exhaustion, but he forced himself to focus the best he could. They moved around the parking lot, filled now with patients lying down on makeshift beds, lying directly on the ground covered by blankets, and sitting on chairs. Some had family alongside. There was one firefighter who had gotten hurt when a half-collapsed building came down on him while he was trying to effect a rescue. With a broken ulna, he was out of commission for a few weeks, but at least he was alive to tell the story.

The little girl with the head injury who had come in last night before he started surgery was still unconscious, and Bash was glad to hear the docs agree to evac her today. Her mother and father had not shown up, and Bash wondered if they were dead, or trapped somewhere, or struggling to find their daughter and hadn't thought of coming here. He wondered about McKenna's mother too, who surely could have made it home by now even walking, and he worried that many children had been made orphans today.

Imagine the administrative nightmare of trying to match them up with distant relatives, of making sure those relatives weren't child abusers or sex criminals, of trying to refer them to psychologists and social workers for the next several years. What were the populations of St. Louis and Memphis? Over four million combined, he imagined, probably 40% minors, and how many had been orphaned?

He brought his attention back to the rounds. Most of the

patients he didn't know. A handful were in the recovery room from surgery he had been in on, but he recognized the wounds, not the faces. A dozen patients were brand new, coming in with Liz and Sonja from the medical building rescue.

Suze was still doing triage and looked rebellious when she was told she'd get relieved in a very short time.

He stayed behind until she was done with her current patient, then said, "You've done a good job, Suze. It's time for us to get some rest. There'll be plenty to do in eight hours too."

"The rescue guys went through our building," was all she said. "They found two survivors."

"That's great!" he said.

"Out of 23? No it's not."

"It's better than no survivors," he said.

"Maybe if we had found them sooner," she said. "Maybe if you had helped me."

"I'm sorry," he said. "There was so much to do."

"I'm not about to forgive you."

"Okay," he said, not wanting to argue over it. There was no reason to argue, and he already felt bad enough. He felt bad about Jared and about McKenna watching him die. He felt bad about the man in the Toyota, the first man he condemned to death with triage. He didn't need her blame on top of his own. "Get yourself some rest, as soon as you can."

"*I* have patients to triage," she said.

He let it go.

At the back of the hospital area where they arrived last, Mr. and Ms. Witherspoon were still sitting.

"There's my nurse," said Ms. W.

"How you doing?" Bash said.

"Past ready to have the baby."

"Where's the pediatrician?"

"Busy. Said it'd be sometime today, but not immediately, after looking up my whatsit."

"How far dilated did he say you were?"

"Six centimeters, he said, about 45 minutes ago."

"Getting there." He turned to Dr. Eisenstein. "Can we get her evacced?"

"Not first thing. Maybe last load today, if no one worse comes in before then. There are too many emergent cases. And from how she answered our questions, the labor is preceding normally." She turned to Ms. W. "Right?"

"There's no blood or anything. It hurts, though."

"We'll see what we can do about that," she said, then to Shah, "Sonja may have delivered a baby before."

Ms. W. stabbed a finger at Bash. "I want him."

"Me?" Bash squeaked. "I've never assisted with a birth." He'd watched a few in nursing school rotations, but that was back before the turn of the century.

"I trust you."

"But," he said, and looked hopelessly at the doctor, then at Mr. W, who shrugged and smiled at him wearily. Bash hoped they could move him out too, maybe tomorrow. He didn't like the way the man looked, sallow and tired.

Shah said, "Why don't you stay with her. I think you're pretty much done for surgery."

"I am a little tired," Bash admitted.

"That'll work, Liz?" he asked the new hospital administrator.

"Sure," she said. "And I'll find you two—" this to the Witherspoons "—the very best in delivery of our staff." Then to Bash, "Stay here for now, okay? At least stay off your feet."

Bash nodded and sat down, then watched the assessment team move away toward the last few patients. He had so much to tell them, but if he could only rest for a second.

"Damn," gasped Ms. W., and he watched as she rode out another long contraction.

When it was done, he said, "What can I do for you?"

"Tell me my baby will be okay."

"Oh yes, I'm sure of it. Did the pediatrician listen to its heart?"

She nodded.

Mr. W. said, "Said it was strong and steady. Said everything was normal."

Bash said, "Then I'm sure you'll both be fine."

Ms W. peered at him. "Why don't you take a nap? You look awful."

"I thought you wanted me here."

"To deliver the baby. And I'd like that to be now, but it isn't."

"You wanting to push?"

"No. Not at all."

"Well..." he said. "Maybe I'll grab forty winks."

"Why don't you use that car they examined me in," she said, pointing. "It's right there. Then we can come for you when we need you."

"Promise to wake me up for whatever," he said. "Especially if you want to push."

"I will," she said, struggling to stand.

He got up and helped her balance on her way to her feet.

"I want to walk again for awhile. You go nap."

Every time someone said "nap" or "rest" or "sleep" it was like a stage hypnotist's trick, making Bash want to lie down right where he stood. But he made over to the car—he wondered briefly whose it was, Meggy's or some other dead person's—and climbed in the front bench seat and let out the sigh to end all sighs. What a day it had been. Within moments, he was out cold.

* * *

Bash woke feeling sticky and still tired, but needing in the worst way to pee. Clambering out of the car, he looked up to see the sun halfway up the eastern sky. Across the way, Mr. Witherspoon was asleep on a blanket on the ground. Ms. W was pacing again.

She'd probably walked miles, without ever going more than ten yards from her husband. Bash headed over.

"How are you?"

"I'm fine. But I want this to be over."

"Has a doctor examined you since I fell asleep?"

She nodded. "I'm hungry."

"I can get you something," he said, wondering if that were so.

"No. I'm nauseated too."

"Ah, okay. You have water or juice?"

"I'm out."

"I'll get all three of us some. Will you be okay for ten minutes until I get back?"

"I'm fine," she said, but she sounded upset, like there were tears underneath.

Well, he had to pee, no matter what else was going on. He'd tend to her emotions when he came back.

As he walked through the parking lot, he was surprised to see just as many patients as before. The staff, he only recognized two of. His first group had been replaced by a whole new shift, and he was happy that those first few were off getting some rest. The gazebo for surgery he had dreamed of last night had magically appeared. Had he mentioned it aloud last night? Or had someone else gotten the same idea?

He asked the receptionist where the bottled water and juice was, and she pointed while she finished writing something. She glanced up and said, "Wait!"

"Yes?"

"You really need a new uniform."

He looked down at himself. He had dried blood and who knows what staining his front. Not very reassuring to patients. "I don't have anything—"

"Someone found a box of scrubs." She pointed. "Second table from the end."

There was a ratty cardboard box under that table with scrubs and patient gowns in a disorganized pile. He rooted through until he found scrubs in large, pants and shirt, and he took them with him into a port-a-potty and peed, blessed relief, and changed his clothes. He found a plastic bag for his uniform, though with what he was hearing about water shortages, who knew when he'd be able to do laundry.

He got three bottles, water, apple juice, and lemon-lime soda, looked around for McKenna and Haruka, and, not seeing them, went back to the Witherspoons. While he was hungry, he could put off a meal for a little while longer.

Ms. W took the apple juice. He left the white soda for her husband and took the water for himself. He lifted the bottle and toasted. "To your baby. You have a name picked out?"

"Ira is campaigning for Diana, but I'm leaning toward Anja."

"They're both pretty names."

"I guess I'll give in to him. He may not be around her whole life, so at least his child should have the name he wants."

"It must be so hard," he said.

Her face looked angry, but Bash thought she wasn't, really, that she was fighting back fear and grief.

"It's okay to be upset," he said.

"Is it?" she said, her eyebrows shooting up, her tone snide.

He knew better than to take it personally. "I can't imagine what either of you is going through."

"But you've seen it before."

"I've seen cancer before, certainly. And what it does to families."

Her face relaxed and showed a hint of the worry she must be feeling. "How many of them die? The ones that you treat."

"Too many. People fight with everything they have, but it doesn't always work."

"I wish he'd fight harder."

"It might not matter—to the outcome, I mean. There's no proof that positive thinking or angry fighting or any particular

146

sort of attitude makes a difference. I know you've heard otherwise on the television, but it's not so."

"What makes a difference, then?"

"The best treatment. The right genes for it to work well. Luck, mostly, just plain old garden variety luck. And probably some stuff we simply don't know about yet."

"How about having a baby on the way? Could that help?"

He gave her a wan smile. "I hope so. I doubt there's been a study done on it." He wondered if she'd gotten pregnant after the diagnosis, if she'd done it to keep some part of her husband alive, even if the outcome of the cancer was the worst.

"If he doesn't make it," she began, and then she gasped and rode her way through another contraction.

Bash moved to her side, ready to help her sit or do whatever she needed. He realized while he'd napped, she'd been dealing with this herself.

She was left panting. "I'm so alone."

"I'm right here."

"I mean in my life," she said. "We moved less than two years ago. I lost my close girlfriends. Email just isn't the same."

Bash understood that all too well. "Do you have family?"

She got a stubborn look on her face.

Bash knew there was something there. Should he pry at it?

From behind him, Mr. W's voice came. "She has a father."

"I *had* a father."

"You still have one, honey. And I think—"

She said, "I know what you think."

"It's time to forget and forgive."

"I can't forget."

Bash had backed off a couple steps to watch both of them. It was like a tennis match, but much more interesting.

She jerked her head. "I need to go to the toilet again."

"I'll help you," said Bash.

"No, I'm fine, if I hurry over there before another contraction comes." She walked away.

Mr. W. yawned and stretched.

"I brought you a soda," said Bash, pointing under the chair.

"Thanks," Mr. W said. "She hasn't spoken to her father for nine years."

Bash was curious and nodded encouragement.

"She was married before." Mr. W leaned down and picked up the soda, cracked it open and took a long pull. "Good. Thanks." He shook his head. "He was an asshole."

"Her father?"

"No. The first husband. And everyone could see it but Melba. Or maybe she could—she's smart. But she was being stubborn."

Not terribly difficult to imagine.

"And her father paid the guy twenty-five thousand dollars to leave her. With the promise of another twenty-five five years later if he stayed away."

"Wow. And did he? Leave, I mean?"

"In a New York second," said Mr. W. "I'm sure it cost Melba's father most of his retirement savings, but it worked."

"Would you do that for your daughter?" asked Bash.

"Only if I could keep myself from killing the guy first."

"It was that bad?"

He nodded and said softly, "She's on her way back. But I want her to call her father. He should see his grandbaby. And if I pass, she needs someone."

Bash agreed. He wondered if he could say anything about it. Probably not. It really wasn't his business. But he'd think on it, come up with something subtle, plant another seed in her mind. If only his mind were working better, this was the sort of thing he usually could do quite well. "A master manipulator," Gale called him, not meanly, and when Bash pointed out that he only used his powers for good, Gale didn't contradict him.

Ms. W. was back. "I think it's getting closer," she said. I'm starting to feel different. There's a heaviness, or something. It's hard to explain."

Bash said, "I'll go get someone." He hoped the new administrators had remembered that a real delivery nurse or midwife was needed. They might have forgotten, as busy as the place was.

He hunted down Sonja and told her he wanted someone to check Ms. W. "And where are we going to do this? Is there a stretcher or a table or something free?"

"That's our worst shortage. We have volunteers out, looking for cots and blankets and so on." She patted his arm. "But we'll get your lady something. I'll send over an internist in a minute."

"We have an internist now?"

"Yes, a volunteer that flew in on the first helicopter run."

"Bless his heart. Or hers."

"Hers. A Doctor Duell."

"You're doing great," he said. "Thanks for taking over."

"Thanks for starting everything," she said, touching his arm. She turned to go.

The Witherspoons were sitting together, holding hands. He stopped several yards from them, not wanting to interrupt what looked like a tender moment. He glanced over his shoulder and saw a big panel van pulling up at reception. The driver and passenger went to the back doors and opened them up, pulling out a big bundle. Bash realized it was a tent of some sort. About time. They could get all the patients and supplies under cover. If rain came—though it didn't look like it would today—they could still treat people. He thought, if it rained, they also needed something to keep all those cardboard boxes of supplies off the ground, pallets or bricks or something. Should be plenty of spare bricks lying around town, that was certain. He'd remember to mention it to Sonja. Or he'd go down to the hospital and gather some bricks himself. No, they needed him to treat patients. He could send McKenna and Haruka, maybe, if McKenna's mom didn't show up.

Two hours later, Bash was gloved and gowned and assisting the birth of baby Diana. Or Anja, whoever won the naming battle. The way Ms. W was cursing at her husband, he'd not bet against her getting her way. She was tough, though, and a good thing, because she was doing this 100% natural. She had insisted Bash be her nurse, and neither he nor anyone else could talk her out of it, so here he was, getting his hand crushed.

Sonja walked by, detoured toward him, and said, "You have a message up front, from a Gale?"

"Thanks," he said, and went back to encouraging Ms. W. She grunted as she pushed, and he thought she might break his metacarpals. Strong woman.

"You want to see this, Dad?" said Dr. Duell "She's crowning."

Mr. W went down to the end of the table and said, "Oh gee. Honey, there's our baby."

"I know that, you fool. I can feel her trying to tear my twat in half."

Bash gave her hand one last squeeze and said, "I'll be right back."

"Fine, y'all just leave me now. Everybody get down there and watch the show."

"I'm here, honey," said Mr. W, moving up and reaching up for her other hand.

Bash went down to help the doc. A dark head of hair was pressing its way out. So cool. "You need anything?" he said quietly to the doctor.

"I want to avoid an episiotomy if I can. We'll wait a few seconds for some stretching. Get ready with the syringe and the towels."

"Opening those now." He had left it until the end, trying to keep the sterile towels perfectly free of contamination. He glanced up to see they had something of an audience, a dozen gapers looking on, and he waved people back. Fools. Did they have no empathy?

"Oh God," moaned Ms. W.

The baby came slithering out, gooey and moving. The doctor transferred her to the mother's belly.

"Is she okay?" said Ms W, straining to sit up.

"She's gorgeous," said Bash, toweling the baby off. The doctor cleared the mouth and stuck a hand out for the syringe. Bash passed it over, and soon the baby's eyes and mouth were clear. It hiccupped and started to mewl, but quietly. Quickly, the doc pressed a stethoscope to its chest.

The doctor nodded to Bash, and smiled, saying, "She's a healthy little girl. Good job, both of you, Mom and Dad."

Bash finished cleaning the baby, and then carefully, nervous as a new father about breaking it, eased her up Ms. W's body to her chest. "Hang on to her, Daddy," he said to Mr. W, who was looking at the baby with tears in his eyes.

Bash kept half an eye on the three of them and tidied up what he could. "How long to the placenta?" he asked Dr. Duell.

"A few minutes, no more than fifteen." She smiled at the parents, then at Bash. "This was your first delivery?"

He nodded. "First hands-on."

"You did fine."

"Well, she had to do most of the work."

"That's the truth," said the doc. "Okay, here we go." The placenta was coming.

Ten minutes later the doc was gone to attend to arriving patients, and Bash was finishing cleaning up. He wished he had a pretty baby blanket to wrap the baby in, but that hadn't been among the supplies that had found their way here, nor was a hat. He had stuffed a small surgical bootie with gauze and was going to pop it onto little—whoever's—head. Luckily, it was another warm day, warm for late October, but the new baby needed to be kept warmer than adults.

He took a second to enjoy the sight of the new family. They didn't have what most women in American had at such a time—a baby weight, a baby picture. Oh, wait. He took out his cell phone and powered it on—still no signal—and took a picture of the three of them. He moved up. "You want a baby picture?"

"Thank you," she said, showing him the first real smile he'd seen on her face. "For everything."

"I only watched. You did the hard part." He took several close shots of the baby, then saddled her with the ridiculous bootie-hat.

"Man. I had no idea it was going to hurt like this," she said. "However does the human race keep going?"

"At least we'll be able to give you a little pain med now."

"I'll still be able to nurse?"

"We won't give you anything that will hurt little—Diana?"

"Yes, Diana."

Mr. W. looked proud and happy. And very, very tired.

"I'm going to find you some place to stay. Someplace safe, and someplace with a roof, if there's a safe roof in town."

"We don't know about our house yet," Mr. W. said. "It may be fine, but we never got back there after getting discharged from the ER."

"Give me the address, and I'll get it figured out through the fire department," Bash said. "For now, you three enjoy each other. I'll have the pediatrician come over in a little bit and talk about nursing. Since it's your first, and all." He'd also have him double-check little Diana.

The couple smiled at each other, and Bash backed off.

He bundled up the dirty paper sheets and put them in one of the sealable red medical waste bags that had gotten flown in. He turned to walk it over to the dumpsters—they had two now, one for medical waste, one for regular—and was surprised to see McKenna come toward him out of the dispersing crowd.

"That was pretty amazing," she said.

He looked at her face. She seemed much better than last night, but he wanted her out of here. Babies were a happy ending, but there'd be more blood and pain to see as people were still being pulled out from under collapsed homes. He heard a male patient yelp in pain.

"Have you found your mother?"

Her face fell. "No. We've been walking around my neighborhood, looking for her. And we made sure the notes to her are still up at the house."

"Keep thinking positive," he said, hoping he wasn't giving her false hope.

"Can I help you with that trash?" she asked.

"No, I have it." He made his way to the dumpsters, and Haruka came out of a patch of visitors and fell into step with them. Bash felt like a mother duck with two ducklings—or rather geese, or puppies, considering his expertise with teenage girls—who had accidentally imprinted on him. He threw away the trash. "Okay, let's find you something to do." Something without blood and painful moans.

He looked around an increasingly organized field hospital. Two men were being assisted by several visitors in getting up the big tent. They needed something like pallets, he reminded himself again. Reception was busy with the walking wounded. Triage was going smoothly—and it was no longer his job to make sure it was. His gaze drifted further, out into the street where an ambulance was pulling up, and further still. Aha.

"I have a really important job for the two of you," he said.

"We're ready," said McKenna, straightening up. Haruka nodded. McKenna said, "What's the job?"

"Feeding us," he said, and marched them over to the reception area to check if the job was already taken. It wasn't. He grabbed the message from Gale and scanned it.

The two girls followed him across the street. The sandwich shop key had been hidden inside a drainpipe, and the word of its location spread around to the staff last night. Bash opened up the door and led them inside, sniffing. It was musty, but so far there was no odor of rotting food. With a big industrial refrigerator and freezer, as long as people hadn't been opening it and closing it all night, the food could stay good for a while. Maybe one more day for the fridge, and maybe two or three for the freezer. By then, he hoped that roads would be open and more food would be arriving via truck.

He found paper and pen and set them to an inventory of the front room first. He thought it through, wondering what sort of danger he was putting them in this time. Looters? Could be. He'd find an adult male to work alongside them if he could, someone big and tough. What if the owner came back? He wrote a note to the owner or cops or anyone who might challenge the girls, explaining the situation and signing his name.

In the front room he said, "Next, do the fridge, but don't leave it open. We'll lose the cold air and the food will spoil."

"I have a cell phone," said McKenna. "I'll take some pix, close it, and we'll use the pictures to make a list, then check it out to make sure we were right. How's that?"

"Great idea. I'm running across the street for a minute, and I'll lock you in. Be right back."

He hunted down Sonja and explained to her about the arrangement he had made with the sandwich shop manager, told her he'd have sandwiches ready to serve over there in an hour or so.

"Good. I'd like to get these visitors out of the way if I can. We just don't have the space."

"That's going to be a challenge. Everyone is so upset."

"If they have food, that's something to do. It'll distract them."

Bash considered. "All the tables from the restaurant are over here, but there's some stools and a high counter."

"They can sit on the floor there or eat standing up too. No biggie."

"And I was thinking. If it rains, all the boxes need to get up off the ground. So we need wood pallets, or we can build platforms with bricks. I can do that."

"No, I'll get it taken care of somehow. We need you for medicine. Or, rather, you need to sleep. You still haven't?"

"I slept for nearly four hours. It'll do me for today, but I'd like a full night's sleep tonight, if possible."

"Sure. I'll put you on days. We're going to have medical problems all week, especially as people run out of meds."

"Days are great, thanks."

"In a way, days are harder."

"Why's that?"

"At night, no evacuation. And fewer people will be getting themselves into trouble crawling around debris."

"Maybe we shouldn't have done any surgery last night. Waited for evac instead."

"From what I can tell, you did what had to be done. We'll be doing some surgeries tonight too, I imagine."

"Let me take an hour to eat and get the girls set up with the sandwich thing. And then I'll report back, okay?"

She made a note on her clipboard. "When you come back, bring me a veggie sandwich if you can."

"Cheese okay?"

"Yes, thanks."

Bash ran back across the street and let himself into the shop. The girls had made good progress in that short time. They were pulling a stuffed trashcan back into the kitchen.

"We decided to throw away some of the salads. Either they were wilted or they had mayonnaise in them, and my mom says to never eat warm mayonnaise."

Actually, it didn't matter—commercial mayonnaise wasn't going to contain salmonella, but he didn't say so. He hoped they wouldn't regret tossing out edible food. From the look of the trashcan, though, there hadn't been that much of it.

He helped them do a quick estimate of what was in the freezer, and then they sat down to make sandwiches, covering each with white paper and labeling them. He ate a turkey and

Swiss and put together a half-dozen vegetarian sandwiches, putting one aside for Sonja. In forty-five minutes, they were nearly ready for customers. He praised the girls, and asked them to clean up after people had been served.

Then he got back to work, getting assigned to a suture station.

At three, Gale showed up and he took a twenty-minute break, sitting in Gale's car in the sandwich shop lot and talking. They were both exhausted. Gale said he'd meet him at home no later than nine and took off again.

Bash got home just after 8:00 p.m., looking through the house with a flashlight and mourning lost items. He was tired. He wanted a shower, but he'd ask Gale first if they could afford to do that. He started cleaning up the kitchen while he waited for Gale, put drawers back together, looking for food that would rot—potatoes, probably they had a week before those would go bad. The fridge was almost empty, which he assumed had been Gale's work. He wanted to do the dirty dishes in the dishwasher, but again, he wasn't sure if they could spare the water. He retrieved the box of antibacterial baby wipes they kept in the bathroom and wiped every dirty dish, then put it back in the dishwasher. At least they wouldn't be smelling of rotting food now. He added the dirty wipes to the trash bag of broken crockery, tied it up, and took it out to the garage, making sure to seal the trashcan well. Who knew when they'd get trash service again?

Then back to the kitchen to clean up scattered utensils and cutlery, giving everything a wipe with a fresh dishtowel before adding it back to the drawers. Might not be perfectly sanitary, but good enough for now. It wasn't as if he'd be doing any gourmet cooking any time soon. He doubted he'd found every item. In the daylight, he'd go looking in corners and behind the fridge for the stragglers.

He was using garden gloves to pick up broken glass in the living room when Gale came home, carrying a paper grocery sack.

Bash met him in the kitchen.

"Food," he said, setting it on the table. "We have some in our emergency supplies, but I grabbed our bag of perishables at the market anyway."

"Our bag?"

"I didn't tell you about the rationing? Food and gas?"

"We have a lot to catch up on." Bash peered into the bag. Cheese, milk, fruits and vegetables.

"The stores should have enough for a week."

"But we're okay for longer, right?"

"With this and one or two more bags, what there is in the garage, what's on our shelves, at least two weeks."

"I'll be able to eat at work tomorrow and the next day, I think," said Bash, thinking of the sandwich shop.

"I'll make do with only breakfast and supper." He looked around. "You've been cleaning."

"Sure. You know me."

"I do." Gale pulled him into a hug.

Bash squeezed him tightly for a moment, then relaxed into the comfort of his husband's arms.

"We'll clean again tomorrow morning at dawn, if you want," Gale said in his ear. "And talk more. But I need some sleep now."

"I need a shower."

Gale backed out of his arms.

"Okay. Take something—" He stepped over and opened a cabinet, and came out with a plastic container, a quart capacity. "Like this. Fill it with water from the hot water heater, pour a little over yourself. Soap, then rinse with the rest."

Bash tried to look cheerful at the prospect. He hoped the dim light made it look more convincing.

"I'm afraid we're going to have to adjust to it for a while. I can't promise running water, or safe water, for at least a week." He explained the plan for public faucets along a main line. "So I'll get some on the way home every day, if I can figure out how to carry it."

"What about the solar shower thing we bought last year for camping? It's five gallons, right?"

"Perfect," Gale said. "I'll dig it out tomorrow."

"I guess we could both shower and even do some dishes with five gallons."

"Showering, we might have to skimp on," said Gale. "I know it sucks, but think of it this way. We're alive, and our house is standing, and we have each other. That's better than a lot of people in the fault zone can say."

Bash knew it for the truth. "I have a favor to ask of you."

"Sure."

"There are these two girls." He went on to explain how he had come across McKenna and Huruka and how he was worried about them. "So I left them alone at their house tonight, but it's pretty wrecked. And if the mother doesn't appear...."

"You want them to move in here."

Bash nodded, searching Gale's face.

"It will halve the time our food will last us."

"I know."

Gale sighed. "Of course we can't just leave them alone. If the mother doesn't show up tomorrow, yeah, bring them back here."

"Thank you."

"You're a good man, Bash."

"I feel like a man waking up from a dream, to find himself again."

"How so?"

"The last year has been hard on me. Hard on you too, I know. But I feel like I've been paying attention to the wrong things, to the little problems, when so much about my life was good. Something like this...." He lifted his palms, unable to find the words.

"I know. Makes you think about what's important."

"Exactly."

"You're important, the most important piece of my life. Don't ever doubt that." Gale reached for his hand. "Leave the kitchen for now. Let's go to bed."

After a quick wash each, they both did. It took no time at all to settle down, after the day Bash had just had. Or was it more than a day? He was trying to count the hours since the quake when exhaustion overtook him.

Chapter 10

Gale

Sunday morning, Gale woke before dawn to the sound of rain, a light but steady patter against the window. He had burrowed under the blanket in the night. Temps had dropped, maybe as much as twenty degrees.

Not good. Not good at all.

He wasn't sleeping outside, but half of his staff was, and so was half the town. Some were bedded down in their own driveways or back yards, their houses too damaged to risk staying inside, but enough of their belongings left intact that they didn't want to abandon them. This rain would ruin some of what hadn't been destroyed by the quake already.

Other citizens were living in the new tent cities. The lowland city parks were unusable for that because of sulfurous fumes. Those parks were also too close to the Mississippi and all the disease and danger it carried. There was a tent city on the high school grounds, two at green spaces on the outskirts of town, and a third, potentially the largest, up beyond the interstate on the highest ground around, outside the city limits on the fallow field of a generous farmer.

Gale crawled out of bed, trying not to disturb Bash, and

walked down the hall to peer into the guest bedroom. The girls, McKenna and Haruka, lay side by side. He and Bash had become foster parents to these two. He had been worried about taking them in, a worry not about having enough food or about extra responsibility, but about being gay in an anti-marriage-freedom state. And the Japanese girl's parents wouldn't love it either, he was sure. Japan was a generation behind the U.S. on the gay issue, he had seen firsthand, on a professional trip to an earthquake conference in Kyoto. But Bash had asked, and Gale hadn't been able to say no. Other people were just going to have to suck it up, and admit that keeping these two girls safe and fed was more important than their bigotry.

As he watched, McKenna flopped over in her sleep, as big in her gestures, as aggressive in sleep as she was awake. He liked the girl, but Bash had taken to a father role as easily as he took to breathing. Haruka was more of a cipher, quiet and thoughtful, hard to get to know.

Gale went into the kitchen and used the toilet in the half-bath off the mudroom. It turned out you could flush without power or water, but you didn't do it for everything—there simply wasn't water to spare. Last night, having heard the forecast for rain, he had set buckets under the downspouts on the house to gather water for just this purpose.

A flashlight set on its end on the kitchen table functioned as a table lamp. He switched it on, sat down and started his to-do list.

Most important was food. He, Bash, and the girls had groceries, the last two bags of the rationed groceries still sitting on the counter, what was left in his trunk and their year-old emergency supplies. But the people in the tent cities and even a good number who were still in their homes were running out. People who had shared freely on day one were rethinking that strategy now. And he couldn't blame them, because he was hoarding what he had too.

That was the first order of business with FEMA this morning.

LOU CADLE

Get an airdrop of food, MREs or whatever was available. And have a talk about water. Smart locals had listened to official advice and taken care with what water was left in their hot water tanks, saving it for drinking. Stupid people had wasted theirs on showering and were out, except for the little coming from the city's water tower. The police had to take over rationing water at the central taps yesterday, limiting the take to three gallons per household. So those who hadn't learned smart water practices before were forced to learn it now. The Guard took water out to the tent cities but, again, there was only enough to drink. People were going to be smelling pretty ripe by now out there.

The flashlight rattled on the table, giving warning, and Gale grabbed for it as the aftershock built. It wasn't much of one. When it passed, he balanced the flashlight again and went on with his list.

"Good morning."

He turned to see Haruka standing in the doorway, rubbing at her short black hair.

"Good morning. Would you like something to drink?"

"No thank you," she said. "May I sit?"

"Of course." He gestured to a chair. "Did the shock wake you?"

"Shock? Oh, aftershock, the tremor. Yes."

"What it is called in Japanese? An aftershock, I mean?"

"*Yoshin.*" Pointing to his pen, she said, "I'll show you, if you wish."

He passed her the pen and paper and watched as she drew in quick strokes two ideograms for the word. "That's lovely," he said.

"With a brush, it is more nice," she said.

"Is English writing hard for you to learn? I can't imagine trying to learn to read in Japanese."

"It is easier to speak," she said. "And I practiced speaking more."

162

"You must miss your home and family. Now more than ever."

She nodded slowly. "But they know now? That I am not dead?"

"Yes, they should by now. The radio people here read out all the survivor names on their radio yesterday. Those people who heard it put it up on the internet." They had also read all the confirmed dead over the airwaves, and that had gone up online too. "Your parents can find your name there."

"I think rain has stopped."

He listened. "I think you're right." Faint light shone through the blinds on the window. "I'm going to start a fire outside so we can have tea and breakfast."

Once the EOC had better cooking arrangements, he had brought their hibachi back home and set it up on the deck. He went out to light a fire. Damn, but it was cold out here. Rain dripped from trees and pattered on the autumn grass.

The charcoal bag was nearly empty. Not enough left to cook meat—not that there was any raw meat left in town to buy—but enough to heat water two or three times. He carefully stacked five pieces and lit them. Then he went inside and poured drinking water from a two-gallon container into two saucepans and went back to set one on the fresh flame. There was tea, and there was plain instant oatmeal from the grocery rationing bag, along with some brown sugar and canned fruit from their own cabinets. He hated oatmeal—loved the smell, but hated the taste, oddly—but he'd eat it. And be grateful for it.

By the time the water was hot enough for tea and oatmeal, the whole household was stirring, woken by the growing daylight. People were reverting to their natural states, he thought, rising and resting with the schedule of the sun. He found he didn't miss television or artificial light or noise—though he liked the few minutes of music he got to hear in the car every day.

Inside, he put away his notes and let Haruka set the table with paper bowls and cups, also from the rationing. He and Bash weren't paper-plate kind of guys, usually, but water couldn't be spared to wash dishes.

After breakfast, everyone used the toilet, and Gale flushed just once with the rainwater. Bash insisted on using a half-cup of the rainwater to scrub the toilet too. If it didn't continue raining, he'd have to get over that, Gale thought.

McKenna wanted to go with Gale to the EOC, but Bash insisted they stay here and do homework. "School starts again tomorrow," he reminded them.

"I cannot believe we have to go to school," McKenna said. "Seriously. Now?"

"I'll be fun. It's outside."

"What if it rains?"

"They'll figure it out," Bash said, brightly.

Gale was reminded of his own childhood, his mother trying to stay cheerful through his surly adolescent mornings.

"It's not like we can have organized classes," McKenna said. "People won't have all the same book."

"I'm sure the teachers will know what to do. You can read here too. We have some classic novels on the shelf."

McKenna sighed.

Gale thought, Bash sounds just like my mother, and now I'm about to become my father. "I really don't want you two wandering around on the streets today."

"Why not?" McKenna said.

"Because I don't trust people," he said. "The golden days are over. People are getting hungry. Some will be getting violent."

"Like me that first day," she said.

Gale had heard the story of her attack on the drug thief. He got the boy's name from McKenna, checked it against the known dead list, and saw the kid's name wasn't on it. Nevertheless, he had told Flint the whole story. Flint had said, "Without a corpus delicti, I don't give a shit. I have bigger fish to fry." Apparently, that was going to be the end of it.

To McKenna he said, "I'm glad you can take care of yourself."

"I miss Facebook," she said, in some inexplicable teenage link of logic.

He said, "Maybe the cell phones will work again today."

"Really?" Both she and Haruka perked up at that.

Gale said, "They're working on it. I promise you they're going as fast as they can."

Another aftershock stopped her reply, and the four of them sat and looked up in unison as the house shook.

"You sure it's safe here?" McKenna said.

"No," he admitted. "And if there's another big quake, run outside. If you can't get outside fast enough, get under the kitchen table. Check?"

"Check," she said.

Bash said, "We have a couple games and puzzles you guys can play today. Let me show you where those are."

"I'm not a kid," she said.

"Good. They're not kids' games."

"I'm sure enjoying this Brady Bunch moment," Gale said, "but I have to get in to work."

"What's a Brady Bunch?" McKenna said, and when he looked at her in surprise, she grinned. "Gotcha, old man."

He followed Bash down to hall to catch a quick private goodbye kiss. There was a moratorium on sex with the girls in the house, and they had agreed not to kiss or hug in front of them. It was irritating, but not impossible to live with. Bash and he had been together a long while, after all, and didn't need to stay draped over each other all the time like newlyweds.

He left for work. He was early, but he wanted to get lists of supplies needed from everyone for the radio call to FEMA at nine. The Triumvirate met at eight. An early arrival would give him a full hour to catch up with Angela and his team leaders before the meeting.

The aftershocks kept up all morning, five or six during his two meetings, many more than there had been the day before. None were strong, but the endless grind of them put everyone on edge. By the time he radioed in to FEMA, he was a little edgy himself.

"I don't want rice and beans," he said into the mike, straining to keep calm. "We don't have the water or fuel to cook them. I want MREs or canned foods, something like that."

"The weight of cans makes that impossible."

"At least they'd have safe liquid to drink in them." He had passed the word this morning to his teams and to Flint and Dan to tell all citizens. Everybody needed to drink the liquid in those cans of vegetables and fruit from here on out. It may not taste great, but it's potable liquid. Do not waste it. "What's the news on the barge?"

"The Corps is still working on the river. It's not the river it was, and they don't have a clear channel much south of St. Louis."

"And you can't get one of those fixed wing planes from the military? Something that can land in the limited space we have?"

"We're working on it. You don't understand. I have St. Louis to worry about, and Memphis is the hardest hit and taking a lot of the national resources." She went on complaining, and he let her—not that you could interrupt with this radio set-up. You had to wait for the "over."

When that word finally came, he said, "I appreciate that. I appreciate your position. But you appreciate that we're maybe 24 to 48 hours from a food riot here. Which reminds me. Our police chief wants more riot equipment. I have a list." He read it out to her. Rubber bullets and tear gas. A town their size didn't have a big stock of such things. Though he had begged Flint to not use the tear gas unless it were the last resort, truly a life or death situation. With the water shortage, how the hell would people wash their eyes after a dose of tear gas?

He read off the last of the other supplies. "But I'd rather have food than any of this. And I'd rather have water than food. A tanker of water."

"We're working on it, truly we are, Mr. Swanton. You know FEMA has always...." And it was off to the political races again, sound bites and ass-covering. He exchanged glances with Marilyn, who was manning the radios this morning.

"Yada yada yada," she said, with a wry smile.

Gale snorted and asked her, "You two are still set for food and water?"

"Yes. Luckily, we had just gone shopping the day before the quake, but in four or five days, we'll be down to the dregs too."

The FEMA director was winding her stump speech to a close, so Gale turned back to the radio.

"We've cleared out the Walmart parking lot and towed all the cars," he said. "We've bulldozed light posts there too, painted a big old X for you. So there is a clear space for landing bigger helicopters in town. Or even for dropping by parachute."

The problem was, he knew, water weighed an awful lot. What 24,000 survivors needed in water was eight pounds per day per person ideally, four pounds at the bare minimum. That meant 50 tons of water per day just to keep his townspeople alive. And that was one small town out of the whole earthquake zone. He did understand that they weren't the only ones needing help. But his understanding of the scale of the disaster didn't make his neighbors less thirsty, did it?

They had one of the biggest rivers in the world flowing by their doorstep, but it was a polluted, chemical-laden cesspool. It had been for three generations or more, but after the earthquake, it was a real danger. Benzene, chlorine, arsenic, mercury, many in high amounts, had been added to the regular pollutants. Really, at this point, you probably didn't want to sit within a mile of the river, but his outdoor Emergency Operations Center was closer than that, as were the fire and police stations. And the hospital, and hundreds of homes. He couldn't help that. His town was built on that polluted river.

He ended his frustrating conversation with FEMA, thanked Marilyn, asked her if their gasoline situation was okay—it was—and he drove back to the EOC.

He saw the smoke of the morning trash fire from a distance. They were making people separate out trash—anything that could be burned was being burned. But since there was plastic in there, and they didn't want people to breathe those fumes, they had put it as far away from the residential areas as they could, right at the edge of where the river was lapping up into the lower part of town. Dan had said it would also give them a way to put it out too, if it got out of control. Two firefighters with respirators and hand pumps stood guard over the fire.

He dropped by the police station and caught Flint on his way out the door. "Your equipment is coming," he said. "Bullets, they can get us. Water?" He shook his head.

"Maybe it'll rain more, like the forecast says. A lot more would be great."

"A month from now and we'll be thinking about snow." What a terrible image.

"I forget you're not from here. We seldom get snow. We get sleet."

Was that any better? "Two months earlier, and the bodies would have been smelling worse."

"Bad enough as it is. Glad burying's your job and not mine."

"Speaking of which, I have to go check with my people on burials." And everything else.

He drove back to City Hall. A bulldozer was there, pushing bricks down the street. Every street had, at its lowest end near the river, a pile of debris they'd shoved in place with bulldozers. The debris piles backed up the levees and replaced breached levees on the north side of town. Ron Woodham had been very good in offering his equipment.

He had shaken Gale's hand when they met again. "I guess you're going to say you told me so."

"No, sir. I'm going to say I'm glad you're alive and thank you very much for the equipment and men."

"But you did tell me so."

"Earthquake prediction's a fuzzy thing. I could have been off by 200 years, just as easily," he had said, and they had gotten on with business.

The bulldozing had to be done with care because there were still bodies in the collapsed buildings. A rescue worker worked alongside the dozers, body bags ready. All over town, slowly they were clearing out the last of the dead, following the markings the search and rescue teams had painted, and sometimes finding unpleasant surprises where none had been known and marked. On certain blocks, you could smell the decomposition, a rich smell, sweet and bitter and indescribably awful. Once you got a snootful, you smelled it for hours.

Gale did not envy the bulldozer operators or those scooping up the decomposing bodies. Among his requested equipment from FEMA yesterday had been more respirators. He hoped they'd come this afternoon.

And at some point, not too long off, they'd run out of diesel and gasoline, and this equipment and the cars would all sit dead in the streets, so much useless metal. Diesel had to last until the final body was buried.

As he walked through the lawn to the ECO, yet another aftershock hit. He muttered curses at the earth under his breath. He stopped walking to jot a note to himself—Ask FEMA if the USGS has any idea why this increased shock activity today.

Kay was manning the EOC radios. She handed him another stack of messages, mostly reports from his department heads. He was standing there, at the edge of the tent, going through them, when yet another aftershock hit. As it faded, a starling fell like a rock to the ground near his feet.

Kay and he both stared at it. It lay there, panting, its black sides heaving in and out.

"What the hell?" Kay said.

"Is it the sulfur fumes? Or something worse coming off the river?" he asked, feeling cold fear at the thought. If so, he would he have to evacuate the EOC right now to protect his people. And evacuate the lower town and the people living there. As if things weren't bad enough.

She stood, walked out of the tent, and tilted her head back. "Look up there."

Gale stepped to her side. Overhead, dozens of birds were wheeling in interlocking circles, all sorts of birds, not just the same species flying in formation. It was a crazy ballet he'd never seen before.

Kay said, "Do they know something we don't?"

Slowly, a few birds here and there found spots on tree branches. Then another small aftershock hit, just a tiny one that lasted no more than three seconds, but the birds that had just roosted lit out for the sky again. Gale said, in awe, "They're exhausted."

"What?"

"The aftershocks. They won't roost during them, and so they've been flying all morning, and this guy fell out of the sky from exhaustion." He looked at the starling on the ground. "He's catching his breath, see?"

As they watched, the bird staggered to its feet and waddled off, still too tired to fly, but uninterested in staying quite so close to humans.

"Holy crap," said Kay. "But I get it. I'm starting to feel that way myself. If flapping my arms would get my fat ass off this shaky ground, I'd be flying too. So what's up with all these shocks?"

"I don't know," he said. "But it makes me nervous."

"Me too."

At lunch, the staff shift change happened like clockwork. He still had most of those people he had started with that first full day, and he was proud of them for not leaving. Some townsfolk who had lost their homes had strapped backpacks on and hiked off to the west, trying to get past the ruined roads and to someplace safer, some town with plentiful water and food. They had even seen strangers coming north. Flint had the Guard stationed on the south road, hurrying the strangers through town. They didn't need more refugees straining the limited resources, and they couldn't even spare a bottle of water for those begging for it. Flint had found it possible to harden his heart to their pleas. Gale was glad he wasn't the one having to do that.

They had heard via radio that cities like Rolla and Columbia, the nearest sizeable cities that were out of the worst of the damage zone, were also suffering from severely strained resources because of refugees. In those cases, food and water could arrive on highways from Kansas City and points west, so the big problem there was housing. Public buildings there were like Houston's Astrodome after Katrina. There were more refugees this time, and there were fewer places to house them. People were being bussed to Kansas City, to Indianapolis, to Cincinnati, even to Chicago, George had told him. He wondered if it helped build sympathy that those towns had felt two minutes of shaking themselves, if far less intense than what had been felt here in the heart of the seismic zone.

He read a written summary of funerals and burials, which were moving along more quickly now that everyone in town had the experience of smelling rotting bodies. There were double and triple funerals, burials of whole families without funeral or mourners, and careful note-taking for each of the town's three cemeteries, so that if someone wanted the bodies moved later or cremated, they could be located. Many townspeople had donated garden rotary tillers, tractors, and shovels to speed the grave-digging. It didn't take many whiffs of decomposing flesh to motivate those donations.

He was moving on to talk to his shelter co-chairs when Kay

shouted his name. "Radio for you."

He turned, went back and took the radio from her.

"George here, Gale. I have that woman you've been looking for."

"What woman?"

"The mother of the girl you have. McKenna Lind. Her mother is Donia Lind, right?"

"Yes, yes! Is she—"

"Safe and sound. Or rather safe, if not entirely sound. She's in a Rolla nursing home, overflow from their hospital, with a badly broken leg. I can have her on radio any time you say."

"Thank you. Thank you, George. Does she know her daughter is safe?"

"I believe so. I passed the message along, at any rate, through my radio buddy there."

"If you don't mind, tell your contact 90 minutes from now they can talk on the radio, and apologize to the mother for the delay."

"Will do. See you then. Over and out."

He was smiling, and Kay said, "Good news?"

"For one family, yes, the very best."

"Lucky them," she said. Like almost everyone, Kay had lost someone—an aunt and a disabled cousin, in her case.

Gale went through the remaining staff meetings as quickly as he could, made sure his walkie-talkie was charged, told Kay he could be reached on it at any time, and drove home.

When he got to the house, he knew immediately something was wrong. The front door was wide open. The garage door was open. Tools were off their pegs and scattered on the floor.

Sick with fear, he jumped out of the car, yelling, "McKenna? Haruka?" He ran in the front door and saw more damage, items knocked off shelves. He stuck his head in the kitchen and saw it was entirely trashed. Cabinet doors stood open, the food cabinets empty, the grocery sacks gone. The back door to the deck was wide open. This was not aftershock damage.

He spun and ran down the hall, calling the girls' names again.

When he heard his name being called softly in return, he felt dizzy with relief. "Where are you?"

The linen closet opened and the McKenna crawled out, shedding a blanket. Then Haruka unfolded herself from behind McKenna and edged out. McKenna said, "Some guys. Two guys broke in." Her voice was shaking.

"It's okay. You're fine," he said, going to her. He pulled her up into a hug, and she clung to him.

Haruka stood but gave off a "don't hug me" vibe. He smiled at her. "You okay?"

She nodded. "Afraid. Afraid they could find us."

McKenna disengaged and said, "I'm sorry."

"Sorry? For what?"

"I should have fought them. They stole the food, didn't they?"

"It's fine. You *shouldn't* have fought them, and food can be replaced."

"No it can't. You talked about it last night, how it's a problem now. I was too scared to fight them, and now we'll starve."

"We won't starve. You did the very best thing by hiding. All I care about is that you're both okay." But if these guys were still in the neighborhood, looting empty houses...or looting houses with people inside.... "Hang on," he said to the girls. He grabbed his handheld radio and told Kay, "I need a police car at my house, now, right now—emergency." He rattled off the address. "Unmarked would be best. No sirens."

"We're safe," he told the girls, wondering if they were. "Let's shut all the doors again."

The three of them shut the house back up tight. He opened every closet and looked under both beds, to make sure no intruder was still inside. The front door was where the thieves had broken in, and it was askew, refusing to shut well enough to lock. He'd need to fix that, or nail boards across it before they could sleep tonight.

A green sedan pulled up out front while he was examining the door, and he jogged out to greet the cop who stepped out, relieved to see it was one he recognized. He explained the situation and that the looters were probably still nearby, maybe only a door or two down. The cop radioed in for help, and Gale returned to the girls.

They were in the kitchen, already cleaning up the mess.

"Everything's gone," McKenna wailed. "All the food."

"I hated that oatmeal anyway," he said.

She shook her head at him, seeing through his attempt to shake off the loss. The truth was, they couldn't afford to lose any food. "Let's check the garage," he said.

Gale thought maybe he was missing some tools, but he couldn't see at a glance which. He went straight over to the emergency stores in the big trashcan and opened it up. He breathed a sigh of relief. "Look, they didn't even find this stuff," he said to the girls. "And I still have a little food and water in my car. We'll be fine."

"Really?" said McKenna.

"And better still," he said, remembering why he was here in the first place. "We found your mom. She's alive."

"Seriously?" McKenna's face lit up. "You're not lying to me?"

"No, I'm not lying. And you can talk to her on the radio in—" he checked his watch "—about thirty minutes." But first he had to deal with the situation here. "Let's clean up a little more and then go talk to her."

"Is she here?" said McKenna. "In town?"

"No, she's in Rolla, but she's okay."

"I am very happy for you," said Haruka.

McKenna said, "Yes. Thank you, me too. I mean, I'm relieved."

Gale said to Haruka, "And I bet she can phone to your parents in Japan from where she is."

"Do you think this is true?" said the girl, her face shining with hope.

"I'm pretty sure of it," Gale said. "Now you two help me find, somewhere in this mess on the floor, a hammer and my coffee can of nails so I can get the front door secured."

They made quick work of nailing the front door shut, and the three of them wrestled a heavy sideboard in front of it too. Try getting in there, assholes. By the time they were done, it was time to get to the radio, and so he left a note on the windshield of the unmarked police car, telling the officer how to get in touch with him at the EOC. He'd figure out later if the cops had caught these looters or not.

He felt he'd been awfully lucky that the thieves hadn't found the stash of emergency food, and that the girls hadn't been harmed. They could have been killed or raped. He supposed they couldn't be left alone now at all, and he was glad that school was starting the next day so at least part of the day they had guaranteed adult supervision.

But what about the rest of the day? How did real parents juggle all this stuff? Of course, real parents, in the States at least, typically didn't have to worry about the decay of civil order at this level.

The three of them arrived at George and Marilyn's. All five of them stood in the basement while George got through to the ham operator in Rolla, who had gone to the nursing home and set up there, some sort of relay that George tried to explain but which was beyond Gale's understanding. Gale stood tense, waiting, but not as tense as poor McKenna, who was bouncing on her toes and seemed ready to snatch the microphone from George's hand.

At long last, a female voice came over the radio. "McKenna, honey, are you there?" then "What? Oh, over."

McKenna stepped forward to the microphone and said, "Mom?" then she burst into tears and couldn't say anything at all for several seconds.

George said "over" for her.

"I'm here. I'm here, McKenna."

George said, "Give her a second, over."

"We'll be together soon, I promise," said the mother. "Over."

McKenna pulled herself together. "I know. But I thought you were dead."

"I know. I was awful worried for you too. But I'm fine. And you are okay, and Haruka isn't hurt?"

"She's fine. She's standing right here."

"Tell her I talked to her parents today, just an hour ago. They know she's alive."

Haruka gave a quick nod. The girl didn't show a lot of emotion, Gale thought, but having gotten used to her quiet ways, he could see she was feeling the news deeply. He felt a little embarrassed to be witnessing all these emotions, and backed off a few steps, giving the girls a little more space, ending up next to Marilyn.

The woman was wiping at tears on her face with a dishtowel and gave him a sheepish smile. She whispered, "A happy ending is good every once in awhile, isn't it?"

He nodded and stepped closer to her to speak softly. "Without you and George, they couldn't be doing this, you know."

"Oh, pooh," she said, brushing it aside. But she looked pleased.

"We can't keep talking forever," McKenna's mother was saying. "But we'll see each other soon. And maybe talk again before that."

"Gale says the cell phones will work again. And he had mine charged from his car, for when they do."

"Good."

Gale stepped forward again. "I'd like to talk to her when you're done."

"Gale says he wants to talk with you. I'll see you soon, Mom. I love you." McKenna handed over the microphone.

"This is Gale Swanton, Ms. Lind," he said. "McKenna and Haruka have been staying at my place. Our house made it through the quake safely."

"I'm so grateful to you," the woman said. "I can't have her here, and I can't even move on my own yet. Can I impose on you to hang on to my girls another day or three, until I make some sort of arrangements?"

"I'm happy to." He looked around at his audience and thought, Well, I don't like the public nature of this, but it has to be said. "I think you should know, Ms. Lind, that I'm gay. The girls are living with my husband, Bash, and me. They seem to have really taken to him. But if you have a problem with that, tell me, and I'll find them another place to stay."

She was laughing when she came back on. "You think I give a crap about that? I'm grateful to you for caring for them, and I don't care if you're gay or black or Jewish or Martian, for that matter, as long as they're safe and fed. Besides, this way, at least I know you're not sex-criming them."

Gale felt a twinge at the word "safe," thinking about the break-in and the danger that had put the girls in. He wasn't about to mention it, though. The woman had enough worries, and he wasn't about to add to them by telling her about details that were out of her control. "The roads out are getting cleared, slowly but surely," he said. "As soon as we can make arrangements, we'll get the two of them to you."

McKenna got to say goodbye one last time, and then they signed off. She politely thanked George and Marilyn and beamed at Gale. "I feel a lot better now."

"So do I," he said. For her sake, and for himself, having official permission to have the girls in the house.

He thanked George and Marilyn and took the girls out to the car. There, he hesitated.

"The thing is, I don't want you alone at home," he said. "Not now. Not after this morning's break-in."

"We can just hang out somewhere," McKenna said.

"Not alone. Either we find some of your friends who have their parents at their house, or at a tent city, or...." He trailed off, thinking of possibilities.

"We could go to the hospital again," McKenna said, hopefully.

"Maybe," he said, remembering Bash's unwillingness to traumatize them with more blood and guts. He probably should check in with Bash and they could figure out together what to do with the girls. There might be something innocuous for them to do there, or they could simply sit with visitors and read books, under the eyes of many responsible adults. At worst, he'd take them back to the EOC and set them to entertaining the littler kids there. Somehow, he had to keep them out of harm's way, and with adults who could protect them. He had no illusions. He knew civil disorder would increase. They were lucky looters had held off this long.

He radioed Kay to tell her of his detour. She said, "We can do without you, no offense, for a little while. Everything does seem to be under control for now."

He signed off and drove the girls to the hospital. It was much more organized there too, than it had been in those first chaotic hours. There was a designated waiting area of folding chairs, parking spots marked off with spray paint, a person in a police auxiliary vest directing traffic, and not quite the jam of patients he had seen before. They had customers, it looked like, but they were arriving mostly on their own, walking wounded rather than serious injuries being brought by ambulance. The seriously injured were evacuated by now—or dead. He parked half a block down the street, where he could see rubble from the hospital being taken away in dump trucks and taken down toward the river to shore up the levee. Bodies were still being removed at the wreck of the old hospital, blue body bags lined up on a sidewalk, and someone walked along the row, unzipping them one by one, maybe to try and identify them. Other people were going through equipment as it was uncovered, salvaging what they needed for the field hospital.

He and the girls checked in at reception, then sat to wait for Gale to get free. In a few minutes, he came over, snapping gloves off, and gave them all a big smile as they stood. "Come to take me to lunch?" he said.

McKenna snorted. "Like where?"

"Oh, a picnic, I guess, would be the most exciting option."

Gale said, "Tell him your news, McKenna."

"They found my mom. I talked to her!"

"Really?" Bash glanced at Gale, and Gale nodded. "I'm so happy for you. No, don't hug me until I ungown." He untied his gown and slipped it off.

Gale said, "And her mom knows she's with us, and she says it's fine."

They exchanged a glance over McKenna's head, as Bash gave her a hug.

Gale confirmed, "Really fine."

McKenna was no idiot—she caught what he was trying to say. "She's no bigot."

"She said it was fine if we were Jewish Martians even," said Gale.

Bash laughed.

"That's not quite what she said," McKenna pointed out.

"I was just making a joke for Bash," Gale said, a little embarrassed. The mom had been very good, really, and he shouldn't be indicating anything else in front of McKenna.

"I mean, she wouldn't have had the idea of sponsoring an exchange student if she were a bigot, right?"

Gale had no doubt there were exchange student families who were homophobes, but he made a pleasant noise of agreement. He asked Bash, "You haven't had lunch yet?"

"I'm tired of salami and cheese, and that's what we're down to at the sandwich shop. Also, the owner showed up and demanded we sign IOUs for the food, and that pissed me off, considering how many others in town are pitching in for free. I think I'd rather starve than promise to pay him." He patted his belly. "I still have a little extra to live off of here."

Gale said, "Hon, you need to e—"

And with a shriek of noise, the second big quake hit.

Chapter 11

Bash and Gale

The noise was fearsome to Bash, a low-pitched metallic screech, like a freight train taking a curve too fast, but an octave lower. He felt adrenaline flood his system. A powerful jolt rocked him. He saw the rows of empty folding chairs fall as one, their crash a descant to the bass scream of the earth.

Haruka has been knocked to her knees. That looked like a smart place to be. As the ground jerked again beneath his feet, he dropped to a sitting position, laced his hands behind his head and leaned forward, making himself as small as possible, protecting neck with his hands. The earthquake noise itself, from the ground, lowered in pitch and lowered, away from that horrible first sound, and finally fell to the lowest end of his hearing range. But he could *feel* the sound, still, vibrating his bones and clenched teeth.

Gale and McKenna were sitting on the ground now too. They were all as safe here as anywhere, Bash realized, and he glanced up to make doubly sure that nothing could fall on their heads. Behind him he heard a *whumph* as the big tent collapsed. Turning his head, he could see it covering people and tables and beds and all, a lumpy ruin. Probably the least awful roof to fall on your head, though, and better than a brick building—he doubted there'd be serious injuries from it unless someone had been pitched off a stretcher. He curled up again and rode out the quake.

Inside his mind, part of him was thinking, timing it, planning what to do when it stopped—and part of him was a terrified animal who wanted to run off in a blind panic. He had treated a farmer the first day who had been trampled by his own cows as they did just that. At this point, he sympathized with the cows. He wanted to bellow and stampede.

A woman started screaming and kept screaming, which wasn't helping her one bit. Nor was it helping his nerves. He wished she'd shut up. As the ground gave a particularly sharp jerk, a man somewhere close said, "Well, fuck *this*," like you'd say just before deciding to back up to detour around a traffic jam. But there was no way around the quake. There was only forbearance.

Still the shaking went on. Distant low booms sounded, like in a TV report from a war zone. Falling buildings? Something in the earth itself? Bash didn't know. He was glad it was someplace else, whatever it was.

There were sobs and moans coming now from several people as the quake went on, seeming endless. Jerk, roll, jerk, over and over, long enough to give him a touch of seasickness.

When it finally stopped, there was a second of stunned silence, then cacophony erupted as a hundred people started talking or crying or calling out for loved ones all at once.

Bash leaned over and reached to Gale, grazing his knee with shaky fingertips. "You okay?"

Grimly, Gale nodded. He stood, pulled out his radio and moved off from the crowd noise, shouting into the radio.

"You two girls?" Bash said to them. "Are you hurt at all?"

"No," they both said. McKenna said, "I'm glad my mom is somewhere else. Somewhere safe."

"Yes. And you're safe too, now. It's over." He stood, brushing off the seat of his scrub pants.

Gale was calling into his radio, "Roger that. I'll be back as soon as I can. No idea how the roads held up. It might take a few minutes to get back."

He looked across at Bash. They wanted, like everyone else, to connect, to get some comfort from those they loved. But they both had to get to work.

"What about the girls?" Gale called.

"I'll keep them. It's safe here," Bash said. "As safe as anywhere."

"We can help again," McKenna said.

Gale hesitated only for a second, raising a hand in farewell, then turned and ran off down the street.

Bash turned back toward the tent and saw chaos, as people crawled out from the edges and three dozen pairs of hands tried to do different things all at the same time, pushing the tent's edges about.

"Wait!" he yelled. "We need that tent. Don't rip it!"

He said to the girls, "Help me out, okay? We'll try to get this organized. Each of you run to a corner of the tent, there and there."

It took almost ten minutes of screaming at dazed people to turn the chaos into useful action, but finally he had a row of twenty-odd people folding the tent back with care. Ten minutes later the tent was a neat burrito of fabric, and the patients and staff were all clear of it. Sonja was only working nights now, so Dr. Liz Eisenstein was here running the place days, and she directed triage of the newly injured while he tried to put the field hospital back together. There'd be seriously injured people coming in soon, and they had to be ready for them.

He set the girls to righting chairs and fallen equipment and picking up. Some tables had collapsed, boxes of supplies had been flattened, and many small items were scattered about the cracked asphalt. Instruments had hit the ground and would need resterilizing. He checked on a staff member who was still sitting on the ground, holding her neck.

"Are you hurt?" he said.

"My neck's killing me," she said, trying to get up.

"No, wait. Let me find a collar for you."

"I'm not *that* hurt."

"Sit still," he ordered and made eye contact with her to make sure she obeyed.

She nodded.

"And don't do that—don't nod or shake your head or move it at all until we have a doc see you."

He went off in search of a cervical collar and was back in no time. He had to slap her hand to keep her from helping him put it on. "Quit that. You just went from staff to patient. Now lie down if you want, but carefully. I think I saw the orthopedist earlier. I'll get him over here."

He stood and hunted for a glimpse of the girls, saw them still working at cleanup, and went to hunt down the doctor.

An ambulance siren sounded in the distance, coming closer.

Oh man, he thought. Here we go again.

* * *

Gale was having problems getting back to the EOC. The roads were buckled in new places, and the routes he had gotten used to weren't clear. He had to try four east-west streets before he could get through, and his path led him by the police station. He decided to pull over and run in. A few officers were trotting out to their cars then tearing off, sirens wailing, to deal with crises.

Gale poked his head in the chief's office, where Flint was barking orders at someone over the radio. When he was done, Gale said, "What's the worst news?"

Flint tossed his hands up in exasperation. "We probably haven't heard it yet. So far, a new levee breach is the worst I heard."

"Damn." Gale shook his head. "Anything else need attention? No? Let me know if it does. I'm at EOC in five if you need me." He left and drove the block to the fire station, saw them gearing up for more rescue work, decided not to check in there, and went on to the EOC.

What had been left of City Hall after the first quake had fallen now, and what had once been a pretty building of age-dark bricks was nothing but rubble. He hoped none of his people had been nearby when it had gone down.

As with the hospital, their shelter tent was down, but his people were already working to put it back up.

"No, this support is bent. We need tools to put it aright—like a vise and a wrench," one of the husbands was yelling.

Kay was on the police-fire radio. "Here he comes," she said, and handed him the mike.

"Gale Swanton, over," he said.

"Gale, this is Dan. The water tower is down, over."

Oh, shit. He couldn't think of what to say for a moment. "Anyone hurt by it?"

"No, but it's breached. The last of our water supply is gone."

Gale took a deep breath and let it out slowly. "Okay. There wasn't that much left anyway."

"There's none now. The hospital was using that and they're already screaming for more. We have to get water in here, and damned fast."

"FEMA's going to focus on the big cities first. Even more so now I'm afraid."

"And there's another levee breach, on the north end of town."

"I heard."

"We should redeploy everyone we can toward that. My guys need to find the injured and deliver them to the hospital, so they can't get on it. But all the earth moving and construction equipment, we need to divert that to shoring up the levee."

185

"Check," Gale said. He saw Kay pointing frantically toward the east. He looked and saw water—river water—creeping toward them. "Uh, Dan? I think the river's going to get us. Your building too. It's coming up fast."

"Damn."

He could smell the river now. And sulfur, always that background stench of sulfur from the bowels of the earth. Gale thought about getting sandbags, then he thought, No. Who knows what the next quake would bring, or the next. Sandbags wouldn't stop the river for long. "We need to set up someplace else," he said to Dan, deciding as the words left his mouth. "The EOC is moving. And you should too."

"No, we need our equipment," said Dan. "It's all right here. But what about the police station?"

"The river's going to get up to them too, I think." And it was creeping up faster now. He could smell the awful water, the deep scent of sewage with a sharp, bitter chemical scent riding over that. "They'll have to move. This isn't safe."

"Even the jail?" Dan said. "Over."

Kay, listening, said, "Oh, God." They exchanged a glance. The jail was two levels, one underground. He couldn't think of an alternative jail site anywhere in town.

"I'm signing off to warn Flint," said Gale. "Over."

"No. I'll do that. You're closest to the river. Evacuate."

"We'll set up by the Walmart," Gale said. There was an open field there, a commercial property that had been for sale the whole time he'd lived here. They could use that as their new home base. "Over."

"Good. Out."

Kay was calling to the others about the plan. Everyone went into action, picking up blankets, sleeping bags, and tossing them onto benches to keep them dry. They let the tent fall back to the ground for the moment.

Gale yelled, "Everybody with a car, get it. Drive it up here, over the grass, get as close as you can." He said to Kay, "We need to save these records too." Every paper he had been using to organize the recovery, he couldn't bear to lose. There was no way to replicate some of this information, like the tax list with dead and living recorded and the maps.

As Gale sprinted for his own car with a half-dozen others, he saw a backhoe operator pulling his rig past. Gale waved him to a stop. "I need your help."

"I need to go check on my family."

"Fine. Just make it fast, please. There's a levee breach. See the water?" He pointed east. "We need to get that levee shored up, or we're going to lose all of downtown. Can you get that out request out to the rest of the heavy equipment operators?"

The man nodded grimly and drove off.

He hoped the man would call for help, and soon. He couldn't spare a moment to organize that himself right now. He tried to think through where all his missing department chairs were working out in the city. He'd have to leave word where the EOC had moved to, make sure his people had all survived the second quake, reprioritize. They had to make a big sign to leave here, for staff and citizens both, and he regretted not pushing for more radios from FEMA so that everyone on his staff had one. He'd been counting on them getting cell service back soon, but he knew that would be delayed again.

As he got in his car, the urge washed over to him to just leave. Drive to Bash, pick him up, drive cross-country if need be, walk when the car got stuck in some ditch, head west and out of this mess. Instead, he steered his car across the grass, back to the EOC, and he started loading boxes and stacks of paper into the back seat. Communications equipment went in the front. He never had emptied his trunk of his personal supplies, but he managed to tuck a few smaller items in there too.

He was relieved to see one of his staff driving up a big pickup truck. Staff and family members were packing blankets and food into their cars. They tossed office furniture into the bed of the truck, with an effort hauled the generator up, threw in the emergency lights and cords. A man leapt up into the bed of the truck with two blankets and stuffed them around the lights.

Two of his staff were wriggling the big iron grill out of the ground. He almost stopped them, but no, they would need to eat, and if damned FEMA dropped nothing but rice on them, they'd need to be able to turn it into edible food by boiling. And possibly they'd need to boil water to make it safe to drink. Water. Where the hell were they going to get water enough to keep all these people alive?

He said to Kay, "Where's your car?"

"Wrecked—smooshed. I've been walking to work."

"I'll clear out my passenger seat."

"No, I'll walk out of the way of the water. I'll grab a ride from someone along the way if I can. I'll just walk straight up Center Street. Get going and claim us that spot. We'll get all the gear loaded, don't worry."

"We need to leave a sign here that says we're going to set up by the Walmart."

"Right. I'll do that next."

"Do it quick. Stay out of that river. It's dangerous."

Gale wanted to be five places at once. But once again, he had to delegate. And trust that Dan and Flint would do their jobs too. The priority for him now was, set up the EOC in the new site, get back in contact with his missing department heads.

Whatever new problems the second quake had brought, number one on the priority list would be getting potable water. They'd be twenty thousand dying people in three days without water.

* * *

Bash was back on triage. A row of cars, ambulances, and a fire truck were lined up at the curb, discharging people with serious injuries. He pointed two paramedics carrying an open fracture straight to the orthopedist, then leaned into the ambulance to check their second patient.

One paramedic called back, "We lost that one. DOA."

Bash was already inside anyway, so he leaned over to double-check.

And his heart dropped. It was Trevor, his six-year-old leukemia patient. The boy's head was covered with blood, and it was pooled around his head where it lay on a stretcher. Bash reached out without thinking to touch his hair, but stopped short of it. Can't afford to contaminate the glove, and the boy was beyond feeling any comfort.

Bash moaned with the pain of it. This tough little guy, with his awful last months of life, was gone. He'd never grow up or fall in love or have little guys of his own. The world swam before him, and he realized tears were leaking from his eyes.

Backing out, he stood on the sidewalk, too shocked to move. The paramedic from the back passed him on the way back to the ambulance, took a look at his face and said, "I know. The kids are the hardest."

"Wh—" Bash started, but his throat closed. With an effort, he cleared it. "Where are you taking the body?"

"Up to the Founders Cemetery. Can't use City any more. It's flooded, they say."

"Thanks," Bash said. As the ambulance sped off, he grabbed his scrub shirt collar and lifted it up to wipe away his tears. He went over to the fire truck and pushed the grief to the back of his mind. It was time for more triage, for helping those who could still be helped.

It wasn't as bad an influx of patients as the first day, but it was bad enough. With half the town already dead, or in tent cities, or having walked away to the west, there weren't as many to *get* hurt, and not nearly as many in buildings. He had two cardiac arrests, three asthma crises, a serious mental health break, many broken bones and head injuries, and contusions and cuts galore. He knew in an hour, they'd start seeing the bad crush injuries as victims were dug out from under whatever had fallen on them. They'd all learned a lot about such injuries, but the main lesson was, evac them as soon as possible.

When the rush temporarily slowed down, he scanned the scene, looking for the girls, but he didn't see them. The first free second he got, he'd hunt them down and make sure they were okay and away from the blood, if possible. His name was called by a dentist taking vitals, and he had to turn back to work. He hoped the girls hadn't wandered off. Surely they'd have more sense.

He was finishing with emptying a church bus pressed into service as an ambulance, filled with mostly minor injuries, when he turned and saw, at the edge of the sidewalk, Trevor's mom scanning the crowd.

Degloving, he walked slowly toward her, trying to form the right words to say. She turned in a circle, craning her head. When she caught sight of him her face lit up for a second, but then the expression faded as he came closer. By the time he reached her, she was shaking her head.

"No no no no no," she said, backing away from him.

"I'm sorry," he said.

A wail was torn from her throat and she fell to her knees. Bash went down on his and held her, crying on her shoulder as she wept on his. "I'm sorry," he kept whispering.

He had work to do with the injured, but he couldn't bear to leave her like this. After long moments of weeping, she pulled away. "It's not fair," she cried.

"It's not." He wiped his tears again, knowing that you're not supposed to show patients and families your own feelings, but these many hard days had destroyed those walls. "He was such a wonderful little boy."

"Was," she said, so awed by the word her tears stopped.

"I'm sorry." Such a stupid phrase. It didn't help a thing.

"Where is he?" she said.

"They took him to Founders Cemetery."

She shook her head slowly. It was too much to grasp, he could see. Trevor had probably been playing two hours ago, and then the quake, and the ambulance taking him. And before she could even say goodbye, they were talking about cemeteries.

"I guess I'll walk over there."

"No. No—I'll find you a ride."

The church bus was still there, and he walked her over, explained to the driver where she needed to go, and the fellow nodded a reluctant okay.

A last squeeze of her hand, and Bash needed to get back to work.

He turned to see Haruka and McKenna staring at him from several yards away. He managed a wan smile, called, "Stay out of trouble," to them, and turned back to check a car with just two walking wounded. More minor injuries. He tagged them green, gave them four by fours to hold on their bleeding bits, and looked around to see McKenna was standing behind him.

"What's up?" he asked her.

"You've been crying," she said.

"It's been a sad day."

She opened her mouth to say more, thought better of it, then shook her head. "You need to see something." She jerked her head off to the left and started to walk that direction.

"What?" He had patients to triage.

When she saw he wasn't following, she turned. "That guy I killed? He's not dead."

"No?"

"He's here."

"The—" Oh crap. "The drug thief."

"Uh-huh," she said, indicating again with her head where to look. "Blue hoodie. Black boots with jeans tucked into them."

He scanned people until he saw him. The kid was loitering, trying to look casual and failing. This didn't look good.

"I, uh," he said, looking around, wondering what to do. Okay. What not to do was let this guy get his hands on their drug supply again.

"I guess I could hit him again," said McKenna.

"No!" Bash felt faint at the thought. "You stay well away from him." He turned and saw the person directing traffic. "You both walk in the other direction, and don't make eye contact with that kid. Go do something useful over there—*way* over there." He strode over to the traffic person. "Are you a cop?"

"Auxiliary," said the man.

"We need a cop. There's a drug thief here, stole some stuff on day one, and he's back again."

The face before him smiled. "You don't say?"

Oooh boy. "We don't need any more patients," said Bash, sternly.

"I'll take care of it."

Bash was not trusting this person's tone and attitude. "I do not want some sort of shoot-out at the hospital. You hear me?"

"I don't have a weapon on me," the man said, sounding as if he regretted that.

"But the kid might. Maybe you can radio the—the regular police?" Bash had almost said "real," but knew that wouldn't have gone over very well.

"I don't have a radio, either," the man began, and just at that moment, a fire truck pulled up.

"They will," said Bash and hurried over and explained what was happening to the fire crew.

"We'll deal with it," one said.

"Save me from cowboys," Bash muttered, but he felt more confident in them than in the auxiliary cop. He described the boy and where he was, watched their eyes scan the crowd and catch on him, and they looked at each other. "Hey, wait," Bash said, "what's the injury you're carrying?"

"Crush," one said. "Compartment injury. Pretty bad."

Shit. He'd have to wait a minute to get to that person, though. He went back over to the girls, who hadn't moved far enough away for his taste.

He said, "You two, come with me," and he walked them behind the fire truck, out of sight of the loitering druggie, and he hoped out of harm's way.

"We can't see anything from here."

"Exactly. You can't catch a stray bullet from here, either," Bash said. He needed to give them something to do, to distract them, but he couldn't think of a thing. "Just stay right there." He climbed up the side of the truck to check the injured person. Adult woman, young, crushed arm up past the shoulder, broken clavicle, dazed but conscious and clearly in agony. The arm looked very bad. They'd evac this one, maybe first load. Come to think of it, where are the first helicopters? Have we arranged for that? He'd ask Liz what the schedule was on evac, first chance he could spare. He grabbed a red tag from his pocket and tied it on the woman.

A shout drew his attention, and he looked up to see the drug thief leap off the curb and the firefighters take off after him.

They were all running this way.

Bash jumped to the edge of the truck and called down to the girls, "Get underneath."

They both looked up at him, confused.

He motioned them down. "Get under the truck!"

But he was too late. The thief came tearing down the street, came up the side of the fire truck and pulled up short, seeing the girls. "You!" he said.

Bash grabbed the rail at the side of the truck and held to it while he flung his legs off. His back was to the street for a split second and he let go of the rail, dropping, hitting the pavement hard, his knees collapsing. And then he was up again and had his balance. He whirled, and there was McKenna, wrestling with the drug thief. Damn that girl!

He leapt on the kid as the firefighters came around the truck and joined the fray. For a moment, Bash was pressed into a rugby scrum, and then he popped loose and the firemen had the kid's arms and were forcing him to the ground.

Bash turned to McKenna. "You crazy girl!" he said. "It's not a movie. It's real life. He could have had a gun!" He grabbed her and hugged her hard, but she wriggled out of his grip, anxious to see what was happening. *She* seemed fine, at least. Bash's heart was going so fast, he might have a cardiac incident.

The auxiliary cop was there now too, trying to figure a way to make himself part of it, Bash could see. The fake cop no doubt would make himself the hero when he told the story later on.

One fireman had the kid firmly penned. The other was digging through hoodie pockets, and came up with a handful of syringes. "Ha," he said. "That's enough for the cops to hold you." Then he said to his partner, "I'll get some line to tie him with."

The thief was struggling, and the auxiliary cop got down and held his legs. Between the two of them, the kid wasn't going anywhere.

The other fireman jumped down—much more gracefully than Bash himself had—and they got the prisoner tied up and up on his feet.

The kid looked right at McKenna and lunged at her, but four hands held him fast. "This is your fault, you bitch. You'll be sorry you ever fucked with me."

Bash stepped forward and got right in the kid's face. "You'll leave her alone."

The kid snorted. "What you do going to do with me, faggot?"

"That's Mr. Faggot to you, dickhead, and I could fill those syringes full of potassium and insulin and shit that will kill you dead in ways that they'll never be able to figure out. And you'll leave these girls alone, or I swear I'll jab you with every one of those drugs." He was so mad he was losing his peripheral vision.

"We'll take him to the jail," one firefighter said.

"The jail is flooding," said the other.

Good, thought Bash. He could drown there for all Bash cared. That people like this lived and Trevor died? What a world.

Then he felt a stab of guilt. Some nurse he was, wishing death on people. He should be wishing the kid drug treatment and a good therapist. But he couldn't get there right now. He'd be nicer in his thoughts later, when he was sure the girls were safe from this little jerk.

Turning to McKenna and Haruka, he searched their faces to make sure they were okay.

Haruka looked pale, but McKenna grinned up at him. "That was pretty badass of you."

"Oh, well, you know. I have my moments," he said. "Now let's all get back to work."

The thief was taken away, the crush injury was moved to treatment, and ninety minutes later the first helicopter came and took her and two other redtags away.

McKenna was swaying on her feet by then, probably exhausted by the dual adrenaline rush of quake and fighting the drug thief. Supporting her arm, Bash walked them over to visitor's area and made them sit down while he hunted for food for them. It was getting sparse, he knew.

Over at the sandwich shop, Nathan was minding the store once again. Bash smiled to see him. "Hey! How is your family?"

"My gran died. In the nursing home, in the first quake."

Bash's smile fell. "I'm sorry."

"But the rest of us are okay. We did pretty well. Better than most."

"I'm glad. What food is left?"

"Not much. Salami and Swiss cheese, no bread, and some

crushed bags of pretzels. All the good chips went early. And we're out of stuff to drink."

"Anything will do. I have two hungry girls to feed."

Nathan put two wrapped packages on the counter and added two sad-looking bags of pretzels.

"Where do I sign for it?"

"Don't worry about that," he said. "The jerk owner wants me to charge twenty bucks now for this pitiful stuff, and I'm not going to do it."

"You're a good guy," said Bash and gratefully took the packages.

He passed the food to the girls and got a small bottle of drinking water from the staff supply. People can't eat, especially not this salty stuff, without water to wash it down and process it. He left them sitting and eating, warned them not to wander away, and got back to work. He wanted to give them a chance to talk to him about whatever they were feeling about today, but that'd have to wait until tonight.

Chapter 12

Gale

As Gale pulled up to George and Marilyn's house, he saw that they had taken some damage this time, with the front picture window of their house riddled with cracks. And the whole house looked out of true, the rectangle no longer square to the ground. He hoped he wasn't walking into a death trap, but he had to talk with FEMA. Now.

When he knocked, the door opened two inches and jammed. George's voice said, "Back up. Don't want the door to hit you when I pop it open."

The door shuddered once, twice, as George threw himself against it, and then it banged open and slammed back against the frame.

"Should I use a different door?" Gale asked.

"No, this is as good as it gets. We took some damage, and I barely got things set up in time for you." He led the way into the living room.

Gale drew up short when he saw several pieces of radio equipment strewn around. "What's up?" he said.

"I don't trust that the basement is safe. If the house falls on me, I'd prefer it to be the roof only, not the roof and the main level."

"You should move, maybe."

"To where? And besides, all the antennas are here."

"I guess we're lucky they're still up."

"They won't fall until the house does," George said with confidence. "Anyway, here's the radio."

Gale stood while George contacted FEMA—or not simply FEMA, now a joint state-FEMA force, but the same contact person. When the connection was made, he took George's chair and began to talk.

"Water," he said to the director, first thing. "You get us water tomorrow morning, or we abandon the town to looters and vagrants. And become vagrants ourselves and bring twenty thousand thirsty refugees down on the nearest town to the west."

"We're doing our best." She sounded short-tempered, a hint of a whine in her tone.

"You have to do better. This is a life and death situation—or will be within hours."

"We have some filtration units coming for St. Louis. I guess I can divert one load to you."

She guessed? He bit back an angry response. "It's a start. What time? Over."

Twenty seconds of dead air passed. He was starting to think something had gone wrong with the radio when she spoke again. "No later than nine. You know, we're buying loads of water microfiltration devices, like they used—still use—in Haiti, but the scientists say even with those, you don't want to drink the river water. They won't filter out chemicals. Sewage, or water out of a lake, yes, they'll work on that."

"We have two small lakes. And the reservoir at the water plant."

"We can get you six suitcase-sized filters. Assign someone to operate them full-time, and they'll give you five hundred gallons per day. Each."

"We need more than three thousand gallons. A lot more."

"We've had to start all over with clearing the river after the second quake. But there's a loaded barge at Davenport that has your name on it—cans, juices, vitamins, the equipment for the water facility you asked for, generators—all the heavy stuff. As soon as the Corps dredges a path through, you'll have it."

"When?"

"Not for at least a couple days, and possibly a week."

"And until then?"

"We'll have something for you tomorrow by air. I don't know what yet, but I'll get you something."

Gale explained his other problems. The levee breach. The hospital not having running water any more, and the growing sanitation problems because no water could be spared for anything but drinking. The new medical director at the hospital requested antibiotics, as the rate of infection was climbing and she expected it to climb more. Lists of equipment everyone else had requested followed. It took nearly an hour to get through it all.

"I can't get you all this in only a day, but I'll do what I can."

When he signed off, he felt as if he'd run a marathon. Slumped at the chair, he closed his eyes and tried to clear his mind and remember what he had to do next.

A hand touched his shoulder. Gale opened his eyes and saw George, looking at him with furrowed brow. "You look done in," the man said.

"I've had better weeks," said Gale, and they smiled at each other.

"You're doing fine, son," said George.

"Do you two have everything you need?"

"Yeah. The new priority-only gas rationing means there's plenty for the generator, still. We'll have food problems in a few days, but by then I guess everyone will."

"At least you don't have little kids. If I had a dollar for every temper tantrum I've seen over kids not wanting to eat what's there. 'Why can't we go to McDonald's?'"

"They'll get hungry enough. Then everything will look good."

"You'd think."

"They're spoiled," said George.

"We all are. We're not used to walking a mile to get water, or functioning on short rations, or running out, or making do. Myself, I'd kill for some real brewed coffee and a long hot shower."

"You should have ordered up some coffee from FEMA."

Gale laughed at the idea of taking space with such a luxury. "Hey, what's the weather forecast?"

"Rain tomorrow and the next day, turning colder with the front."

"Will it freeze?"

"No. But down to 40 tomorrow night, they say."

"I hope I still I have a roof after this morning's quake," Gale said. "Those tent cities are going to be mighty unpleasant places once it freezes."

"I imagine more people will decide to leave now. Take their chances on the road."

Gale didn't have the option to leave. He had work to do here. "If it rains, make sure you two collect rainwater."

"We will."

"Well, thank you, George, again."

"You getting any rest tonight?"

"I have to. I'll work until dark, but after that, I don't think I'll be doing much good, as wiped out as I am. Luckily, I have damned good people working with me, sharing the load. And people like you making it possible for all of to survive."

Gale drove to the new EOC. Someone had rescued the tent, repaired a gash in it with blue duct tape, and put it up once more. The tables were set up underneath. Someone had found tarps at some point, and the sleeping bags and blankets were laid out on those several yards away. They'd have to move those all under the tent when it rained. People would be tucked under tables and fighting for dry space, he thought. Every shelter in town was in use, though, and unless they built some sort of shelter from the scrap of ruined homes, they'd have to make do with the one tent.

Angela didn't show up when he expected her to at 8:00, and as the minutes passed, Gale began to really worry. He asked if anyone knew of her, or lived in her neighborhood. When no one had an answer, he handed the EOC over to Kay, who volunteered to work until he found Angela, and he drove off to the south side of town.

He passed people filling sandbags, close to the river, and he pulled over. "You need to stay out of that water," he said. "It's dangerous."

"Piss off," a man said. "We're trying to save our houses."

"Just be careful. The river has awful chemicals in it, and you don't want it on your bare skin."

"Yeah, yeah," the man said.

A woman stood up and brushed sweaty hair back and said, "You could help, you know."

"I'm sorry, I can't." Gale got back in his car and thought, This is the start of it. Or the end of it, whichever way you wanted to think. It was the end of communal spirit and friendliness, and the start of short tempers and anger. He didn't own a gun, but he was going to ask Flint about some other kind of weapon for self-defense. Pepper spray, Taser, something. People would be looking for someone to blame, though there wasn't anyone *to* blame, and he'd be a public target.

He wondered if he shouldn't hand the girls over to someone else, someone less in the public eye. But everyone he knew well enough to trust with their care was working for him, and none of them could take on an added burden. Chances were, he had as much extra food as anyone in town to feed them if FEMA didn't come through soon. His mind flicked back to the thought of a weapon. He was going to have to do something to protect Bash and those girls.

Angela's neighborhood had taken a bad hit from the second quake. Liquefaction left cars buried up to their axles in the ground and many houses canted as one side or another of the foundation had sunk into what was effectively, during the earthquake, quicksand. Angela's house appeared, the front wall half-collapsed back into the interior. The whole house wasn't down—there was space in there still where people might be trapped—but it certainly wasn't livable.

He found a solid-looking bit of sidewalk and pulled his car up there. He jumped out and started calling for Angela and Michael, her husband.

A kid on a bicycle stopped and watched him, suspicious. Gale turned to him. "Do you know the people who live here?"

The kid shook his head.

Gale walked the perimeter of the house, calling out every few seconds. He stopped to listen, hoping to hear a voice, or a banging, or some sign that they were in there and okay. As much as he wanted to, he couldn't risk going inside to search. He hoped they were safe, or were getting treated at the hospital for minor injuries. It'd even be better if they had just left, jumped in their car and driven as far west as the roads would allow. Though he knew Angela wouldn't do that, not without telling him.

He radioed the address into the EOC and asked them to get Fire on working rescue here whenever they could. He knew it wouldn't be soon. Single-family homes were the lowest priority, no matter who lived in them.

Back at his car, he looked around. The kid on the bike was gone, and no adults were visible. The whole block looked deserted. Damn. Weighed down by worry and frustration, he got back in his car and drove back to work. There were still a hundred crucial tasks to accomplish today, starting with getting out the news to everyone to collect rainwater.

By the time he got home that night, it was after 10:00. He

entered through the garage. Bash was waiting up for him in the kitchen, in the flicker of candlelight.

They hugged, and then he collapsed into a chair.

"I can't find Angela," Gale said. "She's just vanished."

"I'm really sorry. One of my patients from the clinic, a little boy, died," said Bash. "It's just grief piled on grief these days."

"I'm sorry about your patient. How are the girls?"

"They're asleep."

"Is the house safe? From the earthquakes, I mean?" He made a face. "Or from thieves?"

"We didn't get home until after sundown. So I haven't really checked that carefully yet."

"We will tomorrow morning. I guess we'll have to take the chance of sleeping here tonight. I also want to drive nails into all the windows too, try to keep anyone else from breaking in." He looked around. "You cleaned up in here."

"I have some bad news."

"Oh, God," Gale said. He didn't know if he could stand more.

"The thieves. They drained most of the hot water tank."

"Shit. I didn't even know they were here long enough to do that."

"How could you know? I guess they went robbing places with empty bottles in their hands. Can you imagine?"

"We have bottled water in our emergency supplies. But we're going to have to give up on showers and hand-washing."

"We can't give up on hand-washing after using the toilet. Or for whoever prepares meals. At least we did laundry not long before the first quake. When we stink too much, we can just change into fresh clothes."

"How is our supply of wipes holding up?"

"Not great. I think there's a dozen or so left."

"We should cut them in half, stretch them out for hand-washing. It should rain tomorrow and the next day. We have to set up caches to get more of that. We can wash our hands with that water," he said, "but no more toilet flushing."

"What?" Bash sounded horrified.

"No more toilet, period. We need to dig a latrine in the back yard."

"Oh my God."

"Without the city system working, we couldn't flush forever anyway. It's probably just accumulating in pipes under the house as it is."

"Stop, please."

"Sorry." Gale reached over and gave his arm a squeeze. "So tomorrow morning, first thing, at dawn, we nail shut the windows for security and start digging our outhouse. And set up for caching more rainwater." They'd have to work fast. They both had critical jobs to get to.

An aftershock rattled the house, fading after a few seconds. Gale shook his head. "I hope the house is structurally safe."

"It's a little cold to sleep outside."

"I know. And it's getting colder. But we might have to move outside at some point. Thousands already have." He thought of the long expanse of quake zone, stretching from northern Mississippi State all the way up to St. Louis. "Maybe a million are out there tonight, sleeping on the lawn or sidewalks. Some probably don't even have a blanket."

Bash sighed. "Did you eat?"

"No time."

"I'll make you something."

"No. I'm too tired."

"Gale," Bash said, exasperated.

"Okay, okay. Just hand me a can of fruit or something easy. That'll do."

"I haven't unpacked the emergency stuff yet. We three ate supper at the hospital."

"Never mind. I'll get the stuff I have in my trunk. I'll go get it." He started to rise.

"No, you sit. I'll do it. Give me your keys."

Gale sat too tired to even think coherently, while Bash carried in bottled water and sacks of groceries. He put them away, just like it was a normal shopping day. The routine of the act seemed surreal. Gale's vision blurred, and he felt he was on the verge of hallucinating from emotional and physical exhaustion. Damn, he needed to sleep.

Bash set a box of cheese crackers in front of him, opened them, and Gale ate a few.

"Dessert," Bash said, and put the hazelnut chocolate bar in front of him.

"No, sweetie, that was a gift for you. For being an ass that morning."

"What morning?"

"Before the quake." A million years ago.

"Were you an ass then?" Bash said.

"I was, and I'm sorry. You deserved better. I think the last year, I could have been a better husband in a lot of ways."

"Shh," said Bash, stepping behind him and wrapping his arms around his shoulders. "Never mind. That's all done now. We're fine. We're alive and we're fine."

"But the chocolate bar is yours. It's a present."

"Okay, okay."

"I need to sleep."

"We'll sleep, then. But promise to eat more for breakfast."

Gale nodded, stood, and stumbled back into the bedroom. He let his clothes fall to the floor, made it over to the bed, and crawled under the comforter.

* * *

If not for the pressure in his bladder, Gale would have slept twelve hours. He got up and threw on yesterday's clothes, then went through the garage to get a shovel and work gloves. The phrase "call before digging" popped through his mind, and he had to shake his head at himself. Like there were any live power lines anywhere in town to cut into.

In the dim gray light of dawn, he peed in the far corner of the yard, and then he began to dig the latrine, as far from the house as possible. The site would be half-hidden by the stranger's garage that had slid through the fence. He pushed the point of the shovel into the grass. The ground was hard and didn't want to yield. The whole point of buying this house was that it wasn't built on sand like so much of the town. Now he wished he had sand to dig in. But with sand in the yard, he probably wouldn't have a house any more. He jammed his foot down. The shovel clanged off a rock and the vibration shook his joints. More than anything, he wanted to lean on the shovel and rest, but he'd only been at it two minutes. Forcing himself past his weariness, he kept digging, making slow progress.

The sun rose, revealing scattered clouds overhead. You could tell they were gathering into rain clouds. Gale found his rhythm and dug faster. He wasn't digging into power lines or natural gas lines or phone lines, just into pebbly clay.

Forty-five minutes later, with a short trench hardly more than two feet deep, he heard his name and turned to see McKenna coming toward him.

"Bash said we're going to have to pee outside now?"

"Yes. We can't afford to use the rainwater to flush any more. The hot water tank is empty. All we have on hand is water to drink for maybe five days, and whatever rainwater comes."

"I don't really like the idea of peeing out here."

"No one does. But lots of people in town are." He wiped his forehead with his arm. "At least we have a fence for privacy."

McKenna was looking at the hole. "I'm not a guy, you know. I'd kinda like to sit."

"I tell you what. We'll take off one of the toilet seats from inside, and I'll figure out how to support it." He drew a line with the toe of his shoe. "So if I dig narrow and long, find some boards to put on either side, that should do it, don't you think?"

"Won't this stink?"

"Yes. But we'll shovel some dirt back in every day. That'll help keep the smell down."

"Gross." McKenna gave a theatrical shudder. "Bash says come in for breakfast, anyway."

He wanted to finish out here. But he could feel the need for food in his brain and muscles. He needed to get in to work on time too. And he wanted to secure the house better against break-ins. Too much to do, and less light to do it in every single day as winter approached. He dropped the shovel, shoving the work gloves into his back pocket as he trailed McKenna back to the house.

At the table, Bash had set the table with cans, spoons, cloth napkins, and the last of the package of antibacterial wipes. Gale took one and cleaned his hands, then his face. Getting the grease off his nose made him feel a little better.

Bash smiled at him. "Everybody has a can of fruit. If you don't like yours, or if you get bored halfway through, we can trade. And there's crackers. And a treat." He held up a jar of instant lemon-flavored tea. "For a change from plain water."

"And for some caffeine," Gale said. He could use a good dose of that. Maybe today he'd ask for caffeine pills from FEMA. Or maybe they'd air drop him some amphetamines to keep him and police and rescuers going. No, probably a bad idea, just wearing them down more in the long run, making them more aggressive in the short-term. But some mild caffeine would be appreciated this morning. "Where'd you get the napkins?"

"I cut up an old sheet. And I wrote everyone's names on theirs."

Gale looked, and indeed his name was neatly written at the edge of the napkin in black ink.

McKenna wanted the can of pineapple, and Haruka the pears. He left the peaches for Bash, as he knew he liked them, and took the mixed fruit for himself. "Don't forget to drink the juice," he said.

"Mine is syrup," said McKenna.

"Drink it anyway. This is no time to diet." Indeed, survival was a calorie game, and the more you could manage to find, the better. When it got down to 40 degrees and they had no heat source, their bodies would want even more calories. But what was this meal—maybe 400 calories? Times three—or one yesterday—and that wasn't nearly enough food to fuel him. FEMA had better come through with that promised food soon. Or—and he realized he had no "or else" to threaten. The whole town was entirely at their mercy.

"Is there still school today?" Haruka asked.

"Yes," Gale said. They'd lost people in the second quake, but not as high a percentage, as more people were staying outdoors, and the percentage was of a lower population. The first quake had killed nearly 10,000; the second quake, less than an eighth of that number. There were still enough teachers to keep the town's kids busy for five hours today. "Ten o'clock to three. Bring paper and pencils, and whatever books you had with you in your packs."

"Where?" asked McKenna.

"West of town, between the two tent cities, in the Catholic church parking lot." When the river breached the levee, they'd had to integrate the downtown tent city into the other two. The one nearest a small lake was the best one to be at. The lake water wasn't safe to drink without filtration, but it provided wash water. "It's there so that kids from both tent cities can walk to school."

"We can walk too," said McKenna.

"I'd rather not leave you alone on the street," Gale said. "There are the looters and thieves and people are getting...well, testy."

"Violent? Like the survivors in a zombie movie?"

"Maybe not that bad quite yet. But headed in that direction, yes. So you two can come to work with me, and you can walk to school with the other kids there, in a group." There were thirteen children now and six spouses, and seven of his staff living there full-time. Some of the other staff members were sleeping outdoors, but in front of their own homes to protect them from looters. He knew most of them were taking the chance, even with severely damaged homes, of dashing inside twice a day to get clothes, food, and books or toys for their kids. He and Bash were damned lucky to have a relatively safe home.

Which reminded him. He hurried and drank the rest of his lukewarm tea, willing the caffeine to take hold, and he got up. "That was good, thanks, hon," he said to Bash. "I need to go check the house out, and put another half-hour into digging."

"We can help," said McKenna.

"I'll take you up on that offer," Gale said, then to Bash, "Is there any way you can take off work at like 3 today, pick up the girls, and come back here and get some more stuff done?"

"I'll try to get off. I could pick up everything that fell again."

"And nail all the back windows shut if I don't finish that this morning."

"What about if we have a house fire?"

"We'll keep the dowel jammed in the back sliding door, so that they can't get in but we can get out. But otherwise we should keep the front door barred and only use the sliding back door and the entrance from the garage."

"I wish we had an extra key for that to give the girls," Bash said.

"So do I. But locksmiths aren't a working business right now." He said, "I have to go drive a few nails and get to work."

He took ten minutes to secure all the front windows and make sure the front door was impossible to budge. A five-minute inspection of the house convinced him that they were safe to sleep inside. A third quake might bring it down, but for now they were okay. The second quake had only been a 7.8, he had heard last night just before coming home, but it was centered closer to them. A third quake might be closer still, if the quakes were traveling north up the fault line. He hoped there wouldn't be a third big one. The aftershocks were bad enough.

He went to the back yard and spelled Haruka at shoveling out the latrine. He was pleasantly surprised when McKenna came out of the back door, toting a toilet seat.

"It was pretty easy to take off," she said. "I just had to stare at it awhile to figure it out."

"Thanks," he said. "Let's measure it against what we've dug."

After they had, he sent her into the garage to hunt for lumber scraps. Two by sixes would be nice, if he could find some. They could run them on either side, balance the toilet seat on them, and just move it along the trench each day. After a week, slide it all the way down to the starting position, adding dirt over the waste. If he got this deep enough today, the latrine could last for a month before it was full and another had to be dug.

And in a year or two, he thought, it'd probably be a great place to plant a tree or flowers, the soil enriched by the decomposing waste. He liked the idea of a tree being a sort of memorial to the bad times of the quake. Bash had admired the blooming crabapples here in Missouri. Maybe one of those.

The pleasant fantasy of a future without constant emergency, with time for niceties like gardening, energized him, and he got another half-foot of the length dug before it was time to change clothes for work. With some added effort tonight, the latrine would be usable by bedtime.

Overhead, the clouds thickened.

"Hey, girls," he said, staring up at the gathering clouds. "Let's get every pot and pan and plastic container in the house outside in the back yard to catch rain. Set them anywhere flat."

Bash joined the project, digging out an old dishpan, a cleaning bucket, and a stack of disposable aluminum cake pans, as well as his precious designer cookware. Within fifteen minutes, the backyard looked like a thrift store for kitchenware, with more than a hundred receptacles for rain. If they got even a half-inch of rain, they'd end up with a couple gallons of drinking water.

Gale took the girls into work with him and set them to copying notices about avoiding touching the river water on poster board using permanent markers. He'd have his people nail them up all along the downtown and the neighborhoods closest to the river. The rain would destroy them within a few days, but the message would, he hoped, be conveyed by then.

Helicopters had arrived before he got to work, bringing a four-foot-tall swimming pool. Two men in the helicopter had jumped out and assembled it in no time flat.

Sophie, who had been his second-in-command since Kay went home at midnight, and in the absence of Angela, said, "About eighteen-foot diameter, looks like. And they say they'll airlift water into it."

Gale went over and looked at it, and there was a tag on its side that said, "6200-gallon capacity." 6200 gallons wouldn't be enough for the 18,000-plus remaining citizens, but it would come close. With 3,000 gallons produced from the lakes using the suitcase-sized filters that had come in the other helicopter load, they could survive on that, barely, if they didn't have the hospital to think about.

But the water to fill the pool hadn't arrived by the time Gale arrived at work. He kept his eyes out, and his heart lifted at the next sighting of a helicopter, a big-bellied cargo helicopter. Communicating with staff was impossible with them landing this close, so everybody stood and watched as it came down in the parking lot.

Gale ran over to see what it was. They had supplies he had requested, including antibiotics, hand cleaner, and food. But only two kinds of food—powdered potato flakes, and powdered milk, hundreds of pounds of them. Nothing else.

Well, damn.

He thought about it, and he realized on reflection it wasn't a terrible choice. You could mix one with the other, douse it with room temperature water, wait five or ten minutes, and it'd surely turn into an edible paste. Without salt—and there was no salt in the delivery—it'd not taste good, and the kids who had whined about no McDonald's two days ago weren't going to like this at all—but it'd keep everyone alive. He was glad to see a carton of gallon-sized zipper plastic bags in the load—somebody had been thinking ahead. He'd try and get the same people who had given out food at the grocery store in here to bag up the potato flakes and milk and get it distributed around town.

The morning meeting of the Triumvirate was coming up, so he gave Sophie some quick instructions, wished the girls a nice day at school, threw all the medical supplies in his trunk, and took off for downtown.

They'd managed to save the police station and jail with levee support and sandbagging the crap out of that one block, but the prisoners had all been moved to the upper level of the jail, just in case. The three of them met in Flint's office, which reeked of chemicals from the river.

"Flint, you sure you're safe in here?"

"I'm sure I'm not. I'll probably end up sick or dead or on disability. But what can we do? We can't move the jail."

"We could let them go," said Dan.

"Fuck that," said Flint. "We have to send a message about looting and theft and violence and being a bad citizen."

"I'm not sure that last is a crime," said Gale, holding up his hand to forestall Flint's reply, "but I hear you. We can't allow the looting or violence. And as food gets shorter, I'm afraid violence will increase."

"The natives are getting restless already," said Dan.

"How so?" Gale said.

"Some were screaming threats at my guys during rescue operations. I know they're stressed out, and I know they're worried about their families, but it nearly got out of hand a couple times."

"I had someone yelling at me too," said Gale. "Out by my assistant's house, for no real reason."

Flint snorted. "Welcome to a cop's pre-earthquake life."

Gale turned to him. "Is there anything better we can do to keep the peace?"

"Warnings, cajoling, threats, then arrests. Pretend to listen, nod, and then repeat the order. What we typically do."

"But it's not a typical situation. The aftershocks alone..." Gale said.

"Amen to that," muttered Dan.

"And people are getting hungry and thirsty. Though there's some hope on that front." He told them about the water filters and empty pool.

"Don't forget we need food and water here at the jail."

"And for our guys," said Dan. "If you want police and fire to function, we have to have water to drink and sufficient calories."

"I know. And I want my staff to be fed too, even if it's reduced calories, and the couple with the radios who are keeping us connected to FEMA, and the Guard people helping. But then there's the hospital, and the school, which has to hand over something for lunch, and the heavy equipment operators, and everybody else who's crucial to the recovery. What sort of rationing do we need to do?"

"How much water is there?"

"Full, the container is 6,000 gallons. But it's empty right now, and I can't swear how much they'll put in there."

"Maybe they'll fill it twice a day for us. Or three times."

"We can hope," Gale said, but he knew his voice betrayed his lack of confidence in that hope. "We're begging them, and I know they feel like they're helping us as much as they can, but we need more."

"You know what we need? We need media," said Dan.

"Oh man," said Flint, shaking his head. "I can hear it now. I'll be arresting some looter, and it'll be police brutality all over the TV and internet."

"I have no idea why we haven't gotten any coverage before now," said Gale.

"They're staying in the big cities," said Dan. "We need to get word out that there are stories here too."

"Are there?" asked Gale. "I mean, how can the story of a tiny town—tinier each day—that's managing to hang on compete with riots and millions of rotting bodies and fires that are so pretty to watch on video?"

"We could set something on fire," said Flint, grinning at Dan.

"We could probably set the damned river on fire, if it doesn't self-combust on us first."

"You're joking, I hope," said Gale.

"Polluted rivers have caught fire before."

The thought was horrifying. "Maybe we should move the jail," said Gale. "Maybe we should temporarily get the whole town off the lowlands, and transfer everyone to...." He trailed off.

"Yeah, to where? More tent cities?" said Dan. "Empty fields? We don't have the supplies or manpower. And you know you'll start to get epidemics up there in those tent cities. Maybe just flu, or E. coli infections, but maybe in a few weeks something worse."

Gale sighed. "Maybe we should encourage people to leave. We'll get water today, we have lightweight food that we can bag up. Which reminds me." He asked Flint about getting the spouses to volunteer again to bag up and distribute food. Flint nodded the whole time he was talking. "So they have their half-gallon of water per person, and they have their bag of instant potatoes, and they can start walking." And hope to find water somewhere the next day along their route.

"Is the State still working on getting the roads clear?" said

Dan.

"Roads and river both, with the Corps working full-time on the river," said Gale. "But all we can do is wait until it happens. Maybe I should ask for buses to meet refugees as close to us as they can, and we should just empty the city, send people out there. But I'm pretty sure it's still fifty miles or so before the roads are navigable by car. I can't guarantee they'll find water or food along the way."

"The radio—commercial radio, I mean—said they were getting refugees in Wichita, Omaha, Oklahoma City. Dallas, Chicago, Indianapolis too."

"I wonder how many of those people will never return to their homes," Gale said.

"They went back to New Orleans."

"Not all of them," Flint said. "Two thirds, three quarters only."

"You remember the house trailers from the news?" Dan asked. "FEMA set up trailers then."

Gale nodded. "And they had half the population still living in them a year later."

Dan said, "We'd take that. Take it and be grateful."

"Not until after they're sure the quakes are done," said Gale. "There's no reason to set up housing and have it fall down again a month later. Besides, without roads, you can't get trailers here anyway."

"How can we know when the quakes are done?" asked Dan.

Gale shrugged. "You'd have to ask a geologist, but I'll be confident they're over maybe six months after the last big one, when the aftershocks aren't coming any more often than a small one every week or so."

"Six more months," said Dan.

"With next to no aftershocks," Gale reminded him. "And we're not nearly to that point." He sighed. "In 1812, there was a third big quake. There's no reason to think that there won't be this time, or maybe there'll be four."

The three of them just sat quietly for a long moment, thinking about that.

"Well." Flint slapped his hand on his desk. "I need supplies *today*. Six months from now is too far ahead to think."

After Dan left, Gale stayed to ask Flint about a weapon for personal use.

"You should have thought of that day one," snapped Flint.

"I wasn't thinking ahead. And I didn't have two teenage girls to defend then. I don't want a gun. I really don't know anything about guns. Just something, even pepper spray, a Taser."

"We don't have Tasers to spare."

"You have less population to zap now."

"But we have strangers coming north all the time too. Some are going to find places to hole up here. And from what you say about food and water, we can't afford to take in even one. I have to be able to move them along. On top of that, behavior in town is going to get worse, and soon. You can count on that."

"True enough. Well, I'll just make do."

"I tell you what," said Flint. "When my kids were little, they had BB guns. I'll have my wife run one over to you this evening. It won't hurt anybody much, not unless you're a dead shot and get them in the eye, but it'll be something to wave. Maybe from a distance, you'd scare off teenagers or fools."

"I appreciate it." And a hammer and kitchen knife would have to do otherwise. Didn't he have a hatchet in his tools? He thought so. He wished he had some way to train himself and the girls in self-defense in a day or two, how to fight with fists or a knife, but that was silly, just wishful thinking. It took years to get any good at a martial art. And if someone had a powerful gun aimed your way, fighting with fists was a stupid idea. What the girls did—hide in the closet—was the very best course of action. Run, hide, and only fight when you had no other choice.

The question was, he considered as he got in his car, did

defending your food and water supply constitute "have to?" When a household is down to its last can of soup, is shooting a looter "self-defense?" A moral conundrum to consider another day. He swung by the hospital and delivered the antibiotics and other supplies, and headed to George and Marilyn's again.

As he was walking up to the house, his walkie-talkie squawked at him.

"What's up?" he said.

Sophie was on the line. "They brought water, like you see them do with forest fires, one of those buckets?"

"Great. Is the thing full?"

"No. That's why I radioed you. Maybe a third full."

"That's not good enough." That gave him five thousand gallons to spread between more than 18,000 people and the hospital.

"No, it's not," she agreed.

Gale signed off and went to the door, backing off again while George rammed the front door open.

"Maybe I should just leave it open," he said with a rueful smile.

Gale shook his head. "Cold tonight, and people are getting more bad-tempered out there." He told him of being robbed and the fire chief's experience, plus Flint's sense that people were getting worse. "Keep it shut and locked. And if you have a gun, keep it handy."

George nodded. "I guess we shouldn't be surprised that people are acting up."

"It's normal," Gale agreed. "Usually for seventy-two hours, people are cooperative, and then they turn and become selfish and impatient. If anything, we got some extra hours over and above the textbook average out of our neighbors."

"So those drug dealers in Katrina who rescued people in their neighborhoods went back to being bad guys, huh?"

"In no time flat. Now get me FEMA. I have an ass to chew."

He said that just as Marilyn walked in with a tray. "Sorry about the language, Marilyn."

She laughed. "No problem. I have a present for you." She handed him a steaming cup.

He caught the scent. "Coffee?" he said.

"We had some instant in the back of a cupboard. Probably stale, but George mentioned you missed it."

"Wow, thanks." He took a sip. "You have a working camp stove?"

"No. I can warm water by putting a covered pan on the generator. It gets damned hot there, and the lid seems to keep out the gasoline taste."

"Smart." He drank more coffee. It was funky-tasting, but it was still a treat. And a kindness he appreciated. It was good to know as some people got worse as the stress didn't abate, some people stayed decent. Of course, George and Marilyn and he and Bash still had a roof and a bed and had buried no bodies. Maybe he shouldn't judge those who had it worse.

From his seat at the radio, George said, "They're ready for you."

"Thanks for the supplies," said Gale into the mike, "but less than two thousand gallons of water? That doesn't begin to take care of it."

"It's the maximum the helicopter can carry."

"Is there any way we can get more? More deliveries every day? Over."

They haggled back and forth, and finally Gale was able to wangle one more afternoon water delivery. He was up to 7,000 gallons, still not enough, especially with the dehydrated food. She said they had to find ways to cache rainwater, that it was the only long-term solution. She could maybe get more personal microfilters, and they could drink the rainwater, even if it had been runoff from a roof or street first. Or they needed to get to old farms, where there were hand pumps, and start taking water out of underground.

Both the director and Gale were testier today than they had been. He tried to find a balance between being serious, letting her know how bad it was going to get, and spreading enough honey on his speech to keep her feeling positive toward him and prone to helping. It was an impossible tightrope to walk. He wished for the town's sake that Evelyn had survived. She really had been the better politician.

When he signed off, he turned to George. "I have a project for the two of you."

"Sure," George said, sounding eager to help.

"We need press. We need to get a television reporter to helicopter into this town and do human-interest reporting. We need to put pressure on FEMA to push us up their list."

"I don't know of anyone in the news industry."

"I don't either. But I know you and Marilyn are smart. You can use your radio contacts, you can figure out some way to sell the story to a hungry newsperson. Start with Rolla and Springfield radio and TV and move on out from there. Go national if you can."

"They say if it bleeds, it leads. What can they take pictures of?"

"We have a hospital that's rubble, breached levees shored up by debris, and rows of bodies from the second quake still awaiting burial. We have tent cities where people are getting hungry and thirsty and angry about it. We have some photogenic sand blows in the yards of middle-class houses, and a town jail kept dry by a sandbag wall. There's plenty for them to work with. And push the small town angle. If they've been focusing their reports on Memphis and St. Louis, they might be getting bored with the repetition. Hell, you and Marilyn are a good human interest story, the couple who keeps us in contact with the real world."

"I wouldn't say that."

"I would. There are plenty of stories. We're a true blue

American small town fighting to stay alive."

George's eyebrows shot up. "Is that what we are?"

"It's exactly what we are. They can sell that, and they'll know it. If we don't get enough food and water, and soon, this town is going to die. The right person, broadcasting our story, can keep us alive. I need you to find that person."

Chapter 13

Bash

Bash's day started off on a pleasant note. There was a letter at the receptionist's desk for him from the Witherspoons, who were catching a ride out on a supply helicopter. They thanked him and left their email address for the baby pictures.

And then the day started going downhill.

Nathan came by first thing to tell him that the sandwich shop was entirely out of food and that, under the orders of his boss, he was locking it. He presented a bill for food, for tables, for chairs, all with an apology. Bash thanked Nathan for all his help, and they shook hands. He took the bill over to Dr. Eisenstein.

"So we have no food. At all?" she said.

"No. Staff need to bring their lunches, I guess. Patients and visitors? I don't know what we can do for them."

"At least we can evac long-term patients now that the worst of the injured are out." Absentmindedly, she tapped her stethoscope's earpiece with a fingernail. "We need to not keep patients around more than eight hours. They're either serious enough to be evacced, or they go home. If we need to observe, that's going to have to be our limit, if at all possible. If they're here for very long, their family can bring them food and water."

"If they have family surviving." They looked at each other hopelessly. "Will the evac helicopters keep coming? Now that the rescue from the second quake is over?"

"I may have to twist a few arms."

"We'll probably have cardiac and asthma and random injury cases that need evacuation for awhile. Surely they won't refuse those."

"And burns. With more and more open cooking fires, we're getting more burn cases."

Bash had seen one yesterday. "Any bad ones last night?"

"One three-year-old boy, both hands. He was evacced this morning, just before you came."

"So what else do we need to think about?"

"What I'm more worried about is water. We need it to sterilize instruments with the powdered compound, and we need it to wash, and staff need it to drink."

"Do we have enough?"

"I've put in the request several times. It's your boyfriend who's running that end of things, I hear. Maybe you can put in a word."

"My husband. He knows our situation. I think he's having a hard time convincing FEMA how desperate it is. And he says they're focused on the metro area of St. Louis, so that smaller towns are getting forgotten."

"People here die just as they do in big cities. It's as ugly and horrible. Medical help can save the same percentage. The grief of survivors is just as bad."

"I know. You don't have to convince me." He felt a twinge as his mind scanned, unstoppable, through the images of friends and patients he lost. Meggy, his coworkers. None hurt more than Trevor. He hoped the boy's mother was holding up okay. Though how could she be? There could be no "okay," just terrible enduring for her, for years to come.

The doc was called away and Bash returned to his job, triage once again. He had inadvertently become an expert over the last days, able to push aside his empathy for their pain and quickly prioritize dozens of patients in no time at all. The flow of patients was so slow now though that anyone could do it. He had plenty of time to assess, and even precious extra time to offer an encouraging word to patients and anxious family members.

He had green-tagged a woman with a glass cut on her arm and sent her to the waiting area when a medium-sized aftershock hit. They had experienced a dozen or more like this since the second quake. Always, at first, the catch of breath, and nearly everyone froze in place, waiting to see if it climbed in intensity to another big one. The few who didn't freeze threw themselves to the ground immediately, taking no chances. Maybe they were the smart ones.

But this one stayed moderate. After five seconds of it, with the shaking easing off, the cancer clinic building's curved front wall fell. With a resounding crash, glass flew everywhere, scattering for yards. Bash watched as a full panel of glass bounced like a basketball and flung itself, still whole, into the middle of the street. A car screeched to a halt, just avoiding it. An avalanche of old debris skittered down the slopes of the building on every side. Several people screamed, adding to the noise. You'd think they'd be all screamed out by now, but no.

As the aftershock trailed off, Bash yelled for stretchers, grabbed his box of triage tags and ran over to the front of the building. He could see a half-dozen people injured, one struggling to his feet. Yellow at worst, ignore him. Two sets of legs together, buried from the waist up—aim for that.

Pulling the biggest pieces of glass aside, he revealed a woman and a smaller body. The adult had fallen over or perhaps leaped onto the child to protect it. Blood pulsed from the woman's neck. He swiped his glove over the pulse. Location and flow, looked like the carotid. Bash rolled her over. Without full hospital facilities and a vascular surgical team, prepped and ready to sew, she'd be brain dead in five minutes. He didn't even bother with the black tag.

Beneath her, the child, a girl, maybe ten, was covered with blood, but as he checked her over, he thought it was mostly from the woman. As he palpated her head with quick fingers, she moaned. Her eyes didn't open. He lifted the eyelids. One pupil was slow to contract. He rolled the mother off her, slapped a red tag on the girl and moved on.

Two orderlies came up with a stretcher. "Neck brace this one, take her," he said, pointing to the girl. Tearing off the old gloves and digging in his pocket for new, he moved on. Citizens were pulling debris off other victims. One rescuer said, "Ow, damn," and sucked at his hand. On the way by him, Bash said, "Get yourself to first aid," and pointed back at the hospital. "And the rest of you, be careful."

An elderly victim was being helped to his feet by another person. Bash said, "How do you feel? Can you walk?"

"I'm okay," he said, softly. He reached his hand to his head and looked at it. "Am I bleeding?"

Bash said to the other person, "Support him, please, and walk him over to the field hospital."

He heard the old man say, as he was led off, "I was just coming to get my wife."

Bash knelt by a group of volunteers uncovering another victim from debris. In his peripheral vision, he could see another stretcher loaded with another person, one he hadn't checked, off toward the hospital.

The patient at his knees, a man, said, "Dammit," then, "thank you," to one of his rescuers.

"Don't move," said Bash and did a quick exam. "Can you move your arms? Your legs? Does anything hurt?"

"My arm."

As it was uncovered, Bash could see a spike of thin metal had plunged into the man's bicep. As a volunteer rescuer reached for it, Bash snapped, "Leave it." To the man he said, "Don't move," as he hesitated only a moment before choosing a red tag. He stood and called out, "Stretcher!"

Bash turned and scanned the scene. He didn't see anyone else who needed immediate help. A white-smocked person kneeled by the woman with the carotid injury. He walked over and saw it was Suze.

She looked up at him, holding the woman's hand.

"Hey, Suze," he said.

She glanced back. "Fuck you."

"Did I do something to upset you?"

"Look at this woman! She's dying. Why isn't she tagged?" Her voice grew louder.

"I hope she isn't someone you know. But she was beyond our help."

"Bullshit. We could have saved her."

"No we couldn't, hon."

She leapt up and pushed him in the chest. "Don't you hon me, you cold bastard!"

"Suze, shh."

She shoved him again. "You don't care! You don't care about anyone. You didn't care about Meggy. You just let them die up there."

A small crowd was gathering.

"It's okay," he said to Suze, trying not to take her attack personally. She was exhausted from days of stress. He was exhausted too.

"You *like* this!" She made a fist and threw a punch at him.

He grabbed her wrist and tried to make his voice commanding. "Stop it. You're hysterical."

She kicked him in the shin, hard. It hurt, and he let go of her wrist. She was sobbing now and still yelling at him, but her tears made the words impossible to make out.

Dr. Eisenstein came trotting up. "I have her," she said to

Bash.

He backed away and watched as Suze pointed to the fallen woman. The doc glanced down, where the woman's heart was barely pushing blood out of the wound in a slow welling. A puddle of red seeped out of the pile of debris, moving toward his feet, like a finger of accusation. She was nearly bled out. By brain function, she'd been dead for a minute or two now. Should he have red-tagged her, gotten her treated first? He felt a moment of doubt. But no, there had been four minutes at best for that woman. He hadn't the equipment to do anything himself. They weren't set up for that level of trauma surgery. A minute to get the stretcher, a half-minute to run her back. There'd have been time to make an incision, but then what? A doc might have clamped both ends of the carotid with fingers. Could he have gotten a stent in? Maybe. Just maybe, if everything went exactly like clockwork, they could gotten one in, and have saved her with only minor brain damage, no worse than a mild stroke, recoverable. They probably had some AB blood and plasma in coolers. They might have pumped every bit of it they had into her. Probably used up the whole supply for the day, but they just might have pulled it off if everything had gone perfectly. If anyone else needed blood later that person would die instead.

Who would he choose to die instead? The little girl? The metal fragment? The unconscious person? The one on the stretcher?

The weight of the days of triage grew heavy in his chest. Maybe he had made the right decision. Maybe he hadn't. How could he know? You can't run it back and replay it the other way to see how it might come out. She was dead, and that's all there was to it. Don't let it eat at you, he told himself.

But it ate at him.

He limped back to the hospital and sat down in a chair, checking where Suze had kicked him, probing the wound. It was tender, and there'd be a big bruise by the end of the day. He grabbed an alcohol swab and a bandage and treated himself. He had to get himself ready for more triage.

The doc was leading Suze past him, and he kept his head down so Suze didn't see his face. He didn't want to set her off again. The doc led Suze to a bed, got her up, and said something to an LPN. Within two minutes, the LPN brought a capped syringe over, and the doc gave Suze a shot. She looked around and found Bash, then walked over to him.

"She'll be okay."

A stab of new guilt pierced him. He hadn't really been thinking about that. He still didn't know if he gave a shit. He nodded and fiddled, unnecessarily, with his bandage.

The doc kneeled down in front of him. "You did great in triage. Nothing she said was real, you know that?"

He couldn't meet her eyes. "I hope so."

"No, you did fine. She just...broke, I guess. Too many days of the ER life for people not used to it. I'm surprised we haven't had more psychotic breaks or weeping staff collapsing, or people just not showing up for another day or night of it."

"Most of us are doing okay."

"We're doing too damned much with too little in the way of a hospital, but yes. We have every reason to feel proud of ourselves. You as much as anyone."

He squeezed his eyes hard, worried that the lump in his throat would turn to tears. Once he had control, he asked, "What'd you give her?"

"Diazepam, 10 mg IM."

Valium. He could use some himself. "Thanks," he said to the doctor. "I'll stay away from her."

"That'd be best, I imagine, but I'm sending her home for three days, minimum. Luckily for her, she still has a home. I'll find someone to drive her."

"Okay. I better get back to work."

She put a hand on his arm, keeping him from standing. "You

haven't hurt anyone, Bash. The earthquake has hurt people. Buildings have hurt people. Fires have hurt people. You're doing fine."

He nodded, feeling a fractional bit better at the pep talk.

"Do you want off triage?"

"No," he said automatically. Then he thought about it. "I think I'm fine. But if I want to change, I'll come to you, okay?"

"That's great. Do that." She stood and brushed her hands off. "I have to get back to work."

"Yes, me too."

As she walked away, he could hear her mutter to herself, "We need fresh staff."

Ouch. He wondered, was he losing it as much as Suze, but in his own way? If he wasn't good at his job, he should back off. But then who would do it? They only had fifty or so staff, including aides and orderlies and dentists and vets, most of them emotionally and physically wiped out after long hours, some of them in bandages and splints themselves, most of them short on rest from sleeping on the hard ground through increasingly cold nights. He was better off than most, having a roof and a bed and no dead family to mourn.

He had to pull himself together, forget this moment, and soldier on. Rain started, a patter that quickly picked up. Just great.

Down where the glass had fallen, he saw two orderlies by the carotid woman, unfurling a blue body bag. Bash walked a few steps toward them, watching. He sent a silent apology to the woman—*If I screwed up, I'm sorry.* An apology didn't do any good for either of them. He thought about the girl, probably her daughter, possibly an orphan now, and felt guilt anew.

An ambulance pulled up and he forced himself to go over to it and start triage again.

* * *

The day didn't get any worse after that, but it didn't get much better. The rain continued, relentless, and patients came in soaked and shivering. The hospital didn't have enough blankets. The weather cooled further as a cold front followed the leading edge of the rain. It was going to be a nasty night for those sleeping outside on the ground.

He skipped lunch, not having thought to bring food from home, and saw the afternoon's patients. They were getting nearly every sort of case an ER or a acute care clinic might get, plus doctor's office issues too. He saw a patient who had contracted what sounded like crabs. He wondered if people out there, bored with no TV or internet, were having more sex. A population like the tent cities, STDs could sweep through the sexually active people in no time at all.

As Dr. Eisenstein had predicted, he saw two new burn cases, neither worse than second-degree. There was a chest pain, a mental health case, and countless contusions, abrasions, and sprains. Three broken bones—a foot, an ulna, and three fingers. Two of the patients from the wall collapse this morning were evacuated by helicopter—the little girl, identity unknown, and the old man, who had grown increasingly confused and disoriented. He needed a brain MRI or CT, far beyond their level of technology here.

By six o'clock, the rain still hadn't let up entirely, the sunlight was almost gone, and Bash was more than ready to go home. Hunger gnawed at him. He walked to his car, got in, and only then remembered.

He was supposed to pick up the girls at 3:00 from school.

Panic swept over him. Were they okay? It was three hours too late. Where would they be? If they were hurt, he'd never forgive himself.

He drove up to the school site, but no one was there. He drove home, taking the route he thought they might have walked. No one was at the house, either. Had something happened to them? What if they had been assaulted or worse? It would be his fault.

Driving up to the Walmart, he thought it was his last reasonable hope, that they were somehow with Gale. He drove into the parking lot, surprised by the sight of the swimming pool in his headlights—what the heck was that about? He parked and walked to the tent, looking around for Gale or the girls. Lanterns threw dim light around the area. There were sleeping bags and bundles of blankets piled under one tent's edge. A few people were at a table, eating. Others were bent over paperwork or talking in small groups. He wove through the crowd, anxiety pushing him on.

And he saw the girls, sitting on a blanket, playing with a toddler. They were laughing.

He started shaking, his legs feeling weaker and weaker until he just sat down where he was, cross-legged, on cold damp grass. His breath was coming so fast he thought he might pass out, but he forced himself to slow it down. In a few minutes, his head cleared. But his hands were still quivering.

"Bash?" It was Gale's voice.

He looked around.

Gale's eyebrows shot up and he came over, squatting by Bash. "What's wrong with you?"

"I forgot the girls," he managed to say. "I forgot totally to pick them up."

"It's okay. They walked back here."

"Oh, Gale, I can't believe it. They could have been hurt."

"They weren't, though. They hung with some other high school kids for a while, and when you didn't show, they came back here. We all figured the hospital had gotten crazy and you couldn't get away."

Bash shook his head, ashamed. "I just forgot."

"It's okay, really," Gale said, concern on his face. "It's not like we had kids last week. This instant family thing is a little confusing. Looks like you've had a rough day."

"Oh yeah," Bash said. He held his hands out and looked at them. The tremors had ceased.

"Do you need a ride home? We can all go together."

"Don't you need to stay until eight?"

"Lots of people here know what to do. I have the radio. I can leave an hour early for a change."

"If it's okay, yeah. It'd be better for me not to drive right now, and definitely not with the girls in the car."

"I'll close things down here from my end. It'll probably take twenty minutes or so."

"Thanks."

"Go talk to the girls," Gale said.

Bash pushed himself up and walked toward the girls, who were playing with the little kid again, some sort of game about freezing until he released them.

Haruka glanced up and smiled when she saw it was him. "Hello," she said.

McKenna bounced up and gave him a hug. "Hey, Bash. Come and play with us."

The toddler said, "Play play play," bouncing up and down on his rear.

Bash stifled the urge to apologize to McKenna. As far as the girls knew, there was nothing to apologize for. And they were having fun—no need to ruin that with his worrying. He sat down on the blanket and said, "What's the game?"

It was a half hour later when Gale finally came to get them. On the drive home, McKenna talked about school and a fight two girls had which had included a lot of nasty language. Bash wondered if she was this forthcoming to her own mother. McKenna mentioned Haruka's Japanese language lessons. He and Gale held hands as they drove and listened to McKenna's chatter, and Gale kept shooting him worried looks. It'd be good to unload some of his worries tonight, in bed. First, though, he had a meal to prepare.

The girls gathered water from their back yard caches while he put together food. Gale handed him the mashed potato mix, and he said, "We should warm water on the engine block on the way home tomorrow, now that we're out of fuel. Get a closed metal container, put it in there somehow. Then we could have these warm from now on, as soon as we got home."

"I haven't the foggiest idea how to do that. I couldn't identify an engine block if you dropped one on my foot."

"It'd be the heavy thing lying on your foot." Gale grinned.

Bash shook his head at Gale, then pulled out a can of Spam and three cans of vegetables. One was artichokes in dressing, and he'd just add the other cans to that and make a salad and slice the Spam on top, paper-thin, to give the illusion of more food. More crackers on the side. It was almost like a real meal, except for eating Spam instead of chicken breast. "The potatoes are helpful. I doubt we have food left for four of us for a week."

"We'll get by, somehow," said Gale. His tone had a bite to it.

"Troubles?"

"I'm tired of mine. I want to hear about yours."

"Later in bed," Bash said. "We can dump all our woes then."

The girls came back in, carrying two saucepans with caution. A waft of frigid air came in the open door, and Bash moved to close it after them. "There was less than an inch in everything," said McKenna, "but it added up."

"I'll go check the rainspout caches in front while you're finishing getting dinner ready," said Gale.

Twenty minutes later they sat down to eat almost like a normal American family. Except for the gay parents, unrelated child and foreign child, thought Bash. They drank water from the vegetable cans and washed that salty concoction down with rainwater. So maybe not entirely normal.

In bed that night, Bash told of his day, and Gale soothed him the best he could. But there was no real soothing of either of their worries. "I don't know how long I can do this," Bash said.

"I know," said Gale. "I'm stressed out too, and tired, and I don't even have life and death decisions in my hands. I know it must be harder for you."

"You do too have life and death in your hands. It's just death delayed a little. If you don't get enough food and water, if you don't take care of the bodies and the sewage, people will start to die."

That gave him some strange comfort, to remember that many other people bore terrible burdens and that, like Gale and him, they were doing the best they could. Misery didn't love company, but it took some solace in it.

Chapter 14

Gale

"We need to evacuate as many people who will agree to go."

Gale had come to the decision while finishing the home latrine that morning. The weather had been damned cold, and misty, and he knew thousands of the people he was responsible for helping had awoken shivering, hungry, thirsty, and afraid. If the dampness didn't abate, they'd go to bed in wet blankets tonight. So FEMA wouldn't bring enough relief to them? Okay. He'd send the townspeople to them.

Flint said, "We have less than half a town now."

"Fewer people would mean less strain on our resources," said Dan.

"Fewer people to work at recovery would mean it'd take longer to get back to normal."

They sat quietly for long moments, Gale letting the two others think it through.

"If we could march out the prisoners, that would help a lot," said Flint. "We could relocate the police station, up to safer ground, and free up staff." He squinted. "We could send a handful of reservists to guard them on a march out. Two of the Guard I can think of off the top of my head are homeless anyway, might appreciate getting out themselves."

Dan said. "Where to?"

Gale said, "Wherever is the quickest to get to a functioning road. I'll tell FEMA to have buses there waiting for them." He hoped he could actually make that happen.

"You know where that would be?"

"I know Rolla is okay. Probably up that direction, but not so far as that, of course."

"Due west, up the hill," said Dan. "It's a direct route, and if you get up in elevation, that's more solid ground, right? In case of another quake."

"Usually," said Gale. Unless it was landslide country. "I can ask George and Marilyn to confirm about the best roads, via their ham radio contacts rather than ask through official channels. The more I know from independent sources, the stronger my bargaining position with FEMA will be."

"We need a map of Missouri," said Dan. He got up to search for one. They were meeting this morning in the new temporary fire station, a block of buildings up in the industrial section of town. Dan's files and equipment had been moved, but much of it was still in boxes. Who could have predicted that cardboard boxes would become another shortage, as people tried to rescue and store what belongings they could, and as rain ruined any boxes left outdoors.

Flint said, "I know the roads are impassable up through Johnstown. That's nine miles. But if they're bad all the way out to Fredericktown that's more like fifty miles."

"Or they should aim southwest," Gale said.

"That'd be no farther from the epicenter, though. And who knows how Arkansas is handling it."

Dan came back with a state map, and they all studied it for a few minutes. Gale could tell they were getting used to the idea of a large evacuation, seeing how it could work.

Dan said, "If you had little kids in tow, you'd be lucky to

make ten miles a day."

Gale said, "Most people could make more the first day."

"They'd need to carry, what? Eight pounds of water per day, food, blankets. No way is everyone going to own a good backpack. It'd have to be blanket rolls, and for that, we'd need rope."

"What about shopping carts?" said Gale. Most of the stores still had carts stored outside, and many had survived the quakes. "Just pile everything in and push it when you can. Bad patches of road, two adults could lift it up and over obstructions."

Dan's eyebrows flicked up. "I'd sure not want to try it."

Flint said, "I think it's a good idea. Have you been in those tent cities? They're getting worse every day. And people are tearing down bushes, trees, trying to get cooking fires started. Trying to stay warm."

Gale said, "I hear they're seeing more burn injuries from that at the hospital."

"We'll be damned lucky if they don't set the whole county on fire. But the worst part of 'em is the stench."

The latrines had been necessary, and ones that only a few families used could be kept tidy and odor-free, but the tent cities' human waste was much harder to manage.

"If people quit using them—and they may if they're too unpleasant to use—disease will start spreading," Flint said.

"The thing is," said Dan, "I'm afraid of this becoming a ghost city. And if strangers come into an abandoned town, they'll loot."

"I have an idea," said Flint. His voice was hesitant, as hesitant as Gale had ever heard it.

"Go on."

"Two ideas, really. One, let's block off the south with debris. Little chance of that being fixed before the west roads. We're starting on bulldozing hospital row, right? You're done picking through that stuff?"

"We're nearly done," said Dan. "We salvaged what we could,

but with the rain, some that we missed will be damaged anyway, stuff like bandages, gauze, anything in cardboard boxes."

"And...." Again Flint hesitated. "I think we should be doing some looting ourselves."

"I'm sorry?" said Dan.

"I think we should send my people door to door, break into houses that aren't inhabited, and try to salvage whatever food and beverages they have. If FEMA won't send us enough, we have to find it some other way."

"I was thinking about organizing hunters to make up the difference," Dan said. "There are lots of deer out there."

"I think the deer have all taken to higher ground too," said Flint. "They're not idiots. Better at survival-thinking than we are. Have you seen any?"

Dan shook his head. "Maybe the reek of the river drove them off. Like you say, they're pretty smart about self-preservation."

Gale stayed silent as the other two talked about wildlife, trying to get his head around the idea of official looting. But damn, there probably was food out there, the owners gone or dead, the occasional thieves having surely not gotten all of it. When the others paused in their conversation, he spoke up. "I think it's a brilliant idea," he said. "There are dozens of full hot water heaters too, I bet you. Yes. Definitely. Go through the houses and take what's been abandoned. Drain the water. Do as little damage as possible getting in, and don't risk your lives in unsafe buildings, but yes. I say to do it."

Dan still looked uncomfortable.

Gale addressed him. "It's survival. It sucks, I know, legally or morally or any which way you look at it, but we need the food and water. And if we can give the departing refugees the lighter-weight food, dried stuff like the potatoes, to walk with, keep them marching on that, the rest of people in town can survive off what we scavenge."

"It seems—I don't know. I wouldn't want people pawing

around my house."

"If you were dead, Dan, wouldn't you want your neighbors to survive on what you'd left behind?" Gale said. "You wouldn't begrudge them that."

Flint said, "Who knows what else we might find—tarps, sleeping bags, camping tents, stoves tools, propane."

"Let's hope the looters didn't find it all first," said Gale.

"I don't think we have any active ones out there right now. We got them all, or they've gone away."

Gale said, "If we don't feed people better, even decent people are going to think about looting anyway." He turned to Dan. "We're decent people. You know that. We need to get control of the food supply that's out there and distribute it fairly."

Dan sighed. "I guess you're both right."

Gale said, "Before we continue, I need to get on my radio to George." But it was Marilyn who answered his call, and he asked her to find out the information about the roads, where they were open, how far people would have to walk to be able to meet a bus. Or a fleet of buses, more than likely. He wanted to convince lots of people to leave.

Then the Triumvirate continued with the morning's business, a surprising amount of it. Midway through, Gale got a call on the handheld radio that linked him to the EOC. The helicopters had come with the water buckets, and they had about 3,000 gallons to last them until late afternoon's delivery. They also had finally gotten the filtration systems, five large ones, not the six promised. No small ones at all. His staff was already out at the lakes, turning that water into drinkable water.

When he got off the radio, he said, "I hope everybody knows to collect rainwater. Can we repeat that information at every opportunity?"

After they broke off the meeting, Gale swung by the EOC, to see if anyone had heard from Angela.

Kay was there, being his deputy. "No, I'm sorry."

"I asked Fire to check through her house. They found no one there." No bodies, either.

"You think she just left town?"

"Without telling us?" Gale said, shaking his head.

"Maybe she was embarrassed," Kay said. "She liked you. She wanted your respect. Maybe it was too hard to say it to your face."

"Surely she could have left a note, told someone else to tell us."

"You could be right. I don't know. She could be dead somewhere, though she's not on the death rolls." She shook her head. "I guess it's just going to have to be a mystery for now."

"Maybe forever." He raised a hand in farewell and got going to his regular morning call to FEMA. He was tired of begging them for supplies. He thought it was time to *tell*, not ask.

Marilyn and George had a map of the state out and showed him what they'd found about clear roads. They also had called out to as many newspapers, radio stations, and television stations as they could, and they'd tried to encourage people to ask questions on internet sites about what was going on in smaller cities, like their own. "Hoping to create a sort of groundswell, where public demand drives what news crews might do."

"Thank you. Great job, really," Gale said. "I can't begin to tell you how important you two are to me."

Then it was time to have another fight with FEMA. He began, though, by thanking her for the extra water. He read off a list of supplies, including water-free hand cleanser and antibacterial wipes, which took up a lot of space but were needed at the latrines. He had his whole staff busy yesterday at a rough census, getting neighborhood leaders to report in, counting heads at the tent cities and the churches that had become dormitories, and they had about 2750 private households—some entailing people sleeping on their driveways or in their backyards—and two tent cities of over a thousand each, the hospital, and the jail.

A population of about 17,000. Less than 40% of what it had been ten days ago.

And then he told the FEMA director his plan for evacuating the tent cities on foot. "We know that you could get us transport just east of Fredericktown, over," he said.

"And then what?"

That's your job. "You bus them to Kansas City or wherever the nearest refugee site with open cots might be. They're going to freeze or starve or get sick if they stay here."

"You don't know what it's like out here," she said. "You still don't have a television, or a radio, over?"

"I wouldn't have time to watch if I did have one. And no, we're too far from television signals to get much more than static. I think someone on my staff got an Illinois radio station night before last for a while. And no, before you ask, we don't have Internet. We don't have electricity. We don't have cell service. Autumn is here and winter isn't that far off."

"You know the stock market dropped another 12% yesterday? The president had to freeze trading again."

He took a breath, calming himself. *Gee, I have a retirement account in an index fund too, but somehow that's not seeming all that important right now. I have a growling belly and fingernails caked with dirt from digging my own latrine, and there are babies crying all night at the tent cities because they're cold and hungry. Which do you think matters more to me?* But what he said was a toneless, "Thank you for the news."

"We're running out of resources. People who were once generous have turned. They're resenting refugees, now. They want their hospitals and stadiums and hotel rooms back. They don't want the government to keep throwing money at this, over."

"My people want safe drinking water," he said. "A roof over their heads. A blanket that isn't soaked with rain. I don't think that's too much to ask, over."

They argued back and forth for another few minutes, and finally Gale said, "I'm sending these people out. I'll have a reporter imbedded with them too. That'll be an interesting story, when they show up and there are no buses to meet them." It was an empty threat, as he doubted he could get some stranger to walk dozens of miles in the cold rain for a news story, but she didn't know that.

"I'll see what I can do," she said, and signed off.

He hadn't been done with her, actually. He checked his list. It'd have to wait until this afternoon.

"You know," said Marilyn. "Once upon a time, back in World War II, people collected bits of aluminum, kids took their wagons around for it, so that it could be recycled and we could build airplanes. And they planted victory gardens. And had meatless Mondays, all so the soldiers could get fed. I guess we're not that country any more."

Gale nodded. "I suppose we don't have it in us."

"I wonder what makes a thing like that go away," she mused. "Could human characters change so much?"

"I don't know. I do know some people out there are saying we're stupid for living in an earthquake zone."

"Flood zone, tornado zone, ice storm zone, big city crime, hurricane coasts, San Andreas fault, droughts. Heck, everybody lives where something bad can happen," she said. "You think people would have more sympathy."

Gale sighed. "We can hope people will be at their best in a crisis...and protect ourselves the best we can when they aren't." He studied her face. "Do you and George want to leave? We can get you out with the refugees."

"No. This is our home, for twenty-two years now. We'll stay here, even if it falls down around us."

"You're the best, Marilyn. You know what else you could do for me?"

"Anything," she said.

"If we walk the people out, starting tomorrow morning, if people along the way could offer just water—not food, necessarily, but water—that'd help a lot. It'd let us keep more water here, and it'd save the walkers the weight. Maybe your radio pals could organize something. Those communities could have churches or Kiwanis or whatever organize it. Some rural people with a well might be willing to share."

"That's a good idea. Tomorrow? That's soon."

"After a second night of this cold weather, I think many will want to leave. In fact," he said, "I have to go and start organizing the exodus now."

And indeed the rest of the day was taken up with that. He barely spared a thought for missing Angela, or for Bash, or for the girls—not until they were dropped off at the EOC at 3:00 by a friend's mother. And he put them to work too, loading up grocery carts with packaged supplies for the evacuees. At dawn tomorrow, over a thousand people would be walking away from town, some of them forever.

A large part of him wished he could go with them. He hadn't lied to FEMA that morning about feeling the pinch personally. He and Bash were rationing the calories of the emergency food. His belly was growling most of the day, he was tired to the bone, and he was getting bored with canned room-temperature food. Not to mention, he'd punch his own mother in exchange for a long hot shower. Sorry, Mom, he thought, but I think I really would.

Just before five, the rains started again, heavy, but without wind. Which was a damn good thing, because the helicopters were still able to drop the promised water. They didn't land, just hovered over the pool and lowered the red buckets, then splashed it in. Some of it splashed back out and Gale felt a wrench at the loss. They zoomed off to the west, and when the noise faded, the staff was able to talk again.

Everything in the grocery carts was sealed in plastic bags, so the rain wouldn't do it any harm. There were over three hundred of the carts. The police had brought by some of the newly-looted supplies—he couldn't think of what they were doing as anything but looting—and there had been a few small first aid kits, some boxes of trash bags, garden trowels—for burying their own waste along the way, and he hoped they'd understand how important that was. People would not want refugees camping on their lawns.

He left with the girls at 5:30 to radio FEMA again, his afternoon people still hard at work organizing the exodus. He had taken a treat from the looted goods, which he had in a trash bag, to take home to his little family. He had taken less than their fair share until now, knowing he still had emergency food at home, so he didn't feel bad at all about taking this one small treat.

He hadn't arranged for McKenna to talk to her mother again, but he swung by to take the girls with him to the radio. George had gotten hold of the radio operator in Rolla who recorded what they said on an iPhone. Haruka spoke in rapid Japanese. He promised to transfer the sound file via email to Haruka's folks in Japan.

They didn't pull into the driveway at home until 6:49. Bash had been hard at work since coming home and seemed in better spirits today. The house was picked up. He had rainwater ready for them to wash their hands and faces, and dinner was on the table, along with two lit candles.

Gale brought out his surprise, a six-pack of diet root beer. Useless, calorie-wise, but precious liquid and a taste treat. "Dessert!" he said, lifting it onto the table.

Bash smiled. "That's nice."

They sat down and heard about the girls' day at school. Outdoor school was quickly losing its novelty value.

"It's cold," said McKenna. "And we can't sit down much because it's wet from the rain. We take turns using the chairs."

Haruka added only a few words, as usual, but Gale thought

she understood everything being said. He wondered if everyone in Japan was this quiet and polite, or if with each other they whooped and chattered.

As they finished eating, he passed around the root beers. He told the plan to walk a thousand people to safety. "So my question for all of you is, should McKenna and Haruka go too?"

Bash looked surprised. "Oh, I hadn't thought." He trailed off and frowned. "I guess it would be better for you to be with your mother."

"They can't stay with her in a medical facility."

"What is the set-up for children without parents?"

McKenna said, "We're not children."

"You're minors," Bash said. "And I can't even imagine what one of those big places with refugees might be like. Can young people just disappear from them? Who'd know to report it?"

"I don't know actually," said Gale. "I mean, I haven't researched what would happen to them. I'm sorry, but I've been too busy."

"If I can't be with my mom, I'd rather stay here," said McKenna.

He looked at Haruka. After a long moment where she studied her plate, she looked up at him and said, "You must decide."

Gale knew she was right. The decision was on him, and on Bash. If he said they should stay, and there was another earthquake, or something else went wrong, and the girls were hurt, that'd be on him. If he sent them off and they were raped along the way, or killed two weeks down the road at some disorganized refugee camp, that'd be on him too. He looked at Bash. "I never thought I'd be worrying about refugee camps and what might happen to kids there. Not in America."

"And who knew there'd be such hunger. I mean, without it being a fad diet sweeping the country."

Gale glanced at his diet root beer. He had known people in California that put low-fat and low-calorie foods in their earthquake kits. They were idiots. "You have to wonder what it's like in the big cities," he said. "Memphis, St. Louis." He had wanted to manage zoning for a big city, but the challenge of helping fewer than 20,000 people survive this quake was too much. He got back on track and said to McKenna, "So you're saying you want to stay here."

"Yes. I have friends here, and you two have been good to us, and I'm dry at night. I know things here," she said. "I know the streets and the people. If something went wrong, I know alleys to run down and doors to knock on."

"Okay," Gale said. "Bash?"

"Yes, I'd rather know for sure they were okay, here with us."

Gale said to the girls, "You know there'll be more aftershocks. And there could be another bad quake."

"We did okay in the others," said McKenna, and Haruka nodded.

"Okay," he said, feeling less certain than he made himself sound. "So you'll stay, until your mom can get on her feet and take care of you."

Bash looked pleased.

In bed that night, he said, "Bash, you know those girls aren't ours."

"I know. But I like them."

"When all this is done, I think we should talk about adopting. You'll be a good dad."

Bash kissed his cheek. "So will you. But I don't know if gays even can adopt here in Missouri."

"Who cares? We'll go elsewhere, out of the country if we need to. Or back to California."

"California," Bash said, with a wistful sigh. "I wonder how they'd have handled this in L.A. or S.F."

"It wouldn't have been so vast an area there. Because of population density, as many people would be affected, but only in one corner of the state, just the Bay Area or L.A. If it had been way up north, or out in the desert, the numbers of dead and homeless would have been really low. The buildings on the coast are better. The zoning is better. The prep is better." He winced. "I guess that's my fault that it isn't better here."

"Oh Gale, you couldn't have done more than you did. You've been good for the city. Wonderful."

Maybe not wonderful, but barely good enough. A new thought struck Gale. He'd be able to move himself and Bash to California again, now. With this experience under his belt, any city in the Ring of Fire would be happy to have him on staff. If he didn't screw up and got the surviving citizens through it okay, that is...or if the deaths would fall on the shoulders of someone else, lawmakers who hadn't adopted better construction standards, FEMA for not helping enough, or the Earth itself.

Horrible thinking, and shame on him for giving it even a few seconds of attention. But it was the truth—he'd be able to write his own ticket now professionally. He could even consult, he imagined, travel internationally while Bash kept a home base in L.A. or S.F. Then he ruthlessly pushed that line of thought away. Focus on the day's problems, and let the future take care of itself.

After he'd started to doze off, a thudding knock came at the front door. Gale told Bash to get into the spare bedroom with the girls and lock the door. He walked through the living room and peered out a curtain, but it was pitch black out there.

"Who is it?" he called.

"Oralee. I'm Flint's wife?"

"Oh, hi. Go around to the garage, would you?" He hoped she was who she said she was as he went to grab the flashlight from the kitchen. He heaved open the garage door and shone the light out. It was just one person, a woman, also with a flashlight, now aimed at the ground. "Come in."

"I can't stay but a second, or Flint will get worried. He wanted me to bring you this." She raised her light and shone it into the garage, then stepped over to a workbench and put down a towel-wrapped bundle. She unfolded it to show him a gun.

Gale thought it looked even more sinister in the low light. He wasn't a gun person, but whatever it took to protect Bash and the girls. "I thought he said he'd give me a BB gun."

"As they're going through the houses, you know, looking for supplies, they're finding plenty of firearms too. He said to bring you these." She brought a box out of her jacket pocket and slapped it down. "Ammunition too."

"Except for pointing and pulling the trigger, I really don't know how to use it."

"It's a revolver, dead simple. But it's unloaded for now, until you learn how to use it. Hang on." She dug into her other pocket. "Here are some handouts I found you from a gun safety course. Don't point it at anyone when you're figuring out how to use it, even if you think it's unloaded. Only point it at someone when you're confident about, and if you're willing to pull the trigger. Read this, and if you still can't figure it out, ask Flint tomorrow. K?"

"I appreciate it." In equal measure, he hated having the thing, and when she left, he was half afraid to touch it. But he brought it inside and stored it temporarily on the top shelf of his bedroom closet. Then he knocked on the spare bedroom door and told them it was fine.

The next morning before dawn, he went into work, leaving the girls to Bash, and taking the gun, a handful of bullets, and instructions with him. He had no doubt someone at the EOC—maybe everyone—could explain to him how to use the thing.

Leaving the gun in his locked glove box for now, he started organizing the tent city's exodus. When dawn came, he had twenty staff working hard.

Before any FEMA supplies were delivered that morning, another helicopter came in, a bright blue and yellow copter with "NEWS" painted in white on the side. Gale stared at it, unsure whether he should be happy or not. He'd get the news coverage he needed, but he had so much to do this morning. Damn. This was not the best time to have to stop and deal with reporters.

But when would be a good time? He smoothed back his hair and looked around for Megan, the staff member who, that first day, had stuck around longer because she had only her cats to worry about. He saw her, realized she was photogenic enough, and called her over. "You're on communications, right?" he said. "Congratulations, you're now our press officer. Come on."

"But I don't know anything about that," she said, trotting to catch up.

"On-the-job training," he said. As the helicopter's engines started to wind down, he leaned over and yelled into her ear, "Pretend you know everything. Shoulders back, head high. Stand straight, no matter what."

"Oh, shit," she said, then smiled. "Wait. Should I smile for the cameras? Or be serious?"

"Good question. Serious, I think. Worried, but calm and professional. You can do it."

He walked forward and met four people who piled out of the helicopter. There was a Faye something, a reporter from channel 7 in Denver, wearing a blue jacket and high-heeled boots, and Patrick O'something, a reporter from channel 9 dressed in multi-pocket khaki like he was reporting from the war in the Middle East.

After he introduced himself, Patrick explained, "Our stations share a helicopter." And he introduced two cameramen, both in their 30s, both named David.

"You're the town's mayor?" asked the Faye, beautiful in that over-polished TV news reporter way.

"Acting city manager," he said. "Our manager and mayor both died in the first quake, in the City Hall collapse."

"And you run the city?" she said.

"A lot of people make the town run," he said, "but three of us, the police chief, A.J. Flint, and the fire chief, Dan Bickham, and I share responsibility for major decision-making."

Patrick pulled a small notebook from one of his pockets and jotted down the names.

Gale said, "This is Megan, who will be your press liaison for the duration. She'll give you that and any other information you need. Let me tell you what all this morning's activity is about." And he went on to describe the preparations for the exodus.

He was still orienting them when the FEMA helicopters came in with the morning's water buckets and dumped them in the pool. He then had to describe that. "But the best thing for you to see would be our tent cities, I think, so you can see how in need those people are. And the temporary hospital, which is in a parking lot near our collapsed former hospital. And check out the downtown and our makeshift levees too."

They decided to start with a visit to the tent cities, where Patrick and David 2 would do citizen interviews with Megan. The other team, Faye and David 1, went with him to the Triumvirate meeting.

Gale waited, aware of all that he could be doing elsewhere instead of this, as Faye did interviews with the other two. Dan came off just as he was, patient and competent and thorough, and Flint seemed uneasy and barked out terse answers. He needed a media coach, Gale thought. And then he thought what a stupid thing to think about that was at a time like this. Then he drove the reporters to George and Marilyn's house.

"We couldn't do a fraction of what we have done without these two," he said, and sat in the background while they did brief interviews with both.

David 1 said, "I'll get a shot of the antennas outside when we leave. Editors might want to cut that in."

Gale sat down as George got FEMA on the line. He warned Director Hayes first thing. "I'm sitting here with the news team from Denver television, Director, ready to give you our lists of supplies and to talk with you about the refugees who will be coming your way in a couple days, walking from the tent cities here."

"How nice," she said, and Gale heard the strain in her voice. "We appreciate the news coverage."

With witnesses—hell, with potentially the whole world as witness, Gale repeated every request he had made the past week and had not gotten filled. He explained there'd be about a thousand people walking out in a very few hours, and how they'd arranged additional supplies and water stations along the way on their own, through the ham radio community. He was performing for the audience as much as getting something accomplished, but then, the audience was what was going to get more things accomplished for his city in the coming days. He hoped, at least. Maybe this play would piss her off so much, he'd make things worse.

Director Hayes even answered a few direct questions from Faye before the questions started getting tougher, and then she said she had an emergency call from St. Louis she had to take. No one believed it.

When they were done, Faye said, "Has FEMA been cooperative?" The camera was still running.

Gale debated how to answer. Again, he wished for Evelyn's expertise. He thought she'd know the right tone to take. "I understand they've done the best they can in a very tough situation. But you'll see the tent cities in a moment, how cold and wet and hungry and filthy the people are. I understand that FEMA is trying to put out a lot of fires at once, and that to them, we're just a tiny blaze. But this is America, an America a lot of people recognize, those from any medium-sized town or suburb, a heartland community with salt-of-the-earth people, people just like those watching this report. Some of these people have lost everything. They've lost their homes, family members, their jobs, their futures, and they're frightened, and cold, and hungry. It's harder for them to think about what others have lost in the big cities, when they've lost so much themselves."

Not awful, he thought. He'd stomped on some hot-button keywords there, but his sentences were too long, harder to edit. Something to work on over the course of the day. Short, pithy sound bites, that's what he needed.

After that, he drove them to the hospital. McKenna and Haruka were there, sitting in the visitor's chairs. He led the news team over to them and introduced them.

"So you took in these girls you'd never met."

"It's a small town. We're all neighbors here," he said, thinking, *Short sound bites.*

McKenna on camera was glib and charming, a child of the YouTube age, aware how she looked on video and how to present herself well. Hell, he should have Flint get coaching from a cadre of teenagers, instead of paying a media consultant money.

The medical director led the news team on a quick tour while Gale found Bash. "I can take the girls to school when I leave here," Gale said.

"Great. So who are those two?"

"News team from Denver, Faye something and David something. Giving them the tour of town."

"Be careful." He studied the newspeople. "And stay away from that David. He's awfully cute."

"I have the only man I want," said Gale, and he was rewarded with Bash's smile.

The two girls crowded into the car's backseat with David and his equipment, and Gale dropped them off at school, explaining how many teachers had died, how they'd organized this, and why. Faye seemed less interested in this, so their visit was quite short—which no doubt the teachers appreciated—and Gale drove them down to the levee and let them interview a backhoe and dump truck driver while he checked in on radio to the EOC and asked how the exodus was going. "Noon," was the word. That was as soon as they could realistically get some people going, though a few had already started on their own, wearing backpacks.

He flashed on how a news report would look about this. Three minutes tops, edited, ten seconds with the focus on a few of the people she had interviewed, half of it Faye narrating, turning the mess of the city into a coherent story. He hoped she'd call them all brave and hardworking, because they were, but he hoped just as much she'd call them victims and helpless, people who needed a lot more help from the federal government than they were getting. They were that too.

He took the news team by the tent cities, which were in chaos, and back to the EOC just before noon. On a whim, he mixed up some cold potato flakes for their lunch. Faye loved it. That is, she nearly gagged at the cold, saltless, lumpy potato flakes, but she loved the shot of the paper bowl, loved mugging her disgust at the camera while she explained this was all some people had been eating for a few days.

Gale tried to imagine the 90% of the country who hadn't been hurt at all seeing this, sitting in their recliner chairs, bags of Doritos in their laps, central heating keeping them warm and dry, feeling safe and taking that entirely for granted. In his imaginary scene, the viewer grabbed the remote, flipped to ESPN 2 for a rerun of *Highly Questionable*, and sighed in contentment. Cold potatoes and stinky refugees might not compete very well with that.

Did people out there have enough empathy so that the images would make them realize, "Gee, that could be me"? Had it happened during the Indonesian earthquake? During Katrina? Would it help white people to empathize if they saw mostly white faces here? He realized that catering to the mass media this morning was making him dislike humanity. And himself.

By two that afternoon, the newspeople were done, anxious to get to a news station to edit their reports before the early evening broadcasts, and Gale breathed a sigh of relief to see the news copter take off.

He drove to the edge of town, where families were still leaving, pushing carts over the rubble of the interstate highway and along the edges of the state road that would lead them west. Those who had left early this morning, who were young and fit and not weighed down by kids, might make it to transportation in two days. The ones just setting off now with children or a grandparent, the out of shape ones and the injured, would probably be there in five or six. With aching muscles and blisters all over their feet, he thought, but rescued.

With a sigh, he turned. Time to get back and check in on water, the tent cities, and how the controlled police looting was going. Now a full day's worth of work had to get done in four hours.

Chapter 15

Bash

"Be still," the father snapped at the girl Bash was trying to examine. She was six years old and so wrapped around a filthy stuffed tiger that Bash couldn't see what was wrong with her.

He got down on a knee in front of her chair, trying to meet her eyes. "What's your tiger's name, sweetie?"

She made a noise, but if it was an answer, he couldn't catch it.

"Can you tell me where it hurts?"

The girl squeezed her eyes shut and shook her head.

Bash looked up at the father. "Can you tell me where she's hurt?"

"Her stomach, I think," said the father. "She won't talk and she won't eat."

"Is her mother here?"

"Her mother got taken, the second day."

"Taken," Bash asked. He flashed on a scene of alien abduction, but of course that was ridiculous. "She passed away, you mean?"

"No, no," the man said, impatient. "Taken away from here. In a helicopter."

"Oh, evacuated," said Bash. "I hope she's okay."

"How the fuck should I know? Nobody tells anybody anything," said the man.

Bash saw the little girl flinch away from his anger. "That must be really hard," he said.

"Stephanie, let the doctor examine you."

"I'm a nurse," said Bash. Sometimes "doctor" was too scary of a word. "Just a nice nurse who wants to make sure you're okay." He reached forward and patted two fingers on the head of the tiger. "And maybe we should make sure your tiger is okay too."

"Hey, are you a faggot?" the father said.

Save me from this nonsense. Bash stood up and met the man's eyes. "I'm a nurse," he said, patiently. "And your daughter needs to be examined."

"I don't want no fucking faggot touching my daughter!" shouted the father. Heads turned toward them. "You'll give her AIDS."

Oh for pity's sake, AIDS, really? Then he noticed the little girl cringing away from her father and wondered, Is this a child battery case? Even more, he wanted to examine the child, see if this creep had hurt her. "Sir, we just want to see if your daughter's okay."

"You don't touch her," the fellow said, his face turned ugly by his anger.

Nearly as ugly as his insides, thought Bash. "Fine. I'll get another nurse. Just stay right here."

He turned, but Dr. Eisenstein was not ten steps away, coming toward the commotion. "Sir, please lower your voice. We have other patients here."

"I don't want this faggot touching my daughter. It's because of people like him that we had this earthquake. It's God's vengeance."

Bash lost it. "Then why are me and my husband fine and thousands of straight people dead? What's that say about your God's opinion of me?"

Dr. Eisenstein held up a hand to shut him up, which was probably good, as he wanted very much to add, "you ignorant, inbred, Midwestern troglodyte" to the end of that sentence. It wouldn't have helped anything.

The doctor lowered her head and said firmly to the troglodyte, "I'll take a look at your daughter. Why don't you have a seat in the waiting area?" She turned to Bash. "Take the next patient, will you?"

Bash was gratified to see the girl look up toward the doc. When Dr. E. reached down for her, the girl actually reached back. Aha, he thought, maybe she wants a female. That didn't bother him at all. The father, on the other hand? AIDS, really? Was it 1985? And God's vengeance instead of plate tectonics causing quakes? More like 1785, such people and their backward craziness.

He set up another triage station and called the next patient, a fat middle-aged woman with very little wispy hair covering her head. She walked slowly to him and sat heavily on the exam chair.

"What's the problem today?"

"I was hoping you could get me my thyroid meds. I took my last pill the morning after the first quake. I'm so exhausted without them. And there's so much to do." Her eyes welled with tears, and she didn't seem to notice as they spilled over.

Did they have any thyroid drugs? "I'll check what we have. I might have to order them in tomorrow's delivery. What were you taking?"

She handed him an empty pill bottle.

"I'll be right back," he said, and went to the pharmacy, which was in a blue camping tent off to the side of the temporary hospital grounds. They had a real pharmacist now working days, a man still sporting bandages on head and right arm but soldiering on despite his injuries. The controlled substances were now in a key-locked safe. Though two strong guys could probably lift it and carry off the whole thing, it deterred casual thieves.

Bash and the pharmacist tried to solve the thyroid med issue.

And so the day went, patient after patient, the emergency cases tapering off until there were mostly minor injuries sustained through trying to function in this strange new world, with no lights or electricity, with open cook fires, and people scrambling through the wrecks of their homes, trying to find enough supplies to survive the frigid nights and hungry days. He saw a kidney stone, a chest pain, a probable miscarriage. Pain was exacerbated, Bash suspected, by people trying to function without medication—including regular booze drinkers missing that. Pain might feel worse for other people poleaxed with grief.

And everyone was running out of adrenaline and the initial "we can do it" spirit. We're all understanding we *can't* do it, Bash thought, that we don't have the skills, that everything we once took for granted, like running water and flush toilets and telephones, is as lost to us as if we were time travelers visiting the Dark Ages.

He took a break mid-morning and checked with Dr. E. about the little girl from earlier, the one with the bigot father. "Did you see any signs of abuse?"

"Not physical. The guy's an ass, but I don't think he's beating her. She says her stomach hurts, but I'm relatively certain it's anxiety. She sure is skittish of him. And she misses her mommy."

"Thanks for stepping in."

"I'm sorry he yelled at you like that. You've been working your ass off for these people, and the last thing you deserve from them is abuse."

Bash felt his throat closing at the words of sympathy, but he steeled himself against the urge to well up. "I hope he didn't realize you're Jewish."

She snorted. "No shit."

"Ah well, Southern Missouri," said Bash with a shrug.

Dr. E studied him. "Have you had a day off yet?"

"Since the quake? No. I was on for—well, you saw me that

next morning—22 hours straight, a nap, then another six-hour shift. I've worked ten or twelve hours a day ever since."

"You need a break."

He felt a stab of guilt. "Am I screwing up?"

"No, no, not at all. We're just slowing down here, and there are staff who didn't start until the second afternoon or third morning. It's your turn for a day off. Past your turn."

"But can you staff it okay?"

"Let me worry about that. You go home today at lunch, and take tomorrow off too."

"Really?" Bash could feel relief washing through his body, heightening the exhaustion he'd been working overtime to ignore. He could feel himself wanting to collapse and nap right here. "You're sure?"

"I'm sure. We'll get it done without you for a day."

"Thank you."

"Unless there's another big quake, in which case I'll have to ask you to come right in. I'm sorry about that."

"Please, no more big quakes," he said. He wished he knew some effective magical sign to ward off bad luck when people said that. They all were thinking about it now after the second big quake, but he wished no one would say it aloud. It seemed like tempting fate. He realized that sort of superstition was another symptom of his emotional stress levels. Maybe he wasn't so different than the bigoted man in that way...though he'd never blame another human being for what was clearly a geological event.

When he got home, it was raining, a steady, light rain, and he had an urge he couldn't ignore. He stripped off his clothes in the kitchen, grabbed a bar of soap from the guest bathroom sink, and stood outside naked, taking the coldest shower of his life. He had to stand in the rain for a good five minutes to feel sufficient rinsed. Shivering, he checked the indoor-outdoor thermometer when he went in and it said it was 52 out there, 54 inside. The number made him shiver harder, but it felt great to be thoroughly clean, from his scalp on down. He took his clothes to the overflowing hamper and pulled out fresh jeans and a thick sweater.

Outside, the rain sped up, the pattering growing to a steady drumming, and he thought, Hell, there won't be a better chance for this. Quickly, he stripped both his and the girls' bed sheets, hurried to the laundry room and grabbed liquid detergent and bag of clothespins and ran outside. He set everything on a deck chair, strung the clothesline, and hung the sheets. Once they were thoroughly wet, he doused them with soap and squeezed it through the fabric. He left them hanging to be rinsed by the rain. It was a crazy way to do laundry, he thought, but you worked with what you had.

For the next two hours, he straightened the house with renewed energy. He dusted with a rag he dampened in the rain, cleaned up messes remaining from the second quake, picked at little pieces of paper and fluff on the carpet, and dug out boxes from the garage and packed away the few breakables that had survived two big quakes. He wouldn't risk them in a third. He took a broom to the kitchen and bathroom floors and wiped them with his damp dust rag. He made sure the plastic box by the latrine had plenty of toilet paper.

At quarter to three, he drove into the school to pick up the girls. The rain had let up, the kids were still in class, and so he parked and walked up to watch from a distance. McKenna sat with a group of other teens, writing in a notebook. Haruka was with a group of younger kids, maybe eight or nine years old, and as he wandered nearer, he could hear her giving them Japanese language lessons. Her voice was quiet and the kids attended closely to what she said. She held up a pencil, and the kids said something like "*enpitsu*" all together. Then she held up her notebook, and they said "*noto*," easy to understand. She stood and pointed to her chair. Bash smiled as he listened to the

LOU CADLE

children obediently naming items in Japanese.

A teacher in the distance blew a whistle three times and the kids all jumped up as one, happy as kids always were to hear the end-of-school bell. Bash waved hugely to get McKenna's attention—Haruka was listening to one of her charges. McKenna wound her way toward him and Bash felt a warm glow at the simple family moment. Soon the three of them were in the car.

"I want to get you girls more clothes. From your house, McKenna."

"It's pretty wrecked after the second quake."

"I know. But I'll do what I can, okay? Where is it again?"

When they got to McKenna's home and he saw the leaning walls, Bash almost changed his mind. But no, he wanted the girls to be as clean as he was now. It really improved the mood to be clean and have clean clothes, at least every other day.

"Where's your bedroom? Or did you each have your own?"

"I'll show you," said McKenna.

"No, just point it out or describe it. I'm going in alone."

"But I know where everything is."

"I need you two out here in case I get in trouble. If I do, you can go get the fire rescue guys to pull me out."

McKenna got the stubborn look he was getting to know well. But when he handed her his car keys, she relented.

"If I scream or you hear a crash, drive to get help. If I'm not out in twenty minutes, or if I don't answer your shouts, do it."

"Okay. Don't, like, paw around in my underwear for too long. That'd be disgusting. We should go around back," said McKenna. "There's a window with a broken lock."

At the back of the house, McKenna pointed to the window. Bash pushed at it, but it was well and truly stuck. The earthquakes had not totaled the house yet, but they had not been kind, either. The window may have been perfectly functional a week ago, but it was out of square now. "Is there something I can stand on? I need more leverage."

McKenna went to the back side of the detached garage and came back with a couple pieces of firewood. "We can stack some of this up, maybe."

"Okay. But I need more than that." And, he thought, we should take that wood with us. It could fuel the hibachi.

In ten minutes, they had a stable stack of wood piled under the window. Bash climbed onto it and pushed at the window. Nothing. He took a breath and went at it fast, *shoving* the thing. With a screech of wood against wood, it moved almost two inches. After two more hard shoves, it was open far enough for him to wriggle through. As he made it halfway, his bum catching against the window, he could hear Haruka stifling a giggle. He probably did look ridiculous. With an ungainly wiggle, he slipped inside.

The house was a mess. Plaster dust coated everything, and furniture had fallen. Small items littered the floor. He moved through the house, skirting broken glass, opening drapes and blinds to light his way. In McKenna's room, the roof had half-fallen, so that he had to carefully clamber over a lot of damp debris. At least the hole in the roof let light in.

Damn, he should have brought trash bags or something to carry the clothes. He dug around in the debris until he found pillows, stripped off the cases, which were slightly damp but not mildewed yet, and started pushing in what clean clothes he could find. He had to move fallen ceiling panels and a tangle of wiring to get the closet open, and he grabbed more clothes, grabbing up a skirt and finding a set of old sneakers on the floor. As he walked back with two full pillow cases, he could hear McKenna calling, "You okay?"

He popped his head out the open window. "I'm great. Sorry. Took longer than I thought it would." He handed out the pillowcases. "These are yours, McKenna. I'll go get Haruka's now."

The guest bedroom was in, if anything, worse shape, though

the roof was intact for now. Again he used pillowcases as luggage, packing clothes—she had many fewer than McKenna—and then a pile of small Japanese comic books that had slid off some surface or other and were scattered across the carpet. The closet door was stuck shut. He yanked at it and finally kicked it until it popped open. At the back of the closet, he found a suitcase with international flight stickers on it and grabbed that too. At some point, she'd get out of here and fly home, and at least he could get her one piece of the luggage she came with. As he transferred clothes into the suitcase, he wondered where her passport was. He should find it now.

An aftershock hit and he froze, glancing around for someplace to dive under, but there was only the bed, too low for a grown man to crawl beneath. He braced in the closet doorframe, knowing it for poor protection, and waited there, tense and poised to run, as the house rattled around him.

The rattling quieted and he felt the tension ease out of his body. Bash stepped back into the room and, with a crash, a chunk of ceiling fell. He heard the rending sound of splitting wood and a beam began to fall.

Bash leapt to the side with more agility than he knew he had. The shattered beam fell, barely missing him. It was still attached at the far end of the room. It left a triangular space with just enough room for him to crawl through. Looking out at the crushed bed, he realized how close he had come to dying.

Shakily, he stood, gathered up the suitcase and pillowcase—screw the passport, he wasn't staying in here one second longer. He could hear the girls calling to him, and he hurried back through the house to the window. A new crack bisected the window glass.

"We were worried," Haruka said.

"We heard the crash. You hurt?" McKenna asked.

"I'll live," he said. "Glad to see you didn't take my car and go joyriding."

"As if," she said.

"Let's get home and make something great for dinner."

"Maybe we should go by the hospital? You're bleeding." She pointed to his head.

He touched his head and looked at his fingers. Blood, yes. He swiped his palm across his head and looked again. It wasn't much. "I can fix myself up at home just as well."

"If you say so," said McKenna. "By the way, I hate that skirt you brought."

He shook his head at her. "Deal with it. Let's take your firewood with us."

"We'll get it. You just sit in the car and rest."

He was relieved that by the time the trunk was loaded, his adrenaline shakiness has ebbed. He was able to drive the girls home.

Back at the house, he set them to the task of trying to get a fire going in the hibachi with the wood while he doctored himself. The bleeding had slowed to a trickle. He had been lucky, he knew, and he swore to himself never to enter a damaged building again.

Moving between the kitchen and emergency supplies still in the garage, he looked through their food and tried to come up with an interesting meal. He finally decided on canned ham, one of the last bits of meat in the emergency supplies, and if they had a fire, he'd even make a glaze from canned pineapple in syrup. If not, cold canned pineapple on the side. Canned peas with baby onions, which would taste much better warm than cold. After his close call this afternoon, he wanted a decent meal. If the girls could get a fire going in the hibachi, he'd heat the peas. Otherwise, more cold mashed potatoes. It'd be a feast compared to some of their meals.

When Gale got home and got a look at his bandaged head, he demanded to know what had happened. When he learned Bash had gone into a wrecked house just for clothes, he freaked. It took many minutes to reassure him that no, he wouldn't do anything that stupid again. If the girls weren't around, the argument might have gone on for longer.

He called everyone to dinner and was pleased to see McKenna arrive in the skirt. "You look lovely," he said.

"Well, you could have died getting it for me," she said.

"It wasn't that bad," he said, not wanting her to set off Gale again.

"So not to wear it would make me some kind of ingrate," McKenna said. "Please pass the peas."

He was almost full after the meal. That feeling lasted about a half-hour, and then the hunger crept back. By the time he was in bed, it was a vicious burning in his belly, and he could easily have eaten another whole meal just like dinner.

"Hunger sucks," he said, punching his pillow.

"I know, hon. Go to sleep and you won't feel it," said Gale.

Eventually, he did.

Chapter 16

Gale

The media visit had worked, Gale thought, and with a vengeance. That Friday, a crew comprised of state, federal, and Red Cross workers descended on them just before 9:00 a.m. With only about 13,000 people left in town, and over 60 new staff and volunteers, it averaged out to a new relief worker for every 200 citizens. Helicopters discharged staff, equipment, and more staff, all morning long. There were new medical workers, communications workers, counselors, administrators, and a structural engineer.

It didn't take long that morning for Gale to realize he was living inside one of those Chinese curses, like "be careful what you wish for," though, come to think of it, he didn't think that one was actually Chinese. He rubbed the bridge of his nose, willing an encroaching headache away.

Megan and Kay walked up to him, Megan red-faced. "They're telling me I'm doing it all wrong!" she said.

"I know." It wasn't the first such complaint he'd heard. "I think they're late for their annual sensitivity training update."

"It's not funny," she said. "Vinya was in tears."

"Damn it." Oops, had he said that aloud? He had to be more

circumspect than that. "I'll talk to her."

Kay waved it off, saying, "We have that covered. You talk to *them*."

"I will." He needed to somehow get control of this, or the situation would deteriorate quickly. "You know, though, that the Red Cross will be doling out money. That's nothing to sneeze at."

"What good is money?" said Kay. "Can you eat it? Can it keep you warm?"

Megan said, "It's not as if our ATM cards work. I've heard a rumor that the whole country's banking system is screwed up from this."

With City Hall a shambles, Gale wondered, was someone out there recording his automatic pay deposits every two weeks? As far as he knew, all city operating funds were frozen, or spent.

Jeanine came over to join them, interrupting his meandering thoughts, and said, "Megan, George is on the radio. Or Gale, maybe you should take it. Seems *someone* ordered him off the channel." She darted a hostile glance over to a Red Cross worker.

"Gals, realize, we're late to the assistance table here. After more than a week, we may be getting one of the less trained, less experienced teams. The experts are probably all in St. Louis or Memphis. In any case, we'll have to figure out a way to work together."

Megan, still flushed with anger, said, "But they're trying to take over! We had it under control. We're getting things done, our way, and they have all these—" She waved her hands around, searching for a word. "*Procedures*," she said, over-enunciating every syllable.

"I know," he said. "I'll...." He really didn't know what to do first. The head Red Cross person, a high-energy older woman named Phyllis Hambrick, was over at the hospital, possibly driving them nuts too. "I'll talk to George first."

He got on the radio and said, "George, it's Gale, over."

"What the heck is going on up there?"

"We got some new help. There's a team of government staff and volunteers from the Red Cross now."

"Who don't know their heads from their patooties, over," said George.

"I'm sorry. I should have warned you before they came in. I think they have their own protocols and regulations and ways of doing things."

"We have ours too. We've been getting by."

"We have. You've been great, you and Marilyn both. I don't know what I or this city would have done without you." That wasn't just appeasement. He meant it. "Can you lay low for a little bit?" He hated to ask it. "I mean, just stay off the airwaves, take an hour break or so, and I'll get it sorted out. And." He reconsidered. "F—scratch that. Come in here, both of you. We'll meet face to face and deal with it right now. Can you get here?"

"We'll be there in a half hour. Out."

It was not a fun half-hour. Of course, there hadn't been any fun at all in days, just putting out figurative fire after fire, working with too little equipment too few staff, and impossible challenges, but his staff had been getting along all right, with damned few arguments between them, even though they were worn to a frazzle. Citizens were getting angrier, though. Inevitably, that anger spread to his staff.

And so the stress levels were rising faster, as people who had once been friends and neighbors turned on the very people who were sacrificing sleep and sanity to help them. He wished, selfishly, that Evelyn had lived and this was her problem.

But it wasn't. It was his.

He got on the radio to Flint and Dan and invited them to the meeting as a courtesy. Flint said he might send someone to listen in. Dan just said, "Nope. Let me know if anything changes on my end." Gale tried to get the Red Cross supervisor on the radio. When he couldn't, he decided to drive over and haul her back.

"Kay, you're in charge. I want most of these newcomers at the

meeting. Get them gathered and tie them to seats if you have to."
Kay was good, but he missed Angela. He hadn't seen her for days
now. Where the hell was she? Dead? Trapped somewhere? No, by
now if she were trapped, she'd have died. Lost? Murdered? Ran
away? No time to worry about that, either. He made his way to
the hospital and hunted down Ms. Hambrick.

Forty minutes later he was looking out at a sea of faces at the
EOC. The ones he knew were lined with stress, topped by greasy
unwashed hair, and there was more than one set of arms folded
stubbornly across the chest. These were mightily irritated people.

The new relief workers, on the other hand, were well-scrubbed
and energetic-looking. They were curious, not pissed. But that
probably wouldn't last for long.

He turned on the bullhorn someone had found for him
several days ago, but which he had seldom needed to use. "First,
we want to thank our new team members for showing up and
taking some of the load off our shoulders. There's not a worker
here who isn't tired and ready for a break. So, welcome, and
thank you, especially those of you who are volunteering to help
complete strangers." He put down the bullhorn and applauded.
The more polite of his staff joined him, but no one would call the
sound enthusiastic.

"And if I haven't said it enough in the past week, let me tell
the city staff that you've been wonderful. You've taught yourself
brand new areas of expertise and gotten competent on the fly,
under the toughest of conditions. You've helped keep your
neighbors fed and housed and safe. With our terrific Fire and
Police Departments, we've rescued who we could. And we've
done as well as is humanly possible with burials, being respectful
but also taking care of public health by expediting the burial of so
many thousands of our friends and family.

"So now we all—the new and the old—have to learn to work
together. The new people have their ways. The staff have their
own. We need to remember that the most important thing is

keeping as many people as possible safe, dry, fed, and healthy. There's so much to do in recovery, and we'll be working together not just for days, but for months and years. Rebuilding a city this torn is a long-term job. We need help. We need money. We need expertise. We have a lot of that available, now. There are people here who know the city and what our neighbors want and need. There are people here who know disaster relief inside and out. Please, let's work together."

He hesitated. "I know there's some resentment building up today. I know that's normal too. I've had disaster training, and I promise you, every local group hates the new people at first." There were a few chuckles, mostly from the out-of-towners. "And I know that no one who hasn't lived through two huge quakes, and a hundred aftershocks, and the death of people they care about, like Evelyn, and the disappearance of others, like Angela, can't quite understand what it feels like to experience all that and work long hours and try to fuel that effort with sleeping on the cold hard ground and too little food.

"I know it doesn't feel like we have time to spend at a long meeting right now, but I want to call you up and have you talk about what it has been like for you—either here in the thick of it, or preparing to come in to help. " He glanced out. "Oscar, you're an eloquent guy. Come on over here and say something."

He let Oscar talk for almost ten minutes, then thanked him and called up an EPA worker with a lanyard around his neck who talked about the chemicals in the river and trying to protect people against long-term effects, which he understood was not at the top of their minds right now. He talked about the years it would take to clean up the river, and what measures he'd like to put into place now and how if they skipped over this work they'd regret it five or ten years down the road, when their kids started getting rare cancers.

Next Gale called George over and handed him the bullhorn. Back and forth, using a full hour he would have loved to use in some other way, letting a few people from each side talk. He learned something about his own people. Vinya had lost a sister in the first quake—but until now he hadn't heard her say a word about it. George referred to his days in cryptology back in the service—Gale hadn't even known he was a veteran.

"Can I ask all of us—old and new—to come together in a spirit of harmony. We all want the same things—the most people alive, the most people healthy, the most people fed. We want our city back, as soon as we can have it, and our homes, whole once again. The people who arrived this morning want that. They do want to help. What I'd love to see is some assumption of good will on everyone's part, appreciation for what the other guys knows, and cooperation. And a chance for my staff to work a few eight-hour days for a change. Come talk to me if you have individual issues. Now let's all get back to work." He turned off the bullhorn. "George, if you and Marilyn can come over here, I'd like to introduce you to some radio people from the Red Cross."

He started with them because he knew how to approach this one meeting. All he had to do was show George some of the bells and whistles on the radio equipment being set up, and he knew George's curiosity would overcome his resentment of being supplanted as the lead radio guy for the town. After ten minutes, he was able to leave George and Marilyn and the two guys, both volunteers who had flown in that morning, geek-chatting their way to cooperation.

The next two hours he spent reassuring people, one by one, group by group, acting by turns as mediator and supervisor, grateful disaster victim and no-nonsense leader. He tried to remind himself to listen rather than let his mind wander to his to-do list, which only got longer as he dealt with the human element, and to thank people profusely.

He really just wanted to be efficient, to get things done already, and forget all the massaging of egos. But the way things got done, he knew, was to first massage the egos, and once everyone was well-massaged, feathers unruffled, they'd be more likely to work well. In some cases, he succeeded. In some cases, he gave himself a "D" on his work. With Vinya, he wasn't sure she'd come out of her hurt mood for several days.

By mid-afternoon, he was desperate for someone to come and massage his own ego and unruffle his feathers. His face ached from forcing smiles and concerned, interested, listen-y expressions onto it. He wanted a vacation, a month's vacation. But even a day. Bash had gotten a day off—why couldn't he? He recognized the inner tone of that question as a whiny child's, and he tried to shut it down.

As the sun inched down toward the horizon that afternoon, his shoulders were hunched, his smile felt strained, and his head was pounding. Did they have some Vicodin at home, or anything stronger than aspirin? He wanted to knock himself out. Go home, choke down more potato flakes, and sleep for ten hours without moving.

But he couldn't. He still had to help get the new people set up with a place to sleep. They'd brought blankets and cots for a hundred, so he set Oscar's teenagers to setting those up. The rain had backed off yesterday, but it was still cold. Was it November yet? He honestly couldn't remember. Without TV news, the internet, or an office calendar, a person lost track. But what were day and month names anyway? There was only each challenging hour, and the next, and the next.

Once the cots were half set up, he realized he'd need another shelter, a tent or roof. What he really needed was a Quonset hut, now that autumn was full upon them. He needed to ask—uh, he wasn't sure who to ask. Corps of engineers seemed overkill for such a minor request. He'd ask around these Red Cross people how you could get one.

The cots got his own staff off the ground too, which he was grateful for, though he wondered if wind whistling under a cot was really any warmer than just lying on the ground. Not for the first time—hell, not for the first time that day—he realized how lucky he and Bash were to have a standing house.

When the head state guy had to repeat something he'd said three times for Gale to understand it, Gale said, "I'm not tracking. I'm sorry."

"You must be exhausted. Not what you thought you'd be doing when you signed on as City Manager, I'm sure."

"I'm not even the City Manager. I'm the flippin' Planner. My worst worry ten days ago was trying to convince people to toughen earthquake standards in our zoning laws."

"I think they're convinced," he said, wryly.

"Will the state adopt the California standards now, you think?"

"If they do it fast, before they forget. The dollar figures for the loss will convince where warnings didn't. It'll cost—hell, we don't know—say thirty billion dollars in just our state to minimally rebuild. It would have cost a fraction of that to retrofit, and nothing at all to mandate safer new construction."

"Where's all that money going to come from?"

"It's not. I mean, we don't have it. The federal government doesn't have it, and they can't charge a 10% extra income tax across the board next year, can they? People in Vermont or New Mexico won't stand for that. The stock market has taken a terrible hit, and insurance stocks are—well, you don't want to know. But you know who's probably the most worried?"

"Who?"

"People in California. Whatever it takes to rebuild the Midwest after this, there's going to be less willing to do it all over again when L.A. or San Francisco gets hammered in a few years." He shook his head. "But I'm keeping you here. You look done in, man. Go and get some rest."

On the way home, he realized that the best part of the influx of new people might be that he had strangers seeing firsthand the increasing desperation of their food and water situation. A week on shorter and shorter rations, a week without a shower, and he'd have several people with real connections demanding action. State, federal, Red Cross voices added to his own had already won a promise from the state to clear roads sooner.

I

Chapter 17

Gale and Bash

But a week later despite the outside help and louder pleas, the town was not much better off. They had gotten a few more supplies, but the public frustration was mounting. Incidents of violence were on the increase.

The police and fire squads were in slightly better shape than the average citizen. They were still getting allotted 1500 calories of food per day. The adults at the tent cities were down to half that. Most people had never been hungrier than what one got on three weeks of a half-assed stab at a New Year's diet. And with a self-imposed diet, you knew that somewhere out there, ten minutes away, there was a big bag of chips, if you really wanted it. Not here, not now. People were finding hunger very unpleasant indeed, and fights had even broken out over bags of the dreaded potato flakes.

Gale sympathized. He had dreamt one night about his friends and workers turning into potato flakes, big shambling yellowish flaky hulks of people speaking with eerily familiar voices. With a crack of thunder, rain had begun falling, and when potato-flake Bash started melting, he had jolted awake with a pounding heart, relieved when he reached out for his husband and found him still there.

More people would have walked toward Rolla, but without food to fuel them, the Red Cross had talked people with children out of making the attempt, while promising more food that didn't arrive. Every day, a few adults without little ones gave up hope of staying and wandered off to the west. The ones who were left were demanding more food and growing angrier with each passing mealtime that they weren't being fed enough.

There was a groundswell of talk of holding an emergency election, to get a new mayor to make the town leaders do more. Gale didn't protest that idea one bit. He knew he was doing everything humanly possible. He'd love a mayor—would cast his vote for anyone stupid enough to run. Let someone else take the blame for the lack of resources. Let someone else be the public face of failure.

* * *

At the hospital, Bash was seeing an increase in injuries sustained in fights, an increase in psychological problems, and more vague pain complaints that he suspected had mental rather than physical bases.

At lunch break, he had a chance to discuss it with Dr. Eisenstein. "Too bad we can't get a big load of tranqs to dump in the town water supply," she said. "Everybody could use a day off stress."

Bash said, "Especially over what we can't control anyway. That's the worst for me, feeling as if I can't do anything to help myself. It must be awful for parents, being unable to help their kids."

"How are those girls holding up?"

"Surprisingly well. They'd both love to talk to their parents, but that's just not possible, or everyone in town would start demanding radio time. Haruka hasn't spoken directly to hers at all yet."

"You know when the cell service might be working? Special inside knowledge from your husband?"

"Honestly, I don't think it's the top priority. Water, food, levees, latrines, better shelter, fuel. Those are still taking up most of his time. Hey, how's that compartment injury from this morning?"

"Holding out for evac if—what the hell?" Dr. E said, looking over his shoulder.

Bash turned and saw a group of people coming around the corner a block up, marching. They were singing. Two in front held a banner made out of a sheet—Bash's mind flashed on how that sheet could be better put to use.

The song resolved itself in his mind—Onward Christian Soldiers. WTF?

"Uh-oh," said Dr. E. "Maybe you should make yourself scarce."

"What?" he said.

"Look at the sign. No, don't. Go, get lost back there in the patients."

Bash squinted, thinking, I think I need some eyeglasses. Then the words on the banner resolved itself. "Homos must go."

Shit.

He wanted to make a stand, but he knew such people were beyond reasoning with. And with the angry mood in town lately...he pivoted and wove back through the patients, back from the street, until he was at the pharmacy tent. He ducked in and took a seat in a folding chair, hunkering down.

"Need something?" the pharmacist said.

"No, just taking a break."

He peered out toward the front of the hospital where the protestors were being stood off by Dr. E and the auxiliary police officer. A man in cleric's collar was waving a book—Bible, no doubt—and shouting, but Bash couldn't make out any words.

The crowd behind the Bible-wielder surged, and Bash could hear more voices raised in anger.

Maybe he should get out of here. Make it to his car. Run and hide in the rubble along hospital row.

Just as the thought crossed his mind, he saw a man he recognized—the angry bigot father of that little girl, the troglodyte—grab Dr. E by the throat and start to shake her.

The auxiliary cop grabbed the man's arm, shouting. Bash was out of his chair, running forward to help Dr E before he could think.

And then all hell broke loose.

A protester waded forward to punch the auxiliary cop, and then another and another. Dr. E was lost in a crowd. Some of the other protestors fell back from the violence, but a dozen leapt forward. A few peeled off and began to upend chairs. The receptionist screamed, and one went over and threw over her table, knocking her off the chair.

Patients and visitors stood up, some shouting. Some tried to get away. A few tried to stop what was clearly a riot in the making.

Bash stood rooted to the spot, watching, horrified. A man spun out from the central knot of violence and staggered. He caught himself, looked around, and caught sight of Bash.

It was the troglodyte father. He pointed at Bash. "There he is."

Bash turned and ran in the clearest direction he could see. He didn't plan. It was an animal stampede of pure unthinking terror. By the time his mind came back to him, he was on the street, running for his life, with at least a dozen people running after him, a half-block back. He could hear shouts and the sound of breaking glass behind him. He spared a thought of concern for Dr. E, but he kept running.

He realized the best thing to do was to lead this part of the mob away from the hospital, away from Dr. E and the innocent patients. If they caught up to Bash, he was in bad trouble. But the innocent didn't need to get hurt along with him.

He heard the thumping sound of a helicopter behind him. He could hear the crowd too, their yells, the word "faggot" and the word "God." The chopper noise built and, with a roar, the medical evac helicopter swooped over his head, spinning dust into his eyes.

Though blurry vision, he saw the chopper about to land in the street, a half-block ahead. He thought, Get out of my way, damn you. And then he saw the medic at the open door, waving at him. Waving him inside.

The crowd hot on his heels, Bash put on a last burst of speed and ran for the medic. Just as he leapt for the door and grabbed at its edges, he felt it lifting. He hauled himself half in, grabbed for the seat. His feet scrambled for purchase. He could feel the chopper lifting. The medic grabbed the collar of his scrubs and shouted something at him, lost in the noise of the rotor.

Bash screamed, "Help!" as the engine noise went up in pitch. He could feel the thing swing around and rise more, with him barely hanging on. His feet scrambled for purchase on the side of the machine.

His grip slipped, and he thought he'd fall, flashing on Gale and how torn up he'd be. He was accepting that he was about to be horribly injured, just as his feet found the landing skids. His hands caught the door. Hanging on in the open door, feeling the medic hanging on to his scrubs, Bash tried not to look down. The chopper skimmed thirty feet above the street, away from the angry mob.

All things considered, he thought, I'd rather die in a three-story fall from a moving helicopter than be torn limb from limb by a mob of crazed bigots. He closed his eyes and put all his energy into hanging on.

Long, tense seconds later he sensed the chopper coming down. The engine noise changed pitch, and he felt the bump as the thing landed. He opened his eyes to see a bare field under them, stubbles of corn against damp dark soil. Farmland, so they had to be at least a mile from the hospital.

The medic helped him scramble into the front seat next to the pilot. "Belt in," he heard someone say. It took him a few moments to figure out the seat harness, but he finally got it. With shaking hands, he snapped himself in. Someone behind him handed him a headset and he slapped it on.

The pilot was talking to him. "What was going on down there? They were chasing you?"

"They hate me because I'm gay. Some religious people," said Bash.

"Christ," said the pilot. "Idiots. Anybody with half a brain knows that if your religion preaches hatred, it's the wrong religion."

Another voice, the medic's, came on. "We were supposed to pick up an injury."

"Right," said Bash. "A compartment injury. She needs to get out today."

"We'll get you someplace safe first," said the pilot. "Where to?"

Bash's mind was reeling with fear, still, and it took him a few seconds to an answer. "There's a landing site at the Walmart parking lot, about a mile due south of here, next to the city government. It's where supplies are brought in. Go there."

He had to direct the pilot toward the interstate, and then he followed it until Bash saw the Walmart and the tents of the EOC. "Right there."

The pilot landed the machine, and he thanked both him and medic profusely.

When he got out, he ran over to the center of the EOC and said to the radio operator, "You have to get the police to the hospital. There's a riot."

Then Gale was there, and he was in his arms, safe. The relief made him cry, and the fear he had felt came out in gulping sobs.

"What?" Gale was saying. "What's wrong? What is it?"

Bash pulled himself together, wiped his face, and told him what had happened at the hospital.

Gale's face turned to stone. "I'll kill them. I swear."

"They'll kill you, more than likely. There's two of us and dozens of them."

A nearby fat woman said, "There's more than two of you. We all have your back."

"I have to talk to Flint," said Gale.

"We should get safe," said Bash. "You didn't see them. They might know about you. They could come here next."

Gale was clearly torn. "All right. Let's go."

"Let's go home."

"If it isn't safe here, it's even less safe there." He turned to the fat woman. "You have the EOC."

"Sure. Just take care of your fella."

Gale led him over to his car. They drove away from the EOC. Gale seemed to know where he was going.

"What are we going to do? Do you think it'll pass, or...?"

"I won't take that chance with you. As of now you are retired from public service in this town."

Bash said, "The girls! Oh no, do you think they're at risk?"

"No. They're at the school with a hundred people or more around them. But I'll make sure they're okay. Just as soon as you're safe."

"Will I be safe until we can get out of this town?"

"Same old argument," said Gale, but his voice was kind and he smiled at Bash.

He appreciated the effort. "This may admittedly be a little worse than not having anyone to invite to a brunch."

"A little," said Gale.

Bash managed the first deep breath he'd been able to take in ten minutes. "Shit, Gale, I thought I was going to die. You should have seen them."

"I'd like to see them," Gale said, "with my new gun in my hand."

"Don't even think such a thing."

"I can't help it."

"I'm safe. Let's try not to make it any worse."

"They'll see justice. I'll make sure of that."

"Fine. Just don't get yourself hurt doing it."

The car pulled over in front of a frame house, and Gale looked in the rearview mirror, then all around them. "Wait here. If you see anyone, duck down out of sight."

"Where are we?" asked Bash, but Gale was already out of the car and halfway to the front door. He knocked on it, and it opened. Bash tried to see in but couldn't. After a short conversation, Gale trotted back to the car and motioned Bash out. Then he rushed him up the walk and into the open front door. It shut with a squeak behind them.

"Bash, George. George, this is my husband, Bash."

Bash shook hands as a woman came in through a back entrance.

Gale said, "And this is Marilyn. They're the ham radio people I've told you about."

"Of course," said Bash. "So nice to meet you."

George said to Marilyn, "Sweetie, they need our help."

Gale explained to the woman what had happened. "I need someplace to hide Bash. I thought no one would guess he's here. I don't trust that he's safe at our house. Not today. Not tonight. Maybe not for awhile."

"Of course," Marilyn said. "We'd be happy to help. We even have a spare bedroom, if you don't mind sharing it with some boxes of radio parts."

Bash said, "You're too kind." He turned to Gale. "You really don't think they'd come to our house?"

"I know they would."

"But won't they be arrested?"

"If I have anything to say about it," said Gale. "But others will get away, and there may be others out there just as hateful and dangerous."

"If I'm not safe, you're not safe. And you're more visible. Surely you won't keep working?"

"I have to."

A wave of weakness swept over Bash. "Do you mind if I sit?" he asked Marilyn.

"Of course. Here," she said, pointing him to an easy chair.

Bash collapsed into it and took some deep breaths.

"I'll get you both some coffee," said Marilyn. "You look like you could use it."

"Try and get Flint on the radio, please," said Gale to George.

Bash rested his eyes, trying to calm his nerves. He was just feeling a full reaction, now having a chance to think about what had nearly happened to him. A wave of guilt over damage done to the hospital swept over him. But no, that wasn't right. It wasn't his fault, not at all. It was *theirs*. All he had been doing was his job.

He felt a touch on his shoulder and looked up to see Marilyn offering him a steaming cup. "Instant coffee," she said.

"Thank you." He reached for the hot drink and cradled it in his hands, oddly comforted by the heat coming off the crockery and into his fingers. "You're awfully nice to offer to help out."

"We're happy to. We really like Gale," she said.

He took a sip of the coffee. It tasted stale and flat, but it was somehow reassuring to drink something warm. He shivered. "Do you have an afghan or blanket? I'm sorry to bother you, but I'm a little—" He wasn't sure what. Weak. Faint. Aftermath of the jolt of adrenaline.

She left the room and came back with a fleece throw. "Here you go."

He pulled it over his chest and arms and focused his attention on Gale, talking into the radio about the attack on him at the hospital, his anger obvious in his clipped words. When he signed off, the three of them stood around Bash's chair.

Gale said, "The riot's contained. He'll do what he can arresting people. He's happy to hold people for a day or two, just to cool them off, even if there's not a reasonable charge to make against some of them."

"Fools," said George.

Gale looked at the man. "I don't feel good about imposing on you. If it gets out that Bash is here...." He shook his head. Turning to Bash, he said, "I think we should get you out on the last evac helicopter today. Or on the supply helicopter tomorrow morning, at the latest."

"I don't want to leave you." He set his coffee cup on a nearby table. "I *won't* leave you."

"We can keep him well hidden here," said Marilyn. "Like as not, this thing at the hospital will blow over."

"I hope," said Gale. "But people are hungry, and angry, and irrational, and wanting to blame someone."

"Nonsense," she said. "There's no one *to* blame."

"Gale," said Bash, "what about the girls?"

"We're going to need to find another place for them to stay, that's for sure."

"They can stay here," said Marilyn.

Gale was shaking his head. "No. They need to not even know where Bash is."

"They wouldn't tell those people," said Bash.

"Not on purpose. They're teenage girls, though. They might let something slip. And if they are seen coming and going from here, it'll get around."

"I can't just let them go."

"I'm afraid you're going to have to. For their sake. For your own."

Bash couldn't stop the tears from welling up. "Can't I talk to them? Explain?"

"I'll explain to them. They'll understand, I think."

All the things that might happen flashed through Bash's mind. Another quake. The girls getting hurt, or worse. He himself getting out without ever being able to say goodbye to them. He grabbed his forehead with both palms and pressed hard. "Haven't we all been through enough?"

Gale settled on the arm of the chair and put an arm around him. "I'm sorry. I want to keep everyone safe. Your being here needs to be a secret. We need to work to keep it that way."

"So someone else commits a crime, and I'm in prison." He glanced at Marilyn. "I'm sorry, I didn't mean—"

She waved it away. "I know what you mean, and no, it's not fair."

He looked over at Gale. "We should both leave."

"I...." Gale looked torn. "I have a job to finish. I don't feel that I can just abandon it."

"When will it be finished? A week? A month? Three years?"

"I don't know." He looked miserable. "I need to at least solve the food and water problems, get some steady supply lines set up so that people don't starve to death over the winter here."

"Even the people who would happily tar and feather you for being gay?"

"Even them," he said.

Gale left soon after, nothing really decided between them, except that he promised Bash to sleep at the EOC where plenty of people would be around to defend him if there were another attack. It wasn't until the next morning and his call into FEMA that he made a decision about their immediate future.

"We'll both leave in two days," he said to Bash after the call. "We'll walk out. The Corps has gotten a channel clear in the river, and there'll be food, and heaters, and more tents barged in. Propane, personal water filters, and some equipment the water treatment facility needs to get water flowing down the mains again. Once the barge is unloaded, and distribution of the food set up, I promise you, we can walk out of here."

"How far?"

George turned from his radio and said, "They have roads cleared to about twenty miles from here now. It's not an awful walk. Two days at most should get you there."

Two days. Two days to freedom and safety, to hot showers and plenty of food. "Yes," said Bash. "I want to. And you'll come too. You promise?"

Gale nodded. "I promise. I've done my best for the city. Now I need to do my best for us."

Chapter 18

Gale

What Gale hadn't told Bash was that Flint had assigned a team of two officers with assault weapons to protect the EOC, day and night.

"Hell, I should have done it sooner," he said, "as the EOC is so important to the town. Fire station too—we'll keep a pair of men there, as well."

Gale didn't like it, while he admitted the need for it. He hated to see the town turn into an armed camp, with martial law. But as people got more unruly, more dangerous, there really was no other choice. Flint personally had taken him back to the house to gather clothes for himself, Bash, and the girls' things, waiting outside, in uniform, his hand never far from his gun.

Gale also hadn't told Bash about his conversation with the girls, when he went to pick them up after school the day of the attack on Bash and had taken them to their new home, to the sister of one of his staff who had a pull-out couch available in an intact house. He handed over half his remaining food supplies to the family, so it wouldn't be more of a burden than it was.

McKenna had tried every trick—and she knew a few—of wheedling, whining, and threatening, to get him to take her to

Bash. Haruka just looked at him with sad eyes, which was worse. He had driven up to their new place and helped them unload their clothes from his car.

"We'll come say goodbye before we leave."

"You're leaving?" said McKenna. "Then take us with you!"

"It's not safe," he tried to explain. "You need to stay away from us."

"Goddammit," she said, throwing her bag down on the sidewalk.

"I'm sorry. It's for the best."

"I'll find him."

"No, McKenna. Please. Don't even look. Don't ask around. You'll be putting his life at risk."

"Then just tell me. I wouldn't tell those people."

"I know you wouldn't. But it's a small town, really small now, and news has a way of getting around fast."

"You don't trust me."

"I trust you. I do. It's them I don't trust." He gestured vaguely down the street at the people he knew were out there, hating him and Bash, blaming them for matters beyond their control. "Let's get you inside and settled." No purpose was being served by continuing to argue with the girl, and he had to get back to work. If he was leaving in a day and a half, there was a lot of delegating to do first.

That night, at the EOC, in the wee hours, Gale was woken from a troubled sleep by, of all unexpected people, Dan.

"Gale."

He came fully awake. "What it is? Is it Bash?"

"I'm sorry. Your house is on fire. Arson."

"Shit." He kicked off his blanket and got up. "What can I do?"

"There's nothing anyone can do. You know we don't have water."

"Take me there."

"Yeah, I will. But you do what my guys tell you. Don't go running in trying to save stuff."

"I know, I know."

Dan drove him in an official city car through the dark streets to his house, the home that he'd selected so carefully for its safety. Not very safe now, was it?

He could see the light of the fire from two blocks away, shooting fingers of light into the black sky.

As they pulled up a few doors down, he could see the flames licking up the sides. Half of the house was burned through, a smoldering ruin. He thought of everything lost, photos and memories of their marriage. Clothes and books and important papers. A life burning down to ruin.

Behind the smoke, the crescent moon shone orange. Gale couldn't watch any more. He turned away and walked back to the chief's car, leaning both arms on the side and feeling dark despair.

Dan came up. "You've done so much for these people. For the city." His voice shook with anger.

Gale looked up. "Never seen you pissed off before."

"You have. But I'm beyond pissed now."

"Are any other houses at risk?"

"Almost no wind. We got some luck there. And you have a big lot."

"Yeah, it's a double. Was a double." He sighed, feeling all the weariness from the last half-month of effort settling on his shoulders. "How am I going to tell Bash?"

"He doesn't deserve this, either."

"I have to be the one to tell him." He glanced once more at the fire, burning lower now, then away. "Should I wake him up? Or let him sleep?"

"I don't know, man. I don't know what I'd do in your shoes."

He looked at his watch. Just after three. "I guess I'll wake him up around six. I don't want him to hear from anyone else but me."

Dan drove him back to the EOC. Gale checked in with the staff awake this early—or this late—and then drove around town for an hour, wasting gas, he knew, but right now he didn't care. He looked at the intact houses, at the fallen ones, at the distant humps of tents at the tent cities, and he wondered which of these people hated him and Bash so much that they'd burn down their house. He found himself parking in front of a fundamentalist church and staring at it, trying to see through the white walls to whatever was in there that stirred such hate.

He thought of everything it took to build a house—plans, people felling timber somewhere, the timber being shipped, pipe being manufactured, wire extruded, the hundreds and hundreds of people who worked together to make the things that others built into a house, the care of furnishing and decorating it, thousands of hours of labor. And one idiot turns it into ash in the space of a couple hours.

At quarter to six, he pulled up to George and Marilyn's house on the darkened street. He made his way to the front door, and he knocked. When no one answered, he went to the windows and began knocking on those, saying, "It's me, Gale." He went back to the front door to wait, and a few minutes later Marilyn pushed the door open.

She was in a flowered robe, barefoot. "Is something wrong?"

"Not anything big, no. Not big to anyone but me. It's personal. I need to see Bash."

She led him to the spare bedroom, where amongst all the boxes of equipment, Bash was sitting up in bed, wearing a sweatshirt.

"Give us a minute," Gale said to Marilyn, and she murmured about coffee and left them alone.

He sat on the edge of the bed and took Bash's hand. "Our house is gone."

"Oh my gosh. Did it collapse?"

"No." In two short sentences, he told him about the arson.

"Did they get the fire put out?"

"There's no water, Bash."

"Right. Stupid me."

"You're not stupid."

"We have to get out of this place."

"We will. Tomorrow, noon at the latest, we're going to be walking out of town. I promise."

"But. But our things! How will we get our things out?"

"All gone, sweetheart." Ashes.

"Gone." He shook his head, dazed.

Gale could see it'd take the news a couple minutes to really sink in. He watched Bash and waited.

"Our wedding pictures?"

"They're mostly backed up online too."

"But...everything?"

Gale nodded.

"Oh. At least you weren't there. Or the girls."

Gale pulled his husband into his arms, and they mourned together until gray morning light began to filter in.

The last day, he thought. Let me get the barge unloaded today, and arrange getting the goods out to those who need them, and it'll be done.

Chapter 19

Gale

At the morning meeting of the Triumvirate, held at the police station for safety's sake, he handed in an official, hand-written resignation. The other men accepted it, with frowns and shaking heads, but they didn't try to argue him out of quitting—or leaving. "Who's best to replace you?"

"Kay, the city clerk. I talked to her about it last night, and she's okay with it. Nervous, but willing to step up. She's been my back up since Angela disappeared."

"Yeah, Kay Perkins, I know her," said Dan.

"The town will miss you," said Flint.

Gale moved them on to other business, and they began talking about curfews and martial law, just how far they should go to control the violent part of the populace, when Kay called him on his handheld radio.

"The barge has an ETA now," she said. "Nine-thirty, just upriver of the bridge." All the men checked their wristwatches.

"Thanks, Kay," he said. "Over and out."

Flint stood. "We should get over right now and set up for that. I'm putting every man I can spare on crowd control."

Dan said, "I'll get the trucks down there to load the goods."

Gale said, "I'll radio water treatment, so they can come and get their equipment. Start fixing the system first thing." With that repair done in a few days, he thought the city could survive. People could eat light rations for months, but no one can live without water.

Despite everything, he still felt guilt at leaving town, felt he was leaving a job only half-finished. But he couldn't put his and Bash's lives at risk here any longer. It didn't matter if it was only half a percent of the population who wished them ill. Only two people were in jail from the riot at the hospital of the couple dozen who had taken part. Maybe only one person had burned down the house. Just one other, with a gun and a will to use it, would be one too many.

He grabbed a ride in a police cruiser to get down to the unloading point. A dump truck had brought scrap lumber, and Gale watched as workers pounded nails to make a ramp to reach from the shore to the barge. They didn't know how long it'd have to stretch yet, so they were erring on the long side.

Flint was deploying police officers along the landing site. He had traffic barriers set up two blocks down, and armed Guardsmen stood there, only moving the barriers for police, fire, and the water truck. Slowly, the street near the landing zone began to fill with the vehicles and people awaiting the barge.

Gale checked his watch. 9:10. He recognized Oralee, Flint's wife, and made his way over to her. "Morning," he said. "What brings you here?"

"Food. A group of us will get it divvied out and distributed."

"Right, of course. That's good work you've been doing all along."

"Good work you've been doing too. I'm sorry to hear you're leaving us, but I can't say I blame you."

"Thanks."

"Without you, this barge might not be arriving today."

He shrugged. Maybe, maybe not. Surely someone else would

have stepped in had it been he who died alongside Evelyn in City Hall. He was just glad the barge was coming, that he could see this one last result of his efforts before he left.

A gunshot made him start. He turned to the noise, but Oralee had him by the shirt and was dragging him backward toward a police car. "Get under cover."

It hadn't been that close. He could see down to the traffic barriers and saw a crowd had gathered beyond them. Hungry, thirsty, angry people, wanting to get to the food delivery first.

"Ah, crap," he said. "Why don't they just wait? They'll get it in a few hours if they just sit and wait it out."

"People aren't logical," she said. "They're emotional."

They both half squatted behind the cruiser, watching up the street. No more gunfire came, but Gale could hear the noise from the crowd increasing. They hadn't panicked and run at the gunfire. Maybe it came from one of them. "You think it was a warning shot?"

"I think it's trouble," she said. "I hope Flint can manage."

He could hear her worry for her husband in her voice. He knew what that felt like. "Flint's a strong guy. He knows what he's doing." He checked his watch again, and he kept checking it obsessively every minute or so between watching the situation at the barriers. More and more people gathered, and there was a good deal of shoving. Some tried to climb over the barriers and were shoved back by the Guardsmen. Flint waved some of the police officers forward to the barricades.

Then he heard a sound to his left, and he saw six to eight men had skirted around the road. They had to have climbed the makeshift levee to get through. "Flint," he called, standing. He pointed at the oncoming group.

Flint turned and drew his gun. He called to some other officers, two with riot shields. In formation, they walked toward the interlopers. Flint said, "You all get out of here. Get back behind the barriers."

"Fuck you," one of them yelled. "My kids are hungry."

"Everybody will be fed. Let us get it unloaded, and everybody will get the same food in just a few hours."

"Bullshit," another man called. "I hear the police have been getting twice what everyone else has."

Gale thought, Well yes, that's true, and the medical staff too, but surely you can see the reason.

"I don't trust you to bring me my fair share," said the first man. "I'll just take it with me."

"I'm telling you, get back behind those barricades," said Flint. Then, with a signal, the men beside him, the ones without the riot shields, began to shoot.

Gale's heart leapt into his throat. It was overkill, way too much reaction to the situation. What the hell was Flint doing? Then he saw the group of angry men, not falling dead, but flinching. He realized they were firing the rubber bullets.

A few interlopers cut and ran back the way they had come. Two others turned up the street, jogging toward the barricade. But three came right toward the line of cops. One pulled a gun. Crazy man.

The riot-shield bearers had truncheons out. Flint still had his service revolver in hand. Gale saw something fast flick out, like a snake, and he watched as one of the attackers fell, jerking on the ground. Taser, he realized. Then he heard another gunshot—a real one, and he heard a man squeal. Gale dropped to the pavement and got himself out of the line of fire.

Oralee still peeked over the car, and this time he dragged her by her shirt. "He'll be fine. Just stay down."

After a few tense seconds, there was no more gunfire, and, exchanging a glance, he and Oralee both risked looking over the car again. The citizen with the gun was down on the pavement, bleeding. A cop was down but moving, being attended to by a paramedic. Flint was handcuffing another of the men who had come at them, treating him none too gently. A third citizen was on his face, sat on by a solid-looking woman police officer. One of the truncheon-wielders was circling the injured people, looking like he wanted to beat the crap out of anyone he could get to. Gale and Oralee stood up, and she moved forward a few steps.

Gale glanced upriver. Still no sign of the barge. Up the street, the crowd was still surging forward, being pushed back, surging again. From this distance it looked like the breathing of some giant creature. "The damned barge better get here soon," he said to himself.

"I don't think that'll help things," said a familiar voice, and Gale turned to see Dan standing twenty feet to his right.

"Hey," he said. "What should we do to help?"

"Let Flint handle it," Dan said, but doubt was clear in his voice.

Gale understood. The citizens down there looked to have the Guardsmen and cops outnumbered by 10 to 1, or worse. He imagined Flint, of all of them, appreciated that they might not be able to control a crowd that big.

He looked upriver again, and this time he saw something in the distance. "I think it's coming," he said.

Oralee, fixed on her husband, didn't hear him, but Dan did, and he too turned to watch. "Yup. That's gotta be it. But it's not a barge. Too tall." He glanced once more at the subdued rioters and then again down the street. "Well, we gotta get to our jobs." And he turned to organize his own men to help with the unloading.

Gale hunted for the water company employee who was here to pick up their supplies. That man was at his truck, standing with his hand on the door handle. "You ready?" Gale asked.

"I'm ready to get out of here any second."

"Hang tight. We need the town water flowing again, as soon as possible. I'm sure the police have things under control."

"Do they?"

"Yes," Gale said, though he wasn't certain of that. He didn't want to be in Flint's shoes right now.

Dan had been right—it wasn't a barge he was seeing but a boat. As it drew nearer, he could see pipes hanging off its sides, muddy water blowing out of them. He realized it must be a dredging boat of some sort. It flew a flag he didn't know, a red castle on white background.

As it came close, he could see, a couple hundred yards behind, the actual barges. His pulse sped at the thought that there was food, and water, and shelter and heat for the townspeople who so desperately needed it.

He looked back at the barriers. For now the crowd was still behind them, but it seemed larger than the last time he'd looked.

The dredger passed him, wafting a stronger chemical scent from the river in his direction, and the barge made its way slowly along after. A half-dozen khaki-uniformed people stood at the front lip of the barge, under a U.S. flag. As it came closer, he could see it was a double line of small barges connected together somehow, with the tug pushing it set back three or four lengths behind the last barge. Six or eight barges was a lot of supplies.

Relief flooded him, and a weight seemed to lift from Gale's chest. He knew he had to leave town. But at least, with these supplies on hand, the town he had worked so hard to help would have a chance at surviving the winter.

The barge began to slow, dawdling its way up toward the landing site. The heavy equipment operators fired up their engines and pushed at the makeshift dock, moving it slowly out to meet the barge, which slowed more. Gale heard the tug engines reverse as it braked the barges, slowing their momentum. When it was finally stopped, the dock was pushed out until its end kissed the edge of the lead barge.

Gale went, accompanied by an assistant chief of police, Dan, and Oralee, to the end of the dock. He stepped onto it where it floated in the murky river. As he moved cautiously forward, the thing bounced beneath him. He offered his arm to Oralee. "I'm fine," she said.

"I'm not," he admitted, and she shot him a tense smile.

At the end of the dock, awful water sloshed up and over his shoes. The shoes would have to be not just tossed out, but thrown into a toxic waste dump. Many hands reached down to offer him help up a ladder. He, then the other two, were hauled up onto the barge's metal deck. Despite the choking chemical smell of the river below, Gale smiled at the sight of the tarp-wrapped wooden boxes. The tarps could be used as ground cover. The pallets and boxes would heat food. Here was, if not salvation, relief for thousands.

A uniformed fellow stepped forward and saluted. The assistant police chief returned the salute, but Gale settled for a nod.

"Major Callahan," the army fellow said.

"Thanks for coming."

"So how do you want to—" The Major stopped, looked over Gale's shoulder and said, "Shit, not again."

Gale turned to see the crowd had surged over the barrier. As he stared in horror, the leaders picked up steam and came barreling down the road toward the dock. A person in front fell and got trampled.

"Get that dock out of here," said the major, at the same time signaling someone else behind him.

A woman officer said into a handheld radio, "Move 'em forward."

Gale yelled at the workmen on the shore to push the dock out of the way, sink it if they needed to, but they couldn't hear him over the noise of yelling people and the tug's revving engine. He pointed and gestured wildly. But by that point, the crowd was nearly to the end of the dock.

People ran out on the dock. Gunfire started—whether from the police or the citizens themselves, impossible to say. The crowd spilled out from the dock, and several people were pushed into the water.

Gale could finally feel the barge start to move, and as it slowly picked up speed, it scraped against the end of the dock. The far section of dock got torn away from the rest, sending more people tumbling into the polluted river. A few had made it to the barge, and without hesitation, army officers peeled their hands off and dumped them into the river.

Gale was yelling for everyone to calm down, but he may as well have been a songbird singing in the middle of a war zone. It *is* a war zone, he realized, as he heard more weapons fire. Feeling helpless to do anything but watch this craziness, he glanced to Oralee. "You see Flint?" she said, her voice high with strain. Beyond her, the assistant police chief had a weapon drawn.

"I can't see anything that makes sense," Gale said, and then something big hit his leg like a battering ram. He spun, lost his balance, and found himself falling from the barge, scraping his back along its metal sides before he hit the water with a muddy splat.

As he sank, he closed his eyes and lips tight, trying to keep the poisonous river out. Would the tug push the barge right over him? His last thought was of Bash, and then something hit him in the head and it was all he knew for a long while.

Gale woke on a hard bed. His eyes were wet. Something was dripping in them. He blinked to clear them and saw Bash leaning over him, drawing back a small squirt bottle. The chemical smell of the river was still everywhere. Gale was naked under a sheet. And it was painfully noisy.

Bash leaned close, yelling into his ear. "You're on an evac chopper. We're about to lift off."

"What?" He had a hundred questions.

The noise increased and Bash leaned back, shaking his head and pointing to his ears. He mouthed, "You're going to be fine."

Gale reached out, and Bash took his hand.

Then Gale closed his eyes again, hanging on to his husband. He felt the helicopter lifting, turning, and picking up speed.

Epilogue

In their rented efficiency apartment in Long Beach, on Christmas Eve, Bash sat in a chair pulled up to Gale's bed and read aloud from the snail-mail letter from Dan.

"There's a cold, hard frost this morning in southern Missouri, with freezing rain predicted for later.

"Even more people have left town in the past two months since you got out. At least no one is still living in a tent city. Where deaths are verified and homes of the dead still standing, we've decided to let the homeless squat there for the time being. Stand-alone propane heaters and canned propane, brought in by barge, have been distributed, and there's just enough water being pumped out to houses, so most people will survive the winter, barring another big quake or a major epidemic. Fewer than 8,000 people remain, and if there is another 8.0 quake next year—and you told us there could easily be—this once healthy community will, very likely, turn into a ghost town.

"The only way this all works is with much tighter martial law, and after the barge riot, Flint let it be known that a day of punishment for so much as a fistfight is guaranteed. He's kept the promise. There are no trials, just prison, in the dank, smelly jail downtown. No one-day prisoner is even fed. The long-term prisoners, including looters, the barge rioters, and our one post-quake murderer get one meal a day, 600 calories. They've grown too weak to complain, much less riot. The crazy preacher who instigated the attack on Bash is there, too weak any longer to preach hellfire, much to the relief of the other prisoners, I don't doubt.

"I have mixed feelings about all this, as you can imagine. We'll probably get sued a year or two down the road.

"There's not going to be much celebration in town this Christmas. There are no presents to buy, no roast turkeys coming in, and no electricity to run blinking lights. There's a bit of loud preaching planned at a couple churches in town and some more decorous candlelight services at others, including a lay mass at the Catholic church, where I'll take my family. Attendance will be sparse, though. Many have lost their faith.

"The hospital and EOC are still functioning, and often a thought is spared there for the two men whose quick work helped mitigate the disaster's effects. I'm sorry to end on a sad note, but Angela and her husband are still listed as missing. There's no hint of what happened to them.

"I wish you both the best of New Years and hope you're on the mend."

"Thank you," said Gale, from the bed. "Have you heard from McKenna again?"

"I'm sure she'll text me tomorrow," said Bash, folding the letter. He was happy the girl was out, reunited with her mother, and safe. Haruka had made it back to Japan the second week of December.

"Nothing in the mail on my disability judgment?" asked Gale.

"Not yet." Bash's insurance had finally started paying a few of the bills, but with both of them unemployed until now, they were worried about money. If the stock market ever recovered, they could pay the debts off, but if they tried that now they'd lose everything they'd worked years to save. With unemployment and food stamps, they were barely covering their basic needs. Bash said, "I hate to leave you to go back to work."

"I'll miss you. But I'll be fine."

"And you'll do your PT."

"Three times a day, I promise. I want to get back to work too." The experience had made Gale even more determined to help other communities prepare for disaster. He was thinking about consultant work, but based in a more progressive city where they would both be happier and safer outside of work.

"I'm going to make some mint tea—you want some?"

"Sure. Thanks, love."

Bash kissed him and left the bedroom.

We're warm and dry and fed, he thought, as he put water on for the tea. They were eating fresh food every day, and he wasn't taking that for granted. They didn't have much in the way of things, not money, nor furniture, nor clothes, nor treasured mementos lost in the house fire, but they had each other, and they loved each other more than ever. He missed the old things, he still mourned them from time to time, but he knew he was a lucky man. He had what really counted.

The End

About the author and team

Lou Cadle is fascinated with disasters, having been in a few, including the 1989 San Francisco earthquake. A year of work in paleontology helped inspire the series *Dawn of Mammals.* Cadle has been writing professionally since 1991, is on Twitter and Facebook and blogs at www.loucadle.com, where you can also sign up for the mailing list to get information on sales and new releases.

I've had help from many volunteer proofreaders over the past few years, including Peggy, Nancy, Liz, Becca, Shelley, Cathy, and Eric. Experts like friends Ralph (helicopters) and Guy (law enforcement) have helped me get details right. I cannot imagine trying to write researched novels like mine without Wikipedia, and I donate to it every year. Other indie writers—Shelley, Aaron and Hannah, Boyd, Blair, and many more—have shown me several of the ropes and kept me from tripping over yet others. To them heartfelt thanks.

My professional team includes Deranged Doctor Design for covers, Igor Kristc for original art, Nick Bowman for proofreading and paperback formatting, and Podium Publishing for audio books.

My readers might not think of themselves as being on my team, but I see you as the most important members of it. For without someone to listen to my words and care about my characters, I'd be talking only to myself. You make this writing career both possible and worthwhile. Thank you.

Made in United States
Troutdale, OR
08/30/2023

12498234R00192